Christina Lauren is the combined pen name of longtime writing partners/besties/soulmates and brain-twins Christina Hobbs and Lauren Billings, the *New York Times*, *USA Today* and No. 1 international bestselling authors of the Beautiful and Wild Seasons series and various standalone romances.

You can find them online at:
ChristinaLaurenBooks.com
Facebook.com/ChristinaLaurenBooks
@ChristinaLauren

CHRISTINA LAUREN

To Hannah!

the

SOULMATE
EQUATION

[signature]

PIATKUS

PIATKUS

First published in the US in 2021 by Gallery Books,
an imprint of Simon & Schuster, Inc.
First published in Great Britain in 2021 by Piatkus
This edition published in 2021 by Piatkus

23

Interior design by Davina Mock-Maniscalco

The moral right of the author has been asserted.

*All characters and events in this publication, other than those
clearly in the public domain, are fictitious and any resemblance
to real persons, living or dead, is purely coincidental.*

A CIP catalogue record for this book
is available from the British Library.

ISBN 978-0-349-42689-1

Printed and bound in Great Britain by Clays Ltd, Elcograf S.p.A.

Papers used by Piatkus are from well-managed forests
and other responsible sources.

Piatkus
An imprint of
Little, Brown Book Group
Carmelite House
50 Victoria Embankment
London EC4Y 0DZ

An Hachette UK Company
www.hachette.co.uk

www.littlebrown.co.uk

To Holly Root, our Diamond Match

the SOULMATE EQUATION

ONE

J ESSICA DAVIS USED to think it was an honest-to-God tragedy that only twenty-six percent of women believed in true love. Of course, that was nearly a decade ago, when she couldn't imagine what it felt like to be anything but deeply and passionately obsessed with the man who would one day be her ex. Tonight, though, on her third first date in seven years, she was astounded the number was even that high.

"Twenty-six percent," she mumbled, leaning toward the restroom mirror to apply more lipstick. "Twenty-six women out of one hundred believe true love is real." Popping the cap back on, Jess laughed, and her exhausted reflection laughed back. Sadly, her night was far from over. She still had to make it through the entrée course; appetizers had lasted four years. Of course, some of that was probably due to Travis's tendency to talk with his mouth full, oversharing highly specific stories about finding his wife in bed with his business partner and the ensuing messy divorce. But as far as first dates went, Jess reasoned, it could have been worse. This date was better, for sure, than the guy last week who'd been so drunk when he showed up at the restaurant that he'd nodded off before they'd even ordered.

"Come on, Jess." She dropped the tube back into her bag. "You don't have to make, serve, or clean up after this meal. The dishes alone are worth at least one more bitter ex-wife story."

A stall door clicked open, startling her, and a willowy blonde emerged. She glanced at Jess with bald pity.

"God, I know," Jess agreed with a groan. "I'm talking to myself in a bathroom. Tells you exactly how my night is going."

Not a laugh. Not even a smile of politeness, let alone camaraderie. Instead the woman moved as far away as possible to the end of the empty row of sinks and began washing her hands.

Well.

Jess went back to rummaging through her purse but couldn't help glancing toward the end of the counter. She knew it wasn't polite to stare, but the other woman's makeup was flawless, her nails perfectly manicured. How on earth did some women manage it? Jess considered leaving the house with her zipper up a victory. Once, she'd presented an entire fiscal year's worth of data to a client with four of Juno's sparkly butterfly barrettes still clipped to the front of her blazer. This gorgeous stranger probably hadn't been forced to change outfits after cleaning glitter off both a cat and a seven-year-old. She probably never had to apologize for being late. She probably didn't even have to shave—she was just naturally smooth everywhere.

"Are you okay?"

Jess blinked back to awareness, realizing the woman was speaking to her. There was really no way to pretend she hadn't been staring directly at this stranger's cleavage.

Resisting the urge to cover her own less-than-impressive assets, Jess offered a small, embarrassed wave. "Sorry. I was just thinking that your kitten probably isn't covered in glitter, too."

"My what?"

She turned back to the mirror. *Jessica Marie Davis, get your shit together.* Ignoring the fact that she still had an audience, Jess channeled Nana Jo into the mirror: "You have plenty of time. Go out there, eat some guacamole, go home," she said aloud. "There's no ticking clock on any of this."

"I'M JUST SAYING, the clock is ticking." Fizzy waved vaguely toward Jess's butt. "That booty won't be high and tight forever, you know."

"Maybe not," Jess said, "but Tinder isn't going to help me find a quality guy to hold it up, either."

Fizzy lifted her chin defensively. "I've had some of the best sex of my life from Tinder. I swear you give up too quickly. We are in the era of women taking pleasure and not apologizing for getting theirs first, second, and one more time for the road. Travis might be ex-wife obsessed, but I saw his photo and he was fine as hell. Maybe he would have rocked your world for an hour or two after churros, but you'll never know, because you left before dessert."

Jess paused. Maybe . . . "Goddammit, Fizzy."

Her best friend leaned back, smug. If Felicity Chen decided to start selling Amway, Jess would simply hand over her wallet. Fizzy was made of charisma, witchcraft, and bad judgment. Those qualities made her a great writer, but were also partly the reason Jess had a misspelled song lyric tattooed on the inside of her right wrist, had had disastrous not-even-close-to–Audrey Hepburn bangs for six depressing months in 2014, and had attended a costume party in LA that turned out to be a BDSM scene in a dungeon basement. Fizzy's response to Jess's "You brought me to a sex party in a dungeon?" was, "Yeah, everyone in LA has dungeons!"

Fizzy tucked a strand of glossy black hair behind her ear. "Okay, let's make plans for your next date."

"No." Opening her laptop, Jess logged into her email. But even with her attention fixed elsewhere, it was hard to miss Fizzy's scowl. "Fizz, it's hard with a kid."

"That's always your excuse."

"Because I always have a kid."

"You also have grandparents who live next door and are more than happy to watch her while you're on a date, and a best friend who thinks your kid is cooler than you are. We all just want you to be happy."

Jess knew they did. That was why she'd agreed to test the Tinder waters in the first place. "Okay, let me humor you," she said. "Let's say I meet someone amazing. Where am I going to hook up with him? It was different when Juno was two. Now I have a light sleeper seven-year-old with perfect hearing, and the last time I went to a guy's place it was so messy, a pair of his boxers stuck to my back when I got up to use the bathroom."

"Gross."

"Agreed."

"Still." Fizzy rubbed a thoughtful finger beneath her lip. "Single parents make it work all the time, Jess. Look at the Brady Bunch."

"Your best example is a fifty-year-old sitcom?" The harder Fizzy tried to convince her, the less Jess actually wanted to get back out there. "In 1969 only thirteen percent of parents were single. Carol Brady was ahead of her time. I am not."

"Vanilla latte!" the barista, Daniel, shouted over the din of the coffee shop.

Fizzy motioned that she wasn't done being a pain in Jess's ass before standing and making her way to the counter.

Jess had been coming to Twiggs coffee shop every weekday for almost as long as she'd been freelancing. Her life, which essentially existed in a four-block radius, was exceedingly manageable as it was. She walked Juno to school just down the street from their apartment complex while Fizzy grabbed the best table—in the back, away from the glare of the window but near the outlet that hadn't yet gone wobbly. Jess crunched numbers while Fizzy wrote novels, and in an effort to not be leeches, they ordered something at least every ninety minutes, which had the added benefit of incentivizing them to work more, gossip less.

Except today. She could already tell Fizzy was going to be unrelenting.

"Okay." Her friend returned with her drink and a huge blueberry muffin, and took a moment to get situated. "Where was I?"

Jess kept her eyes on the email in front of her, pretending to read. "I think you were about to say that it's my life and that I should do what I think is best."

"We both know that's not something I would say."

"Why am I your friend?"

"Because I immortalized you as the villain in *Crimson Lace*, and you became a fan favorite, so I can't kill you off."

"Sometimes I wonder if you're answering my questions," Jess grumbled, "or continuing an ongoing conversation in your head."

Fizzy began peeling the paper off her muffin. "What I was going to say is that you can't throw in the towel because of one bad date."

"It's not just the one bad date," Jess said. "It's the exhausting and alien process of trying to be appealing to men. I'm a freelance statitician and consider my sexiest outfit to be my old *Buffy* shirt and a pair of cutoffs. My favorite pajamas are one of Pops's old undershirts and some maternity yoga pants."

Fizzy whimpered out a plaintive "No."

"Yes," Jess said emphatically. "On top of that, I had a kid when most people our age were still lying about enjoying Jägermeister. It's hard to make myself seem polished in a dating profile."

Fizzy laughed.

"I hate taking time away from Juno for some guy I'm probably never going to see again."

Fizzy let that sink in for a beat, dark eyes fixed in disbelief. "So, you're . . . done? Jessica, you went on three dates with three hot, if dull, men."

"I'm done until Juno is older, yeah."

She regarded Jess with suspicion. "How much older?"

"I don't know." Jess picked up her coffee, but her attention was snagged when the man they referred to as "Americano" stepped into Twiggs, striding to the front precisely on cue—8:24 in the morning—all long legs and dark hair and surly, glowering vibes, not making eye contact with a single person. "Maybe when she's in college?"

When Jess's eyes left Americano, horror was rippling across Fizzy's expression. "*College?* When she's eighteen?" She lowered her voice when every head in the coffee shop swiveled. "You're telling me that if I sat down to write the novel of your future love life, I'd be writing a heroine who is happily showing her body to a dude for the first time in eighteen years? Honey, no. Not even your perfectly preserved vagina can pull that off."

"Felicity."

"Like an Egyptian tomb in there. Practically mummified," Fizzy mumbled into a sip.

Up front, Americano paid for his drink and then stepped to the side, absorbed in typing something on his phone. "What is his deal?" Jess asked quietly.

"You have such a crush on Americano," Fizzy said. "Do you realize you watch him whenever he comes in here?"

"Maybe I find his demeanor fascinating."

Fizzy let her eyes drop to his ass, currently hidden by a navy coat. "We're calling it his 'demeanor' now?" She bent, writing something in the Idea Notebook she kept near her laptop.

"He comes in here and emits the vibe that if anyone tried to talk to him, he would do a murder," Jess quipped.

"Maybe he's a professional hit man."

Jess, too, inspected him top to bottom. "More like a socially constipated medieval art professor." She tried to remember when he'd started coming in here. Maybe two years ago? Almost every day, same time every morning, same drink, same sullen silence. This was a quirky neighborhood, and Twiggs was its heart. People came in to linger, to sip, to chat; Americano stood out not for being different or eccentric but for being almost entirely silent in a space full of boisterous, lovable weirdos. "Nice clothes, but inside them he's all grouchy," Jess mumbled.

"Well, maybe he needs to get laid, kind of like someone else I know."

"Fizz. I've had sex since birthing Juno," Jess said in exasperation. "I'm just saying I don't have a lot left over for commitment, and I'm not willing to endure boring or outright terrible dates just for orgasms. They make battery-operated appliances for that."

"I'm not talking just about sex," Fizzy said. "I'm talking about not always putting yourself last." Fizzy paused to wave to Daniel, who was wiping down a table nearby. "Daniel, did you catch all of that?"

He straightened and gave her the smile that had made Fizzy write the hero of *Destiny's Devil* with Daniel in mind, and do all manner of dirty things to him in the book that she hadn't dared do in real life.

And would never do: Daniel and Fizzy went out once last year but quickly ended things when they ran into each other at a family reunion. Their family reunion. "When can't we hear you?" he asked.

"Good, then please tell Jess that I'm right."

"You want me to have an opinion about whether Jess should be on Tinder just to get laid?" he asked.

"Okay, yup." Jess groaned. "This is what rock bottom feels like."

"Or whichever dating site she likes!" Fizzy cried, ignoring her. "This woman is sexy and young. She shouldn't waste her remaining hot years in mom jeans and old sweatshirts."

Jess looked down at her outfit, ready to protest, but the words shriveled in her throat.

"Maybe not," Daniel said, "but if she's happy, does it matter whether or not she's frumpy?"

She beamed at Fizzy in triumph. "See? Daniel is sort of on Team Jess."

"You know," Daniel said to her now, balling the washrag in his hands, smug with insider knowledge, "Americano is a romantic, too."

"Let me guess," Jess said, grinning. "He's the host of a Dothraki-themed sex dungeon?"

Only Fizzy laughed. Daniel gave a coy shrug. "He's about to launch a cutting-edge matchmaking company."

Both women went silent. *A what now?*

"Matchmaking?" Jess asked. "The same Americano who is a regular here in this coffee shop and yet never smiles at anyone?" She pointed behind her to the door he'd exited through only a minute ago. "*That* guy? With his intense hotness marred by the moody, antisocial filter?"

"That's the one," Daniel said, nodding. "You could be right that he needs to get laid, but I'm guessing he does just fine for himself."

AT LEAST THIS particular Fizzy tangent happened on a Monday— Pops picked up Juno from school on Mondays and took her to the library. Jess was able to get a proposal together for Genentech, set up a meeting with Whole Foods for next week, and bash through a few spreadsheets before she had to walk home and start attacking dinner.

Her car, ten years old with barely thirty thousand miles logged on it, was so rarely used that Jess couldn't remember the last time she'd had to fill the tank. Everything in her world, she thought contentedly on her walk home, was within arm's reach. University Heights was the perfect blend of apartments and mismatched houses nestled between tiny restaurants and independent businesses. Frankly, the sole benefit of last night's date was that Travis had agreed to meet at El Zarape just two doors down; the only thing worse than having the world's most boring dinner conversation would have been driving to the Gaslamp to do it.

With about an hour until sunset, the sky had gone a heavily bruised gray-blue, threatening rain that'd send any Southern Californian driver into a confused turmoil. A sparse crowd was getting Monday levels of rowdy on the deck of the new Kiwi-run brewery down the street, and the ubiquitous line at Bahn Thai was quickly turning into a tangle of hungry bodies; three butts were attached to humans currently ignoring the sign for customers not to sit on the private stoop next door to the restaurant. Nana and Pops's tenant, Mr. Brooks, had installed a doorbell camera for the front units, and almost every morning he gave Jess a detailed accounting of how many college kids vaped on his front step while waiting for a table.

Home came into view. Juno had named their apartment complex "Harley Hall" when she was four, and although it didn't have nearly the pretentious vibe required to be a capital-*H* Hall, the name stuck. Harley Hall was bright green and stood out like an emerald against the earth-tone stucco of the adjacent buildings. The street-facing side was decorated with a horizontal strip of pink and purple tiles forming a harlequin pattern; electric-pink window boxes spilled brightly colored mandevilla most of the year. Jess's grandparents Ronald and Joanne Davis had bought the property the year Pops retired from the navy. Coincidentally this was the same year Jess's long-term boyfriend decided he wasn't *father material* and wanted to retain the option to put his penis in other ladies. Jess finished school and then packed up two-month-old Juno, moving into the ground floor two-bedroom unit that faced Nana and Pops's bungalow at the back end of the property. Given that they'd raised Jess down the road in Mission Hills until she'd gone to college at UCLA, the transition was basically zero. And now, her small and perfect village helped her raise her child.

The side gate opened with a tiny squeak, then latched closed behind her. Down a narrow path, Jess stepped into the courtyard that separated her apartment from Nana Jo and Pops's bungalow. The space looked like a lush garden somewhere in Bali or Indonesia. A handful of stone fountains gurgled quietly, and the primary sensation was *bright*: magenta, coral, and brassy-purple bougainvillea dominated the walls and fences.

Immediately, a small, neatly French-braided child tackled Jess. "Mom, I got a book about snakes from the library, did you know that snakes don't have eyelids?"

"I—"

"Also, they eat their food whole, and their ears are only inside their heads. Guess where you can't find snakes?" Juno stared up at her, blue eyes unblinking. "Guess."

"Canada!"

"No! Antarctica!"

Jess led them inside, calling "No way!" over her shoulder.

"Way. And remember that cobra in *The Black Stallion*? Well, cobras are the only kind of snakes that build nests, and they can live to be twenty."

That one actually shocked Jessica. "Wait, seriously?" She dropped her bag on the couch just inside the door and moved to the pantry to dig around for dinner options. "That's insane."

"Yes. Seriously."

Juno went quiet behind her, and understanding dropped like a weight in Jess's chest. She turned to find her kid wearing the enormous-eyed expression of preemptive begging. "Juno, baby, no."

"Please, Mom?"

"No."

"Pops said maybe a corn snake. The book says they're 'very docile.' Or a ball python?"

"A python?" Jess set a pot of water on the stove to boil. "Are you out of your mind, child?" She pointed to the cat, Pigeon, asleep in the dying stretch of daylight streaming through the window. "A python would eat that creature."

"A ball python, and I wouldn't let it."

"If Pops is encouraging you to get a snake," Jess said, "Pops can keep it over at his house."

"Nana Jo already said no."

"I bet she did."

Juno growled, collapsing onto the couch. Jess walked over and sat down, drawing her in for a cuddle. She was seven but small; she still had baby hands with dimples on the knuckles and smelled like baby shampoo and the woody fiber of books. When Juno wrapped her small arms around Jess's neck, she breathed the little girl in. Juno had her own room now, but she'd slept with her mom until she was four, and sometimes Jess would still wake up in the middle of the night and experience a sharp stab of longing for the warm weight of her baby in her arms. Jess's own mother used to say she needed to break Juno of the habit, but parenting advice was the last thing Jamie Davis should be giving to anyone. Besides, it wasn't like anyone else ever occupied that side of the mattress.

And Juno was a master cuddler, a gold-medal Olympian in the snuggle. She pressed her face to Jess's neck and breathed in, wiggling closer. "Mama. You went on a date last night," she whispered.

"Mm-hmm."

Juno had been excited for the date, not only because she adored her great-grandparents and got Nana Jo's cooking when Jess was out, but also because they'd recently watched *Adventures in Babysitting*, and Fizzy'd told her it was a pretty accurate depiction of what dating was like. In Juno's mind, Jess might end up dating Thor.

"Did you go downtown? Did he bring you flowers?" She pulled back. "Did you kiss him?"

Jess laughed. "No, I did not. We had dinner, and I walked home."

Juno studied her, eyes narrowed. She seemed pretty sure that more was supposed to happen on a date. Popping up like she'd remembered something, she jogged to her roller backpack near the door. "I got you a book, too."

"You did?"

Juno walked back over and crawled into her lap, handing it over. *Middle Aged and Kickin' It!: A Woman's Definitive Guide to Dating Over 40, 50 and Beyond.*

Jess let out a surprised laugh. "Did your Auntie Fizz put you up to this?"

Juno's giggle rolled out of her, delighted. "She texted Pops."

Over the top of her head, Jess caught a glimpse of the dry-erase board next to the fridge, and a tingling spread from her fingertips up to her arms. The words **NEW YEARS GOALS** were written in Juno's bubbly handwriting.

NANA & POPS
Get a personal trayner
Take a wock evry day

JUNO
Lern to like brocooli
Make my bed evry mornning
Try Something New Sunday!

MOM
Try Something New Sunday!
Nana ses be more selfish!
Do more things that skare me

Okay, Universe, Jessica thought. *I get it.* If Mrs. Brady could be a trailblazer, maybe it was time for Jess to try, too.

TWO

——————⎍——————

THE PROBLEM WITH epiphanies: they never arrived at a convenient time. Jess had a mildly hyperactive seven-year-old and
a flourishing freelancing career juggling all flavors of mathematical
conundrums. Neither of these things left a lot of time for creating a
bucket list of adventures. Besides, her daughter and her career were
enough for her; she had four good freelancing contracts, and although they didn't leave her with much extra, she was able to cover
the bills—including their astronomical insurance premiums—and
help her grandparents out, too. Juno was a happy kid. They lived in
a nice area. Frankly, Jess liked her life as it was.

But the words *Do more things that scare me* seemed to flash
neon on her lids whenever she closed her eyes between data sets.

Truthfully, her lack of dating was probably more about laziness
than fear. *It's not like I jumped giddily into stagnation*, Jess thought.
*I slid into it slowly, and realize it only now that I'm no longer even
questioning whether the jeans I pulled off the floor should've been
washed before being worn again.* Jess would never complain about

having become a mom when she was twenty-two—Juno was the best thing Alec could have given her, frankly—but it was probably fair to admit that she put more effort into making Juno's lunch than she did into considering, say, what she might look for in a future partner. Maybe Fizzy, Nana, and the cover of *Marie Claire* weren't wrong when they hinted that Jess needed to step out of her comfort zone and dream bigger.

"What's that face you're making?" Fizzy drew an imaginary circle around Jess's expression. "I'm blanking on the word."

"This?" Jess pointed to her own head. "Defeat?"

Fizzy nodded, mumbling aloud as she typed: "'She glanced away from his penetrating gaze, defeat coloring her features a milky gray.'"

"Wow. Thank you."

"I am not writing about you. Your expression was just timely." She typed a few more words, and then picked up her latte. "As we covered in Ye Olden Days of our friendship, you do not consider yourself a heroine of one of my romance novels, therefore I will never make you anything but a side character or villain."

Fizzy winced at what was unlikely to be a very fresh sip—it was clearly time for her to reorder—as her words hit Jess like a Three Stooges slap.

Jess sat quietly, reeling in a tunneling awareness that her life was going to pass her by before she knew it. It would break her heart if Juno ever stopped living life to its fullest. She only vaguely registered that it must be 8:24 when Americano strolled into the coffee shop, looking like a hot man with places to be and no time for any of the hoi polloi at Twiggs. Without a word, he plucked a ten from his wallet, taking the change from Daniel and dropping only the coins into the tip jar. Jess stared, overblown irritation rising hot in her throat.

He's a shitty tipper! It threw another log on her Petty Reasons Why Americano Is Awful mental fire.

Fizzy snapped in front of her face, pulling her attention back to their table. "There. You're doing it again."

Jess frowned. "Doing what?"

"Ogling him. Americano." Fizzy's face split into a knowing grin. "You do think he's sexy."

"I do not. I was just spacing out." Jess pulled back, insulted. "Gross, Felicity."

"Sure, okay." Fizzy angled her pointed finger to the man in question, wearing slim dark jeans and a lightweight royal-blue sweater. Dark hair curled at the nape of his neck, Jess noticed, the perfect length of barely overgrown, almost-needs-a-haircut hair. Olive skin, a mouth full enough to bite. So tall that, when viewed from a chair, his head seemed to scrape the ceiling. But his eyes—now, those were the main event: expressive and soulful, darkly lashed. "*That's* gross. Whatever you say."

Jess shrugged, rattled. "He's not my type."

"That man is everyone's type." Fizzy laughed incredulously.

"Well, you can have him." Frowning, Jess watched him do his customary wipe of the condiment bar with a napkin. "I was just thinking how I can't fathom the idea that he's starting a match-making company. That isn't something an asshole like that does."

"Personally, I think Daniel has no idea what he's talking about. Rich men who look like that are too married to their jobs during the day and their investment portfolios at night to think about anyone's love life."

Americano turned from the condiment bar to leave. In a flash, Jess's curiosity bubbled over, and she impulsively caught him with a hand around his forearm as he passed. They both froze. His eyes were a rare, surprising color, lighter than she would have expected up close. Amber, she could see now, not brown. The weight of his full attention felt like a physical pressure on her chest, pushing the air out of her lungs.

"Hey." Jess charged forward through vibrating nerves and lifted her chin. "Hang on a second. Can we ask you something?"

When she released him, he pulled his arm away slowly, glancing to Fizzy, then back to her. He nodded once.

"Rumor has it you're a matchmaker," Jess said.

Americano narrowed his eyes. "'Rumor'?"

"Yeah."

"In what context did this rumor come up?"

With an incredulous laugh, Jess gestured around them. "Ground zero of University Heights gossip. The rumor mill of Park Avenue." She waited, but he continued to gaze down at her, perplexed. "Is it true?" she asked. "Are you a matchmaker?"

"Technically, I'm a geneticist."

"So . . ." Her brows climbed her forehead. Americano was apparently very comfortable with pointed silence. "Is that a 'no' to matchmaking?"

He relented with an amused flick of one eyebrow. "My company has developed a service that connects people based on proprietary genetic profiling technology."

Fizzy *Oooohe*d. "Big words. Sounds scandalous." She bent, scribbling in her notebook.

"'Genetic profiling technology'?" Jess winced at him. "Gives me vague eugenics vibes, sorry."

Fizzy was quick to redirect Americano's attention away from Jess's dumpster-fire mouth. "I write romance. This sounds like my kryptonite." She held up her pen, shaking it flirtatiously. "My readers would flip for this stuff."

"What's your pen name?" he asked.

"I write under my real name," she said. "Felicity Chen."

Felicity offered a dainty hand as if for him to kiss and, after a beat of confused hesitation, Americano gripped her fingertips for a brief handshake.

"She's translated in over a dozen languages," Jess bragged, hoping to wipe the odd expression off his face.

It did the trick; Americano looked impressed. "Really."

"Will there be an app?" Fizzy was relentless. "Is it like Tinder?"

"Yes." He frowned. "But no. It's not for hookups."

"Can anyone do it?"

"Eventually," he said. "It's a—" His phone buzzed from his pocket, and he pulled it out, frown deepening. "Sorry," he said, pocketing it again. "I need to go, but I appreciate your interest. I'm sure you'll hear more about it soon."

Fizzy leaned in, smiling her confident smile. "I have over a hundred thousand followers on Instagram. I'd love to share the information if it's something my predominantly eighteen-to-fifty-five-year-old female readers might want to hear."

Americano's forehead smoothed, permafrown vanishing.

Bingo.

"We're going public in May," he said, "but if you'd like, you're welcome to come to the office, hear the spiel, give a sample—"

"A *sample*?" Jess blurted.

She could see the small hot flash of annoyance in his eyes when they flickered back over to her. If Fizzy was flirty cop, Jess was definitely skeptical cop, and Americano seemed to be barely tolerating even Fizzy's genuine fascination.

He looked Jess in the eye. "Spit."

Barking out a laugh, Jess asked, "I beg your pardon?"

"The sample," he said slowly, "is spit."

His eyes did a casual sweep of her from face to lap and back up. Inside her chest, her heart did a strange flip.

Then he glanced down at his watch. *Well.*

Fizzy laughed tightly as she looked back and forth between the two of them. "I'm sure we could both manage to spit." She grinned. "For you."

With a wan smile, he dropped a business card on the table; it made an audible *thunk*. "No eugenics," he added quietly, "I promise."

JESS WATCHED HIM leave. The bell over the door gave a single disappointed chime at his departure. "Okay," she said, turning back to her friend. "What's the over/under that he's a vampire?"

Fizzy ignored her, rapping the business card against the edge of the table. "Look at this."

Narrowing her eyes, Jess looked back out the window as

Americano got into a sleek black Audi at the curb. "He was trying to compel me."

"This card is legit." Fizzy squinted at it, turning it in her hand. "He didn't get this shit made at Kinko's."

"'Spit,'" Jess mimicked in a deep, clipped voice. "God, he is definitely not in marketing because that man has zero charisma. Put a pin in this prediction and let's circle back to it when I'm ninety: he's the most arrogant person I'll meet in this lifetime."

"Will you stop obsessing about him?"

Jess took the business card from Fizzy. "Will you stop obsessing about this car—" She stopped, weighing its impressive heft in her hand. "Wow. It is really thick."

"I told you so."

Jess flipped it over to examine the logo: two interconnected circles with a double helix as their point of contact. On the front, Americano's real name in small, raised silver letters at the bottom. "That's not what I would have guessed. He looks like a Richard. Or maybe an Adam."

"He looks like a Keanu."

"Brace yourself." She looked up at Fizzy and smirked. "Americano's name is Dr. River Peña."

"Oh no," Fizzy said, exhaling. "That's a *hot* name, Jess."

Jess laughed; Felicity Chen was wonderfully predictable.

"Eh, the man makes the name, not the other way around."

"Incorrect. No matter how hot the man, the name Gregg with two *G*s will never be sexy." Fizzy sank deeper into her chair, flushed. "How weird would it be if I named my next hero 'River'?"

"Very."

Fizzy wrote it down anyway as Jess read the company name aloud. "GeneticAlly? Genetic *Ally*?" She rolled the word around in her mouth before it clicked. "Oh, I get it. Said like 'genetically' but with the capital A for 'ally.' Listen to this tagline: 'Your future is already inside you.' Wow." She set the card down and leaned back, grinning. "'Inside you'? Did anyone read that out loud first?"

"We're going," Fizzy said, ignoring Jess's snark and packing up her bag.

Jess stared at her, eyes wide. "Are you serious? Right now?"

"You have more than five hours before you have to get Juno. La Jolla is a half-hour drive."

"Fizzy, he didn't seem exactly thrilled to talk to us about it. He couldn't wait to get out of here."

"So what? Consider it research: I have got to see this place."

THERE WERE ONLY four cars in the expansive parking lot, and with a chuckle, Fizzy parked her new but sensible blue Camry alongside River's gleaming Audi.

She grinned at Jess across the leather console. "Ready to find your soulmate?"

"I am not." But Fizzy was already out of the car.

Jess climbed out, looking up at the two-story building ahead of them. She had to admit: it was impressive. The polished wood-slat façade bore the company name, GeneticAlly, in giant brushed-aluminum letters; the second floor boasted modern, unfinished concrete and bright, wide windows. The two-ring DNA logo was printed on the broad front doors, which swept outward when Fizzy gave a gentle tug. Jess and Fizzy stepped into an upscale and deserted lobby.

"Whoa," Fizzy whispered. "This is weird."

Their footsteps echoed across the floor as they made their way to a giant marble-slab desk practically a football field away from the entrance. Everything screamed *expensive*; they were absolutely being filmed by at least five security cameras.

"Hi." A woman looked up at them, smiling. She also looked expensive. "Can I help you?"

Fizzy, never out of her depth, leaned her forearms against the desk. "We're here to see River Peña."

The receptionist blinked, checking the calendar with a wild, panicked gaze. "Is he expecting you?" Jess grew painfully aware that she and Fizzy may have just strolled in and asked to see the person who literally ran the place.

"No," Jess admitted just as Fizzy gave an entitled "He is."

Fizz waved Jess off. "You can tell him Felicity Chen and her associate are here."

Jess coughed out a laugh, and the wary receptionist gestured to a guest log. "Okay, well, please go ahead and sign in. And I'll need to see your IDs. Are you here for a presentation?" She jotted down the info from their identification.

Jess frowned. "A what?"

"I mean—has he recruited you for DNADuo?" she asked.

"DNADuo. That's the one." Fizzy grinned down as she wrote their names in the log. "He saw two beautiful single ladies in the coffee shop and just begged us to come spit into vials."

"Fizz." For the thousandth time, Jess wondered whether she'd always follow Fizzy around like a broom and dustpan sweeping up chaos. Being around Fizzy made Jess feel simultaneously more alive and duller.

The receptionist returned a polite smile along with their IDs, and indicated they should take a seat. "I'll let Dr. Peña know you're here."

Over on the red leather couches, Jess swore it felt like theirs were the first butts to ever sit down. There was literally no dust anywhere, no hint that another body had ever touched this furniture. "This is weird," she whispered. "Are we sure this isn't a front for some organ-harvesting cult?" She carefully fingered a tidy stack of science journals. "They always use the pretty ones as bait."

"Dr. Peña." Fizzy pulled out her notebook and coyly licked the tip of her pen. "I'm definitely naming a hero after him now."

"If I leave with only one kidney," Jess said, "I'm coming for one of yours."

Fizzy tapped her pen against the paper. "I wonder if a River Peña would have a brother. Luis. Antonio . . ."

"And all of this costs money." Jess ran a hand over the supple leather. "How many kidneys do you think a couch like this is worth?" She pulled out her phone and typed into the search bar, her mouth agape at the results. "According to Google, the going rate for a single kidney is $262,000. Why am I working? I could survive with only one, right?"

"Jessica Davis, you sound like you've never left your house before."

"You're the one building his fictional family tree! What are we even doing here?"

"Finding The One?" Fizzy said, and then smiled slyly at her. "Or getting some freaky intel for a book."

"You have to admit you don't look at Dr. River Peña and think, 'Now, there's a romantic soul.'"

"No," Fizz conceded, "but I do look at him and think, 'I bet he's got a fantastic penis.' Did you see the size of his hands? He could carry me by the head, like a basketball."

A throat cleared, and they looked up to find River Peña standing not two feet away. "Well, you two sure didn't waste any time."

Jess's stomach fell through the floor, and the words creaked out of her: "Oh shit."

"Did you hear what I just said?" Fizzy asked.

He let out a slow, controlled exhale. He'd totally heard. "Hear what?" he managed, finally.

Fizzy stood, pulling Jess up with her. "Excellent." She gave River a dainty curtsy. "Take us away."

THREE

———————⋀———————

THEY FOLLOWED HIM through a set of sterile double doors and down a long hall, with offices coming off the right side every few yards. Each door had a hammered stainless steel placard and a name: Lisa Addams. Sanjeev Jariwala. David Morris. River Peña. Tiffany Fujita. Brandon Butkis.

Jess glanced over to Fizzy, who, predictably, was already on it: "Butt kiss," she whispered, delighted.

Through one open office door, Jess saw a broad window displaying a view of the La Jolla shoreline. Less than a mile away, gulls swooped down over white-capped water, and waves crashed violently against rocky cliffs. It was spectacular.

The annual lease on this property had to be at least a kidney and a half.

The trio tromped along in silence, reaching a set of elevators. River pushed the Up button with a long index finger, and then stared wordlessly ahead.

The silence grew heavy. "How long have you worked here?" Jess asked.

"Since it was founded."

Helpful. She tried again. "How many employees are there?"

"About a dozen."

"It's a shame you're not in marketing," Jess said with a smile. "Such charm."

River turned to look at her, and his expression sent a cold wash of sensation down her arms. "Yes, well. Luckily my talents lie elsewhere." His gaze lingered on hers for just a beat too long, and the sensation turned into warm static just as the elevator doors opened.

Fizzy elbowed her sharply in the ribs. *Sexy things*, she was clearly thinking.

Assassin things, Jess mentally replied.

For all of the promises of exploiting this great research opportunity, Fizzy was uncharacteristically quiet; maybe she was also cowed by River's rigid presence. It meant the rest of the slow elevator ride was as wordless as the bleak center of Siberia. When they stepped out, Jess watched her best friend begin scribbling note after note about—she presumed—the building; the handful of buttoned-up scientists they passed in the second hallway; River's composed pace, perfect posture, and visibly muscular thighs. Meanwhile, Jess grew increasingly self-conscious about the obnoxious squeak of her sneakers on the linoleum and the relative dumpiness of her outfit. Fizzy was dressed like she usually was—an adorable polka dot silk blouse and pencil trousers—and River was dressed as he usually was—a glossy magazine version of business casual. It hadn't occurred to Jess that morning as she'd hurriedly pulled on a threadbare UCLA sweatshirt, some old Levi's, and a pair of scuffed Vans that she would later be strolling down a hallway in the most well-heeled part of biotech La Jolla.

At the end of the hall was an open door leading into a conference room. River paused and gestured for them to walk in ahead of him.

"Have a seat in here," he said. "Lisa will join you momentarily."

Fizzy glanced to Jess and then back to River. "Who's Lisa?"

"She's the head of customer relations and the lead on our app development. She'll explain the technology and the matching process."

Frankly this whole thing had become a boatload of confusing secrecy. "You're not staying?" Jess asked.

He looked affronted, like she'd suggested he was the company water boy. "No." With a vague smile, he turned and continued down the hallway. *Ass.*

Only a couple of minutes later, a brunette walked in. She had the sun-kissed, faux-no-makeup, beachy-waved look of perpetually active Southern Californians who could throw on a shapeless muumuu and look stylish.

"Hey!" She strode forward, reaching to shake their hands. "I'm Lisa Addams. Head of customer relations for GeneticAlly. I'm so glad you came in! I haven't given this presentation to such a small group yet, this'll be a blast. Are you two ready?"

Fizzy nodded enthusiastically, but Jess was starting to feel a bit like she'd been dropped into a world where she was the only one not in on an important secret. "Would you mind showing me to the restroom before we start?" she asked, wincing lightly. "Coffee."

With another smile, Lisa gave Jess directions that seemed simple enough. Jess passed a stretch of large doorways with a distinct laboratory vibe. One was labeled SAMPLE PREP. The next was DNA SEQUENCERS, followed by ANALYSIS 1, ANALYSIS 2, and SERVERS. Finally: an alcove with restrooms.

Even the toilets were futuristic. Jess was honestly not sure how to feel about a public bidet, but there were so many buttons on the thing—and hey, warm water—she decided to roll with it. A check of her reflection while she washed her hands informed her that she hadn't put makeup on that morning and looked haggard and frazzled, even in the dim yet flattering light. *Great*.

On the way back, her attention was snagged by an open door. It had been forever since she'd been in a real scientific setting, and nostalgia pulsed in the back of her mind. Peeking into the room labeled SAMPLE PREP, Jess saw a long stretch of lab benches and an assortment of machines with keypads and flashing full-color digital displays like something out of a movie.

And then she heard River's quiet, deep voice: "Isn't there another 10X bottle of extraction buffer?"

"We have some on order," another man replied. "I think I have enough to finish this set."

"Good."

"Did I hear you had two people come in for a demo?"

"Yes," River said. "Two women. One of them is apparently an author with a large online presence."

There was a pause that Jess assumed held some wordless communication.

"I don't know, man," River said. "I was just trying to get my coffee, so I suggested they come in so Lisa could handle it."

Well.

"Got it," the other voice said. "If they send in kits, I'll run them in quadruplicate with some reference sequences."

"There may be times soon after the rollout that we only have a handful of samples at a time, so this'll be a good trial for that."

"True."

She was just about to turn and walk back to the conference room when she heard River say with a laugh, "—an opportunity to prove that there's someone out there for everyone."

The other man asked, "Ugly?"

"No, not ugly." Jess immediately decided to receive this as River's version of a compliment, until he added: "Entirely average."

She reared back, palm to chest in genuine offense, and startled when a voice came from behind her. "Did you want a lab tour after your meeting with Lisa?"

The man behind her held his hands up as Jess wheeled on him like she might throw a punch. He was tall and thin and looked like every actor in every movie playing a scientist: Caucasian, glasses, needed a haircut. He was Jeff Goldblum, if Jeff Goldblum were also Benedict Cumberbatch.

She wasn't sure whether he was genuinely offering her a tour or subtly chastising her for eavesdropping.

"Oh. No," she said, "it's okay. Sorry. I was just on my way back from the restrooms and took a peek."

Smiling, he held out his hand. "David Morris."

Jess shook it tentatively. "Jessica."

"We haven't had clients in the offices for a while. It's nice to see a fresh face." As he said this, his eyes did a quick sweep down her body and back up. "You're doing the DNADuo?"

She resisted the urge to cross her arms over her chest to hide the fact that she'd come to this high-end dating service looking like a hungover college kid. "I haven't decided yet. I'm here with my best friend. She's a romance author and completely lost her mind when Americano—Dr. Peña, sorry—mentioned the business to us this morning."

David gestured for her to lead them both back to the conference room. "Well, I hope you find the technology compelling."

Jess forced a polite smile. "I'm sure we will."

David stopped at the threshold to the conference room. "It was nice to meet you, Jessica. If you need anything else, please feel free to reach out."

With another tight smile, Jess pushed down her bubbling uneasiness. "I absolutely will."

SHE RETURNED TO the conference room feeling roughly ten percent frumpier than she had before. Which was to say, scraping the bottom of the barrel. Fizzy and Lisa were chatting about the benefits and drawbacks of various dating apps, but they straightened like they'd been busted when Jess walked back in. Without either of them having to say it, Jess knew she absolutely looked the part of the friend who had been dragged along to this and would much rather be watching Netflix on her couch.

"Ready to get started?" Lisa asked, swiping through a menu on an iPad. The room dimmed and a massive screen descended from the ceiling with a soft hum.

Fizzy played her role, "Hell yes!" so Jess played hers, too: "Sure, why not."

Lisa strode to the front of the large room with confidence, like she was speaking to a crowd of fifty instead of two.

"What are your goals," she began, "as far as romantic relationships go?"

Jess turned expectantly to Fizzy, who had turned expectantly to Jess.

"Okay, well, I guess I'll take the first shot," Fizzy said, scoffing at Jess's blank expression. "I'm thirty-four, and I enjoy dating. A lot. But I suppose I'll eventually settle down, have some kids. It all depends on the person."

Lisa nodded, smiling like this was a perfect answer, and then turned to Jess.

"I . . ." she began, flailing a little. "I assume there's someone out there for me, but I'm not really in a rush to find him. I'm about to turn thirty. I have a daughter; I don't have a lot of time." Shrugging vaguely, she mumbled, "I don't really know."

Clearly Lisa was used to people with a bit more drive, but she rolled out her spiel anyway. "Have you ever wondered what a soulmate truly is?" she asked. "Is love a quality you can quantify?"

"Oooh, good question." Fizzy leaned in. Hook, line, and sinker.

"Here, we believe it is," Lisa said. "Matchmaking through DNA technology is exactly what we offer here at GeneticAlly, through the DNADuo. GeneticAlly was officially founded six years ago, but the concept of the DNADuo was first conceived in the lab of Dr. David

Morris at the Salk Institute back in 2003." Lisa swiped from the first image—the DNADuo logo—to an aerial view of the Salk, a stark collection of futuristic buildings just up the road. "The idea of genetic matchmaking is not new, but few companies have been able to create anything even a fraction as extensive as what Dr. Morris and his graduate student, River Peña, designed."

Jess glanced at Fizzy, who looked back at her. If River and his mentor invented all of this, Jess figured she couldn't give him too much shit for being a terrible pitch man.

Even if she could give him shit for being a bit of an asshole.

Lisa continued: "The reason the DNADuo has been so successful at identifying genuine love matches is that the idea didn't start with DNA." She paused dramatically. "It started with people."

Jess stifled an eye roll as the slide became animated, zooming away from the Salk research buildings and along a street to a collection of computer-generated coeds standing on the patio of a bar, laughing and talking.

"Dr. Peña first asked whether he could find a complementary pattern in the DNA of two people who are attracted to each other." Lisa's slide zoomed in on a couple speaking closely, flirtatiously. "That is, are we programmed to find certain people attractive, and can we predict which two people will be attracted to each other before they ever meet?" She grinned. "In a study of over one thousand students from UC San Diego, a series of nearly forty genes were found to be tightly correlated with attraction. Dr. Peña then pointed the lab in the opposite direction to look into lasting happiness. Could he find a genetic profile of people who had been happily married for longer than a decade?"

Lisa swiped the animation forward to show an older computer-generated couple sitting on a couch, cuddling. The view zoomed back to show a neighborhood, and then a city, and then farther until the city map looked like a double-helix strand of DNA. "From a study of over three hundred couples," Lisa continued, "Dr. Peña found nearly two hundred genes that were linked to emotional compatibility long-term, including the same forty genes associated with attraction, as well as many other previously uncorrelated ones." She paused, looking at them. "This was only the first generation of the DNADuo."

Beside Jess, Fizzy was sitting up at full attention, completely plugged in. But Jess was skeptical. What Lisa was describing was essentially a slot machine with two hundred reels. Statistically speaking, landing on the right combination was an absurdly low-probability event. Even if GeneticAlly was just looking for pattern compatibility, with the number of variants of every gene in the human genome, this type of algorithm was so complex as to be nearly impossible to calculate manually. She couldn't see how they would begin to process the amount of data they were facing.

Lisa seemed to read her mind. "Two hundred is a lot of genes, and the human genome is made up of at least twenty thousand. Of course, not all of these—maybe not even most—are involved in our emotional satisfaction. But Drs. Peña and Morris wanted to find every last one. They didn't just want to identify compatibility, they wanted to help you find your soulmate. Which is exactly why Dr. Peña collaborated with Caltech to develop a novel deep neural network."

She let these words sink in as the slide became animated again, diving into the double helix, highlighting base fragments as it whizzed along the length of the DNA strand.

"This project has encompassed personality tests, brain scans, longitudinal studies of relationship success, and—yes—well over one hundred thousand samples run through DNA sequencing and analysis." She looked each of them dead in the eye. "The investors have put over thirty million dollars into the technology alone. The app developers have invested almost five million. Do I think we have a truly groundbreaking system?" She nodded. "Between us? In all honesty? I do."

Swiping forward, she lifted her chin to the screen, where a woman stood alone against a stark white backdrop. "Here's how it works. We've developed a kit like many genetic profiling companies, which, very soon, customers will be able to order by mail. We have kits here for purchase, if you're interested."

Jess could sense Fizzy itching to pull out her credit card. Lisa picked up a small box on the table; it was white, the simple DNADuo logo printed in rainbow colors. "Once we fully launch, clients will send in their sample for analysis by our DNADuo algorithm, which now combines findings from over thirty-five hundred genes. Once received, analysis takes only about three days for the results to load into your DNADuo app. While you wait, you can enter information about yourself in your profile—the same way that you would on other dating sites. Information about your age, location, profession—whatever you want people to know about you. Once your results are in, we'll share with you the compatibility scores based on the criteria you've chosen."

Jess swallowed audibly. All of this sounded so . . . thorough.

The slide now showed two people standing side by side before the same empty backdrop. "Through rigorous analysis, we've created scoring bins. That is, we group the scores based on how tightly they correlate to relationship success. If you pull two random people off the street to see whether they're compatible, you're looking at a score on average between seven and twenty-four on our DNADuo algorithm. These scores are out of one hundred, so twenty-four isn't ideal, but it's not zero, either. We call these scores Base Matches."

"Are there a lot of those?" Fizzy asked.

"Oh, yes," Lisa said. "A large majority of random pairings tested against each other are Base Matches. Now"—she swiped forward, and the two people turned toward each other, smiling—"attraction is frequently reported between couples with scores of twenty-five to fifty, but when we follow them long-term, these individuals rarely find lasting emotional compatibility. We call these Silver Matches, and some of the individuals in our beta testing have chosen to explore these relationships." Lisa shrugged, grinning, clearly breaking from script. "Good sex is good sex, right?"

Fizzy nodded enthusiastically, but Jess only gave a vague shrug. "What's your threshold for 'rarely,' when you say they rarely find lasting compatibility?"

Lisa smiled. "Based on our initial studies, only one Silver Match in every three hundred lasts beyond the two-year threshold we consider long-term. But here's where it gets fun," she said, straightening. A new couple appeared on the screen, holding hands as they walked forward together. "Gold Matches are couples with a score of fifty to sixty-five. A third of Gold Matches will find a lasting relationship together. That number shoots up to two-thirds with a score of sixty-six to eighty—what we call a Platinum Match."

"Wow," Fizzy whispered, staring at the new couple laughing together over an intimate candlelit dinner. "That's a huge jump."

Lisa nodded. "But three out of four couples find long-term love with scores of eighty to ninety," she said. "And *those* are the matches we hope to eventually find for everyone in our database." She swiped ahead to a couple getting married under a broad arch of flowers. "We call them Titanium."

Admittedly, Jess had to hide her shock over that statistic. It was impressive. She still had about a million questions, though, and gestured to the couple in the wedding scenario; the woman was Asian, the man of Middle Eastern descent. "It seems from your marketing tools that DNADuo doesn't have an ethnicity bias."

"Correct. It's about finding a soulmate based on a set of biological markers. While there are some genetic variants found across different ethnicities, this technology is about DNA-level compatibility, not symmetry. Not to put too technical a point on it, but in many cases, compatibility is stronger when the two individuals have different genetic markers, rather than the same. And keep in mind, the DNADuo can't take cultural influences into account, so the importance of all of this information has to be weighed by the client personally. Clients can indicate any and all desired criteria in their intake form—cultural background, religion, et cetera. The algorithm discounts any compatibility findings that don't fall within their prescribed criteria."

"So if I'm gay?"

"Sure." Lisa didn't hesitate. "On your intake form, you can select to see female matches, male matches, nonbinary matches, or all of the above. As a company, we don't discriminate based on race, cultural identity, gender, sexual orientation, or religion, and the DNADuo doesn't, either. Only a handful of the compatibility sequence signatures are located on the X or Y chromosomes; certainly not enough to nullify the data set if a particular sexual genotype is excluded."

Jess leaned back in her chair, admittedly—and unexpectedly—impressed.

"Sorry, one more question," Fizzy said. "You said to consider the compatibility scores as one to one hundred . . . Have you ever seen a score higher than ninety?"

Lisa smiled genuinely. "Only three times."

"And?" Jess's heart started slamming against her breastbone. Her brain imagined a different slot machine now, one with 3,500 rows, and a single pull that lined up nearly every single cherry.

For the first time since she walked into the room, Lisa let the hypercompetent surfer-executive façade drop. She looked young, and hopeful, and awestruck: "That's what gives me the most confidence in this company. Yes, three is a low number, but the couples who've tested above ninety are the three couples who've scored the highest on emotional stability, communication and collaboration, and sexual satisfaction. They're *Diamond* Matches. Do we want more of those? Of course. I mean, the DNADuo has been tested on one hundred and forty thousand people and fully validated in nearly twenty thousand couples. That is an enormous study for a start-up of this size, but there are at least five million people on Hinge and an estimated fifty million people on Tinder. Until we can get the whole world of data in our server, we won't know how many Diamond Matches are really out there."

FOUR

Fizzy was calling.

Fizzy never called.

So even though it was 8:13, and Jess was supposed to have Juno at school in two minutes, and had yet to feed her child or have a single sip of coffee, and had a meeting downtown at 9:30, and was barely dressed, she answered.

"You never call," Jess said.

"This app is insane," Fizzy said.

Juno ran out, still in her pajamas. "I'm ready for breakfast!"

Tilting her phone away from her mouth, Jess whispered, "You need to wear actual clothing, my love."

Her daughter groaned as she stomped back to her bedroom.

"I'm—" Fizzy said, and then paused. "Okay, good point. This shirt is pretty transparent." Another pause. "Wait, how did you know what I'm wearing?"

"I was talking to my kid," Jess said, laughing. "What is this about the app being insane? What app?"

"I've gotten twenty-three matches since my DNADuo results came in this morning."

Jess did the quick mental math—it'd only been two days since their visit to the site. Either GeneticAlly was insanely efficient, or it wasn't running many samples these days. She had to admit, begrudgingly, that any company that invested in a unique neural network was taking its data seriously.

"Twenty-three?" She poured a cup of coffee, and Pigeon wound her way between Jess's legs, purring. Jess made the mistake of briefly looking down at the cat, and her cup overfilled, pooling coffee on the countertop. Cursing, she leaned over to open the front door, letting Pigeon out, then dug in a drawer for a dish towel. "That's a lot of soulmates."

"I cast a pretty wide net," Fizzy agreed. "I said anything above a score of thirteen."

"Thirteen?"

"It's fun to just see what happens when you date guys with no expectations."

Coffee dripped from the counter onto the floor, soaking through Jess's lucky socks. *"Goddammit."*

"It's just a potentially terrible date, not plastic surgery."

"I wasn't goddammitting you, I spilled coffee."

"Think of it as a character study," Fizzy waxed on. "What happens when you put two completely incompatible people together? Will they beat the odds? Or come out fighting . . . each other?" She paused, and Jess imagined her friend reaching for her notebook. A weird alert sounded in the background. "Twenty-four!"

Juno wandered into the kitchen dressed for school, but her hair remained a bird's nest. "Mama, can I have a smoothie?"

"Baby, go brush your hair."

"I assume you were talking to Juno again," Fizzy said distractedly.

"Can I, Mama?"

"I was," Jess said to Fizzy, and then, "and yes, Junebug, I'll make one, but go brush your hair and your teeth, too, please." Back in the kitchen, Jess glanced at the clock and groaned. She pulled a basket of strawberries from the fridge.

"Okay," Fizzy said, "I have a lunch date today with Aiden B., a Base Match with a score of thirteen, and a dinner date tomorrow with Antonio R., also a Base Match, twenty-one."

"Don't ever let anyone tell you you're not adventurous."

"Mom," Juno called from the bathroom. "Remember, don't let Pigeon out because the gardener is here today!"

Jess whirled around and stared out the front window, across the cat-less courtyard, and down the path to the open gate.

"Fizz, I've gotta jet."

ONE EXPLODED BLENDER, one four-block cat chase, two changes of clothes (Jess's), one impossibly double-knotted sneaker (Juno's), and one tardy drop-off later, Juno was at school and Jess was finally hustling her ass downtown. A huge meeting with Jennings Grocery that morning, two potential new clients in the afternoon, and then a school meeting at six. Marathon, but doable. But why was it the nature of the universe that on the day Jess was already running behind, there was an accident on the 5, a detour at her exit, and not a single parking space to be found? She passed row after row of luxury sedans and was beginning to wonder whether every rich person in San Diego was in the Gaslamp at the same time, but then, *huzzah*: her prayers were answered by a flash of reverse lights to her right. She rolled forward, flipping on her blinker. Relief pumped adrenaline through her bloodstream like there was an actual prize for parking, rather than an intense meeting with some clients she was fairly sure wanted to cherry-pick their data to match their annual projections.

But just as Jess moved her foot to the accelerator to pull in, a black sedan swerved around the bend from the next row over, gliding into the spot with an impressive *Fast & Furious* screech.

Smacking the steering wheel, Jess yelled an aggravated "Oh, come on!"

She threw her hands up passive-aggressively, hoping the driver saw and felt like an asshole for taking the spot from a woman who'd never done anything more selfish than eat the last Ding Dong and blame it on her grandfather. Exaggerations aside, Jess—always able to keep her cool behind the wheel—was on the verge of laying a heavy hand on her horn. But then the car door opened, and one impossibly long leg stretched out, wrapped in pressed charcoal trousers and capped by a shiny leather shoe. There was something about the shoulders that emerged, the poise . . . and then it hit her. Jess didn't need to see his face to know, because this wasn't just any black sedan, it was a black Audi. *His* black Audi.

River Peña stole her parking spot.

She leaned out her window, shouting, "Hey!" But he was already walking briskly down the sidewalk and didn't bother to turn around.

Jess spotted another car backing out a few rows away, and winced at the audible squeal of her tires as she bolted around the turn. Ready to lay on her horn lest anyone dare take this spot, she pulled in, shoved her car into park, grabbed everything she needed, and shuffle-jogged in heels and her fitted skirt toward the entrance.

Nearly ten minutes late now, but last time Jennings had been running fifteen minutes behind, and she could already see the elevators on the other side of the glass doors. She just might make it . . .

And who was standing at the elevator but River Peña? Jess watched him reach forward, pressing the button.

The light above it blinked on, the doors slid open. He took a step forward, and Jess clutched her laptop to her chest, breaking into a sprint.

"Hold it, please!"

Turning, he glanced over his shoulder and then disappeared into the elevator.

"Motherfucker!" Jess mumbled.

Jennings Grocery headquarters was only three floors up, so instead of waiting, she took the stairs. Two at a time. Visibly out of breath when she jogged from the stairwell into the hallway, Jess immediately collided with a brick wall of a man. For the record, he smelled amazing. It was infuriating.

"Careful," he murmured, eyes on his phone as he stepped around her, continuing down the hall.

But Jess had reached the boiling point: "Americano!"

Hesitating only briefly, he turned. His dark hair fell over one eye and he brushed it aside. "I'm sorry?"

"Apology not accepted. You took my parking spot."

"I took your—?"

"And you didn't hold the elevator," she said. "I'm running late, you saw me, and you didn't bother to hold the door."

"I didn't *see* you." He let out a short, incredulous laugh. "Maybe you should leave a little earlier next time."

"Wow. You really are an asshole."

He frowned, studying her. "Do we know each other?"

"Are you kidding?" She pointed to her chest. "Twiggs? Spit in a vial? Entirely average? Any of that ring a bell?"

Comprehension was a weather front that moved across his face. Surprise, recognition, embarrassment.

"I . . ." His eyes flickered over her and then down the hall as if there might be reinforcements coming at any moment. "You were . . . completely unrecognizable. I didn't know it was you."

For the life of her, Jess couldn't figure out if that was a sick burn or a backhanded compliment.

"I'm sorry, I don't recall your name, Ms. . . . ?" he asked evenly.

"You've never known it."

And there was the look that delighted her—the one that said he was barely tolerating the conversation. Breaking eye contact, he finally glanced down at his watch. "You said something about running late?"

Shit!

Jess pushed past him, jogging ten feet down the hall to Suite 303, the offices of Jennings Grocery.

———————

THIRTY-ONE PERCENT OF California households are run by single parents, but Jess would never have guessed that from the people streaming into the Alice Birney Elementary Science-Art Fair meeting. Being a solo parent at a school event was like being a single person at a couples' party. Minus the wine. If Nana or Pops wasn't with her, Jess was made intensely aware that the other parents had no idea how to interact with a single mom. The longest conversation she'd had with someone there had been at the first-grade holiday recital when a mom had asked if Jess's husband was going to be sitting in the empty seat next to her. When she'd said, "No husband, free chair," the other woman smiled awkwardly for a few beats before rolling on breathlessly for five minutes about how sorry she was that she didn't know any nice single men.

But for the first time at one of these events, she realized as she walked into the hall, Jess was relieved to be alone; she wouldn't have to small-talk. She wasn't sure she'd be able to do that tonight; every meeting she'd had today had been a dead end. Well, except the Jennings Grocery meeting. That was a complete disaster.

One of the biggest sins in statistics is cherry-picking—choosing which data sets to include in analysis after the study is finished. There are plenty of legitimate reasons to drop outliers: the data isn't collected correctly, etc. But if a data point affects both results and assumptions, it must be included. And just as Jess suspected, Jennings Grocery didn't just want to exclude a few data points in the set they sent her; they wanted to eliminate enormous territories entirely in their report to shareholders, because the numbers didn't fit their projected sales targets.

She refused—even though she'd spent four months meticulously designing the analysis, writing the code, building the program. During the meeting, the executives had exchanged extended periods of silent eye contact, and eventually shooed Jess out of the room, saying they'd be in touch.

Was it stupid to be so inflexible with her biggest account? She couldn't shake a sense of panic. If she lost Jennings, she would lose a third of her income for the year. Juno might need braces, and she'd be driving in eight years. What if she wanted to start doing dance competitions? What if she got sick? Nana and Pops weren't getting any younger, either.

Movement in her peripheral vision pulled her attention, and Jess watched Juno's second-grade teacher, Mrs. Klein, and the principal, Mr. Walker, come to the front of the room. Mrs. Klein was dressed as some hybrid of a scientist and artist: lab coat, goggles, beret, paint palette. Mr. Walker was dressed as, Jess supposed, a kid: baggy shorts, knee-high socks, and a Padres baseball cap. They sat in chairs facing the assembled parents.

The principal-child crossed his arms and pouted dramatically, and the room fell to a hush. "I don't even get what a science-art fair is. Do I *have* to do it?"

"You don't *have* to do the science-art fair," Mrs. Klein said, hamming it up for the crowd, "you *GET* to do the science-art fair!"

The room rippled with polite laughter, and the rest of the second-grade team passed out handouts with information as the little play went on. Jess scanned the stapled pages, skimming instructions for helping the children find an art project that was based in some area of science: plant life, animal life, engineering, chemistry. A papier-mâché plant with various structures labeled. A painting of a dog skeleton. A house made out of Popsicle sticks. It was one of the things that Jess loved about this little school—the creative curriculum, the emphasis on integrated learning—but with the murmuring voices rising from the crowd, she was pulled out of her little bubble. In the seats all around her, heads came together in excited conversation. Husband-and-wife teams brainstormed fun projects for their kids, and the dread in Jess's stomach curdled with loneliness. She was flanked by an empty seat on each side, a little buffer zone to protect the other parents from the infection of singlehood.

Mood still low despite—she had to admit—some pretty solid jokes from Mr. Walker and Mrs. Klein, Jess practically crawled across the parking lot. Her car was parked next to a pearl-white Porsche that made her red 2008 Corolla look like an old roller skate missing its mate. Jess couldn't feel ashamed of the clunker, though; this car had driven her home from the maternity ward and then to her college graduation only a month later. It took them on various outings for Try Something New Sundays and road trips to Disneyland and—

"Jessica!"

She jerked around at the sound of a trilling voice and turned to find a tall, thin blond woman waving her down. Dawn Porter: PTA President, Mother of the Year, Zero Gag Reflex, probably. Jess braced herself to feel like a shitty mom for at least five minutes.

"Dawn! Hey." Jess winced in preemptive apology. "It's been a long day and—"

"Oh God, totally. I know you're—like, frazzled all the time. Poor thing. If I can just get one second? I wanted to check on the auction site you were going to build? The fundraiser for the new playground equipment?"

Crap.

The site Jess had been working on when Juno threw up at school and needed to be picked up, then when a client had a last-minute shareholders meeting and needed her to spend twelve hours in LA, then when she'd been interrupted by a phone call from her mom asking for some help making rent.

The site Jess had then forgotten about until this second. *Good job, Jess.*

"I'm totally on it, Dawn," she said. "Just been a little slammed lately."

"Ugh, I know, we are all so *busy*." Dawn pressed a button on the key fob in her hand. The lights on the gleaming Porsche winked and the tailgate drifted open with a delicate chime. Hanging from Dawn's back seat were neat little organized totes, each monogrammed with her children's names—Hunter, Parker, Taylor—and words like *Snacks* and *Books* and *Car Fun!*

In the trunk of Jess's car was a pair of badly tangled bedazzled cat leashes, a dozen mismatched grocery bags, a chain of tampons Juno had constructed while they waited with a flat tire, and at least thirty-two other items she fully intended to take inside . . . someday.

Dawn placed the packet of school papers in one pouch, moving some dry cleaning on a hook out of the way, then pressed the key fob again to close the hatch with a whisper.

She turned back to Jess. "I only ask because Kyle—you've met my husband, Kyle?" She gestured to a man chatting with two other dads across the parking lot. "Anyway, he said he could have one of the paralegals down at Porter, Aaron, and Kim whip something up. It wouldn't be a problem—they love helping out, and every time I look at you, I think, 'Poor Jessica is just running herself ragged!'"

Her defensiveness rocketed out: "I've got it."

Dawn tilted her head, surprised by the force of this reaction, and Jess wanted to reel the words back in. It had required some pretty intense blending with her drugstore foundation stick to get the dark circles under her eyes to disappear this morning, and she was sure the parking lot's sodium lights weren't her *best* lighting. Today had been hellacious, and the last thing Jess wanted was to become the subject of Mom Gossip. She thought of the dozens of things she could do with that time because, really, what did she care who built the stupid site?

Because I want to be a good mom, she thought. *I want to be present for Juno, even if some days I feel like I'm failing.*

"Really," Jess assured her. "It's nearly finished." Thank God. "I should have something for you soon."

"Well. That's great then! I'll let the board know so they stop fussing at me!"

"Great," Jess repeated as Dawn popped into the passenger side of her car. "Great."

"I'M HIDING IN the bathroom, crying on the toilet," she said when Fizzy answered an hour later.

Jess's friend barked out a laugh and an "Aww, I love it when you ignore boundaries. Usually that's my wheelhouse."

"I had a terrible day." Jess swiped a hand across her nose. "I'm lonely. And I feel like such an asshole complaining, but you're always going to be a bigger asshole than I am, so I can complain to you."

"I swear, Jessica, you know just what to say to make my heart melt." The funny thing was, Fizzy meant it. "Let me have it."

Jess closed her eyes, leaning back against the water tank. "It all seems like such little stuff. After we got off the phone this morning, my entire day fell apart. Pigeon escaped, my blender blew up all over my shirt, we were running late. I had a meeting at Jennings Grocery, but Americano stole my parking spot—"

"You saw Americano in the wild?"

"I did," she said. "He continues to be terrible. Then my big meeting went horribly, and I had to jet to the school for this science-art thing, and I sat in the back and just stared at all of these happily married couples who were seeing each other at the end of the day, and I swear to God, Fizz, I've never felt so lonely in my entire life. And then PTA Dawn reminded me to finish the fundraiser website, and I just did but it's probably a holy mess and I cannot find a bone in me that cares."

Before Fizzy could speak, Jess added, "And don't say anything, because I know how this sounds—like 'poor me, and I'm all alone.' I *know* I'm lucky. I have the best kid, and I have Nana and Pops here to help me whenever I need them. I have you—"

"Cutting in now," Fizzy said. "Yes, you have Nana and Pops, you have a great kid, you have me. I am here for you every day, for forever, but please, Jess. It isn't the same. You're talking about wanting to have someone to come home to, to talk to, and yeah—to get naked with. It isn't selfish to want that. You aren't somehow putting Juno second by occasionally putting your needs first. Juno needs a happy mom."

"It isn't only that," Jess said quietly. "Do I worry about introducing Juno to a man someday? Yes, completely. But the idea of putting myself out there is honestly more exhausting than anything. I had to change my shirt twice this morning for the meeting, first for the smoothie explosion, and second when I drooled a glob of toothpaste on my chest."

"Reason number one why I always brush my teeth naked," Fizzy joked, and Jess laughed. "And PS? You probably looked straight-up gorgeous, regardless of what you think."

"Thank you—"

"I'm serious," Fizzy pressed. "Listen to me. You're so beautiful, it's stupid. Your eyes? Like, I try to describe that blue in books, and it just sounds cliché. You have the cutest little bod, and literally the best lips. And for free! People usually have to pay for mouths like that."

Jess laughed through a sob.

"If I didn't know you were such a head case, I'd ask you out myself."

"You see me through that lens because you love me," Jess said, chin wobbling. "Dating in our thirties is different. It requires us to get our shit together, and most days just being a mom and hustling my ass off to keep my head above water takes everything I've got. Where am I going to find the time and energy to hunt for a good guy when most of the dudes on Tinder think a quick drink earns them sex?"

Jess could practically hear Fizzy's gape on the other end of the line. "We just went to a presentation at a company that asks you to spit in a vial and they'll hand over a list of potential *soulmates*." She enunciated the last word so it stretched for three long syllables. "No one is asking you to *hunt*."

"Even the DNADuo still requires dating!" Jess told her, laughing. "It's not like I get a name and we elope! There's still trial and error."

"You could specify only high-level matches," Fizzy argued. "You don't have to do what I'm doing and take whatever comes your way. Hell, tell them you only want matches of seventy or higher. What do you have to lose?" She paused, and then added more gently, "Put yourself first tonight, Jessie. Just for ten minutes. Consider it an early B-day present for the big Three-Oh."

"Don't remind me."

Fizzy laughed. "You don't have to answer any of the matches if you change your mind, but for tonight, just imagine a world where you find someone who's perfect for you, and is there for you, and is the head you can lean yours against at the end of the day."

When they hung up, Jess's eyes landed on the DNADuo box Fizzy had pushed into her hands as they'd left GeneticAlly.

Before she could talk herself out of it, she reached for the box, tore it open, spit into the vial, sealed the whole thing in the enclosed envelope, and walked it out to the mailbox.

FIVE

———⌐———

JESS ADJUSTED THE elastic strap beneath her chin. Was this what thirty felt like? Spending her birthday in a coffee shop with a madwoman who would get the entire room to belt "Happy Birthday" if Jess tried to take off this sparkly birthday hat?

Fizzy looked up abruptly. "You goblin. Leave the hat alone."

"It's itchy! Tell me about your date with Aiden B."

Fizzy waved this off, already over it. "He lives with his sister."

"Is that an automatic disqualification?"

"I mean, they live together as in they share a bedroom." She shook her head, clearly not wanting Jess to ask more. "It's uncharted territory for me. I'm unwilling to explore what it means."

Jess laughed. "Fair enough. If I remember, he was only a score of, what? Thirteen? What about . . . ?" She was blanking on the other guy's name.

"Antonio?" Fizzy prompted. "He was hot."

"He was the twenty-one?"

"Yeah. We had dinner, we had sex." Fizzy shrugged, summarizing. "We won't be seeing each other again, though." As if she remembered something, she picked up her notebook and jotted down a couple of words.

"What did you just write down?"

Fizzy's lip curled. "Dick tattoo."

Jess's curled, too. "What? No."

"Also," Fizzy said, "he wanted me to talk dirty, so I did, but apparently I went too dirty."

Jess burst out laughing again. "You went too dirty for a guy with a dick tattoo? Felicity Chen, my God." She lifted her coffee to her lips. "But to be fair, you're setting yourself up for this. Why are you casting the net so wide? Just filter the results. I don't get it."

Fizzy got that look she had when she was about to get real intense. "Listen. Tinder is the biggest dating app in the world for a reason. Sometimes people just want to have fun. The benefit here is that we get to choose what level of investment we want, and right now, for me, that level is hovering somewhere around *sex with people I don't feel obligated to call again*." She lifted her chin. "I'm testing the waters without all the pressure of forever."

Holding up her hands in defense, Jess said, "I'm not judging. Write this dissertation and mail it to Americano."

Fizzy gave her a casual middle finger. "Anyway, I've got a date with a twenty-three named Ted tomorrow—who is himself only twenty-one—and on Saturday I'm having dinner with a thirty-one named Ralph."

"Thirty-one? Wow, that's a Silver. Moving up in the world."

Fizzy opened her mouth to reply when, on the table between them, a phone delivered a telltale chime.

Jess assumed it was another mediocre compatibility score hitting Fizzy's inbox, and Fizzy seemed to assume the same, reaching for her phone—

So it took them both a second to register that the sound had actually come from Jess's phone . . . and it took Jess another to remember she'd sent her "sample" away for analysis.

Betrayal widened every one of Fizzy's features. "*Jessica Davis.* I'm over here telling you about dick tattoos and you don't even tell me you sent your spit!"

Jess barked out an uncomfortable laugh. "I can explain!"

"You'd better!"

She was unable to control her bubbling laughter. Fizzy looked genuinely furious in a mildly cartoonish way. "It was last Thursday, remember? I called you from the toilet. On impulse, I put it in the mail after we hung up, downloaded the app and filled out the basic info, and then totally spaced on it."

Fizzy picked up Jess's phone, tapping it awake with a punitive jab of her index finger. Entering the passcode, she stared in confusion down at the screen while Jess stared with similar confusion at her. "I don't remember giving you my passcode."

"Juno's birthday. You should choose a more secure code. Never know what brand of crazy can get into your phone."

Jess raised a wry eyebrow. "You don't say."

Fizzy turned the screen to face her. "It's red. What does that mean?"

"What's red?" Jess's amusement at the situation was fading, quickly replaced by the realization that her DNADuo app had just pinged her with an alert.

She'd excluded matches below seventy percent.

She had a Platinum or higher match.

She suddenly understood Fizzy's desire to dip a toe in the soul-mate waters rather than dive headfirst. Jess wasn't ready. She wasn't even sure she was curious.

"The thing," Fizzy said, pointing aggressively. "The little—circle notification thing over the app icon that means you have a result!"

The prospect of making a decision based on a numerical score made Jess immediately tired. She took her phone back, tempted to delete the app along with whatever impulse had told her to spit in that vial in the first place. "Is red bad?"

"All of mine are green," Fizzy explained. "Whether it's a compat-ibility score of twelve or thirty-one, the match notifications have been green."

Okay, if the match notifications were green, at least Jess knew a potential soulmate wasn't just casually hanging out in her inbox. "Might I suggest your intensity about this is now at an eleven?"

Fizzy shot back: "To my romance-loving heart, this app is the most fascinating game ever. Humor me."

"Most likely it means there was something wrong with my sam-ple," Jess said, relief expanding in her. "I did it after I brushed my teeth, and it says to wait an hour after eating or drinking anything before spitting." She put her phone back on the table, screen-side down. "I'll deal with it later."

She should've known better. "Uh. Nope." Fizzy immediately handed the phone back to her. "I want to know what red means."

"It's my birthday, and I can ignore it if I want to."

Fizzy shook her head. "What's a better birthday gift than a soul-mate?"

With a sigh, Jess clicked on the DNADuo icon. No notifications under the tab labeled Compatibility Scores, but she did have a small red bubble indicating a new message. Jess's eyes quickly scanned the words, but her brain was slow to process them. Starting over, Jess read it slowly, word by word, even though there were only eight of them: *Please call our office at your earliest convenience.*

"What does it say?"

Jess handed the phone over. "It's from GeneticAlly. I need to call them at my earliest convenience. That's weird. Isn't that weird? Like, why not just tell me another sample kit is required?"

Fizzy read it, frowning. "They sent it in your app inbox, so you can reply, right? Let's just ask what this is about." Instead of handing the phone back, she did it herself, dictating each word as she typed. "May—I—ask—what—this—is—concerning?" Fizzy stared at the screen, and after only a few seconds, her brows shot up excitedly. "Someone's typing back!"

Meanwhile, Jess's stomach was crawling into her throat. She already hated how intense it all felt; this was way too much investment and expectation for something she'd done on impulse in a crappy mood. "I'm sure it's just a sample thing, just—"

"Shh."

"Fizz," Jess said, "just give me my phone. I don't care about any of—"

Fizzy held up a hand. "They're typ— Oh." Her brows furrowed. "Okay, you're right. This is weird."

She handed the phone back, and Jess's stomach twisted as she read the note.

Do you mind coming in? it said. *We'll send a car.*

THEY'D SEND A *car?*

Good grief.

Jess managed to find about a thousand important things she needed to do immediately. She made a DMV appointment to renew her license, scheduled her and Juno's annual physical exams and dentist appointments. She went for a run; she took a long shower. She even bought herself a new sweater as a birthday indulgence. She had lunch with Nana and Pops, cleaned her apartment, folded every piece of laundry she could find, picked up Juno from school, and read almost an entire Judy Blume novel with her before Juno urged Jess to leave the apartment so Nana and Pops could come over and get the surprise party ready.

Surprise!

With two hours to kill and the notification like a splinter in her thumb, Jess gave up and called Lisa Addams.

The GeneticAlly building was dark from the outside, but a light in the lobby flickered on as the town car pulled up to the curb. Lisa emerged, walking briskly out and opening the car door.

"Jessica," she said breathlessly. "Thanks for coming in on such short notice."

Even in the dusk, Jess spotted the flush on Lisa's cheeks, the way her hairline seemed just the slightest bit sweaty. She tumbled one more tick down the Uneasy Scale.

"No problem. I only have about an hour, though."

"Of course. Come on in."

Lisa turned, leading them into the empty building. None of this seemed like normal protocol, which made Jess feel like she'd swallowed battery acid. "I have to admit I'm really confused about why this is so urgent."

"I'll explain everything once we're inside."

Jess followed her through the double doors and down the long hallway she'd walked the last time she was here. Everyone was clearly done for the day; the offices were dark and vacant in that way that made even innocuous spaces seem creepy.

In the conference room, Lisa gestured to six people seated around a large table. River wasn't among them.

"Jessica, I'd like to introduce you to our executive team."

Their what now?

"This is David Morris, the principal investigator in charge of the original research, and the CEO of GeneticAlly."

A man to her right stood, stretching out his hand, and Jess recognized him as the person she'd met after overhearing River call her "entirely average."

"Jessica. It's so great to see you again."

"You too." She wiped her palm on her pants before shaking. And then it sank in: Original research. CEO. "Right. I guess I didn't realize who I was meeting in the hall the other day."

He laughed a big, open-mouthed laugh. "Well, it feels a little douchey to say, 'I'm CEO David Morris.'"

"Maybe," Jess said, "but you've earned the right."

"I'm friends with Alan Timberland over at Genentech," he said, still smiling, "and he's mentioned some analytics help he had. After looking at your intake information from the other day, I put two and two together and realized you're the brain behind their new high-throughput screening algorithms."

Jess was a wine bottle, slowly uncorked. *Oh, this is about data?* Had GeneticAlly brought her here to talk about algorithms?

"Alan's great," she said carefully. At the prospect that she was here for consulting, not because she had lemur DNA, the nausea slowly cleared.

Lisa gestured to an overly tanned man to David's left. "Brandon Butkis is our head of marketing."

Another hand closed around Jess's, another face gave her an urgent, vibrating smile. All she could see was blindingly white capped teeth.

After Jess had shaken every hand in the room, Lisa gestured for her to sit down in the direct center seat at the table.

"It's probably unexpected to walk into a full room like this," Lisa started.

"A little," Jess agreed, "but I know how important it is to get data organized, and how hard it is to do that when the data set is as big as yours."

David and Brandon exchanged a quick look. Lisa's smile slipped for only a second, but Jess logged it. "That's definitely true. I'm sure you know that better than anyone."

A man—Jess thought his name was Sanjeev—on the other side of the table caught Lisa's attention. "Is Peña coming in for this?"

"He'll be here," Lisa said, and then turned to Jess. "Sorry to make you wait, Jessica."

"Jess is fine," she said, adding unnecessarily, "I mean, calling me Jess is fine." Another awkward pause. "I wasn't referring to myself in the third person."

After some courtesy laughter, the room fell into a pin-drop silence. It seemed that everyone but Jess knew what this was all about, but no one could tell her until River had arrived. Unfortunately, no one knew where he was ("He said he was on his way up from his office ten minutes ago," Sanjeev told the throat-clearing, paper-shuffling table).

Nor could anyone think of something to say. So of course, her mouth opened, and words tumbled out. "You all must be very excited for the launch."

Heads bobbed around the table, and Brandon Butkis delivered an enthusiastic "Very!"

"Have you all given samples as well?" she asked.

There was a strange exchange of looks around the table before David said carefully, "We have, yes."

Jess was just about to break and ask for some bloody information when the door burst open and River made a grand entrance much like his irritating, sweeping arrivals at Twiggs. "I'm here. What's up?"

A tangible energy filled the room. Everyone sat up straighter. Every eye followed him as he moved to his seat. Yes, he was great to look at, but there seemed to be more to the weight of their attention, like the low, humming vibration of hero worship.

River's gaze passed over the group, sweeping past Jess before pausing and jerking back to her face. "Why's she here?"

"Have a seat, Riv," Lisa said, then turned to a petite Asian woman to her right. "Tiff? Do you want to hand out the data?"

Data. Yes. Great. Jess's shoulders eased, and she took a sheet when the stack came around.

The handout contained much less information than Jess would need to give useful feedback on a commercial undertaking of this scale. Two client IDs were listed at the top left and a red circle around a number in the upper right corner. Ninety-eight. Beneath was a table with a simple summary of a data set: variable names, means, deviations, and P values with many, many zeroes after the decimal.

There was a highly significant finding in this data; the urgency of this meeting was becoming clear.

River released a breath that sounded like it'd been punched out of him.

"Wow," Jess said. "Ninety-eight. Is that a compatibility score? I realize I'm new to this, but that's huge, right?" She flipped back to her memory of Lisa's presentation. "Diamond?"

The nervous energy at the table doubled; all but one head nodded. River was still staring at the piece of paper.

"Yes," Lisa said, and her smile was so intense the skin had grown tight around her eyes. "The highest we've seen in the DNADuo is ninety-three."

"Okay, so are we asking about a way to confirm this interaction?" Jess leaned in, looking at the variables. "Without the raw data, I can only guess, but it looks like you've customized your stats using an N-type analysis—which is exactly what I would have used. But I'm sure you know the biggest problem with this is that the bounds we would normally use for a typical algorithm become less effective. Though"—she chuckled—"looking at this P value, I'm guessing with this pair the interactions are everywhere, even with stricter bounds. I could create a non-Euclidean metric, something like a multidimensional data structure—like a k-d tree or cover tree . . ." She trailed off, looking up. No one was nodding excitedly; no one was jumping in to brainstorm. Maybe there wasn't another statistician in the room. "I'm more than happy to dig into your post hoc analyses, though with the number of genes in your array, I might need a couple weeks."

Self-conscious now, she put the packet down on the table, smoothing it with her left hand. The room had grown so quiet, the sound of her palm over paper seemed to echo around them. But no one else was actually looking at their handout, or even seemed to be listening. They were all looking at River.

And when Jess looked at him, at the raw shock in his expression, a current of electricity ran through her, almost like she'd just touched a live wire.

He cleared his throat and turned to Tiffany. "Tiff, did you look through the raw data?"

She nodded, but she was staring at David, who was exchanging another heavy look with Brandon. The room felt deeply, meaningfully silent, and Jess realized she was missing an important context for the gravity here.

Awareness sank as quickly as a weight in water. Jess glanced down again at the client information.

Client 144326.

Client 000001.

Oh, God.

"Um . . . who is client number one?"

River cleared his throat; he'd gone sheet white and gripped the paper in two hands. "Me."

Oh. Well, Jesus Christ, no wonder he wanted to confirm the analysis. A Diamond Match for the original scientist on the project was huge news, especially this close to launch.

"Okay, I get it." Jess took a deep breath, leaning back, ready to get to work. "How can I help?"

River looked at Lisa then, his eyes heavy with the obvious question. Literally everyone else in the room was staring at him, waiting for him to say it: *Have we confirmed the assay? Have we replicated the finding with a backup sample?*

But that wasn't what he asked. In a low, shaky voice, River murmured, "Who is 1-4-4-3-2-6?"

Every head swung Jess's way and—

When she realized what was going on, why they were all there, why they had sent a car, why they hadn't made her sign an NDA for data purposes, why River hadn't known she would be there, and why everyone else was looking at Jess with that fevered, vibrating force in their expressions, it felt a little like falling off a curb, except she was sitting.

It was genuinely so absurd she started laughing.

Ninety-eight!

"Oh." Jess was still laughing as she stood on shaky legs. Her heartbeat was a pulsating cacophony in her ears. "I'm not here to advise on your statistics."

Ninety-eight. P values with at least ten zeroes after the decimal. Her brain scratched around, looking for a way out of this.

"Jess—" Lisa began.

"This isn't right," Jess cut her off, fumbling for her purse.

"We ran the data through all of our standard analysis programs," Tiffany added quietly.

"No, I mean I'm sure your stats are—" Jess started, but realized she couldn't finish the sentence because it would be a lie. Clearly their statistics were garbage and they were all delusional. And unfortunately, Jess hadn't driven herself here. "I can call someone to come pick me up."

Jess glanced at River—who was already watching her with wild, dark eyes—and then at surfer-chic Lisa, and Toothy Brandon, and Jeff Goldblum's Benedict Cumberbatch, and every other person in the room who'd also never dealt with this particular situation. "It was so nice meeting everyone. Thanks so much for having me. Sorry for the ramble about N-type analyses."

She turned, opening the door with a hand she wasn't all that sure was going to cooperate, and practically sprinted back the way she came.

SIX

———⌐———

JESS'S HANDS WERE shaking so uncontrollably that, as she walked, she could barely type out a text plea to Pops to come pick her up with the address of the building. Somehow the hall had stretched; it took her a century to get to the elevator, and when she pushed the button, she heard its slow grind up from the bottom floor.

Feet jogged down the hall. They didn't sound like Lisa's heels, and yeah—when Jess looked up, she saw River making his way toward her.

"Jessica," he said, holding up a hand. "Hold on a second."

Was he serious? Jess turned and continued toward the door labeled EXIT, pushing into the stairwell. Ten hurried steps down before the door clanged shut behind her; the sound was so jarring it actually made her duck. Half a flight above, the door flew open again. Footsteps tap-tap-tapped down toward her, and Jess accelerated, jogging down to the first level and emerging into the lobby.

River managed to get out only a patient, echoing "Jessica, wait" before the lobby stairwell door sealed shut.

It didn't matter; he would invariably catch her outside. Because although Pops had replied that he was out getting the cake and could get there quickly, it wasn't like he could drive to La Jolla in three minutes. At least outside she could breathe a precious handful of seconds of fresh air, could think without the pressure of everyone's stunned attention on her. What were they thinking, dropping something so personal in a room full of strangers?

Wrapping her arms around her midsection, Jess paced the sidewalk in front of the building, waiting. When she heard River emerge, she expected him to start talking right away, but he didn't. He approached her slowly, cautiously, and came to a stop about ten feet away.

For maybe three seconds, Jess liked him for giving her space. But then she remembered that he wasn't usually so considerate . . . and he was supposedly her *soulmate*.

The absurdity of that meeting finally hit her like a slap, and she coughed out an overwhelmed laugh. "Oh my God. What just happened?"

He spoke through the chilly quiet. "It was a surprise to me, too."

His words felt like an echo between them. They surprised *him*? "How? You—you know everyone in that room. Why would they tell you like that?" she asked. "Why would they have everyone there, like some kind of a reality show?"

"I can only assume they wanted us all to have a conversation about how to handle it."

"'Handle it'?" she repeated. "You really are dead inside, aren't you?"

"I meant handle for the company. I'm sure it's occurred to you that the optics of one of the founders having the highest recorded compatibility score is both fantastic and fraught, from a marketing perspective."

"Any woman would be lucky to hear these words from her"—Jess used finger quotes—"'biological soulmate.'"

He exhaled slowly. "I also assume they were worried that if they told you remotely, you wouldn't come in." River shrugged, sliding one hand into his trouser pocket. "Sanjeev—the head of assay development—is a close friend. I'd mentioned our run-in downtown to him, and your blowing up at me—"

"My *'blowing up'* at you?"

"—and word probably spread when the result came in and your name was associated."

"'Associated'?" Unproductive, but the only thing she could focus on was the way he spoke like he was reading aloud from a textbook. God, Siri carried on a more familiar conversation.

"I'm sorry that we have to consider the business implications of all of this," River said, "but I assume you understand this is a really big deal, on several levels."

Jess stared at him, giving him the benefit of the doubt that he was allowing for at least one of these levels being human emotion. "Uh, yeah, I get that. But *we* don't have to consider anything. I mean—there's no way, River. We both know it's an error, right? Or if not an error, that the compatibility paradigm doesn't apply to us."

"Why is it your first assumption that the technology is wrong?"

"Why isn't it yours?"

He laughed dryly, looking past her. "The DNADuo has been validated thousands of times. If we got scores of ninety-eight all the time, I'd be more skeptical."

"I can't imagine being *less* skeptical. Every thought in here"—Jess pointed to her head—"is either 'LOL no' or 'Surely you jest.'" She paused, taking him in. "How can you look at me with a straight face right now?"

He reached up, running a hand through his hair. "Biological compatibility is independent of whether or not we like each other."

A horrified laugh ripped out of her. "Is that the company slogan or your best pickup line?"

"Listen, I'm not—" River broke off, exhaling a long, slow breath. "How do we proceed?"

"I'm not even sure what that means, 'proceed.'" Jess hooked a thumb over her shoulder. "I'm going to head home."

"It means we see if the science has made an accurate prediction."

"You're client number *one*," she reminded him. "If we're having this conversation, I'm guessing you're single and none of your other matches worked out, either. Let's assume this one will follow that trajectory."

"You're my first," he said matter-of-factly, adding, in response to her baffled expression, "I haven't had any other matches. I set stringent criteria."

"How—what does that even mean?"

River took a cautious step closer. "I selected to see only Diamond Matches."

Jess maintained eye contact with him for five . . . ten . . . fifteen seconds. His gaze was steady, unblinking, and rational, and an abrupt thought crashed into her mind: *I bet he's good at everything he sets his mind to. What if, just for one minute, I let myself imagine that this is real? What then?*

His eyes dipped briefly to her mouth, and Jess had the feeling he was asking himself the same question. Her thoughts were unexpectedly hijacked by a flashing image of him staring down at her, shirtless, watching her reaction to the pressure of his hand between her legs.

Jess had to blink—hard—to clear the image away. "Why would you set your criteria that strict?"

She knew her reasons, but what about his? A romantic soul would say that they were only interested in true love, but River's beat of hesitation told her his answer was grounded in something much more logical. "Initially because the goal wasn't to find myself a partner," he said. "It's been a protracted longitudinal study, and we've all been focused on getting to this point. I stopped thinking about my own client information a long time ago."

It wasn't the worst answer; Jess could understand how much focus it took to keep a business afloat, let alone one with employees. This all just seemed completely impossible to her.

She heard Pops's old clunker turning into the parking lot, and River's angular face was briefly illuminated by the headlights. His guarded scowl made his profile aggravatingly more handsome.

Something in her expression must have softened, because he took a few steps closer. "Let's talk about it some more," he said. "It doesn't have to be tonight."

"I'll think about it."

"It's exciting," he said quietly. "Isn't it?"

If she could only make herself believe this result, learning to tolerate his face for the sake of science wouldn't be the worst thing in the world, would it?

"I guess."

River gave her a shy smile that hit her like a thunderbolt. "And the timing couldn't be better for launch."

HALFWAY THROUGH HER birthday dinner, Jess's phone chimed. It wasn't the DNADuo app—she'd deleted that thing as soon as they pulled away from the curb outside GeneticAlly—it was her work email. Normally she wouldn't check until morning, but she'd been stewing all day and there'd been crickets from Jennings Grocery. So while Juno regaled Nana and Pops with a dramatic reenactment of Cole Mason getting his penis stuck in his zipper at school, Jess covertly reached for her phone.

Ms. Jessica Davis,

This is a formal notification that we are terminating your contract as detailed in Appendix IV. The remaining balance owed of $725.25 for STATISTICAL FORMULA + MARKETING ALGORITHM will be direct-deposited as agreed to account XXXXXXXXX-652. We would like to thank you for the work you have provided us during the last three years and wish you only the best.

If you have any questions, please feel free to contact us.

Regards,

Todd Jennings

Jennings Grocery

Jess felt like she'd just pulled the pin from a grenade and swallowed it down. Seven hundred dollars deposited into her account, but the remaining eighteen thousand wouldn't be coming in this year, or ever. Thirty percent of her income was gone. Anxiety tore through her—hot, feverish—and she closed her eyes, taking ten deep breaths.

One . . . Two . . .

She still had three active contracts. After taxes she could still bring in thirty thousand dollars this year. It would be tight, and unless she got some new clients, there wouldn't be much left over for extras, but she would be able to cover rent and health insurance.

Three . . . Four . . . Five . . .

Maybe she could get on a payment plan for Juno's ballet class.

Six . . . Seven . . .

They wouldn't starve.

Eight . . . Nine . . .

They had a roof over their heads.

Ten . . .

Slowly, her pulse returned to normal, but the alarm had left her feeling worn out and dented. Turning her phone facedown on the table, Jess reached for the bottle of wine and poured, stopping only when the liquid formed a glossy meniscus at the lip of the glass.

"Wow." Pops whistled. "Everything okay over there?"

"Yup." Jess bent down, sucking the first sip so that she could lift the glass without spilling. *It's my birthday*, she thought. *I'm getting smashed.*

Pops shared a look with Nana before he turned to Juno. "Miss Junebug?" he said.

She slurped a spaghetti noodle into her mouth. "Hmm?"

"Think you could go back to my place and find my glasses? There were a few crossword clues I needed your mama's help with."

Juno's chair screeched away from the table, and she squinted suspiciously, pointing a marinara-tipped finger at him. "Don't have cake without me."

"Wouldn't dare."

They watched as she raced out the back door and through the courtyard to the bungalow, Pigeon trailing behind her.

"Well, that bought us about thirty seconds," Nana said with a laugh.

"I'll give her sixty." Pops reached into the pocket of his sweater and pulled his glasses from the case. He gave Jess a teasing wink before slipping them on. "Now, it's your birthday, Jessica." He leaned in, pretending to study her. His eyes were pale, watery, full of love. "What's this face? Does it have to do with me picking you up earlier? The man outside?"

"No."

"He sure did seem upset when we drove off."

"He's a jerk, but this isn't about him." If it were just about

River and his stupid test, this would be easy. Jess had deleted the app and could ignore him at Twiggs. Done.

But it wasn't nearly that simple.

"What is it, then?" Nana Jo asked.

Jess leaned her elbows on the table and propped her head in her hands. It weighed about eighty pounds. "Oh . . . just life." She picked up her phone again, opening it before handing it over to let them read the Jennings email. "This was one of my bigger accounts. We disagreed on how to move forward, and they're letting me go."

Nana's face fell and she placed her hand on Jess's. "I'm so sorry, sugar."

"Money can be fixed," Pops said. "We'll always help you."

Jess squeezed his hand in wordless thanks. They had raised Jamie and Jess, and now helped with Juno. She was supposed to be taking care of them at this point in her life, not the other way around.

"It's not just money." Jess took a breath, trying to arrange her thoughts in some sort of order. "I mean it *is*, but it's also me. I feel like I'm in this holding pattern, raising Juno, making ends meet, trying to keep things moving until my life actually begins. I was just starting to think how silly that is and how I need to get out more. But now this," she said, waving her phone for emphasis. "I worked my butt off for this account, and they're going to replace me tomorrow because there are a hundred other people with looser morals who can do what I do." Jess pressed her fingers to her temples. "I need to look for a second job. I don't want you taking care of me."

"Are you kidding?" Pops argued. "Who takes us to our appointments? Who helps us when we don't know how to use a damned iPhone? Who found our trainer and helps Nana Jo with the garden? You work hard, Jessica, and you're raising that amazing little girl."

The amazing little girl herself bounded back in and pointed accusingly at her great-grandfather. "Pops! Your glasses are on your face!"

"Would you look at that!" He adjusted them over his nose, pulling his crossword closer to peer down at it. "I bet you know a three-letter word for 'regret,' don't you, Jess?"

Jess smiled. "Rue."

"See? What would we do without you?" He grinned at her over the top of his glasses before penciling the word in.

ONCE HER GRANDPARENTS were gone, Jess leaned against the closed door. Fatigue settled flabbily into her muscles, aching deep into her bones. She felt much older than thirty. Walking through the quiet apartment, she picked up Juno's shoes, the stray socks, the cat toys, more than one cup half-full of milk, pencils, food orders on Post-it notes from Juno and Pops playing Restaurant. She set the coffee timer, packed up Juno's backpack, loaded the dishwasher, and glanced around the space for any other random detritus before flicking off the light and walking down the hall to her daughter's room.

Juno had fallen asleep with *Frog and Toad Are Friends* open on her chest again, her mermaid light still on. Jess deposited Pigeon on her fancy three-tiered cat post near the window, but she immediately jumped down and onto the bed, happily curling herself into a ball at Juno's feet.

Jess closed Juno's book and put it on the nightstand, tucked the blankets up to her chin, and sat carefully on the edge of the mattress at her side. In her sleep, Juno frowned. Her hair spilled coppery across the light pink pillowcase. Jess hadn't seen Alec in almost two years, but looking at their daughter was like seeing him every day anyway. She had Jess's eyes but got his strikingly metallic chestnut hair, dimpled smile, and grumpy crease in the middle of her forehead. Jess smoothed her thumb across Juno's warm, kid-sweaty brow and gave herself two deep breaths to wish he were here, before remembering that she hadn't loved him in a long time and didn't need his help. Empty companionship was lonelier than being alone.

Alec wasn't a bad guy; he just didn't want to be a dad. He'd never pressured Jess to terminate the pregnancy, but he'd made it clear where he stood. In the end, Jess chose Juno over him, and they both had to live with that. He got to enjoy his twenties, but every one of their friends thought he was an asshole; Jess got a delightful child but had to learn how to hustle to make ends meet. She never regretted her choice for a single breath, though, and was pretty sure he hadn't, either.

Heavy with exhaustion, Jess switched the lamp off and slipped quietly out of the room, startling in the hallway when the doorbell pierced the silence. Pops left his glasses at Jess's more nights than he didn't, and pulling her sweater tighter around her chest, Jess walked quietly to the living room to peek out the window. But it wasn't Pops.

It was Jamie.

Jess used to feel a potent mix of reactions when she saw her mother—relief, anxiety, excitement—but at this point it was primarily dread, and as a mother herself now, she found that realization so deeply bleak.

Taking a deep, bracing breath, Jess hesitated with her hand on the knob before opening the door. Jamie Davis had worn many labels—cocktail waitress, addict, stadium usher, girlfriend, recovering addict, homeless—but none of them had ever been "devoted mother." On the rare occasion she had shown up to one of Jess's school events or a softball game she was usually hungover—sometimes still drunk—and reeking of cigarettes or marijuana. She would make a show, cheering for Jess, being proud of her. Sometimes she would bring a group of her rowdy friends calling themselves "Jessie's Cheering Squad." Inside, Jess would die of embarrassment, and then panic that Jamie would see it all over her face, that she would leave in a fit of anger and not come around again for weeks.

And there she was, still beautiful—she'd always been beautiful—but with a powdery finish to her beauty now, something both artificial and dull. A lifetime of bad habits had finally caught up.

"My girl!" Jamie pushed forward, wrapping her daughter in a quick one-armed hug before stepping back and shoving a set of bath bombs in Jess's hands. They'd started to disintegrate inside the cellophane, and the brightly colored dust leaked out onto Jess's fingers. She knew her mother well enough to guess Jamie had bought them as an afterthought while grabbing a pack of menthol lights at the convenience store down the street.

Jamie stepped around her and into the dark living room.

"Hey," Jess said, closing the door. "What's the occasion?"

Her mother set her giant purse on the coffee table and looked at her, wounded. Her lipstick slowly bled up into the tiny lines around her mouth. "I can't see my baby on her twenty-eighth birthday?"

Jess didn't point out that Jamie was off by two years, or the many other birthdays she'd missed. Frankly Jess was surprised her mom remembered her birth date at all; her sporadic visits weren't generally timed to life events.

"Of course you can," Jess said. "Do you want to sit down? Can I get you something?"

"No, no. I'm fine." Jamie walked into the kitchen, tapping her acrylic nails along the counter, and then glanced down the hall. "Juno, honey? Where's my beautiful grandbaby?"

"She's in bed, Mom." Jess shushed her. "It's late, and she has school tomorrow."

Jamie threw her an annoyed look. "Kids should go to sleep when they're tired. All these rules just make them anxious and depressed. That's why we have so many of them on medication these days." She scanned Juno's spelling test on the refrigerator, the birthday card she'd made for Jess, a grocery list. "People need to listen to their bodies. If you're tired, sleep. If you're hungry, eat something. Parents need to stop scheduling these kids to death."

Carefully, Jess set the bath bombs on the counter. "I take an antidepressant every day," she said with careful calm. "Guess that no-schedule theory isn't a sure thing."

Jamie ignored this to continue her perusal of the apartment, casually glancing at the spines of library books on the table, flipping through a few pages on one of Juno's about horses. Thanksgiving was the last time Jess had seen her mother. Jess had transferred five hundred dollars into Jamie's checking and hadn't heard a word since. Jamie had been living in Santa Ana then. They'd met at a Denny's—Jess paid—and Jamie lamented how her utilities had been shut off because the bank made an error. They'd taken the automatic withdrawal early, she'd insisted. Those fees had made other payments bounce, and it snowballed from there. But it hadn't been her fault. It was never her fault.

"So, how are you?" Jess asked now, stifling a yawn as she sat on the couch. "How's . . . John?"

As soon as the name was out, Jess winced. She thought his name was John. Might have been Jim.

"*Oh*," Jamie said with a *You are not going to believe this* lean to the single word. "Yeah, he was married."

Jess's surprise was genuine. "Wait, really? How did you find out?"

"His wife called me." Jamie tapped out a cigarette before remembering she couldn't smoke in the apartment, and sort of toyed with it like that had been her intent all along. "Honestly I should have known. He had a job, good credit, and a prescription for Viagra. Of course he was married."

Jess snorted out a laugh. "Are those the criteria these days?"

"Oh, honey. Don't let the age of men with good circulation pass you by. Trust me." She sat on the edge of the coffee table across from her daughter, resting a hand on Jess's leg, and the whiff of genuine camaraderie made Jess's heart lean forward. "How are you?" Jamie asked. "How's your writer friend? She is so funny."

"I'm fine. You know, working. And Fizzy," Jess said with a small laugh. "Fizzy is always fine."

"Are you dating anyone?"

Uninvited, River's voice rammed into Jess's mind.

And the timing couldn't be better for launch.

"Definitely not dating."

Jamie's disappointment was palpable. "Are you just going to be single forever? I haven't met a boyfriend of yours since Juno's daddy. It's your birthday. You should be out!"

"It's a school night, and Juno is asleep down the hall."

Jamie pointed like Jess might be catching on. "So she wouldn't even know you were gone."

Jess's heart settled back into its familiar cramp, and she said with patient finality: "I don't want to go out, Mom."

Holding her hands up in defensive surrender, Jamie groaned out, "Fine, fine."

Jess yawned again. "Listen, it's l—"

"Did I tell you about my new gig?"

Her abruptly bright tone set off warning bells. "Your new what?"

"My new job." Jamie sat up. "Okay . . . don't say anything to your grandparents, because you know they're old-fashioned and never understand how exciting these opportunities are, but you are looking at Skin Glow Incorporated's newest team member."

Jess searched her brain but no recognition flared. "Who are they?"

"You're kidding." Jamie shook her head in disbelief. "Their commercials are everywhere, Jess. They do in-home facials. God, I want to say it's a good company, but it's more than that, it's a whole *lifestyle*. A way of empowering women. I get a cut of every facial I do and—"

Jess couldn't keep the edge from her voice. "A cut?"

"Well, yeah—I mean, to start. Eventually I'll have girls working for me and I'll make some of everything they make, and the people they bring on board."

"So, like a pyramid scheme."

"Like an entrepreneur." Jamie's words were sharp with offense. "I am capable of more than waiting tables, you know."

"I'm sorry, Mom. I didn't mean it like that."

"Well, this is a really rare opportunity. Maureen said the lady who got her into it is already making six figures! And it's only three hundred dollars to start."

Of course. "You need money."

"Just a loan." Jamie waved a casual hand. "I'll pay you back with my first paycheck."

"Mom, no good job requires you to pay to get started."

Jamie's expression darkened. "Why do you always make me feel like this? Can't I ever dig out of the hole with you?" She stood up and bent to grab her purse. "I've been clean for eighteen months!"

"It's not about you— Wait." Jess was on the verge of telling Jamie that she had her own money problems to worry about. Jamie sat back down on the couch, and the silence stretched between them. "Did you stop at Nana and Pops's?" she asked instead. "They're probably still up."

Jamie half rolled her eyes, and Jess found herself wondering, again, when she'd become the parent and Jamie had become the child. "They don't want to see me."

"You know that's not true. If you've got a new job and you're clean, they'd love to see you. They love you, Mom."

Jamie kept her eyes on the wall. "Well. They know where to find me."

It was astonishing that someone like Jamie came from Joanne and Ronald Davis. At only three, Jess had been spending most nights over at Nana and Pops's house. By the time she was six, Jamie had given up all pretense of trying, and Jess was permanently living with her grandparents. Jamie had been around, generally speaking, but she was never steady. Whereas Nana and Pops were involved in every aspect of Jess's life from birth to this very moment, she learned early on that Jamie would pick drugs and men over family, every time.

As much as she tried not to repeat any of her mother's patterns, Jess did take after her in one way: she'd gotten pregnant young. But hopefully that was where the similarities ended. Jess had graduated from college, gotten a job, and tried to save a little every time a check came. She took her kid to the dentist. She tried to put Juno first every day.

Jess tried to think what Jamie would do now if their positions were reversed. *Would Jamie give me the money?*

No. Jamie would tell her she needed to grow up, stop expecting handouts, and take responsibility for her own goddamned self.

Standing, Jess walked to the counter. She opened her phone's bank app, wincing as she typed in $300 to transfer the money to Jamie's account.

I am not my mother, she reminded herself. *I am not my mother.*

SEVEN

———— / ————

B RIGHT AND EARLY Monday morning, Fizzy walked into Twiggs.
  She marched to their usual table, set her laptop down, and
even though she'd been told what she would see, still did a double
take at Jess standing behind the counter.

"This new situation," Fizzy said, dropping her purse onto her
chair, "is going to take some getting used to."

Jess smiled, swiping a cloth across the counter before pointing to
a steaming vanilla latte at the end of the bar. "If it sucks, lie to me."

Fizzy leaned an elbow on the counter and picked up the cup. "I
feel like I should have made you a little boxed lunch or something.
How's your first day?"

"The steamer is terrifying, and I didn't have the lid on the
blender all the way during the morning rush, but not too bad."

Fizzy blew across the top of her drink and tasted it. Her brows
lifted in surprised approval.

"I guess third time really is a charm," Jess said.

Fizzy looked around the quiet coffee shop. "Is this where we stand and gossip from now on?"

From where he was wiping tables, Daniel uttered a simple "No," but Fizzy ignored him, leaning in closer.

"Listen, Jess, I know you want to think this compatibility score thing is bullshit, but Ralph was *good*. What I'm saying is, if I graphed these compatibility scores relative to my sexual satisfaction, like you nerds might, there would be a definite up-slope to the line."

It took a beat for Jess to connect the dots before she remembered Ralph, the Silver Match. Unease was an index finger jabbing her shoulder, whispering, *Don't ask*. But curiosity overruled discomfort. With a guilty glance at Daniel over Fizzy's shoulder, she stepped farther down the bar to get some privacy. "Oh yeah?"

Fizzy followed on the other side of the counter. "We had dinner at Bali Hai."

Jess hummed enviously.

"He was super easy to talk to. We each probably had one too many mai tais, but it wasn't a problem because we both took Lyfts there and shared a Lyft home . . ." Fizzy grinned. "Incidentally, he has a cute place in PB."

An unexpected kernel of angst pinged Jess's lungs, and she cleared it with a cough and started wiping the bar in front of her. "So, more compatible than with Aiden or Antonio?"

"Without a doubt."

"Do you think you'll see him again?"

"Unfortunately, I get the sense that he's too busy to really get serious with anyone." Fizzy frowned. "Why would he sign up for the DNADuo during their soft launch if he just wanted to mess around?"

Laughing, Jess said, "I think I remember asking you that exact question only a handful of days ago. Look at you, ready to commit after a single night of mai tais and good sex."

From nowhere, Daniel materialized, tapping Jess's shoulder and pointing to the cash register. "You have a customer."

"Oops, sorry." She swatted after him with her cleaning cloth. Jess jogged the few feet to the register before looking up into the gorgeous yet despicable face of none other than Dr. River Peña.

In fairness, Jess shouldn't have been surprised; if she'd looked at the clock, she would have known that it was 8:24 and River was right on time. But somehow her brain had dropped the ball on reminding her that she might actually have to wait on him during her very first shift as a Twiggs barista. And this was the first time she was seeing him after their non-goodbye at the curb four days ago. Although Jess didn't expect to exhale actual fire the next time they came face-to-face, she couldn't account for the transfusion of warmth that hit her bloodstream, either. For a few seconds, she stared dumbly up at him, clocking the same shock in his expression.

He broke his stunned gaze from hers to look down the counter at Daniel, standing behind the La Marzocco. Then, with that trademark unhurried way of his, River looked at Jess again. "What are you doing back there?" His eyes took a leisurely perusal down the length of her body. "In an apron?"

"Oh, right." She gave an awkward curtsy. "I work here now."

When he didn't say anything else, she offered an artificially perky "What can I get for you, sir?"

He frowned, and his dark brows came together; glimmering bright eyes regarded her with skepticism. "You work here? Since when? I thought you worked for . . ." He glanced over to the table where Fizzy now sat alone, watching them hawkishly. Jess raised an eyebrow in amusement as he turned back to her and seemed to be putting the puzzle together in his head. Finally, he managed only, "I thought you worked . . . somewhere else."

Inwardly, she groaned. Why wasn't he just ordering, paying, and stepping to the side to stare at his phone? Had he forgotten that he was too busy to converse with plebeians?

"I'm a freelance statistician," she said, maintaining the polite smile. "But I lost a big account the other day. Given that I have a kid and lots of bills . . ." She held her arms out to say, *Voilà*.

Jess would gladly take sixteen hours a week at minimum wage *and* the hit to the pride from serving River Peña if it meant Juno could keep taking ballet with Ms. Mia.

Without subtlety, River's eyes darted down to her left hand. Was she imagining the way his brow relaxed? Had he been looking for a wedding band?

"One kid," she confirmed quietly, "no husband." For a brief second, she let herself be amused by this potential scenario. "Wow, that would have been an awkward press release for GeneticAlly: 'Founder's Soulmate Is Already Married.'"

"Married people tend to not submit DNA samples," River replied with an amused twinkle in his eye. "And I hear they prefer to cheat using apps with fewer intake forms."

Self-preservation welled up hot in her throat, and she could see the twin realization pass through him: this exchange felt suspiciously like nerdy flirting.

"What can I get for you?" Jess asked again.

His expression shuttered. "Sorry, I would have—" He held her gaze and the contact felt like a swarm of bees in her chest. "I thought you called me 'Americano' the other day," he said.

Holy duh, Jessica.

Scribbling the drink order on a cup, she moved to hand it to Daniel, who gave her a blank look. "I already got it, Jess."

Of course he had. Daniel smiled apologetically on behalf of his new employee, handing the drink to River. Silence fell as they watched her struggle to find the correct entry for *Americano* on the screen.

"It's under espresso drinks," Daniel prompted quietly.

River, hulking, leaned over to peer upside down at the screen. "It's over on the—"

His finger landed on the touch screen just as Jess's did, their hands briefly coming together.

"I got it," she said, humiliated. He pulled away, and she tapped the button, flustered by the contact that she could somehow feel all the way up her arm. No doubt her cheeks looked like she'd been slapped. "That'll be three eighty-five."

He hesitated, and Jess realized her mistake. She upsized to *large*. "Sorry. Four seventy-four."

Their shared discomfort shoved between them, a loud, uninvited guest at the awkward party for two. Jess took his money, counted out his change. But what really wrecked her was that, after the tiniest hesitation, he dropped all of it—including the five-dollar bill—into the tip jar.

FIZZY SIDLED UP to the counter fifteen minutes later when she seemed to assess Jess was done being mortified.

"Hey." She offered a little best-friend-simpatico smile and reached across the counter to offer a fist bump.

"Hey." Jess cleared her throat, meeting Fizzy's knuckles. "I bet an ending like that never made it into a romance novel."

Fizzy laughed. "Are you kidding? That would be the *start* of an amazing love story."

"Not my story."

Jess felt her best friend studying her while she pretended to be very engrossed in rearranging the pastry case. Fizzy had been uncharacteristically mum on the subject of River. After hearing of their DNADuo result, the rundown on the disastrous GeneticAlly meeting, and Jess's theory that the statistics were completely bogus and most likely invalidated their entire business plan, Fizzy had stared at her in silence for a few beats before saying only "I get it."

"You okay?" she asked now.

Daniel decided this moment was a good one to join the conversation, setting two sealed bags of beans down at the espresso bar. He frowned. "What's wrong?"

"Nothing," Jess mumbled just as Fizzy practically shouted, "Did you not see that awkward run-in with Americano?"

"Why was it awkward?" Daniel took a beat to recollect, then

said, "Oh, about the drink? Eh, don't worry about that. It's your first day."

"No, Dan," Fizzy said, exasperated with him for no good reason. "Because they *matched*."

It felt like the entire coffee shop went silent in response.

Jess groaned. "Fizzy, I swear to God, I will barehand—"

"What level?" Daniel asked.

"What do you mean 'what level'?" Jess gaped at him.

He ripped open a bag of espresso beans and poured it into the machine. "If we're talking about DNADuo, I was one of the original samples," he said proudly. "Back in my days at SDSU. When they were still taking . . . *samples*."

It took a second for that to sink in, and when it did, all a blushing Jess could manage was a quiet "Gross, Dan."

"I meant blood."

"Didn't sound like you meant blood."

"Anyway, I did it again about a year and a half ago when they put out the call for people to help validate their spit kit." He pulled his phone from his back pocket and showed them the screen like they might see a thread of matches lined up there. "But I've never gotten anything above a thirty-seven."

Fizzy's interest was piqued. "Did you go out with her?"

"I did," he said. "It was good, but I think we both had this weird expectation that it was nice but statistically unlikely to go anywhere?"

"I did wonder about that aspect," Fizzy said. "I went out with a Silver the other day but, like, if you get anything lower than a Gold, do you just assume it's most likely not to work?"

"Even though," Jess cut in quietly, "if you believe their data, the odds are significantly better of finding a lasting relationship with a Silver than with regular dating . . ."

Fizzy gaped at her. "Says the woman who won't believe her own score."

"What was it?" Daniel asked again.

Jess laughed. "It doesn't matter. Fizzy's right. I don't believe it." She wiped her hands on her apron and looked at Daniel. "What's next, boss? Dishes? Restocking?"

He lifted his chin, undeterred. "Was it a Base Match?"

Fizzy looked at her, one eyebrow pointed sharply skyward. "Yeah, Jess. Was it a Base Match?"

Jess slid a patient look to her friend. "Are you being a pot-stirrer?"

"Guilty."

Daniel turned to Fizzy, who in turn gave Jess a look that either sought permission or delivered a warning.

Warning, apparently, because a few seconds later, Fizzy said, "It was a Diamond."

Jess expected him to explode: *How can you ignore that?* and *If I had a Diamond Match, I'd quit my job and get laid all day long!* But just as Fizzy had when Jess told her, Daniel studied Jess very quietly and very intently.

"You're not curious?" he asked, at length.

"No."

Daniel seemed to be trying to wrap his head around this. "Is River?"

Jess shrugged. "Who knows? We haven't really talked since we found out a few days ago."

"So, you're going to, what? Do nothing?"

She nodded at Daniel. "That's the plan."

Fizzy rolled her eyes and repeated with an exasperated edge: "That's the plan. The boring, *safe* plan."

Jess gave her friend a look of warning. It wasn't that Fizzy was wrong, per se, but Jess had more to think about than just herself. She couldn't throw caution to the wind. That was a luxury childless people had, people with free time and fewer responsibilities. Boring, safe plans hadn't steered her wrong yet.

EIGHT

———/———

B UT THE PLAN, as it were, went up in smoke three days later at about 5:17 in the evening, when a silver Tesla pulled up beside Jess on her walk home and rolled down a heavily tinted passenger-side window. It was in her nature to ignore all cars rolling up at a curb, but this one wasn't catcalling. This driver knew her name.

"Jessica."

She turned to find Brandon "the Teeth" Butkis in the driver's seat. His left arm was wrapped around the steering wheel as he leaned toward her, smiling like he had an entire pack of Chiclets he wanted to show off. He was dressed casually in a blue button-down shirt open at the collar. "Do you have a second?"

"Not really." She pointed down two blocks, toward her apartment building. "I need to get dinner started."

"Actually, I was wondering if there was someone who could watch your daughter tonight," he said, and his smile turned tentative. Despite the intimidating size of his teeth, his eyes were warm and brown, with crinkles at the edges. He did not look like a man who wanted to pull Jess off the street, plug wires into her skin, and turn her into a human battery. Jess registered vaguely that she needed to take it down a notch, imagination-wise.

Approaching the car, she leaned down, resting her forearms on the windowsill. "I'm sure this is frustrating for you, but I'm really not interested in pursuing this."

"And we won't force you to," he said quickly. "Our intention isn't to be intrusive. I know this has been an . . . odd situation. David and I just wanted to make sure to follow up."

Jess had to admit they'd been surprisingly silent given the urgency of the first meeting, the enormity of the finding, and the rushed manner in which she'd fled their headquarters. So far it had been crickets. "You aren't suggesting another meeting, are you?"

She must have looked like she'd relish another meeting as much as she would a root canal because Brandon laughed. "No. That meeting was a mistake. *Our* mistake. And probably the worst way to tell you both. We got overly excited, as scientists—we wanted you to experience that moment of discovery with us, but we should have exhibited more EQ." He shifted in his seat. "We were hoping to take you to dinner."

"Tonight?"

He nodded. "Can you get free?"

She turned and looked down the street again, considering it. Jess wasn't blind—River was objectively gorgeous—but she couldn't even say she liked him as a person. Plus, she still couldn't wrap her logical mind around the number. Her priorities, in order, were her kid, her grandparents, and her bills. She wasn't going to pursue this no matter what they said tonight.

"I have a lot on my plate," Jess told him. "I've taken on another job; I have a young daughter at home, as you know. I really don't think I have—"

"I promise, Jessica," Brandon cut in gently, and when her attention flew back to his face, he gave another tentative smile. "We won't waste your time."

JESS KNEW AS soon as Brandon pulled up at the valet in front of Addison at the Grand Del Mar that this wasn't going to be a laid-back kind of dinner. They wouldn't be eating tacos with their hands or sharing pitchers of beer. A meal at the Addison would cost more than her rent.

She glanced down at her lap, brushing nonexistent lint from the skirt of her dress. Brandon would forever be in the *Like* column for giving her fifteen minutes to change out of her yoga pants and the you-can-barely-see-the-stain Lululemon top Juno had picked out for her at Goodwill. The blue dress she'd tugged on was stretchy, which was why it still fit.

Brandon grabbed his neatly pressed sports coat from where it hung on a hook in the back seat, beamed a reassuring smile, and gestured for Jess to walk ahead of him.

"Right this way, Mr. Butkis." The maître d' nodded, leading them through a stunning circular room lined with arch-capped French doors. Silverware tapped gently against porcelain, ice clinked in highball glasses; all around them, conversation hummed at a low, pleasant murmur. Tables were dotted spaciously throughout the room, framed by low plush chairs upholstered in scarlet and gold.

"Is David meeting us?"

Brandon looked over his shoulder at her. "They should be here already."

They. Jess's stomach swiftly fell to her knees: *they.* David and River stood at their arrival at a table on the far end of the room.

Frozen as Brandon held the chair out for her, she felt River watching, carefully taking in her reaction. His mouth drooped in apology. "I thought—well, I assumed you'd realize we'd all be here."

"It's okay," she said quietly, taking her seat and struggling to regain her composure. River was seated immediately to her right, and his discomfort over *her* discomfort was palpable. "I misunderstood."

She took a risk, meeting his gaze, and his expression remained largely unreadable except for a small crease in his forehead, the hint of concern in his eyes. If he were a more intuitive person, she might have interpreted his look as a question: *Is this okay?*

Jess blinked away, setting her napkin on her lap. As they settled, the table fell into a hush. Jess looked up to find the three men watching as she tried to anticipate why they'd invited her to this dinner.

"It's okay," she said again. "Let's do this."

"Let's take a moment to study the menu first," David suggested, "and then maybe River can tell you a little more about the company and our technology."

They perused in heavy silence before agreeing on the five-course tasting menu. They ordered cocktails, ordered food, and then the four of them just . . . sat. It was unbearable.

"River?" David finally prompted in a fatherly tone.

River cleared his throat, adjusted his napkin. He reached forward to fidget with his water glass. How awkward for him, being put in the position of trying to convince Jess that this was all real when it seemed he didn't want to believe it, either.

"I think I understand the science," she said, before he could launch into whatever pitch he was formulating in that big brain of his. "At least, I understand that you've identified a wide variety of genes you believe are involved in emotional and, uh—sexual fulfillment in a relationship. I understand how the algorithm could work, in theory. I guess what I question is whether this particular finding is real. If you've never had a score of ninety-eight before, how do we know what it means?"

"If we were given a score of twenty-two," River asked, "would you have believed that?"

It was exactly the question she'd asked herself only a handful of days ago. "Yes," she admitted, "because that would align with my feelings about you in general. A ninety-eight, to me, implies that we would be drawn to each other. That we would have instantaneous chemistry."

There was a lull that was mercifully interrupted by the waiter bringing bread and cocktails. When they were alone again, David carefully asked, "And you don't?"

"I generally want to commit a felony when I see him," Jess said, a butter knife held in front of her. "I'm not sure that's a sign of romantic compatibility."

River exhaled, settling back in his chair. "This is a waste of our time."

Leaning forward, Brandon engaged her with his grin. "It can be easier to believe bad news than good news."

"I'm not a pessimist," she said. "I'd believe good news if it was someone telling me I won the lottery. But I'm looking at him— and he's looking at me—and I'm sure we are both thinking, 'There is no way.'"

Brandon turned to River. "Do you find her attractive?"

"This test isn't a measure of attraction," River said blandly. "It's a measure of compatibility."

Jess set down her bread. "You really just said that."

"Jessica," David said, redirecting her attention. "Do you?"

She laughed. "River is attractive. We can all see that." She made the mistake of instinctively glancing his way when she said this and noticed a tiny muscle twitching upward at the corner of his lips. It made her feel softer, bending toward him, and self-preservation swelled up in her throat. She hated it. "But speaking to him is like having a conversation with a grouchy calculator."

David hid a surprised laugh with a cough, gamely tapping his own chest and reaching for his water. To Jess's right, River exhaled long and slow.

"Let me try a different tack," Brandon said as the waiter brought the first course. "We believe in this science." He gestured to the men on either side of him. "I don't just mean that we hope it works because we stand to make a lot of money. That is true, of course, but that isn't everything. Yes, the story of the two of you could be very compelling for our launch, but it's also a scientific curiosity for us. So far, every couple who received scores greater than eighty is still together and scores off the charts on many measures of relationship satisfaction. We have to wonder: How satisfied would a couple be at ninety-eight?"

"*Every* match over eighty has been successful?" she asked, wondering at his wording. "I thought Lisa said three out of four."

"Legally we can't say one hundred percent, because not every Titanium Match has actually connected in person yet."

"That must be annoying for you," she joked.

This time, David's laugh was booming. "You have no idea."

"You're both young, attractive, and single," Brandon said, rolling with this momentary levity.

"We aren't asking you to marry him," David added.

"I'm sorry," River cut in. "Can I join this conversation?"

"Yes," Jess agreed, "where *are* you with all of this?"

The food sat neglected on the table in front of them as they all waited for his answer. "Of course I believe in it," River said. "I invented it."

Do you actually believe our result could be real? That we could be soulmates? she wanted to ask, but the words felt too enormous to push past her lips. She dug into her scallops instead.

"We're asking the two of you to spend some time together," Brandon urged.

"Exactly," David said, nodding. "To get to know each other. Give it a little time."

"Unfortunately," she said, lifting a bite to her mouth. If nothing else, at least she was getting dinner out of it. "Time is what I don't have to give. I'm not sure River's mute five minutes in Twiggs every morning will let us dive too deep."

"What if we compensated you?" Brandon asked.

Her hand froze, dinner suddenly forgotten. A hush fell over the table. River looked sharply at Brandon, but David was watching only her. They'd planned for this.

I promise, Jessica. We won't waste your time.

"I'm sorry," she said hoarsely, "what?"

"What if we compensated you," Brandon calmly repeated. "Allowing you to make time in your schedule to get to know River?"

She carefully placed the knife on the edge of her plate. "You want to pay me to date him?"

River exhaled sharply, reaching for his whiskey.

"Consider it a stipend for participating in an aspect of a larger experiment," David said. "You could quit the coffee shop, have more free time. You're an important part of our research study, one-half of a score we need to validate—or invalidate—our binning paradigm prior to launch."

Jess leaned back in her chair, heart thundering. "So, you need us to . . . *explore this* until after launch?"

Brandon laughed a little at this. "Well, you can explore it until—"

"Assuming we *don't* fall for each other," she clarified, "what is the duration of the study?"

"The IPO is May sixth," David said matter-of-factly. "Today is January twenty-eighth. So, just over three months."

And there was the truth, baldly laid out.

"How much compensation are we talking?"

David and Brandon exchanged a look. Jess lifted her water glass to her lips with a shaking hand, ice tinkling gently against the glass.

"Ten thousand a month."

A watery cough burst from her throat, sharp and urgent. River reached over and laid a hand on her back, rubbing gently.

The touch was steady but electric, jerking a breath from her chest, making her cough again. His palm was huge and warm, a vibrating hum on her skin.

"I'm okay," she finally managed, and set the glass on the table.

He pulled away, curling his hand into a fist on his lap.

"And what does that amount buy you?" Jess asked once she trusted her voice to come out steady.

"You go out for coffee. You date." Brandon held his hands out, shrugging, before picking up his fork. "Maybe you have a public appearance or two. Basically, you give it a chance."

David nodded. "You get to know him, Jessica."

She turned to River. "You're so quiet. This concerns you, too, you know. I realize your default energy level is Cardboard Cutout, but I can't get to know you if you don't speak."

"I'm thinking," he admitted in a low growl.

Honestly, her mind was reeling. She'd never conceived of a situation like this. Was she physically attracted to him? Yes. Obviously *yes*. But so much of him felt inaccessible and deeply aggravating.

"Do you feel . . . ?" She didn't know how to ask the question. She started over. "With everything you know, and everything you've seen, do you think this number is right?"

He lifted his water, taking a long sip. With a steady, unhurried hand, he set the glass down and met her gaze. "I don't know."

In the background, she was aware of Brandon and David digging into their food, trying to be inconspicuous as they listened to what should probably be a private conversation. Jess hated the way her stomach heated, the way it felt like there were bubbles rising from her bloodstream to the surface of her skin. "Do you . . . want it to be right?"

The last thing she wanted to happen was for someone to get hurt, but it was hard to imagine walking away from thirty thousand dollars. How hard would it be to spend a few hours with this man for an amount that'd truly make her and Juno's lives easier?

River closed his eyes and swallowed. When he opened them again, she saw the same conflict on his face that she felt inside. "I don't know," he said again.

"So why are you willing to do this?"

He lifted one shoulder. "I want to prove that I'm right."

Jess wasn't sure what woman would think that answer was good enough. While she could appreciate this take from an intellectual standpoint, that was exactly the problem: this was supposed to be about unquantifiable, instinctive chemistry.

Wasn't it?

Standing, she placed her napkin on the table. "I need to think about it. I'll call you."

NINE

J ESS WAVED TO Nana through the kitchen window and headed toward the back of the apartment. Juno was already tucked into bed with a book. Again. Fail, fail, fail. If Juno talked Pops into letting her have frozen fish sticks for dinner again, it would definitely push Jess over the edge.

Did every mom feel like this? Jess worked too much or didn't work enough. She was spoiling Juno or Juno wasn't getting everything she needed. Jess was a helicopter mom, or she was ignoring her kid. More often than not Jess was convinced that every decision she made was ruining Juno's childhood in some way.

"Hey, Bug," she said, stepping around a basket of laundry and collapsing onto the bed next to her daughter. Pigeon stood and stretched, making her way up the mattress to curl in the space between them.

Juno turned a page. "Did you know female giraffes go back to where they were born to give birth?"

Jess ran her fingers through Juno's hair; the strands were still damp from her bath. "I did not know that."

"The baby just plops onto the ground." Juno threw her arms out in a dramatic *splat*.

"I guess if your mom is a giraffe that'd be a pretty big fall."

Juno angled the book for her, displaying a photo of a giraffe and her baby. "But the baby just gets up and runs." She turned the page. "And their necks have the same number of vertebrae as humans. Do you know how many that is?"

"I think seven?"

"Yep." Juno nodded once. "Good job."

Jess listened as her daughter read, but her head was a spin cycle, the conversation from dinner tumbling over and over and over inside. She wasn't sure whether she was more insulted by the suggestion that she'd agree, or mad that she was thinking about agreeing. She'd be crazy to pass something like that up, right? It would make up for the Jennings account; it'd take care of health care for the rest of the year.

"—that reminds me of when Mr. Lannis had to wear a neck brace because he got a compressed nerve from karaoke. Hey, Mom?"

When Jess refocused, she realized Juno had already closed her book. "What, baby?"

"Why are you making that face?" she asked.

"What face?"

Juno ran a finger across her forehead. "The one Auntie Fizzy can't make anymore because of the Botox."

"I'm not frowning," Jess said. "I'm just thinking. Someone asked me to do something and I'm not sure whether I should."

Now Juno frowned. "Is it bad?"

"No. Not bad."

Purring, the cat climbed up onto Juno's chest. "Is someone going to get hurt?"

"I hope not," Jess said. "I don't think so."

"Do you feel unsafe?"

Jess bit her lips, trying to hold in a charmed laugh. This kid was repeating exactly what she would say if their positions were reversed. "No." Leaning in, she pressed a kiss to her head. "I don't feel unsafe."

Once she sat up again, her daughter pinned her with a stern look. "Will you be lying?"

You're an important part of our research study, one-half of a score we need to validate—or invalidate—our binning paradigm prior to launch.

She shook her head. "I won't be lying."

Juno set her book on the nightstand and scooped up Pigeon before snuggling them both down into her comforter. "Would you learn something?"

Jess felt an intense pulse of pride in her kid, and the knee-jerk negative answer evaporated in her mouth.

Because . . . maybe she would.

SHE CAUGHT A glimpse of herself in the mirror at the end of the hall and wondered how the chaos inside her wasn't more visible. If her outside matched her inside, she would look like a Picasso sculpture: head sideways, nose where her eyes should be, eyes on her chin. Instead she was still just Jess: brown hair, tired blue eyes, and what looked like the beginnings of a stress pimple on her forehead. *Awesome*.

Nana and Pops were playing cribbage in the courtyard; Jess grabbed a beer from the fridge and a sweater from the back of the couch and stepped outside to join them.

Mr. Brooks opened his window when he saw her, his white T-shirt striped by a pair of gray suspenders. "Jessica," he said, leaning outside. "I need to talk to you."

Jess shared a look with Nana, and walked back toward the building again, looking up to the second floor. "Yes, Mr. Brooks?"

"I'm posting two photographs to the Nextdoor app. There are some kids who keep riding their scooters up and down the sidewalks, and I don't like the look of them. There's an entire sidewalk, but they insist on riding right next to my stoop." He made a fist and flattened it against the window frame. "I don't want them knocking over my broom."

"I'll watch for them. I know you use that broom every day."

"Thank you, Jessica. We can't have kids running up and down the street here. Too many cars, too many people. And they don't make that broom anymore. I've already fixed it once."

She nodded in solidarity and, satisfied, Mr. Brooks leaned back inside and closed the window.

Jess popped the cap off her beer and took a seat at the table. "To be fair," Pops said, arranging the cards in his hands, "it is a pretty great broom."

"I am no broom connoisseur so I shall take your word for it." Jess wrapped her arms around Nana and rested her head on her grandmother's shoulder, closing her eyes. "Have I told you how much I love you?"

Nana Jo patted her arm. "Not in the last thirty minutes."

Jess kissed her cheek. "Okay then. I love you a whole lot."

"How was dinner?"

Jess laughed dryly. First of all, she'd left before she finished eating. A crime. Second . . . where to begin? "It was enlightening."

"Oh?" Nana prompted, interest piqued. Nana loved a bit of drama.

Sitting up, Jess drew a line through the condensation on her beer bottle. Nana and Pops resumed their game. "Do you know how much it takes to raise a kid these days?" she finally asked.

"A damn sight more than when we were doing it, I'm sure," Pops said, then played an ace for thirty-one and pegged forward two.

"Estimated to be at least $233,610. That's housing," Jess began, counting off on her fingers, "food, transportation, clothing, health care, child care, and miscellaneous. And that's only to the age of seventeen."

Pops whistled and reached for his own beer.

"Tuition to a school like UCSD is fifty-two thousand for a four-year degree," Jess said. "And that's an in-state public school. Juno could want to go out of state, and it would quadruple the price. I can barely afford ballet lessons." She took a long drag of her beer and then stood up to get another.

Pops looked at her over his glasses; the fairy lights suspended overhead reflected in the thick lenses. A candle flickered on the table; crickets chirped in a planter nearby. "I think you'd better tell us about this dinner."

Jess returned to her seat. "You remember the dating service Fizzy joined?"

Nana laid down a card, and then moved her peg forward two. "The one where you spit in the tube?"

"Yep." Jess turned to Pops. "And you remember the guy outside? The night you picked me up?"

"Tall, good-looking?" He paused, his smile smug. "So your mood that night *was* about him."

"No, but this mood is." She laughed. "That dating service isn't really a dating service. Or . . . it is, but they don't *just* find you dates. You provide a sample, they create a genetic profile, and then they give you a list of matches based on the criteria you select. Fizzy got five bazillion matches because she set the parameters really wide."

Pops nodded. "Sounds like Fizzy."

"And you did this?" Nana asked.

Jess hesitated. "Fizzy bought me a kit for my birthday, and I had a moment of temporary insanity. The night Pops picked me up, the higher-ups had just told me about the person I'd been matched with. Tonight, at dinner, they had a proposition for me."

Nana's brows disappeared beneath her wavy silver hair.

"I gave them very strict criteria. Apparently, I matched at a statistically unbelievable level with the guy Pops saw me arguing with." Jess took a deep breath. "His name is River Peña. He's a PhD, the service's top scientist, and one of the founders of the whole thing."

Pops whistled.

"What do you mean, statistically unbelievable?"

"Most good matches score over fifty. Sixty-six to about ninety would be amazing." Jess stared into her empty bottle, unable to look at them when she said, "Our score was ninety-eight."

Nana reached for her wine.

"Yeah," Jess said, and then blew out a long, slow exhale.

"How often do they get a ninety-eight?" Nana asked.

"Never. This is the highest match they've had to date."

"And do you like this Dr. Peña?" she asked.

Jess cursed the traitorous zing that skyrocketed through her blood. "He's attractive but has a brooding vibe." She put it in Nana Jo context: "Think Mr. Darcy, but without the lovely proclamations. He called me average, didn't hold the elevator, speaks with less emotional fluency than the Alexa in your kitchen, and doesn't know a thing about parking lot etiquette."

Nana Jo gently let Jess's pettiness settle in the space between them as she and Pops played the rest of their hands.

"Okay, parking lot etiquette aside, *could* you like him?" she finally asked.

The quiet murmur of Bahn Thai customers drifted over the fence, making Jess wonder whether they could hear her, too. She lowered her voice. "Aside from the score, I really don't know."

Nana and Pops shared a look across the table. "And the proposition?" Nana asked.

"That we get to know each other." Nana's eyes widened, and Jess quickly clarified. "Not like *that*, jeez. Just—see if the data is right, if we are somehow emotionally compatible."

Apparently satisfied with this answer, Nana Jo looked down at her cards before counting aloud the points she had in the crib. She moved her peg on the game board, and then turned her attention to

Jess. "You seem more conflicted about it than if you simply didn't like him."

"Well . . ." Jess stared into the dark abyss of her bottle. "They offered to pay me."

Nana reached for her wine again. "Oh boy."

Pops fixed Jess with his watery gaze. "How much?"

She laughed. Of course that would be Pops's question. "A lot." They waited. "Ten grand a month a lot."

They both blinked. The silence stretched. A car sped by; someone laughed at the restaurant next door.

"Just to get to know each other," Nana clarified. "No sex."

"Right." Jess lifted a single shoulder. "They need to validate the science. And I would definitely like $30,000."

"But you're hesitating," Pops said.

"Of course I am."

Pops pinned her with a serious expression. "He seems harmless?"

"We don't really get along, but as far as I can tell, he's not a sociopath. He's not nearly charming enough to be one." When neither of them laughed at this, Jess said, "He has a *lot* riding on the company, obviously. I don't think dropping my body in a dumpster would be worth losing the millions he stands to make if they have a successful IPO."

Pops took off his glasses. "Then I don't know what you have to think about."

"Ronald Davis," Nana chastised. "This has to be her decision."

"What?" he said, hands up in defense. "You would turn down that kind of money?"

"Not now, obviously." She motioned to herself before giving Jess a conspiratorial wink. "Ask me forty years ago and you'd get a different answer."

"Nana Jo, I am shocked," Jess said with a teasing smile.

"If you saw her forty years ago, you wouldn't be." Pops leaned back, dodging Nana's playful slap to his shoulder. "Nobody's asking me, but I think you should do it. As long as they're not asking you to lie, or cheat, or rob a bank," he said. "Go to a couple restaurants. Make conversation, hear some stories. At the very least you'll earn a little time to breathe." He picked up his cards again. "UCSD isn't getting any cheaper."

"YOUR KID CRACKS me up."

Seated on a park bench, Fizzy and Jess watched Juno try to teach Pigeon to walk on a leash. The kid took one step forward and patiently waited for the cat to follow. Around them, dogs chased balls and licked faces and barked, tails wagging. Hunkered low to the ground in the harness and suspicious of every shadow, sound, and blade of grass, Pigeon looked like she was about to sprint out of her skin, cartoon-style.

"Other than the Great Cat Chase a few weeks ago, she's never really been out of the courtyard," Jess said. "I'm sure she feels the way we would if we were put in a harness and set down on Mars."

For native San Diegans, any forced indoor time was borderline intolerable, and by three o'clock on Friday afternoon, the first sunny day in over a week, Trolley Barn Park was crawling with people seeking sunshine. The air had that bright, cold smell after all the pollution was washed from the clouds and the dirt was cleared from tree branches. The sky was an unreal royal blue. And Juno's chestnut braids were a streak of playful red against the blue-green backdrop.

"Don't tug her," Jess reminded her gently.

"I'm *not*."

Out of the corner of her eye, Jess saw Pigeon's tail twitch just moments before she dove forward, catching something triumphantly in her paws. All that time she'd been hunkering down, she'd been on the hunt.

Juno squealed, delighted. "Mom!" She waved Jess over, and Jess halted just as Juno said, "Pigeon caught a *praying mantis*."

That was a Hell No from Jess, but Fizzy jumped up, getting an eyeful of the six-inch-long insect Pigeon clearly had no idea what to do with. She trapped it, batted it with a paw, and simultaneously looked semi-disgusted by the entire thing.

"Juno," Jess said, laughing, "baby, just get Pigeon to let it go."

Juno bent, prying the cat's paws apart and releasing the praying mantis, which calmly prowled away.

Fizzy settled back on the bench and, somehow, Jess knew what was coming. "We could all learn a lot from that cat."

"Here we go," she said.

"*Jumping* on an opportunity when we see it."

"Mm-hmm," Jess answered, distracted.

"Like, sure," Fizzy continued, ignoring her, "I get being careful, but when the opportunity arises, take it."

"Like Pigeon did?" Jess said, laughing. "She caught that poor thing and had zero clue what to do next."

She felt Fizzy turn to look at her. "You think you wouldn't know how to use thirty thousand dollars?"

"Actually, that's the part that I'm stuck on—the greatest incentive and the biggest drawback. I need money, but in some ways, I think it'd be easier to do this purely for the sake of science or whatever." She shrugged, tilting her face to the sky. "Being paid to 'get to know River' feels vaguely . . . illegal."

Fizzy laughed. "And see, I put that in the 'pro' column."

"You're the adventurous one."

"All I'm saying is you'd be insane to not do this."

Jess let out a long, slow breath. "Trust me, I'm seriously considering it."

"Good." After a long stretch of quiet, Fizzy added, "Incidentally, I met someone I really like last night."

They'd been together since almost seven thirty that morning, and she was only mentioning this now? "Really? Is he a match?"

"He is what's known in science as an 'organic match,'" Fizzy joked. "Daniel had a few people over, and this guy Rob was there. He's Daniel's brother's friend from college and is now a banker, which I realize sounds so generic it has to be fake, but I made him show me his business card and it's legit. It actually says 'Banker.' He's funny and good-looking, and I was in peak Fizzy mode last night and he seemed charmed by it."

"Peak Fizzy mode as in oral manifesto about the positive impact of romance novels on society? Or peak Fizzy mode as in spontaneously wallpapering your bedroom at midnight with pages from your favorite books?"

"Peak Fizzy mode as in three shots of tequila and recruiting Rob to help me hide Daniel's shoes all over the house."

"Ah." Jess turned her attention back to Juno, who had given up on walking Pigeon and was letting other children pet the cat instead. "You should have Banker Rob tested to see how he compares to the other dates."

"I'm not actually sure I want to," Fizzy said. "I had the scores for those other guys, and we had fun, but going in knowing that they probably wouldn't work long-term made it easy to not take it seriously. I didn't expect my dates to be life-altering, and they weren't. Was it because the test is right, or because I didn't expect them to be soulmates?"

"I mean, statistically you're more likely to get a soulmate with a Silver Match than you are to ever get a Titanium Match."

"You're statisticsizing me."

Jess laughed. What could she really say to Fizzy when she was, herself, grappling with the opposite concern: Did people given a score of ninety-eight just assume that person would be their happily ever after?

"And I keep thinking you're crazy to not get to know River," Fizzy continued, "but if I got a Diamond Match, would I feel overwhelmed with the pressure and bail, too?"

Jess laughed at their mental symmetry. "Mm-hmm."

"Then again, I think if I got even a Gold Match, I'd be pretty stoked." Fizzy pulled a leg beneath her, turning to face Jess. "There's something about knowing you align according to all of these biological factors that makes it easier to imagine compromising on some of the ways I'm set in my routine." She paused. "But still." She exhaled, puffing out her cheeks. "I *like* Rob. I don't want to know yet that he and I aren't *supposed* to end up together."

"So you *do* believe it?" Jess asked, gently poking Fizzy's knee with her index finger. "All of this DNADuo stuff?"

Fizzy caught her hand and interlaced their fingers. "I think the more important question is: Do you?"

TEN

CONSUMED BY A strange disorientation, Jess climbed from her car outside the GeneticAlly building. It was after seven, and the parking lot was empty, but the stillness was somehow more unsettling. Her hands seemed to float ten feet away from her body; it felt like she was gliding more than walking. This physical dissociation wasn't new to her. She'd felt it on and off her entire childhood, and therapy had revealed that it happened when she was avoiding thinking about what it all *meant*. But every time she thought about the prospect that the DNADuo really was right and that she and River might actually be good together, a wall went up inside her and the entire mental monologue just went dark.

And now that she was here, Jess had no idea whether she'd made the right decision by telling David that she would come to the office to meet with them. Their lawyer would be present. They would sign a contract . . . after that, Jess had no clue.

She expected to be met by the receptionist or maybe Lisa.

But this time, waiting for her near the untouched couches was River.

Her breath caught in her throat. Hidden in the shadows, he looked skyscraper tall and angular. The thought of relishing touching him . . . it made her feel light-headed.

He pulled his hand from a pocket and lifted it in a careful wave. "Hey." His hand hesitated, unsure, rising up to scratch the back of his neck. "I didn't know whether you'd actually show up."

"That makes two of us."

What's in it for you? she wanted to ask. *Is this about glory, or money, or something else?* He certainly wasn't here for the pursuit of love.

With a little sideward tilt of his head, he led her back through the double doors, down the hall, to the elevator, where he depressed the Up button with that long index finger.

"How was your day?"

Jess bit her bottom lip, swallowing an incredulous smile. He was trying. "Um, it was fine, how was yours?"

"Pretty good."

"Do you always work this late?"

"Pretty much."

The doors opened; they stepped in and were swallowed into the tiny vessel together.

"Do you have any questions for me?" he asked.

She wasn't fast enough this time, and the surprised laugh escaped. "Yes. Thousands. How nice of you to ask."

"Okay," he said, smiling down at his shoes, "I guess I deserve that."

"The only one I think I really *need* to know before we go into the conference room is: Is it true you're not currently in a relationship with anyone?"

River shook his head. "I would never do this if I were."

"Okay, good," she said, and quickly added when his brows slowly rose: "Me either."

"I do have one question," he said as they reached the second floor. The doors opened, and they stepped out into the hall, but then stopped and faced each other still out of hearing range of the conference room. "Why did you take the test in the first place? You don't seem to be all that excited about the prospect of any match, let alone a Diamond."

"That," Jess said, grinning and pointing at him, "is the question of the day." Her smile faded, hand dropped, and she realized she wasn't going to get out of this with deflection or humor. His was a good question. She'd genuinely felt a desire to start making her own life bigger in the moment, so why was she here now, feeling resistant to the entire process?

Immediately Jess knew: the idea of finding The One—it was just too much.

"I'd had a really bad day," she said quietly. "That day I ran into you downtown. You took my parking spot. You didn't hold the elevator. I lost a big account, had to sit in a room full of smug married couples, went home, and just felt pathetic. I spit into the vial and sent it, but I shouldn't have."

She watched the reaction to this pass across his features.

"We all feel worst at night," she said. "I should have waited until the morning."

He nodded once. "Okay."

And then he turned and continued down the hallway.

That was it? Seriously? He asked the Hard Question and she answered honestly and he nodded and moved on?

What was he even thinking? This man was a vault.

River waited at the threshold to the room for her, and gestured for her to step in ahead of him. She'd expected a roomful of people to witness the ceremonial contract signing between two Diamond Matches who, at best, tolerated each other. But instead, there were only two people inside: David and a man Jess didn't know, but who looked so much like Don Cheadle that she felt an excited smile burst across her face before she realized he was just a very close doppelgänger.

David clocked her reaction, and laughed. "I know. It's uncanny."

"I'm Omar Gamble," Don Cheadle said. "I'm the head legal counsel for GeneticAlly. It's nice to meet you, Jessica."

"Just Jess." She reached out, shaking his hand.

What were they thinking of her right now? *Desperate? Stupid? Opportunistic?* Honestly, though, for that much money, did she even care what they thought?

There wasn't much more to be said, so they all shuffled to their chairs. Omar opened a folder and pulled out a small stack of papers. "We know you haven't brought legal counsel, but wanted to give you some time to look this over."

"Would you like River and me to leave the room?" David asked.

River began to stand, which irked her. At least let her decide.

Obstinately, she said, "No. Stay, if you don't mind."

Slowly, River settled back into his seat.

Honestly, this situation was a first. She and River sat beside each other on one side, facing David and Omar, and she'd just asked them to stay and essentially watch her read five dense pages of legalese. As carefully as she could under the press of their conspicuous attention, she read through the contract.

WHEREAS Individual A (JESSICA DAVIS) has indicated to GENETICALLY LLC and Individual B (RIVER PEÑA) a willingness to engage . . .

. . . Individual A further agrees to limit disclosure of Confidential Information . . .

. . . at least three (3) interactions per calendar week including but not limited to outings, phone calls . . .

. . . publicity appearances and/or interviews not to exceed two (2) per calendar week . . .

. . . explicitly state that no physical contact is contractually obligated on the part of Individual A or Individual B throughout the . . .

. . . will be compensated in the amount of ten thousand dollars ($10,000 USD) per month for the duration of the contract, beginning on the 10th day of February . . .

. . . IN WITNESS WHEREOF, Individual A and Individual B have executed this agreement himself or herself or have caused

this Agreement to be executed by his or her appointed
representative as of the signature date below.

Jess leaned back, exhaling slowly. This was . . . a lot to take in.

"Take your time," Omar said with a smile that filled his eyes.
"It's a strange situation, we get it."

She looked at River. "Have you read it?"

He nodded.

"Did you have any objections?"

He stared at her, blinked. Finally, "My concerns were addressed
before you arrived."

"And they were?"

"I requested item fifteen."

Jess looked down, flipping to the second page. . . . no physical
contact is obligated on the part of Individual A or Individual B
throughout the duration of the Agreement, and any such contact is at
the sole discretion of the parties listed herein. GeneticAlly LLC, and its
agents, assigns, officers, and Board of Directors, are hereby indemni-
fied against any claim of action or resulting damages arising from any
such contact.

Her feminist brain was giving River a standing ovation for en-
suring that she didn't feel pressured into anything physical. But the
insecure beast inside was louder. River wanted it in black and white
that they didn't have to touch each other? Ladies and gentlemen:
her soulmate.

Humor came to her defense. "Got it: I'm not being paid to pet
the beast."

Omar nodded, stifling a smile. "Correct."

"Additionally, if I find myself unable to keep my libido in check," she said, "and River surprises us all and realizes that blood and not silt runs through those veins, and I get knocked up, it's not on you guys."

River coughed sharply, and Omar smothered this smile with a fist. "Correct."

She saccharine-smiled at River. "Not to worry. Great addition, Americano."

"It felt like a necessary clarification," he said stiffly.

Looking back to Omar, Jess said, "One thing I don't see here— and it's good, I guess—but I'd like it explicitly stated that I don't want my daughter involved contractually in any way. I don't want her to be photographed or included in any of these outings or inter- views."

"I agree," River said immediately. "No kids."

It was the tone, like nails on a chalkboard, that got her back up. "Are you just not a fan of humans of any size, or . . . ?"

He gave her a bemused smile. "Do you want me to back you up here or not?"

She turned back to Omar. "Can you add it?"

He made a note on his copy of the printout. "I can make that change on our part," he said with careful precision, "but we'll have no control over what the press writes if a reporter finds out that you have a daughter. All we can assure is that GeneticAlly will not discuss her existence with the press or any of our investors or affiliates."

"I'll handle my side, keeping her out of the spotlight, I just don't want you to assume that you can use her as a prop, too."

Omar looked briefly across the table at the man seated beside her. Jess saw Omar's expression falter for just a moment as the two men shared some silent communication. It was long enough for Jess to register that she'd said something sort of shitty. They were close to the finish line of something they'd believed in for years.

Jess wanted to rephrase what she'd said, but the moment moved on; Omar rolled forward. "I'll get this change made and the contract couriered over to you ASAP."

"Great, thanks for—"

"Actually," River cut in, and then hesitated, waiting for her to look at him. When their eyes met, her rib cage constricted, her blood felt too thick in her veins. "I'd like to confirm," he said haltingly, adding after a long beat of her confusion: "The test results."

Was he serious? He wanted to confirm *now*? When they had a contract in front of them and Jess was about to sign on to be his fake girlfriend for the next three months? "Are we—I mean, I assumed you would have done that already."

"We did confirm with your saliva sample," he rushed to clarify. "But I'd like to take a quick blood sample and run the lysate through the screen. Alongside mine."

Her cheeks decided to go all warm at the suggestion that their blood rest in side-by-side tubes in a centrifuge. "Sure. Whatever."

His eyes refocused on hers, and Jess realized River had just clocked her blush. "Sure," he said with a small smile. "Whatever. Follow me."

HE'D ALREADY GATHERED everything they'd need on a tray near two chairs. A rack with sterile vials. A tourniquet, needle, alcohol pads, cotton gauze, and tape. While they waited for the phlebotomist to arrive, River washed his hands extensively at the sink, dried them on a stack of fresh lab towels . . . and then pulled on a pair of blue nitrile gloves.

"*You're* going to do it?" Jess asked, awareness dropping like a hammer.

He froze just after the second glove snapped into place. "There's no one left in the building tonight who can take blood. Is that okay?"

"Um . . . what?"

He let out a short laugh. "Sorry, I didn't say that right. I'm certified to do it. I'm not just filling in because no one else is here."

Jess wanted to keep emotional distance, wanted to keep this professional. But she couldn't help her playful tone: "You're telling me you're a geneticist, a CSO, and a phlebotomist?"

A small smile appeared and disappeared. "In the early days," he said, "when we were testing whole blood lysate, we recruited a huge cohort of subjects from local universities. It was all hands on deck." He blinked up to her face, then back down to her arm. "I got certified."

"Handy. Can you garden and cook, too?"

Was that a blush? He ignored her question, probably assuming it was rhetorical, and safely returned them to science. "I'm not in the lab much anymore. I used to go through every data file that would come out of there," he said, pointing to one of two boxy pieces of high-tech equipment on the far side of the lab. "Now everything is so streamlined, I'm never needed here."

"Let me guess," Jess said, "you're the meetings guy."

He smiled, nodding. "Endless investor meetings."

"Send the hot scientist in, right?" she said, and immediately wanted to swallow her fist.

He laughed down at his tray of supplies, motioned for her to sit, and holy crap, it was suddenly seven hundred degrees in the lab.

"Could you—?" River gestured for her to roll up her left sleeve.

"Right. Sorry." Awkwardly, she pushed it up and over her biceps. Very gently, but with absolute calm, River cupped a hand beneath her elbow, shifting her arm forward, and ran his thumb over the crease, looking clinically at the landscape of her veins. Much less clinically, Jess—covered in goose bumps from his hand on her inner elbow—stared at his eyes. They were, frankly, absurd.

She found herself leaning forward, slightly fascinated, and wishing he would look up again. "You have really pretty eyes," she said, and sucked in a breath. She hadn't meant to say that out loud. She cleared her throat. "Sorry. I bet you get that a lot."

He hummed.

"And why do guys always get the thick lashes?" she asked. "They literally don't care about them."

The corner of his mouth pinched in with the suggestion of another smile. "A painful truth." Satisfied with the vein situation, he reached for the tourniquet, tying the band around her upper arm. "I'm going to let you in on a secret, though," he said conspiratorially, flicking his eyes up to hers and then back down. "I'd honestly rather be punched in the jaw than get one of those fuckers in my eye."

An unexpected laugh burst free of her throat. River's gaze

returned to hers, lingering now, and her insides rolled over. He was so good-looking it made her mad.

Some of this must have shown in her expression, because his answering smile faded and he returned his attention to her arm, tearing open two alcohol prep pads and carefully swabbing.

His voice was a gentle rumble: "Make a fist."

Is this a horrible idea?

He reached for the needle, uncapping it with a practiced tug of thumb and forefinger. Yes, this was a horrible idea.

Jess needed a distraction.

"What's the story?" she asked.

"The story?" Focused, River leaned closer, and inserted the needle so deftly that she barely felt the pinch.

"*Your* story." She cleared her throat, looking away from the needle in her arm. "The origin story."

He straightened as the first vial filled. "About this?"

"Yeah."

"Lisa didn't go over the early studies in the presentation?" His frown down at her arm felt like professional concern, the beginning of a chastisement he'd deliver to Lisa later.

"She did. About your study on attraction," Jess said quickly, and definitely didn't watch his throat move as he swallowed. "And, um, long-term marital happiness. But I'm more curious about how you got there, what gave you the idea in the first place."

He detached the first vial and screwed on the cap with a practiced press of a thumb, simultaneously securing the new vial in place with his left hand. These displays of dexterity were very sexually distracting.

"You mean, how an asshole like me started studying love in the first place?"

"I'm not sure if you're trying to make me feel bad, but let me remind you: This is the room where you told your friend that I was 'average.'"

He rolled his eyes playfully. "I didn't expect you to hear that."

"Oh. In that case, it's not insulting at all."

"You . . ." He drew his eyes up, over her chest, her neck, briefly to her face, and back down to her arm. "You're a perfect test subject. From a scientific standpoint, average isn't an insult. You're exactly what we look for." She wasn't sure, but in the dim light, the tips of his ears seemed to redden. He switched out the second vial and easily fastened a third, releasing the tourniquet. "Anyway, that morning was busy." He smiled to himself before adding, "And I was probably turned off by your attitude."

"Oh my God."

River laughed quietly. "Come on. I'm teasing. It's obvious neither of us liked the other at first."

"You didn't like when I stopped you at Twiggs."

"It startled me," he said, not meeting her eyes. He cleared his throat. "I get deep in my head sometimes. You may have noticed that I can be a bit . . ." He unleashed the smile again, but only briefly. There and then gone. "Intense."

"I've spotted the trait once or twice."

Deftly, he unscrewed the last vial. "So: origin story. While I was in graduate school, there was a woman in David's lab named Rhea."

A woman, Jess thought. *Of course.*

"We were rivals, in a way."

The way he added the last three words to the sentence clearly communicated *Rivals who also fucked*.

River pulled the needle out and immediately covered the puncture site with a square of gauze. He held it there firmly with his thumb, the rest of his hand lightly curled around her arm. "One night, at a party at someone's house," he said, "we started talking about the Human Genome Project from the nineties."

"As you do at a party."

He laughed, and the full, genuine sound delivered an erotic shock like a spanking. "Yes. As you do. We were talking about the implications of knowing every gene, the way that information could be manipulated. Could you, for example, screen people for certain jobs based on their genetic profile?"

"How very *Brave New World*."

"Right?" He checked beneath the gauze to see if she was bleeding and, satisfied, reached for a fresh square, fastening it to her arm with some medical tape. "Anyway, I guess the drinks flowed and eventually I brought up whether it was possible to identify sexual attraction through DNA. Rhea laughed and said it was the stupidest thing she'd ever heard."

Jess stared at him, waiting for the rest of it, and the heated effect of his laugh slowly faded. "That's it?"

"I mean, that's not *it* it," he said, grinning shyly. "It turned into a real scientific undertaking, but if you're wondering whether the project was sparked in a moment when a woman mocked me, you wouldn't be entirely wrong. But it isn't supervillain levels of insecurity or vanity; it was a genuine curiosity at first. Like a bet. Why did she think it would be possible to profile someone for an engineering job versus a graphic design position, but not for relationships? Aren't both ultimately about suitedness and gratification?"

He had a point.

His face tipped down, he laughed quietly as he checked the labels. "Anyway, Rhea wasn't the last person to mock the idea."

"What does that mean?"

"Imagine being a fairly well-respected young geneticist and word gets out that you're planning to use your expertise to find who'll fall in love with whom."

"People were dicks about it?"

He tilted his head side to side, a yes-no. "Scientists are often pretty critical of other scientists and what we choose to do with our time and knowledge."

"Sounds like the literary world and Fizzy."

His brows went up. "Oh yeah? How so?"

"You wouldn't believe the things people say to her about writing romance. Calling her books 'trashy' and 'guilty,' like they're something to be ashamed of. Even in interviews. She's been asked what her father thinks of her writing sex scenes."

"Yeah, I get that. Early on nearly everyone who knew me asked, 'Are you that desperate to find a girlfriend?' They obviously didn't know that in 2018, fifteen percent of Americans were using dating sites, and that same fifteen percent spent almost three billion dollars a year on them. Imagine that number going from fifteen percent to forty-two point five percent—"

"The current percentage of unmarried people over the age of eighteen."

Their eyes met and held as they shared this deeply—and surprisingly sensual—data-wonk moment.

"Well." She blinked away and back again. "I'm sure you're getting the last laugh, and I think it's cool." He stared at her in disbelief. "I really do. I just . . ." Jess winced and the obvious question hung between them, a swinging sign in the wind. "Does it annoy you that I don't believe our score?"

"Not really. I admire your natural skepticism." He gave her a little self-indulgent grin. "And we have enough data that I feel fairly confident we know what we're doing here. You'll just have to decide what to think if this test comes back with the same score."

"What are *you* expecting?"

"I'll believe the test if it says we are biologically compatible, but I'm not a scientific zealot, Jess. I recognize the element of choice." He pulled his gloves off and dropped them on the tray. "No one is going to force you to fall in love with me."

With his face tilted down, Jess was able to stare at him outright. Smooth olive skin, the shadow of stubble, full lips. Jess wasn't sure, but she'd guess midthirties. She put the mental filter of time over his face, imagining him with salt and pepper at his temples, the small lines of laughter in the corners of his eyes.

She shifted a little on the stool, hit with an unfamiliar ache.

"When you saw the first compatibility score over ninety, what was your immediate reaction?"

He stood and pulled on a fresh pair of gloves. "Dread."

This was . . . not the answer she was expecting. Jess followed him with her eyes as he moved with the rack of vials over to the hood. "Dread? Seriously?"

"Over ninety is where we enter the range of scores that could completely throw off our curve." He set the rack inside and then peeled off his gloves, turning to face her. "We'd already seen great compatibility with scores *up to* ninety. The scores coming off the behavioral and mood assessments tracked. It was all linear. We didn't know what to expect. Could it *stay* linear? How would that look emotionally? A sigmoidal curve made the most sense—the emotional satisfaction scores might flatten out at some point over eighty and reach an asymptote. But to imagine that at higher biological compatibility we might see *lower* emotional compatibility— that's what scared me. We really don't want to be bell-shaped, but we just don't have a lot of data either way."

He seemed to hear his own rambling and stopped abruptly, blushing.

Self-conscious River was too much to handle. Jess shoved fondness away. "You are *deeply* nerdy."

"I'm just saying," he said, laughing self-deprecatingly, "if actual emotional compatibility tanked at higher DNADuo numbers, it would narrow our range of possible matches, and make it harder to argue that we'd been binning them the right way."

"But that isn't what happened," Jess said. "Right? They're all together and happy."

"The ones we know of, yeah. But like I said, there's only a handful at the top of the scale."

He sat down at the fume hood, pulling on a fresh pair of gloves, spraying them with alcohol, and pulling on a second pair over the first.

He wasn't leaving anything to chance. Even Jess knew enough

to know he could do this sample prep out on the lab bench, but she wasn't surprised he was using sterile technique. Still, the anxiety building in her stomach had reached a boiling point: she would need to find a way to explain it if the results came back ninety-eight again.

Even if it was starting to feel like River Peña might not be the worst man alive.

Jess lifted her chin to the two identical hulking machines on the other side of the room. "Are those the DNADuos?"

He followed her attention briefly and nodded. "Creatively named DNADuo One and DNADuo Two." She could hear his smile. "DNADuo Two is down right now. Getting serviced next week. It'll be up and running by May, I hope. You're welcome to stay and hang out," he added, "but the assay takes eight hours, so the data won't be analyzed until tomorrow morning."

"A wild Friday night for you?" she joked.

But with his back to her, she couldn't tell if he even cracked a smile. His posture took the shape of renewed focus. "I'm usually here anyway."

"Spoken like a true dream boyfriend."

He scoffed—appreciating her joke just about as much as she expected him to. Jess realized she was being politely dismissed. Standing, she pushed her sleeve back down. "Think I'll head home to Juno."

"I'll call you tomorrow," he said without turning around. "I'll call either way."

ELEVEN

M OM, DID YOU know the first roller coaster was built to keep
people away from brothels?"

Jess dragged her eyes away from Google to focus on her pajama-
clad seven-year-old, hanging upside down over the back of the
couch. Her hair was nearly to her waist, and Pigeon had made herself a nice little nest where it pooled on the cushion. "Hello, small
human. How do you know what a brothel is?"

Juno peeked at her from behind her book. "I heard it."

She lifted her chin to what Juno was reading. "Your library book
about lizards mentions brothels?"

"No, it was in a movie I watched with Pops."

Jess leaned an elbow on the dining table next to her abandoned
bowl of oatmeal and slid her gaze over to Pops sitting innocently in
the lounger. He scanned his crossword puzzle, saying casually, "It
was on some history channel." He flipped a page. "Practically a
documentary."

"A documentary about brothels, Pops? It can't wait until she's, I don't know, ten?"

Upside-down Juno grinned at her victoriously. "I looked it up in the dictionary *you* got me."

Dammit.

Pigeon darted off the couch barely a second before Juno slid the rest of the way to the floor, landing in a giggling, crumpled pile. Sitting right-side-up again, she flipped her head back, leaving her hair a tangled mess around her head. "It was a movie about Billy the Kid."

Jess looked at Pops again. "*Young Guns?*" she said incredulously. "My seven-year-old watched *Young Guns*."

"In my defense," he said, still not bothering to glance up, "we were watching *Frozen* again and I fell asleep. When I woke up, she'd changed the channel and got invested. You want me to keep her from learning history?"

Juno skipped to Jess's side and peered down at her laptop. Clearly Jess was grasping at straws; she'd actually typed *Second Grade Art Projects* into the search bar.

"I already know what I want to do for my project," Juno said. "I want to do an art tape amusement park with a roller coaster, a carousel, tiny screaming people, and a Tilt-A-Whirl."

"Honey, while I appreciate your ambition, that is a lot of work." Jess paused. And giant, and messy, with five thousand sticky tiny pieces that would end up on Juno, Jess, the furniture, and the cat. "Also, I'm worried you'd tell Mrs. Klein how you arrived at roller coasters for art inspiration."

"I wouldn't tell her that I know what brothels are."

"Maybe we could start by not repeating the word *brothel*." Jess tucked a strand of hair behind Juno's ear. "What about a hot air balloon collage? We can cut pictures out of magazines and glue them to a poster board."

Her daughter was clearly not tempted.

Jess turned back to the screen and clicked on a list of projects. "These pinwheels are pretty. Or a Popsicle stick bridge?"

Juno shook her head, furrowed brow pinned firmly in place. *Hello again, Alec.* She grabbed a book from a pile on the table and turned it to a page listing the Top Ten Amusement Parks Across the World.

"I want to do something cool and enter it in the North Park Festival of Arts." Juno pointed a sparkly painted fingernail at an old photo. "This is Switchback Gravity Railroad. It's the one the guy built so people would go here instead of the"—she leaned in, whispering—"*brothels*." Straightening, she returned to normal volume. "But I don't want to do that one because it only went six miles an hour and that's only two miles an hour faster than Nana's Rascal scooter when she broke her knee."

Pops chuckled from his chair. "I thought she was going to mow someone over in that thing."

Juno turned the page to a brightly colored coaster, one with a loop so huge Jess's stomach lurched just imagining it. "I think I want to do Full Throttle at Magic Mountain," she said. "Since you don't have to work at Twiggs anymore, maybe we could go there tomorrow for Try Something New Sunday?"

Jess had called Daniel on her way home from GeneticAlly last night. He'd sounded mildly relived when Jess gave notice; she'd shown no promise as a barista. "That's a long drive," Jess told her.

"We could take the train," Juno singsonged.

"I don't know if the train goes that far north," Jess sang back.

Her daughter leaned in close, pressing the tip of her nose to Jess's. "It does. Pops checked."

Jess glared at Pops again, but guilt still hadn't induced him to look up from his crossword.

"Are you even tall enough to ride that?" she asked.

"We'll put lifts in her shoes," Pops offered, to which Juno responded with an ear-splitting screech as she ran over to tackle him.

Jess rubbed her temples, looking up when her phone vibrated on the table with an unknown number. Who would be calling at 8:15 a.m. on a Saturday?

The foggy window of her mind wiped clean. *River*.

She should answer. She should. He probably had the test results. But she couldn't make her thumb swipe over the screen. She just let it vibrate in her hand before it went over to voicemail.

It wasn't panic over the possibility that the results were confirmed late last night. It was the opposite: She'd lain awake until after two a.m. thinking of what she would do with the money. College savings. A better hearing aid for Pops. A little cushion in the bank. Now that she'd taken the leap and signed the contract, Jess didn't want it snatched away.

Her phone screen went dark. She waited . . . and waited. No voicemail. Great. Now she would have to call him.

Jess returned to her laptop, finger hovering absently over the keyboard. She'd resisted doing this so far, but the urge was too tempting. Jess typed Dr. River Peña into the search bar and pressed Enter. The results populated the page: medical articles, UCSD alumni posts, awards. LinkedIn, ResearchGate. She clicked on the image tab, and low-resolution thumbnails filled the screen. The first photo was a faculty shot taken, according to the caption, while he was a postdoctoral researcher in the Division of Medical Genetics at UCSD. There were more recent ones, too: pictures with investors at various fundraising events. In each, he looked easy in his skin. In each, he was *smiling*. Jess was so unprepared for the sight of his crinkly eyes and uneven, perfect grin that she felt that weird hot flush of defensive anger. She'd caught hints of his smile in passing, but usually only as smug amusement or flashes of embarrassed laughter. Jess had never seen it like this: bright and sincere. And pointed right at her.

"Ooh, who's that?"

"Nobody." She slammed her laptop shut and picked up her coffee with all the subtlety of a cartoon criminal. "I was just . . ." With renewed focus, she flipped open Juno's book again. "So, roller coasters, then?"

Daughter slyly appraised mother. Suspicion slid across Juno's features, but was quickly replaced by the realization that she'd just gotten her way. "Yes!"

Closing the book, she scooped it up with the others and raced toward her room. "I'm gonna look at the train schedule on your iPad!"

Jess began to argue, but her phone vibrated on the table. It was a text from the same unknown number.

Would you like to have dinner?

(It's River.)

Her lungs filled with helium.

> Does that mean you
> reproduced the finding?

David just emailed the graph.
I called to share the results.

> But it's a yes on the
> finding?

98, confirmed.

Jess stared at her phone while her heart decided to absolutely freak the hell out inside her body. Flipping, flopping, punching. It was real.

It was *real*.

She knew it was her turn to say something, but her hands had gone vaguely numb. Stalling, she clicked on the phone number and entered it under *Americano Phlebotomist* in her contacts.

Finally, the three dots appeared, indicating that he was typing.

Are you free tonight?

Slowly, one letter carefully tapped at a time, she managed to reply.

Bahn Thai. Park & Adams.
7:30

Park in the alley in
the back

"Four letters down," Pops said across the room. "First letter is
L—'hurdle.'"

Pushing her phone aside, Jess bent to rest her head on her
folded arms.

"Leap," she said.

"HONESTLY, JESSICA, I haven't seen outfit panic like this since I
wrote Nicoline in *His Accidental Bride*." Fizzy stepped back to judge
what had to be outfit change number 142. "And you're not even pretending to be a virgin picking out what to wear on your Victorian-era
wedding night. Take it down a notch."

Jess took in her reflection, styled and polished and hilariously
unfamiliar in a padded push-up bra and V-neck sweater with a neck-
line so plunging it nearly reached hell. "Fizzy, I cannot wear this."

"Why not?"

"For starters?" she said, motioning to the mirror. "I can almost
see my belly button."

Fizzy blinked. "And?"

Jess yanked the sweater over her head, tossed it onto the bed,
and reached for a distressed chambray shirt she'd picked up at a
boutique in LA last summer. It didn't fit quite the same with the

benefit of Fizzy's padded bra, but even Jess had to admit she (they) looked pretty good.

She added a layered necklace, tucked the shirt into the front of dark jeans, and turned to face Fizzy. "Well?"

Fizzy looked her up and down, a smile parting her cherry-red lips. "You look hot. How're you feeling?"

"Like I might throw up."

She laughed. "It's dinner," Fizzy said. "*Next door.* You'll have some tom ka, some duck green curry, and if at any point you think you've made a mistake, leave him with the check and come home. Listen to your gut. We'll be right here."

NO EXAGGERATION: THEY were *right there*. The restaurant Jess had chosen was on the other side of their fence, which meant she was already seated at a table outside when River showed up. He was five minutes early, but going by his expression of surprise, Jess could only assume she'd derailed his plan to get there first, get comfortable, and be seated with ease by the time she arrived.

He stopped when he saw her, midstep, uncharacteristically caught off guard. "Oh." He looked around the sidewalk. "I— Sorry, I thought you said seven thirty."

Jess indulged in a quick scan. Even though it was Saturday, she assumed he'd just come from work—he was wearing dark navy trousers, a white button-down shirt with the collar open—but his clothes looked crisp, and his hair was freshly washed and finger-raked.

"I did. I live right there." She pointed to her left and his eyes tracked to the apartment building.

"Oh." Pulling out the chair, he sat across the small table from her and did his own inspection—his eyes skirting the length of her body and quickly back up. A trail of heat followed the path. He cleared his throat. "That's handy."

Rama, a muscular twentysomething waiter who was Jess's hero because he frequently booted people from Mr. Brooks's stoop, stopped at their table. He grinned down at her, and then meaningfully slid his gaze to River. "Hey, Jess, who's your friend?"

Way to make it abundantly clear that she'd never brought a date here before. "Knock it off, Rama. His name's River."

The two men shook hands, and River sized up Rama while he was pouring water into their glasses. "Need a minute?"

"Sure, that'd be great."

When Rama left them to peruse, Jess lifted her chin. "Did you come from work?"

He brought his water to his lips, and Jess definitely did not watch them part and make contact with the glass. She also did not watch his Adam's apple bob as he swallowed. "I stopped at home to change." He answered her smirk with one of his own. "I don't have a partner, kids, or pets. Work is pretty much all I have."

"Is that by design?"

His brows pulled in, and Jess could tell he was giving the question real consideration. "Maybe? I mean, once we got some early results in the attraction study, my curiosity sort of . . . took over. It's been hard to think about anything else."

"Which is funny," she pointed out, "since you're thinking about dating and relationships all day long, but not ever for yourself."

"I see it from a bit of a distance," he said. "I was so far down in the weeds, looking at specific alleles and genetic variants, that until maybe the last year or two, the larger picture was easy to ignore."

Jess wasn't sure if there was a better way to phrase her next question, so she just came out with it: "Is there a part of you that feels sort of inconvenienced by this result?"

River laughed and lifted his glass again. Just then, Rama returned. "You guys ready?"

"Saved by Rama," she said.

River's eyes held hers. "Saved." He lifted his hand, palm up, gesturing for her to order.

Jess sighed and turned her face up. "You know what I'm getting."

"Yup." Rama turned to River. "And you?"

"Wait, what is she getting?"

"Tom ka soup," Rama recited. "And the duck green curry."

River frowned. "Oh." He opened his menu again. "What . . . um, else would you recommend?"

Jess gaped at him. "Do not tell me you were going to get the same thing."

River nodded down at his menu. "Drunken noodles?"

"They're great," she confirmed. "Let's do soup for two and the two entrées." She looked at River. "Want a beer or anything?"

He seemed genuinely tickled by the way she took charge. "Water's good."

They handed their menus to Rama, and Jess stared at her date across the table. "But really: you were *not* going to get the duck."

"I was."

She didn't know where the urge to laugh-scream came from, but she swallowed it down with a cold gulp of ice water.

"Did you work today?" he asked stiffly, clearly hoping she'd forgotten what she'd asked before they were interrupted. Frankly, if he didn't want to answer, Jess probably didn't want to hear the truth anyway.

"Nana's always been a stickler that if I don't have to work, Saturday is a family day."

"You live with your grandmother?" he asked.

"Yes and no. Nana Jo and Pops own the apartment complex. They live in the bungalow, and I live in the apartment across the courtyard."

"With your daughter?" he confirmed, and she nodded. "What's her name?"

After a second's pause, Jess shook her head. Unease twisted through her.

"I know she's off-limits as far as the experiment," he said. "That was just me asking about family. Sharing." He paused, smiling playfully. "For example, I have two meddling sisters."

"Oh, you're lucky then. Meddling women keep the world running."

"They'd love that." He laughed, warm and clear. "Both older: Natalia and Pilar. Both overbearing."

"The youngest. Huh." Jess sipped her water. "I would have lost that bet."

Amusement lifted the corner of his mouth. "Why's that?"

Rama materialized again with a large steaming bowl of soup. He placed it between them and they shared a few moments of easy silence as they dished up their portions, passing the chili sauce and condiments across the table.

Jess bent to smell the contents of her bowl—the tangy, pungent broth was one of her favorite comfort foods—and registered that River had just mirrored her movement precisely.

He noticed at almost the same time and straightened in his chair. "Why are you surprised I'm the youngest?" he asked, moving on.

"Youngest children are usually less 'intense,'" she said with a smile, using his own description against him. "You uptight perfectionists tend to be oldest children."

"I see." His laugh rolled through her, and he bent, taking a bite of soup. The deeply sexual groan he let escape when he tasted was destined to haunt Jess's best and worst dreams.

"What about you?" he asked. "Any siblings?"

She shook her head. "Only child."

He took another bite. "I guess we'd have both lost a bet, then. I would have said oldest, with at least one sibling."

"Why?"

"You seem responsible, smart, conscientious. Bossy. I imagine you emulating your parents and—"

Jess snort-laughed and reached up to cover her mouth with her napkin. The very idea of emulating Jamie was absurd. "Sorry, that was just—" She smoothed her napkin over her lap again. "No, I'm an only child."

He nodded in understanding and, to his credit, changed the subject.

"So, we've talked about how I got here," he said. "But how'd you end up a statistician? I'll admit it suits you."

She lifted a brow.

"You seem very competent," he added. "It's reassuring. Attractive."

Jess watched him pointedly avoid her eyes. He had no way of knowing, but calling her "competent" was easily the best compliment he could have paid her.

He set the glass down again. "But to my question . . ."

Jess hummed, thinking. "I find it soothing that numbers don't lie."

"But they *can* be misleading."

"Only if you don't know what to look for." She took a sip of soup. "I've always been a numbers geek. When I was a kid, I'd count my steps everywhere I went. I would count how many floors were in a building, how many windows per floor. I'd try to estimate how tall a building was, and then look it up when I got home. And when I took my first stats class, I was done for. I love working with numbers that are meaningful more broadly. Predicting earthquakes or natural disasters, political campaigns, customer service survey results or—"

"Genetics," he said quietly.

Ahh. The elephant in the room. She felt the tops of her cheeks warm and looked down, surprised again that her boobs were so much closer to her face in this bra than they usually were. Freaking Fizzy. Jess cleared her throat. "Exactly. As long as you have enough data, you can figure out anything."

"I get it," he said in that same quiet voice. "There's something satisfying about solving little puzzles every day." They ate in silence for a moment, and Jess wondered if she was imagining the way his gaze seemed to linger on her neck, and lower, down her arms . . .

"Are those . . ." he asked, narrowing his eyes and motioning to her right forearm, where she'd pushed her sleeve up a bit, "Fleetwood Mac lyrics?"

"Oh." Her left hand moved to cover the ink. "Yes." She turned her arm over, but he leaned in, wrapping his thumb and forefinger around her wrist, turning it so he could see the soft skin of her inner arm.

"'Thunner only happens,'" he read, eyes moving away from the misspelled word and up to her face. "'Thunner'?"

Jess rolled her eyes. "Felicity." Hopefully he'd gathered that simply saying her name should explain everything.

He must've, because he laughed and lightly swept his thumb across the letters. Nothing like the clinical way he'd touched her last night, this was leisurely, exploring. And she was melting. "And another piece of the puzzle falls into place."

"She—Fizzy—has the other half of the line. 'When it's raining' except there's no *h* in *when*." With him looking at her and touching her like that, it took great concentration to form thoughts and make those thoughts into words. "On my twenty-fifth birthday, she took me out to celebrate. It was a really perfect night and I emailed her when I got home to say thank you. I was absolutely hammered, and Pops thought it was so funny he wouldn't let me use the backspace key to correct my typos." She shrugged. "Apparently I emailed her the full lyrics to the song we'd sung at karaoke to prove how sober I was."

His eyes shone when he glanced up at her face. With a look that might be regret, he released her arm. "That's a good story."

Jess laughed down at the last couple bites of her soup. "Pops is basically a monster."

"A monster with a sense of humor."

"I'm surrounded by jokers," she admitted.

"You're lucky."

There was something in his tone that caught her, hooked her eyes back up to his. It wasn't that he sounded lonely, exactly, but there was a vulnerability there that threw her a little off balance. "I feel lucky." She scratched around inside her head for something to say. "Tell me about everyone at GeneticAlly. Have you known all of them very long?"

"Most of them since we started. David, of course. And Brandon was Dave's friend from college." He stirred his soup and moved out of the way when Rama returned with their main courses. "It's a really tight-knit team."

"Have any of them been matched?" Jess asked, digging into the platters.

"Brandon, yeah," he said. "He met his wife in the . . ." River looked up, thinking, and Jess marveled over his dark-lashed whiskey eyes all over again. "I guess it would be the third phase of beta testing. Maybe four years ago now. They were a Gold Match."

"Wow."

He nodded, dishing some food onto his own plate. "I know. He was the first, and it was a really big deal." *Nothing like this, though* hung unsaid between them. "Then Tiffany—you met her at the

Results Reveal Disaster," he said with a wink, and Jess burst out laughing. "She's our head data analyst—she met her wife, Yuna, when they matched. I believe they were an eighty-four, and Yuna moved here from Singapore to be with Tiff."

"How many countries have you pulled samples from?"

He didn't even have to think. "Fifty-seven."

"Wow."

"Yeah." Wiping his mouth with his napkin, River was a portrait of manners and class across the table from her. Did it make her a terrible person that she was surprised this date wasn't awful? The conversation flowed, the silences were easy. She hadn't spilled any-thing down her shirt, and he'd called her competent. It was the best date she'd had in seven years. "And everyone else has dated pretty broadly, if they're single and interested."

"Do you think it's a bummer for any of them who haven't had a Gold or higher match? Like, do you worry within the company it will become a competitive or—I guess, like, a status thing?"

He stared at her, and then blinked. "You ask really probing questions."

Immediately, Jess was mortified. "I'm sorry. I'm just—" *Ugh*. "Sorry."

"No, no, it's okay, it's very . . . thoughtful."

Warmth spread in a prickly rush along her skin. "I want to know about it," she admitted. "I want to know about you, and this, and what you think about all of it. I mean, we're here right now. I said I would enter into this agreement genuinely."

"I know," he said, and seemed to be quietly appraising her with new eyes. "I appreciate it."

"Will you?" she asked, feeling her heart hit her from the inside like a gloved fist.

"I don't really know any other way to be." He reached for his water and took a sip. "You asked me before whether this result was an inconvenience. It isn't. It isn't an inconvenience, but I admit I'm not sure what to think about it. If I take it seriously, it rearranges my entire life. If I don't take it seriously, I'm discarding everything I've worked for."

"Which, incidentally, also rearranges your life," Jess said, laughing.

He laughed, too. "Exactly."

"Well, in that case," she said, "I can be on board for Project Be Genuine but Cautious."

He wiped his hand on his napkin and reached across the table for a handshake. With her heartbeat in her ears, she took his hand, and hers felt weirdly small in his grasp.

"What happens now?" she asked.

"I guess we get together when we're free," he said, and her brain took off spinning about how that would work, where this could even go.

And where she wanted it to go.

"Okay."

"Otherwise, we wait for marching orders from Brandon about any public appearances."

"*Brandon Butkis*," Jess whispered, partly to break the tension of imagining forging a personal relationship with River after tonight and partly because—how could she not say it? "Come on, you have to admit it's a great name."

Rama dropped the bill off at their table and River thanked him before sliding the small leather folder into his lap. Never missing a beat, River delivered the next bit of information with an admirably straight face: "His wife's last name is Seaman."

Jess gasped. "No."

Finally, a smile broke across his face. "Yes."

"Did they hyphenate?" She leaned in. "Please tell me they hyphenated."

River laughed. "They did not."

Small footsteps stomped along the sidewalk, and the weight and rhythm registered in Jess's brain only a split second before a pair of small arms were thrown around her neck. "Did you save me some duck?"

Jess peeked over her daughter's head to deliver an apologetic-mortified glance at River. Holding her kid at arm's length, Jess gave the most convincing Mom Face she could manage. "What are you still doing up, honey? You're not supposed to be out here."

"I could hear your laugh in the courtyard."

"But what were you doing in the courtyard?"

"Beating Pops at checkers."

"Pops?" Jess called out.

"She's too fast," Pops replied from behind the fence.

Juno giggled.

"I've got her," Jess said back. She relented and kissed Juno's forehead before turning her around to face River. Apparently this was happening. "Sorry for the interruption."

He shook his head and smiled warmly at Juno. "Not at all."

"Juno, this is Dr. Peña."

Juno reached out, and he wrapped her tiny hand in his large one. "River," he said, shaking gently. "You can call me River."

Settling on her mom's lap, Juno tilted her head, considering him. "You have a unique name, too."

River nodded. "I do."

"Do you like it?" she asked.

"Absolutely."

"My middle name is M-E-R-R-I-A-M. I'm named after mountains. What's yours?"

"Nicolas, after my grandpa."

She pursed her lips, less impressed. "Hmm. That's kind of normal, I guess. Did anyone ever tease you for being named River Nicolas?"

"A few times," he admitted. "But I'd rather be teased for having a name nobody else has than one that a ton of people have. I'm willing to bet no one else is named Juno Merriam Davis. Only you."

Jess leaned back, taking this all in, confused by the warm wiggly feeling in her stomach.

Juno shifted on her lap, and Jess heard the tiny bell of the cat on the other side of the fence separating the restaurant patio from the apartment's side yard. "My mom is Jessica Marie Davis," Juno said with exaggerated sympathy. "We looked it up once, and there were four hundred of them." She paused, and with surprisingly good comedic timing added, "In California."

"Yeah." He caught Jess's eye and then smiled back at Juno. "But I bet there's really only one person like your mom anywhere in the world."

W h a t.

"That's true," Juno agreed with unbridled innocence.

He immediately looked away, clearing his throat, and Jess's heart scrabbled up a vine, swinging wildly behind her ribs.

River pulled out his wallet, smoothly sliding four twenties into the bill folder. "I should probably head out."

Jess smiled. "Thanks for dinner."

"Anytime." He smiled at Juno again, and then quickly at Jess. "I mean it."

They stood, and Jess let her pajama-clad kid climb onto her back to be carried to bed.

At the alley, River stopped and looked over Jess's shoulder at the apartment complex behind them. The tender tips of vines could be seen bobbing along the top of the fence. "Thanks for letting me park back here."

"We have a guest spot. Street parking is a total drag."

"People sit on cars out front," Juno added. "Mr. Brooks gets *so mad*."

River frowned, taking this information adorably seriously. "Does he?"

"Our neighbor," Jess explained. "It's a cast of characters here."

River glanced at his watch as he reached for his car door and unlocked it. "I'm seeing that."

Jess searched for it, she really did, but there was nothing in his tone to make her think he was complaining at all.

"Good night, Jessica Marie and Juno Merriam."

Juno squeezed Jess's neck. "Good night, River Nicolas."

TWELVE

———／———

BURNED PANCAKES, ONE missing orange sneaker, cat vomit on the backpack, coffee brewing without water in the tank, and one mother yelling at her daughter that if she didn't want to cut her hair then she needed to let Mom braid it before bed. In other words, a classic meltdown before eight a.m. Jess didn't have a chance to look in the mirror, let alone check her email, until she'd safely dropped Juno off at school, and she was glad for it, because the notification that she and River had been asked for an interview by the *San Diego Union-Tribune* would have had her barfing right beside the cat.

"I got your email," she said as soon as Brandon answered.

"Oh, great!" Teeth, teeth, teeth. It was all Jess could imagine. "Sounds like the date went well?"

She chewed on her lip. It had gone well. Better than expected. River wasn't supposed to be funny, and he definitely wasn't supposed to charm her kid. And yet. "Yeah, it was fine."

"Does the timing for the interview work? I know tomorrow's short notice."

"It's less a timing issue," Jess admitted, "than a bravery one."

"You?" He laughed generously. "You're adorable. Stop it."

"I am very much not used to press." Quickly Jess added, "I know it's what I signed up for, but I was sort of hoping to start small with dinners, then maybe a couple tweets no one notices, a small blog interview about online dating, and *eventually* working our way up to the *Trib*."

"Michelle is doing the piece and she's a love," Brandon assured her. "She's going to adore you. She and River go way back."

Jess wanted to ask whether that was code for banging, but would not ask that.

Brandon read through her silence: "She did a piece on him several years ago. That's all."

"Mm-hmm. So, tomorrow," she said, biting her lip. "Tomorrow at noon, Shelter Island." Jess paused and a clammy chill worked its way up her neck. "Why Shelter Island?"

"Perfect for photos." He confirmed her fears, and she nearly swallowed her tongue. She'd already turned her closet upside down for the dinner date, and a chambray shirt and jeans was the best she could come up with. This was exactly the sort of thing she'd been dreading.

"I have to go shopping."

"Jessica, honestly, whatever you're wearing is fine."

"Brandon. You wouldn't say that if you could see me right now."

He laughed. "I just mean you'll be fine regardless."

Would she? She looked down at her threadbare light gray T-shirt and charcoal-gray sweats. She, honestly, could not stand next to River "*GQ*" Peña in front of the San Diego Bay in anything that was currently in her closet.

On the other hand, at the end of the day, a soulmate loved you for what was on the inside, right?

OF ALL THE beautiful places in San Diego—and there were indeed many—few were as spectacular as Shelter Island. If she took Harbor to Scott, hung a left at Shelter Island Drive and then another left at the circle, a long parking lot overlooked one of the best views in the city: a full vista of the San Diego Bay with the downtown skyline in perfect, crystalline glory. Coronado was visible in the distance. At night, the view was so breathtaking it felt like stepping inside a postcard.

Even during the day—especially after a morning shower that had left the sky bright and clear—it was so beautiful that Jess paused for a second once she climbed out of her car, staring at a side of downtown San Diego she should appreciate more. The buildings looked like sleek, glossy swords in the distance. Big, puffy cotton-ball clouds dotted the sky, and sailboats bobbed on the surface of the bay. Add to that the sight of River, in dark trousers, a long camel coat over a navy sweater, hair blowing in the wind like something out of an Austen movie. Would it be weird if she stood here and just . . . stared at him? Took a photo or two? Nobody would blame her.

For a second—truly, only a second—Jess regretted not being more insecure about her clothing before leaving the house. She had finally settled on black jeans, a white T-shirt, and black flats. Simple but appropriate.

Though maybe too simple. Beside River was a woman—Michelle, Jess guessed. She was pretty in a journalist sort of way, which was to say she had the luxury of never being the subject of her own story; how she dressed didn't really matter. Jess was both amused and aggrieved that she and Michelle were essentially wearing the same outfit, with the sole exception that Michelle had been smart enough to wear a cardigan over her white T-shirt. It was noon on a gorgeous early-February day, but Jess had forgotten how exposed Shelter Island was. With the wind whipping past them in chilly gusts, she was going to freeze her ass off.

Noticing her arrival, they brought their conversation to an end. The two made their way over, and behind where they'd been standing, Jess noticed a man diligently setting up what looked like a whole lot of camera equipment. This was a much bigger production than she'd anticipated.

Her stomach wilted.

Michelle was even prettier up close, comfortable in her skin, with a friendly smile. And of course, there was River, ripped from the thick pages of a magazine, looking so far out of Jess's league that she could only laugh at his approach.

He noticed and gave an unsure smile. "What's funny?"

"Nothing." She lifted a hand and let it fall in defeat. "Of course, you just—look so nice."

He stopped in front of her and dropped his gaze from her head to her feet and back again. His voice was a sandpaper scrape. "So do you."

"Liar."

He quirked a smile. "Nope."

It's all an act, she thought. *Even Dracula was notoriously charming.*

Then, so quickly she wondered how long he'd been working himself up to it, he bent down and kissed her cheek. Jess was so shocked by this turn of events, he may as well have reached a single finger out and touched her forehead, ET-style. Michelle was probably watching this and writing the headline in her head: *Wow, They Are Totally Fake Dating.*

Subhead: *And They Are Terrible at It.*

"Hi," Jess said, because her brain didn't remember other words.

River smiled this unfamiliar, private smile and parroted cutely back at her, "Hi."

Subtitle revision: *And She Is Terrible at It.*

Michelle reminded them that she was standing there, too. "You two are cute."

Jess had to literally bite her tongue to not reply, *No we aren't.*

River seemed to have also expected her to come back with something contrary and offered a proud flicker of his eyebrow before turning back to Michelle. "Michelle, this is Jess. Jess, Michelle."

The two women shook hands, and Michelle gestured to an outcropping of rocks near the water. "Should we get started?" As they walked, she pointed to the man with all the cameras. "Jess, this is Blake. He'll be getting some photos. For now, we'll just chat while he sets up." She tilted her head to Blake but kept her eyes on Jess.

"If you see him snapping some pictures, he's just getting candids. I promise we'll make you look great. Just try to relax as much as possible, be natural."

Jess took a deep breath and exhaled as completely as she could, clocking that in the process her shoulders dropped from up near her ears back to normal shoulder position.

Comfortably, as though he spent most of his day in front of a film crew rather than at investor meetings, River sat on a rock just below waist height and opened his arm, gesturing for Jess to sit down beside him.

Jess took three steps closer and sat down in a stumble, legs awkwardly pinched together to avoid leaning into his long, solid body. With ease, he shifted her closer to a flatter surface, and now she was in a more comfortable position but they were sitting pressed together like people who were effortlessly intimate.

Which they were not.

"Jess," Michelle said, and then added, "I hope it's okay to call you Jess. It's how River referred to you . . . ?"

"Jess is great."

"Great," she repeated. "I've interviewed River before for a piece on the company, so I have some good background there, but this is my first time talking to him as a client. Before we get to him, I'm interested in hearing about how you came into all this. What made you take the test in the first place?"

"Honestly," Jess said, "I was dragged into it by a friend. She and I—and River—are regulars at this coffee shop, and one of the baristas mentioned River was starting some kind of dating site.

Which"—she pointed to him—"I mean, be honest, he looks more like a hot medieval history professor, right?"

Michelle laughed, nodding. "He totally does." She wrote something down.

"But he invited us to come out to the offices," Jess said, and looked up at River to find him smiling at her fondly. It was rattling and threw her off her easy, unselfconscious rhythm. "So, we did."

"And what was it like for you, meeting Jess?" she asked River.

"We hadn't officially met until that day," he said, and reached up to run his hand through his hair like a gorgeous stereotype. "I'd noticed her," he said, looking at her again and letting his gaze move thoroughly over her features. "I've seen her there for a couple years now, but had no idea what her name was."

"Did you want to know?"

He looked at Michelle with a small smirk. "Of course I did. Look at her." He gestured to Jess.

"Above average?" Jess snarked, unable to help herself.

He gave her a playful but cautious smile. "Far above average. Only an idiot would suggest otherwise."

Michelle watched this exchange with interest. "I'm sensing there's a backstory there, but I'll move on. Jess, can you tell me a little about yourself?"

While Jess gave a skeletal rundown of her life—her undergraduate work at UCLA, her first job at Google, and her later work as a freelancer—River's attention on the side of her face was like the press of a hot iron. She could feel him smiling, nodding at these various bites of information. She could even hear the tiny hums of affirmation he offered every now and then. Like a proud boyfriend. He was good at this.

"And what did you think when you got the DNADuo score of ninety-eight?" Michelle asked.

At least she could answer plainly here. "I didn't believe it."

River laughed. "I didn't, either."

"I can imagine," Michelle said.

"Think about it," he said. Jess swallowed about a cubic liter of air when River threaded the fingers of his left hand with her right. He was *very* good at this. "I've seen hundreds of thousands of these scores over the past decade. I'd never seen a ninety-eight. What are the odds it would be *me*?"

"I'd say they were very slim."

"Slim to none. In fact," River told her, "Jess could probably calculate those odds."

"I could, for sure," she said, grinning. "That score is, as we mathematicians like to say, 'deeply fucking unexpected.'"

They both laughed, and River squeezed her hand in a tiny *Good job* gesture. At least, she assumed that's what he meant. It could easily have been more like *Don't say the F-word in front of the reporter*.

"So you get the score, you both take a beat to digest it. Then what?"

"Then," River said with honeyed calm, "we went out for dinner."

"How did it go?"

He looked down at Jess, eyes smiling. "I'd say it went well."

"So," Michelle singsonged gently, "you'd say you're officially together?"

Instantly, Jess's hand went slick and sweaty in River's grasp. As covertly as she could without Michelle noticing, she unthreaded it, wiping it on her thigh. "Uh," she said, squinting at the horizon like the question required deep calculation. "River?"

Just as she said his name, River gave a definitive "We are."

Michelle laughed.

"Yeah, we are, I'm just kidding," Jess said, as he added, "At least, we're open to what the future holds."

Smiling, Michelle bent to write something down again. Jess threw River a murder look. He threw one right back. They probably should have anticipated this sort of question. They turned away and fastened smiles on their faces just before Michelle looked back up.

"So I guess we can agree it's new," she said.

"Very new," they replied in unison, and laughed stiffly.

River took her hand again, and squeezed it emphatically. Meanwhile, Blake the Photographer hovered in the background, arcing around them, planning his attack—or candid shots. Jess's palms went clammy again.

"Sorry," she mumbled.

River bent to pretend to cough into his free hand. "It's fine."

"So, seriously," Michelle said, "I think most people will want to know if this feels different. The first time you saw each other, I mean really *looked*, was there some sort of internal reaction? A score of ninety-eight—you must've known on some cellular level."

There. Right there. She'd found River's vulnerability. The biology of it, the assumption that his body would somehow just *know*. Jess couldn't get past the unlikelihood of the number. He couldn't get past the way he knew he should feel it in every cell of his body.

"Attraction, yes," he said without hesitation. "But we're only programmed to think about first encounters on a very primitive level. Sex. Coupling. We are animals, ultimately."

Heat crawled up her neck, and she was treated to a mental image of River behind her, his front curled over her back, teeth pressed into the bare skin of her shoulder.

"But we aren't really programmed to wonder on first sight whether someone is our soulmate. At least, I'm not." Beside her, he shrugged. "It may be ironic given that I want to find it for other people, but I somehow hadn't self-inserted into any of DNADuo's findings. Truly. Given that we're a couple months away from my first IPO, and having set my own criteria so high, the last thing I was expecting was a notification on my own app. So, if you're asking whether I was surprised by the result, the answer is yes . . . and no."

Her brain felt like it was chewing, digesting each one of his words. He sounded so sincere, but what was real and what was just for show? Michelle's voice jolted her out of her thoughts. "Jess?"

Jess cleared her throat. "Like I said, I took the test on a whim. I wasn't looking for a relationship. Had just sworn off dating, actually." Michelle laughed in easy comprehension. "So yes, I was surprised." She looked up at River's open face and, maybe because her defenses were down, a low hum began in her bones. The deep vibration coursed through her, synchronizing with the high-frequency-static feeling along the surface of her skin. He was so gorgeous it made her woozy. "And no," she added quietly. "In another way, I wasn't surprised at all."

"River," Michelle asked, "I have to ask: Is sharing this finding publicly a conflict of interest?"

"I expected you to be more suspicious that it was a media stunt."

She grinned. "Is it?"

"No."

She gestured around them. "But you're leveraging it, surely."

"It's serendipitous. Doesn't mean it's false."

"Jess," Michelle said, leaning in, "does the pressure to fall in love with him feel . . . intense?"

"Yes," she admitted. "I don't know what it's supposed to feel like to find your soulmate. I've never found mine before, obviously. And in this case, I second-guess every feeling, even when they seem genuine."

"River, hearing that—does it make you uneasy?"

"Not at all." His voice rang true. "We're both scientists. It wouldn't be our natures to dive headlong into anything."

"Maybe that's why you matched," Michelle mused.

Jess looked up at him. He looked down at her. She couldn't help mirroring his new, private smile. "Maybe," he agreed, and dropped his voice, leaning in to whisper in her ear. "Project Be Genuine but Cautious." Jess nearly shivered at the sensation.

Michelle cut a knife through the tension, clapping her hands. "Let's grab some photos over by the benches there." She stood, and if she was aware of the dense emotional fog that clouded Jess and River, she didn't show it. She and Blake conferred, then waved them over. "We'd like to get the water as the backdrop, so if you could stand"—she put her hands on Jess's shoulders, turning her to face the parking lot—"here. River just beside and a little behind her, yes, good, however is comfortable for you. I'm going to be over here, we aren't listening. Just—talk to each other. As naturally as you can. Forget we're here!"

Jess wanted to stare at her with deep, unmasked incredulity. She and River were on what was essentially their second date, and Michelle wanted them to stand together and be knowingly photographed just—conversing intimately? Naturally? For a newspaper with a circulation in the hundreds of thousands? They weren't even good at being natural when they were alone.

"No pressure," Jess mumbled.

"Just," he said, searching, "tell me something about your—car."

"My . . . car?"

He laughed, and stepped closer beside her. "It's the first thing that came to mind. Don't assume I'm any better than you are at this."

"I absolutely assume that," she said, cheesing a grin as Blake lifted his camera to his face. "Look at you."

"What does that mean?" River asked.

"What does what mean?"

"'Look at you,'" he repeated.

Jess laughed.

Blake clicked the shutter.

"It means," Jess said, "that this is what you do. Of course I expect you to be smoother at all things dating and public-appearance related. I mean, I'm—"

"If you say 'average,' I'm going to toss you into the bay."

"I wasn't going to," she said, laughing. *Click.*

River exhaled a long, slow breath behind her, warm on her neck. A shiver ran through her, rattling her spine.

He noticed: "Are you cold?"

"Freezing," she admitted.

Jess felt him shift so he stood fully behind her. Just as she was going to ask him what he was doing, he stretched his arms out and she found herself being wrapped up in soft warmth, pressed against a wall of hard heat. River had tucked her into his coat, enclosing her inside it with him.

Click.

He wasn't shaking or unsteady. He held her firmly, his front pressed all along her back like it was no big deal. Jess's senses went haywire.

Michelle laughed. "Jess, you're blushing."

She couldn't even pretend this was normal. "I'm sure I am."

"So, I take it the physical side of—"

"No comment," River cut in, voice sharp.

But now the image was well and truly sparking inside her mind: Sex with River. Him over her. Sweaty beneath her. Growling and commanding behind her. Jess's body betrayed her, arching back a bit, and his tiny muffled groan told her the movement had registered.

Michelle turned and conferred with Blake over something on his camera screen, and Jess leaned minutely forward for some physical cooldown, but River pulled her back against him again, wrapping his arms around her waist. Pressed to her.

"You're cold," he reminded her, murmuring into her hair.

"Less so now," she said under her breath, and he laughed warmly.

Click.

Jess bit her bottom lip, restraining a hysterical laugh that bubbled up her throat. "Are you turned on?"

His voice was a blend of embarrassed and matter-of-fact close to her ear. "I might be."

"Oh my God."

"You just—pressed yourself against me."

Jess bent, stifling a laugh—

Click. Click.

—but this just pushed her ass back into him further and he let out a quiet hiss, pulling her closer. "Jessica."

She unleashed the laugh. For just a tiny beat, she wielded the power of the entire universe. Jess had turned on the formidable River Peña.

Click.

"You're enjoying this," he growled.

"Of course I am. So are you, apparently."

"I'd enjoy it more if we didn't have an audience."

Click.

"Are you hitting on me?"

"It sounds like I am." He seemed as surprised as she was.

"Do we even *like* each other?"

He adjusted his arms around her, heavy and secure. "Still under review."

Click.

He sighed. "I think . . . well, I don't know about you, but I'm starting to like you."

Easier to be brave facing the parking lot instead of his handsome face, his arms grounding her from floating away. "I don't know about soulmate, but I'd admit to lust." She turned her face to the side. His mouth was so close to hers.

River stilled, glanced down at her lips. "Is that right?"

His tone snagged Jess, who finally felt brave enough to meet his eyes. Heat melted through her.

Click.

THIRTEEN

———————————

IT PROBABLY SHOULD have occurred to Jess that her wrapped up in River's coat would be the perfect candid, but it absolutely did not occur to her that they would end up on the front page.

Of the *San Diego Union-Tribune*.

Fizzy dropped a copy onto the table before unloading her bag from her shoulder.

"Holy shit, Jessica Davis."

Jess brought her mug to her lips, hiding a grimace behind it. "I know. I saw it on my iPad this morning."

"How fucking adorable are you two?"

She set the mug back down. "Stop it."

Fizzy cleared her throat, reading aloud. "'The pair have the sparkling gleam and nervous tremble of new love. Seemingly without realizing it, Jess leans into him when she speaks. River looks at Jess like he's waited his entire life for her. But despite the outward impression that love is in the air, neither believed the result when it first came in. "We're both scientists," Peña said plainly. "It wouldn't be our natures to dive headlong into anything." Even so, it's hard to not believe it when you see them together.'"

Jess groaned. "Seriously. Stop, please."

"No, no," Fizzy said, holding up a hand and flipping to the second page. "The next part is my favorite. 'When the wind picked up and Jess was visibly cold, River wrapped her up in his coat. My photographer and I went quiet, witnesses to the love story unfolding in front of us. GeneticAlly may be entering a crowded sea of seasoned dating services, but it's clear they're getting the important things right.'"

By now, Jess was leaning her head on the table, wishing for the building to collapse. "Can we stop now?"

"If we must." She heard Fizzy fold up the paper and set it down on the table. "Was it fun?"

"No," Jess said immediately, reflexively. She sat up, and the lie hung filmy between them. "Yes?" She took a too-hot sip of coffee and coughed. "I mean, *no*. It wasn't fun in the sense you mean. It was weird and awkward . . . but good?" She squeezed her eyes closed. "Stop it, Fizzy."

"Stop what?"

"Stop looking at me like that."

Fizzy laughed at her. "Your mainframe is actually melting."

"He's a good-looking man, okay?" Jess conceded. "So, yes, there's a proximity effect there."

Pointing to Jess's giggling smile in the picture, Fizzy said, "You look like you want him to eat you for dinner."

"Okay, nope." Jess sat up straighter, dragging her hair into a bun. "I don't want to talk about it anymore."

"Melting." Fizzy stared at her in wonder before shaking herself into action and unpacking her laptop. They got to work; Fizzy wrote, Jess crunched data. But she could feel Fizzy look up at her every once in a while, studying her like a sample in a dish. And she felt the weight of her scrutiny so physically that Fizzy might as well have been standing behind her, hands on her shoulders, pressing down. Lucky for Fizzy's head and the external hard drive on the table between them, she looked away just before Jess reached for something to throw at her.

Jess knew Fizzy probably had a thousand questions about all of this. She did, too. What in the fresh hell were she and River actually doing? How did she feel about being so physically attracted to someone she wasn't sure she actually liked? What should she do with all of this interest in her loins? And in all this silent questioning, it never occurred to Jess that 8:24 was coming soon.

The door opened with a jubilant ding, and her heart skipped away, double tempo.

Stride, stride, stride.

River passed through the room with the sweeping confidence of a king through a court, and Jess felt the air shift all around them, an honest-to-God change in atmospheric pressure.

Fizzy leaned to the side, spotting River, her eyes going wide. "Holy shit."

Jess didn't have to turn to know that everyone was watching him. And then, even with her back to the room, Jess felt them all turn to look at *her*.

Ignoring the feeling, she turned around. River was smiling . . .

at people? A healthy flush to his cheeks, a tiny yet unmistakable upturn to his mouth.

Fizzy's voice glimmered with wonder: "What did you do to him?"

"We did *not*—"

"He's smil—"

"I *know*," Jess snapped. "It's weird. Shut up."

She did not shut up: "When you two actually—"

Leaning in, Jess hissed: "*Shhh!*"

She pretended to be very, very engrossed in her work, but it was useless. And she knew without having to watch him that once he'd picked up his drink, he was headed their way.

He set down two cups on their table. "Hey."

Jess and Fizzy stared dumbly up at him. He was so gorgeous and commanding that all Jess could manage in response was a flat "What."

He nodded to the drinks he set down. A flat white. A vanilla latte. "I thought you might want a fresh one soon," he said.

"Thank you," Fizzy and Jess said in monotonal sexbot unison.

The left corner of his mouth tucked in. "You're welcome." He held Jess's gaze, and the dark weight of it lit the fuse leading to the bomb in her libido. "Did you see the *Trib*?"

Her neck and cheeks flushed as she remembered how it felt to have him behind her. "Uh, I did, yeah."

River smiled knowingly, waiting for more, but she was unable to mentally undress him and make words at the same time. Finally, he offered, "I thought Michelle did a good piece."

Why was she out of breath? "It was really good. She was . . . nice. Even though she mentioned my clammy hands."

He laughed, shaking his head. "You were great."

"Thanks." Imaginary River was naked and beneath her on the floor, which explained why it took her a few seconds to add, "So were you."

He looked to his watch. "All right, well . . . catch you later." With a final amused pursed-lips smile, he turned to leave Twiggs with his Americano in hand. Stride, stride, stride. The bell over the door cried when he left.

Fizzy stared after him. "What just happened?"

"He bought us coffee." Jess was extremely casual. Not at all unsettled. "Calm down, Fizz."

Meanwhile, her brain was shouting in all caps.

"My vagina just unfurled like a flower," Fizzy said, still staring at the door.

"No."

"A fucking *flower*, Jess."

Jess cupped her forehead in her hands. It was going to be a long day.

HOURS LATER, FIZZY'S attention was back on the newspaper. "Look at this goddamn chemistry." They'd left for lunch but, both being on deadline, had returned to crank out a bit more work before calling it a day. "It drips from these goddamn pages. Tell me you don't believe this shit."

"Stop."

"You're going to set the town on fire. *Everyone's* humping tonight."

"Oh my God, would you—" Jess stopped abruptly, realization falling like an anvil. "Oh *shit*."

"Can you just bang him and then describe—"

"Fizz. Seriously, wait." Jess looked up at her. The effect of River's thoughtfulness this morning had worn off, and the chill of dread washed over her, head to toe. "Today is Monday."

"So?"

"Juno and Pops go to the library on Monday."

"So?"

Jess jabbed her index finger down at her copy of the paper. "Fizzy, there are about seventy copies of this picture in the library! My kid is going to see me on the cover of the *U-T* wrapped like a horny cat in River's coat! Do you know how many questions she has about giraffe vertebrae? Do you know how many she'll have about this?"

Fizzy bolted upright, turning left, turning right, before hastily shoving her laptop into her bag. Jess followed suit, packing up like Twiggs was on fire.

IT WAS NORMALLY a ten-minute walk from Twiggs to the University Heights library. They made it in six.

Fizzy stopped on the sidewalk just outside, hands on her knees. "Holy shit. Why did I pick such a sedentary job? When the zombies come, I am screwed."

Jess leaned against the bus stop and panted, "Same."

"If the point was to get here fast, we could have, I don't know, taken a car?"

Jess straightened, glaring at her. "I panicked, okay? It feels a lot easier when I walk it."

She took a deep breath, marveling over how deeply winded she was. *Add to the to-do list: More cardio.* She checked her watch. "Juno's school got out four minutes ago. They'll be here in about ten. We need to bust ass."

Fizzy brushed the blunt ends of her dark hair behind her shoulder. "What could possibly go wrong?"

They headed up the ramp that led to the main entrance, smiling nonchalantly at an older woman as they passed. *Nothing to see here. Just your average trip to the library to hide every copy of your daily newspaper.* Emily, Juno's favorite librarian, was on the computer at the main desk, and Jess slowed to a stop.

"What are we waiting for?" Fizzy said over Jess's shoulder as she collided with her back.

"Emily is up there," she whispered. Emily was Juno's favorite partly because she was a sweetheart and knew where everything was, and partly because her hair was pink and she rode a sparkly blue Vespa to work every day. "If she sees me come in, she'll want to say hi. Juno will see us, and we're toast."

"A friendly librarian," Fizzy said sarcastically, narrowing her eyes. "The worst kind."

Jess glared at Fizzy over her shoulder. "Hush."

"You hush. I feel like I'm committing a crime even being in here," Fizzy whispered behind her. "I'm late renewing my library card!"

"It's not like an alarm's gonna go off," Jess said. "They don't scan them as you walk through the door." A patron stepped up to the counter, and she watched as Emily listened, smiled, and then nodded, motioning for the person to follow her. Jess reached for Fizzy's hand. "Come on."

They slipped through the door and headed straight for the back near Adult Services, darting behind a bookcase when they saw an older man standing right in front of the giant rack of newspapers. Fizzy looked around nervously.

"Would you stop it?" Jess whisper-hissed. "You wrote an entire romantic suspense series about a female assassin. We're hiding newspapers. Why does this look harder for you than the time you realized halfway through a game of pool that you'd bet a bunch of Hells Angels that we could kick their asses?"

"I'm not good with peer pressure, okay? Usually I'm the one talking you into doing something stupid. This is all backwards."

Jess looked around the corner, groaning when she saw the man still standing there. "I can see six copies of the front page right there. We just need to grab them all."

An older woman walked down the aisle, and they both tried to look casual. Fizzy leaned against the bookcase; Jess picked up an escargot cookbook off the shelf and attempted to appear engrossed. The woman eyed them warily as she passed.

Fizzy took the book from her and shoved it back into place. "Do we really have to do this?" She looked around. "This feels oddly naughty."

Jess honestly never expected Fizzy to have a pearl-clutching side. "Do you remember when you were writing *My Alter Ego* and you asked me to hoist my leg behind my head to"—Jess made air quotes—"'see if a normal person could do it'?"

Fizzy frowned, thinking. "Vaguely."

"I pulled my hamstring and could barely walk for a week. For you and your book. But you still told Daniel I'd pulled a vaginal muscle in a sex accident. You *owe* me."

"I'm going to kill you off in the next Crimson Lace book."

It wasn't the first time she'd threatened it, definitely wouldn't be the last. "Sure."

They both peered around the bookcase again, relieved when they saw that the coast was finally clear. Jess could already see herself seated across from the bad cop down at the police station, given sludgy coffee in a Styrofoam cup and shown surveillance footage of her skulking over to the Adult Media section, unspooling an armful of *Union-Tribunes* from the rack, and jogging away. She made a silent promise to Juno and San Diego County that she would volunteer and read at story time until her kid was eighteen if she could just keep Juno from seeing these papers . . . or her.

They walked through the library as if they had every right to be carrying two armloads of newspapers, and then arranged them carefully behind a long row of Mary Higgins Clark paperbacks.

"Is that all of them?" Fizzy asked, face flushed as she checked over her shoulder.

"Yeah. Let's get out of here."

They walked down the aisle and stopped short just as the entrance came into view. Jess pulled Fizzy back, ducking her head out just long enough to see Juno and Pops walk through the door.

"Oh my God," Fizzy said. "That was close."

"Yeah." Jess looked again, heart racing as she watched them walk straight to the newspapers. "Let's go. She'll leave Pops at the papers and head straight for kids' nonfiction. We have about thirty seconds."

Fizzy nodded, and with Juno's and Pops's backs turned, they ran straight for the doors.

FIZZY STAYED LONG enough to finish a glass of Nana's iced tea and jot down the details of their adventure before heading home to do some social media stuff and get ready for a night out with Rob. Jess had a few texts from River mentioning the possibility of a party, and that Brandon would be emailing them both . . . definitely nothing to warrant the flash of heat that moved up her neck. She was tempted to launch into a brilliant retelling of her and Fizzy's little crime spree but stopped herself for fear of beginning a conversation she didn't really want to have. Jess wasn't upset that River had met Juno, but she wasn't sure she wanted it to happen again, either. Future Jess would definitely have to deal with it, but after the day she'd had, *this* Jess just wanted to have a glass of wine and make spaghetti.

As she straightened the apartment and began dinner, she fell back on a new and still unfamiliar comfort: reminding herself that she didn't have to worry about money, at least for a few months. She'd never had the luxury of a cushion before, and it was almost indulgent to imagine paying a year of insurance premiums in advance or splurging on real Tylenol instead of the generic. Wild times.

Pigeon wound around her feet and Jess was just adding pasta

to the boiling water when the door burst open and Juno rushed inside.

"Mom! *How to Build the World's Best Roller Coaster in Ten Easy Steps!* I got it!" She kicked off her shoes and opened her bag in the middle of the living room, spilling the contents across Jess's freshly vacuumed floor.

Setting the wooden spoon on the trivet, Jess turned away from the stove and leaned against the island. Did she look guilty?

"I was number two on the waitlist, but somebody didn't pick it up, and so when I was there, Emily said I could check it out." Juno slapped the book on the counter and finally came up for air. "I gotta start my project."

"Hello to you, too." Jess stopped the whirling dervish with an arm around her shoulders and reeled her daughter in to press a kiss to the top of her head. "Where's Pops?" She looked out into the courtyard but didn't see him.

Juno disappeared into the living room, returning with a blue folder, at least a dozen pieces of paper trying to escape it. "He's taking Nana for Ethiopian food." She toppled a neat stack of mail as she spread the papers out on the counter in front of her. Jess picked them up again. "The instructions say to use a nine-by-twelve piece of cardboard but I can also use a thirty-six-by-forty-eight." She paused. "Do we have that?"

"You're asking if I have a four-foot piece of cardboard lying around? Sorry. Fresh out." Jess stirred the pasta and turned off the stove. "Baby, let's try and keep it manageable? Where would we even put something that big?"

Juno looked around the apartment and motioned to the dining room table.

"And where would we eat?"

"At Nana and Pops's."

Jess looked at her daughter over her shoulder as she drained the noodles. "What else do you need to start this project?"

"Art tape, the big kind. Lots of it. Did you know that in Philadelphia somebody made a one-hundred-twenty-eight-foot cocoon out of translucent tape? Twenty-one miles of it! You can climb in it and everything."

"Wow." Jess pulled down plates and brought them to the counter.

"I also need glue and regular tape and construction paper to make the people." She pointed to Jess's iPad on the table. "Can I look it up?"

"May I," Jess said reflexively, and dished noodles onto the plate, topping them with sauce.

Juno picked up Pigeon from the chair, lifted the iPad to wake it up.

"How was school today?" Jess asked, turning just as an image loaded on the screen.

A picture of her and River.

The cover of the *Union-Tribune* she'd been looking at this morning. *Fuuuu*—

"Mom!" Juno yelled. "That's you and River Nicolas!"

Was it possible to lose all the blood in one's body without actually bleeding?

"Is he your boyfriend?"

How was Jess supposed to answer that? That she was only pretending with River because they were *paying her*? That they were friends who just happened to be photographed wrapped up in each other's clothes? How was it that she tried so hard to protect Juno, but consistently screwed everything up?

She set down their dinner with shaking hands. "That's . . ." Jess searched for words, panicked, sweating, spiraling. "We were—"

I am not my mom. I am not putting Juno last. I can explain.

Before Jess could speak, though, Juno tilted her head. "You look pretty with your hair like that." And then, just as quickly, her attention was drawn to her plate. "Ooh, spaghetti!" She took a humongous bite, eyes closed as she chewed.

Stunned, Jess could only stare as Juno tilted her glass to her face and set it down, leaving a bright moon of milk over her top lip. She grinned winningly at her mother. "Can I order tape after dinner?"

"Yes, as much tape as you want," Jess said.

"Okay!" Juno swirled more noodles onto her fork. "Can I get different colors? Like blue and orange and green and red?" She took another giant bite, and Jess moved back to the kitchen.

She opened the fridge and pulled out a bottle of wine. "Sure," she told her, and poured herself a drink. *Pink? Purple? Polka dot? Knock yourself out, kid.* Jess had never had the luxury of being frivolous before; it felt strange but also wonderful. She watched Juno finish her dinner and pull out the iPad again, humming as she added art supplies to her cart.

Whoever said money couldn't buy happiness had never seen this.

FOURTEEN

B Y BRANDON'S RAVING account, Trevor and Caroline Gruber were completely lovely people. Yes, they were GeneticAlly investors, and yes, after that *Union-Tribune* profile they wanted to host a cocktail hour to meet Jess along with some of the other major donors, but *They're unpretentious, Jess*, Brandon had insisted. *You'll love them.*

Trevor was some sort of tech genius from Detroit, and Caroline was a pediatric orthopedist from Rhode Island. Worlds colliding, true love, all of that.

That they'd chosen to give a cool few million to a company whose goal was to match people up with their soulmates gave Jess hope they and their guests wouldn't all look like the Monopoly man. There were a thousand good investments in this booming biotech area, but as someone who manipulated data and helped companies evaluate risk, even Jess couldn't say for sure that, under different circumstances, she'd choose to give money to GeneticAlly.

That said, one look at River when he picked her up out in front of her building, and she would happily throw her wallet and banking passwords at whoever was asking. He was in a tailored navy suit. Polished shoes. Perfect almost-too-long hair, bright eyes. The Adam's apple she'd thought of licking more than once since the Shelter Island interview a week ago. Brandon had talked her off a ledge earlier, insisting GeneticAlly would spring for her dress and send someone to do her hair and makeup. A thoughtful and generous gesture, it had mainly served to highlight that the event was Very Fucking Important, which sent Jess deep-breathing into a paper bag.

And just when she'd convinced herself she was both socially adept and attractive enough to handle being on Dr. River Peña's arm all night, he stepped out of his car looking like solid muscle and sexual energy poured by a fancy German-engineered machine into that suit.

Jess took a flying leap off a mental bridge. She was so completely screwed. She'd lowered the drawbridge to sex thoughts and now they were stampeding across. Frankly, if she and River ever managed to get it on, he was going to have a lot to live up to. Fictional River was a wonder in bed.

He bent and kissed her cheek again—this time she was at least prepared for it, but she was not prepared for the assault of sensation. He smelled . . . different.

He did a similar deep inhale near her ear.

They spoke in unison:

"Are you wearing perfume?" "Are you wearing cologne?"

Her question echoed last, and louder. *Is he blushing?*

"A little. My sisters—" He cleared his throat. "They told me to go to Neiman Marcus, get some recommendations."

Jess pulled out a mental bag of arrows and took aim at the imagined saleswoman who'd dabbed his skin with various colognes and gotten close enough to smell him. "Your sisters told you to get . . . cologne?"

"They're invested. In this." He sighed, but she knew he was only pretending to be exasperated.

His sisters were invested in them? Was that adorable or terrifying? "That's very sweet," Jess managed.

River laughed dryly. "That's one word for it."

"Well, the cologne is nice." Understatement of the ages. Jess wanted to eat him up and wash him down with the rest of the bottle.

He leaned in again. "What is it I'm smelling?"

Jess was thrown for a moment when she registered that they were *smelling* each other. And recognizing a difference. Was this normal? Was this weird? She decided to roll with it.

"It's—okay, it sounds weird, but it's grapefruit. It's a grapefruit roll thing—" She didn't know how to say it. "It's not perfume, exactly. Like an oil? It's a little roller—" Jess shut up and just mimed rolling something on her wrist. "Perfume gives me a headache, but this"—she felt the tops of her cheeks flame—"this I can do."

"I like it." He seemed to struggle for words. "A lot."

What was she hearing in his voice? Weird tight restraint. It sounded like he was telling a platter of buttery beef Wellington, *I could stand to take a bite*, when really he meant, *Get in my face*.

Did River Peña . . . want *her* in his face?

Jess had to take it down a notch. She might have been consistently obsessing since their Shelter Island snuggle, but she could make no assumptions about where he was with all of this.

Also, as they climbed into his car, Jess reminded herself that they would soon be standing inside an investor's penthouse for a cocktail party. That is, River—and everyone there tonight—had a financial interest in her looking at him with horny eyes. Jess knew already that River chose his words carefully; for all she knew, his sisters might be *actually* invested, not just sentimental and meddling. Her obvious attraction to him helped boost confidence in his company, which helped his pocketbook, and also helped confirm everything he'd been saying from a scientific standpoint all this time. Jess knew how important it was to River that the world saw the impact of his data.

And frankly, look what Jess was willing to do for thirty thousand dollars. No, it wasn't a hardship to buy dresses with GeneticAlly expense accounts and walk hand in hand with dressed-up science-brained sex on legs into a fancy party, but her thirty thousand was a drop in the bucket compared to what River stood to make. Millions.

"What are you thinking about over there?" he asked, cutting into her pondering silence.

It couldn't hurt to be honest. "Oh, just questioning every choice I've made."

This made him laugh. "Same."

Doubtful. "Give me one example."

He glanced at her and then back to the road as they took the 163 on-ramp. "Really?"

"Really."

After a long pause, during which Jess assumed he'd decided to ignore her request, River finally spoke. "Okay: Did you think of me when you put on that dress?"

From chest to forehead, her skin flushed hot. Jess looked down at her gown. It was deep blue, with black spaghetti straps. Delicate metallic stardust embroidery was scattered in small, artful clusters across the entire gown, giving it the feel of a gently starred sky. The subtle black lace trim crisscrossed above and beneath her breasts and purred *evening wear meets* evening *wear*, but Juno and Fizzy— her two jabbermouths—had literally gone speechless when she came out of the dressing room wearing it, so Jess trusted their reactions over her hesitation that she might be showing way too much skin.

"I know you're getting paid to be here," he added quietly. "So, there's my question. Did you?"

"Same question, but with the cologne," Jess said through a cork of emotion in her throat. "And you're getting paid a lot more."

"Potentially." He laughed.

"But that's exactly it. If we do a good job tonight, you stand to make a lot more than thirty thousand. Your sisters told you to get some cologne—that would be smart seduction advice, especially if they're shareholders."

"They are," he acknowledged.

They fell back into a thick silence; Jess was unwilling to answer until he did. She bet her entire thirty thousand that he felt the same.

"So, smart seduction advice, then?" he pressed, grinning slyly at her before turning back to the road.

"It smells really good on you," she admitted quietly, and was instantly mortified about the growling bass in her voice. She cleared her throat.

Jessica Davis, get your shit together.

Beside her, River shifted in the driver's seat. "Well, for what it's worth, that dress is . . ." His voice also came out hoarse, and he coughed into his fist. "It is also really good on you."

TWO GOOD-LOOKING GUYS in their early twenties jogged over as River pulled the car up to the curb.

"Every bit of fanciness just makes me more nervous," Jess admitted quietly after River tipped the valets—nephews of the hosts, they'd learned—and met her on the sidewalk.

He stepped closer, looking down at her with concern. "Everyone who'll be here is incredibly nice."

"I'm sure," Jess said. "It's just that as of yesterday, my fanciest outfit was the only other dress you've seen me wear. This dress cost more than two months of Juno's ballet lessons."

"It's worth every cent, if that makes you feel better."

"It does," she said, smoothing her hands over the front of the dress. "Just keep telling me I'm pretty and it'll be fine. Oh, and wine. Wine will help."

Laughing quietly, he let her lead them inside the building. The marble-floored lobby was empty except for a security desk, a beautiful leather settee, and two elevators at the end.

The security guard looked up as they approached. "Here for the Gruber event?"

River's warm palm came over the small of her back, and every thought in her brain was incinerated. "River Peña and Jessica Davis," River confirmed, and the man checked their names on a list before programming the elevator from where he sat.

"Head on over to the car on the right," he said. "It'll take you straight up."

As the doors closed, Jess was reminded of the other times she'd been in an elevator with River—the strained silence, the unspoken disdain between them. Going back to that felt like it'd be simpler than this unmeasurable, unmanageable attraction.

River cut into the quiet. "I think I need to clear something up." Jess looked up at him in question, his eyes fixed on the wall ahead. "About my sisters."

"Oh?" She had no idea where this was headed, but the pace of the world's second-slowest elevator suggested there'd be plenty of time to find out.

"They *are* investors," he said. "They both put in money at the very beginning of the project. But that isn't what I meant by 'invested.'" Finally, he looked down at her. "About the cologne."

Jess bit back a laugh. He was so serious. "Okay."

"They think this"—he gestured between them—"is very . . ." He paused, and then gave her a sardonic smile. "*Very* exciting. But," he quickly added, "please don't feel pressured by their enthusiasm."

Nodding, Jess gave him another quiet "Okay."

"And I'm telling you this now because up there is waiting a roomful of people who, you already know, are deeply financially invested in how you and I interact, and I don't want you to go in there thinking that everything is for show." River reached into the inside pocket of his suit and pulled out his phone. He swiped it awake, opened it to his photos, and began scrolling. Finally, he found what he was looking for and turned the screen to face her.

For a second, Jess had no idea what she was seeing. River's doofus doppelgänger was her best guess. He was in his early twenties, but his posture read even younger, way less confident.

"Do you recognize him?" he asked.

She was afraid to guess. This scrawny, hunched, mismatched child could not be—

"It's me." He swiped through a few more, showing her several photos of the same dorky alternate-reality version of himself.

"Plaid shorts and striped shirt was a real style choice," Jess said, laughing.

"I moved away from home when I was sixteen," he said, and the elevator doors opened.

Her stomach vaulted into her throat because for the past ten seconds, she'd forgotten where they were. They stepped out, but River paused in the marble foyer leading to a single front door.

"I graduated high school early and started at Stanford when I was about four months shy of turning seventeen."

"Holy shit."

"I was probably twenty in this picture—although you'd never guess it—and you can see that once my sisters could no longer exert daily influence, I had no idea how to dress myself."

Jess burst out laughing, sparking a return smile.

"If it weren't for them, I'd probably still be wearing those plaid shorts."

"Please, no. Your sisters are doing a much better job."

He laughed now. "It's just how they are. They left for school on the East Coast when I was in high school and . . . it wasn't always . . . They feel responsible for me." River licked his lips and glanced up at the door before back to her. "All of this is to say: I wasn't thinking of this roomful of people when I put the cologne on earlier. I was thinking of you."

She didn't know what else to say besides "Thank you for telling me."

Jess was split in half—turned on by his confession and terrified by it.

Luckily, he didn't seem to need a bigger response. Straightening, River turned to face the Grubers' double front door and took a deep breath. She expected him to ring the bell, but he didn't.

After a few long, increasingly awkward moments of silence, Jess asked, "You okay?"

"I hate these things," he admitted.

It was a little like being hit in the face with the obvious stick.

Of course: River wasn't a callous, gruff asshole. He was *shy.* Having to do this part of the job was probably miserable for him. Jess felt this as clearly as if she'd just read it on a pamphlet entitled *Instructions to Your Soulmate*. Framing every one of their past interactions through this lens only solidified for her that River was nothing like Brandon—all smiles and easy charm. He was most comfortable when facing the fume hood with his back to the room, just him and some tubes and billions and billions of paired-up nucleotides.

She was going to have to be the brave one here. Reaching

down, Jess laced her fingers with his. Warmth spiraled up from her fingertips, crackling along every inch to her shoulder and across her chest.

"We've got this," she said.

He squeezed her hand. "We don't have much choice."

"Let's just stay together, okay?"

"Yes," he whispered. "Good plan."

In unison, they took a deep, bracing breath. Reaching forward, River pressed the doorbell.

FIFTEEN

T HE MOMENT THE door swung open, they could hear the commotion inside come to a brief halt before it broke out into glass-clinking, jewelry-rustling, jacket-straightening mayhem. A chorus of voices whispered their names and *They're here!*, followed by a smattering of applause.

A valet stepped unobtrusively to the side as a tall, angular Black man approached, casually gorgeous in a stylish suit, and gave Jess a smile that somehow communicated a warm *You can trust me* vibe. His hand was outstretched, and only a few paces behind him was a woman, playfully shuffle-jogging in sky-high heels to catch up.

"Trevor Gruber," he said to Jess, shaking her hand.

"Jess Davis."

"Great to meet you, Jess." He pulled River in for a hug. "Good to see you, man. And this," he said to Jess as the petite Asian woman arrived at his side, "is my wife, Caroline. Thank you so much for coming tonight."

"Hi, you two!" Caroline embraced Jess first, and then stepped forward to hug River. Her dress clung to and flowed over her body in such a graceful balance that Jess wanted to high-five her. When Caroline moved back, Jess noticed a caterer practically materialize out of thin air.

Caroline offered River a mischievous little smile and reached back to grab a highball glass from the tray held aloft by the waiter. She pressed the drink into River's hand. "See? One step in the door, just like I promised." He laughed, and she stretched, kissing his cheek, stage-whispering, "I told you it wouldn't be so bad."

Jess immediately loved her.

River looked over their shoulders, deeper into the room. "*This isn't bad?*"

Jess followed his gaze and did a quick estimation that there were upward of fifty people in the expansive living room with floor-to-ceiling windows overlooking San Diego Bay and the Coronado Bridge. Every one of them in formal attire, every one of them staring at the Diamond couple.

Turning to their hosts to compliment the view, Jess stopped at the sight of River's expression, swallowing her words. He'd gone vaguely pale and clammy. He lifted the drink to his lips, and then hummed appreciatively, murmuring with recognition some obscure alcohol name Jess didn't catch, and thanking Caroline under his breath.

With a smile aimed at Jess, Caroline turned and grabbed the other item off the caterer's tray—a glass of white wine. "River said you like semidry whites." She glanced sweetly at him for confirmation. "This is a viognier-marsanne."

"Gesundheit," Jess joked dorkily, and to her relief, Caroline laughed. River had paid attention to what she'd ordered at dinner with David and Brandon and remembered all this time?

He wore cologne for her.

He wanted to eat her like beef Wellington in this dress.

Caroline turned to face the party. "Everyone is dying to meet you, Jess." She angled back to them. "But let's let them sweat it out for a few. It's my party." Threading her arm through Trevor's, she leaned in conspiratorially. "We loved the profile in the *Trib*—River is my favorite guy ever, other than the one I married, and those pictures? Oh my God. The one of you in his coat?" She lightly smacked Jess's arm. "Forget it. I dropped dead on the spot. But I'm afraid this party got away from me as soon as I mentioned the idea to my friend Tilly." She pointed vaguely across the room to where this Tilly must have been. "I said, 'Wouldn't it be so fun to have Jess and River over?' She talked to Brandon and it turned into a whole *thing*." Caroline rolled her eyes in apology. "I meant like *dinner*. Of course, the two of them had the entire GeneticAlly board and all the investors invited before I'd even told Trevor."

Trevor laughed, nodding. "So, see? You aren't the only one who was dreading it."

"I wasn't dreading it!" Jess insisted, smiling her best liar smile.

"I meant River," Trevor joked.

"Come on," Caroline said, and took Jess's arm. Jess grabbed blindly for River's free hand before they could be separated, feeling oddly panicked. "Let me introduce you to some people."

Of course, River already knew everyone here; she was the novelty.

First up were the Watson-Duggars, a fiftysomething couple

who, within thirty seconds, suggested—without subtlety—that it would be great if Jess and River could get married before the IPO. And then there were the Lius, who owned the building they were standing in. Mrs. Liu admitted to Jess in a breathless whisper that they'd been married for twenty-seven years but she hadn't been at all surprised to find out they were a Base Match. Awkward!

The Romas seemed to want to punch holes in Jess and River's possible connection, and Jess reminded herself—as they quizzed her about River's history, most of which she got wrong—that they were just trying to protect their investment, not attack her.

Albert Mendoza couldn't stop staring at Jess's chest. Worse, she was worried his wife might actually reach forward and stroke River's biceps, the way she kept eyeing him with such blatant sex eyes. Dr. Farley McIntosh and his husband were prominent San Diego architects and mostly wanted to know whether Jess had heard of any of their buildings.

Through all of it, River's hand grew sweatier and sweatier in her grip.

They moved from group to group, like a bride and groom at their reception. They were specimens to be poked at, prodded, questioned, and quizzed.

Is it a connection you can just feel *when you look at him?*

Is the sex, you know . . . unreal?

How long before wedding bells?

Have you met River's sisters yet?

Your children are going to be stunning!

What happens if you match like this with someone else?

Jess and River had stumbled through their answers together,

hands clasped desperately, tight smiles in place, but that last question pulled Jess up short, and she made an excuse about needing the restroom, following River's directions down the hall to the second door on the left. The condo was enormous, and Jess itched to escape, to explore, to see how many rooms were actually furnished.

But it was enough just to step out of the melee and into a quiet space for a few minutes. Her heart was on a rampage, tearing everything up in her chest. If she hadn't been wearing such artfully applied makeup, Jess would've splashed water on her face, but as it was, she just leaned forward, taking a few deep breaths. Every time she thought she had a handle on what all of this meant, another question came at her around the corner, like a curveball. First, she hadn't believed the result, and then she hadn't needed to because— money. And then she'd suspected the DNADuo score might be true, but it didn't matter because she wasn't looking for love, dammit. And now, being by River's side all night and feeling like they were in this as a team from the very first step made the charade feel so real. When someone had asked about another soulmate out there somewhere, she'd wanted to vomit.

Too much, too fast.

Jess washed her hands, reapplied her lipstick, and gave herself a hard but encouraging stare in the mirror. This party had to have cost thousands of dollars. She was wearing a dress someone else had paid for. Who was she pretending to be? *Just get through it and get home.*

But when she stepped out into the hall, River was there waiting, one ankle crossed over the other, leaning casually against the opposite wall. His posture was so unconsciously confident, so sensual that Jess felt her legs clench together hard in response.

He straightened. "You okay?"

"Yeah, just—" She pointed over her shoulder. "Needed a second."

A relieved smile played at his lips. "I did, too."

She blew out a slow breath. "This isn't my world at all." The effect of his proximity simmered just beneath her skin and she felt the words slip out: "I hope I'm not messing it up for you."

A flash of emotion moved over his face, and he burst forward a step. "You're— No. You're amazing." He looked back down the hall. "And I'm sorry Brandon isn't here. This is his scene. Not mine."

"I get it," Jess said quietly. "They want to see their investment in action."

She could immediately tell he didn't love this phrasing . . . but also couldn't disagree.

"It must be especially surreal to you," she said, "to already know these people and have them see you tonight not as the lead scientist, but as one of the big findings."

"Yeah. Maybe three people in that room knew anything about my personal life. Now all these strangers feel comfortable making comments about our sex life and asking me when I'm going to propose."

Jess barked out a nervous laugh. "Right."

"It occurred to me," he began, and then turned his face up to the ceiling. "When Esther Lin asked us about, you know, matching with someone else . . ."

Jess waited for him to finish, her heart beating like a racer's at the starting line.

"Were you married to Juno's dad?" he finally asked.

She exhaled. "No." There was a long pause where it felt like he wanted more, but they were standing in a hallway at a party, and she just honestly didn't know how much more there was to say about her and Alec. In hindsight, their footing had never been solid. The pregnancy hadn't ended things; it had just sped the demise along. "He's not in the picture," she finished, eventually. "He never really has been. We broke up before Juno was born."

She could see his curiosity visibly sated. They turned and started walking leisurely back down the hall toward the party.

"You mentioned you've always lived near your grandparents. Did your parents pass, or—?"

"My mom struggled with addiction—still does—and relinquished custody of me when I was six. I never knew my father."

"Oh." He stopped walking and turned to her, eyes wide. "Wow."

The pain in his expression seemed genuine. Jess nodded slowly, unsure where to look. "Yeah."

"I'm sorry, Jess."

"No, really, Nana Jo and Pops are the best people I've ever known. I knew from a really young age that I was better off."

"They sound amazing."

She suddenly felt naked. Here she was, her ex-boyfriend didn't even want to raise a kid with her, mother chose drugs over her, raised by grandparents and still living with them. River had two sisters who adored him so much they helped him figure out how to dress to reach his full hotness potential.

"What is that expression?" he asked, leaning in. "What did I say?"

Jess was made uneasy by how quickly he read her. A panic she didn't completely understand rose in her throat, making her want to look for an exit. This party was the kind of thing that happened to the heroine of the story, not the best friend. What was she doing here?

Humor, as usual, was her best defense. "Just imagining how from your perspective your Diamond Match has a truckload of baggage."

He didn't laugh. "Don't we all?"

Her smile faded. "Do we?"

"We do. But come on. I know you well enough to know that you're not carrying baggage." He was holding her gaze, and she felt physically unable to look away. "You've chosen your circumstances, Jess. I like that about you. You take what you want and leave the rest behind. You decide."

He was right. She felt herself stand up straighter, lean toward him.

"There you are!" a voice called out. "River, come on down here, and bring that young lady of yours."

Still holding her eyes, he fought a smile. "Is this young lady of mine ready for some more mingling?"

Jess laughed. "I've sufficiently recharged my battery, yes."

Taking her hand, he led her back down the hall to the party, toward the tiny old man who'd called out his name. He had to be in his eighties, wearing wire-rimmed glasses and a well-worn black suit. Beside him was a woman with a thick braid of white hair around the crown of her head and makeup-free crepe-lined features. She was wearing a simple black dress with a lace collar and pearls. Somehow she was even smaller than her husband.

"How'd they convince you to come out?" River asked, grinning.

"Caroline leaned on Dorothy," the man said in a thick German accent.

"And by 'leaned on,'" Dorothy chimed in, "he means that Caroline promised me I'd get to see you."

River bent to kiss her powder-soft cheek. "Johan, Dotty, this is my Jessica."

My Jessica.

Her heart fell in a swoon, from her chest to her feet.

"Jess, Johan and Dotty Fuchs."

She didn't even have time to recover; both tiny octogenarians were coming toward her, each wanting an embrace.

She bent, hugging them in turn. "Hi. Nice to meet you, Mr. and Mrs. Fuchs."

"Jess," River said quietly, reverently, "Johan and Dotty were our very first Diamond Match. Their granddaughter brought them to us back in 2014, and she was right: they came through with a score of ninety-three. Our first score in the nineties."

Dotty nodded, squeezing Johan's arm. "We've been married since 1958. Sixty-three years."

Jess wasn't an emotional person by nature; she adored her daughter and grandparents to the stars and back, but she wasn't one to cry at commercials and was the only person in her life who could listen to Adele's "Someone Like You" without weeping. But the moment caught her like a hook, and she felt a swell of emotion rise, salty, in her throat.

Through this deep, sweeping emotional moment—as she struggled to balance reverence and enthusiasm—Jess noticed Johan's outfit. He was wearing a blazer and dress pants, but beneath the coat was a T-shirt, not a dress shirt. On it was a benzene ring with iron atoms replacing the carbon, and beneath it the words FERROUS WHEEL.

"I realize this is a fancy affair, but I wore it for River," Johan said, noticing her amusement. "He loves terrible science puns."

"Does he?" Jess asked, looking at the man in question.

Mr. Fuchs cleared his throat, raising a finger. "What did Gregor Mendel say when he discovered genetics?" He waited a beat and then sang, "Whoopea!"

It was corny, but his delivery was fantastic. Besides, he might have been the smallest, sweetest old man Jess had ever seen. She would laugh at any joke he told for the rest of time.

"Very clever," River agreed, eyes twinkling. "What is the fastest way to determine the sex of a chromosome?" he asked. "Pull down its genes."

Everyone groaned.

"Potassium and oxygen went on a date," Johan said, grinning as their game started rolling. "It went OK."

Dotty groaned just as Jess said, "Okay, that one is cute."

"I wish I was adenine," River said, and winked down at her. "Then I could get paired up with U."

Everyone *Awww*-ed audibly, and then three pairs of eyes turned to Jess with anticipation. After a beat, it sank in: she was up to bat. "Um," she said, digging around the dusty reaches of her brain for a science joke. "Okay, anyone know any good jokes about sodium?" She scanned their faces, grinning. "Or Na?"

Mr. and Mrs. Fuchs looked at each other. "I don't think I do," Dotty said, frowning. "Do you know any, darling?"

"No, it's—" Jess stammered.

"I don't," Johan said. "Well, let's see now. That is a rather specific request. Sodium. Sodium jokes . . ."

"No," she said, "the joke is—" She gave up as they continued to confer, mumbling to each other.

"Sorry, dear," Dotty said. "No sodium jokes, but I am so delighted to meet you." She smiled up at River. "It's good to see you, darling. You take care of her, okay?"

"I will." He bent, kissing her cheek again. Jess and River watched them walk off together, holding hands.

Silence settled over the two of them, and Jess laughed out a quiet "Wow."

"Only the best jokes require explanation immediately afterward," he said, eyes dancing at her.

"They do call me the Party Cooler."

"Do they?" he asked.

"If they don't, they should." She grinned up at him. "They were freaking adorable."

"Aren't they? They are the nicest people, too."

"Lucky for them they were already married when they found out they were a Diamond Match."

He nodded, eyes softening. "Takes some pressure off, I'd imagine."

Jess would look away, but she couldn't. Her feelings weren't growing in a measured, linear way. In the past hour they'd expanded exponentially, like a wave inside her. It was the way she imagined a tsunami might approach San Diego: calm ocean surface until a wall was suddenly crashing over the shore. She stared at him, and all she could think about was how much she wanted him to touch her.

A clinking rose in the room; it was quiet and unobtrusive at first but built into a clattering of silver on crystal all around them. Jess looked around, confused. Awareness sank in, but River was still wearing an expression of frank confusion.

"Oh shit," she whispered.

"What?" he asked frantically as everyone began to chant, "*Kiss, kiss, kiss.*"

River's eyes widened, and Jess witnessed the moment comprehension landed. "Oh, God."

"It's okay." She put a warm smile on her face and turned to face him. They had an audience. River was shy and Jess was deeply private, and this was a nightmare! But no big deal! Soulmates! As presented to this room full of investors, Jess and River kissed, like, *all the time*.

He mirrored her grin, but Jess hoped hers was way more convincing. "We should have anticipated this," he gritted out.

"Well, we didn't," she whispered, running a coy hand down his chest. The feeling was a bit like being submerged in warm champagne. "We don't have to if you don't want."

"No, we can," he said immediately, leaning in and toying intimately with a strand of her hair. "I mean, unless you don't want to?"

His breath smelled like mint and whiskey. Frankly, Jess wanted to.

River looked at her in question as the clattering intensified. But then his eyes flickered away nervously.

"Hey. It's just me."

His brow relaxed, and he nodded, breath trembling. "Okay."

River's eyes dipped to her mouth.

Are we doing this?

He stepped to her—

I guess we're doing this.

—bending, sliding one hand up her neck to cup her jaw and leaving a trail of carbonated heat on her skin. He leaned in—she stopped breathing—and his mouth came over hers.

Together, they exhaled in relief, and everything fell away: sound, light, other people. She felt the sag in him, too, the confirmation that they were right to think it would feel this good. One short kiss, and then a longer one, just his mouth covering hers and then coming back to taste again. Just to see.

A valiant collection of neurons in her brain screamed a reminder that fifty pairs of eyes were on them right that second, but even that awareness didn't keep her from reaching for the lapels of his coat, pulling him flush up against her.

Jess swallowed a moan when his other arm came around her waist, his fingers spreading wide below her ribs. It felt so good it sent a fevered ache straight from her mouth to her navel, corkscrewing through her. River veered slightly away, and Jess expected the kiss to close off, it probably *should*, but she realized he was only shifting his footing, coming at her from a new angle, sending his fingers into her hair.

She let out the smallest sound, a helpless moan she thought

only he could hear, but it seemed to shove him into awareness, and he pulled away, remaining only an inch or two from her face.

Breathless, they stared at each other with wild, shocked eyes. It was probably only a few seconds, but the kiss shifted the trajectory of them, immediately. She wanted more, and she could see in his eyes that he did, too. Jess didn't question for a single second that the physical attraction was mutual.

She startled as the entire room broke into sound and commotion. She looked away for a beat, and then back to River. His attention, it seemed, had remained entirely fixed on her mouth.

"I think we just made your company a lot of money," she mumbled, grinning as she carefully pressed her fingertips to her tingling lips.

He didn't crack a smile. Jess wasn't sure he'd even heard her.

"I'd suspect most people comment on your eyes," he said quietly, running a fingertip across her collarbone. "That startling, bright blue."

Surely he could feel her heart scaling her windpipe. He didn't seem to remember there was anyone else in the room.

"But I prefer your mouth."

"You do?" Jess managed.

"I do," he said, and bent, kissing her forehead. "You don't give those smiles away for free."

SIXTEEN

———————⟋———————

THANKS TO A friend of a friend of a friend, Jess met with a potential new client on Tuesday. She didn't really have room in
her schedule for anyone new—*who knew fake dating would be such
a time suck?*—but the gravy train would be over when GeneticAlly
went public in May, and Jess didn't intend to be caught with her
proverbial pants down when it happened.

Kenneth Marshall ran a small engineering firm in Wyoming and
was in town to see clients of his own. They agreed to meet for
lunch at his hotel, which had the added bonus of overlooking the
convention center and the San Diego Bay. Unfortunately, it also
had views of Shelter Island and the Grubers' high-rise condo, which
meant that it took monumental effort for Jess to focus on the conversation about probability study and regression analysis and *not*
the searing kiss from the cocktail party.

How did someone learn to kiss like that? Did River take a class?
Watch YouTube videos, like when Jess learned how to fix the toilet
fill valve? She'd lain in bed last night thinking about his mouth and

the urging press of his fingers to her jaw, about the sobering reality that Jess had had actual sex that left her less satisfied than River's kiss.

Sex with River might actually end her.

She was all too happy when the meeting with Kenneth wrapped up, and even happier when he offered a deposit to hold his place on her schedule until late spring. But instead of immediately heading toward the valet, she walked out to the back patio of the hotel to take in the view. Seagulls soared overhead and waves gently rocked the boats docked at the marina. Snapping a photo, she sent a quick text to Fizzy, who was in LA meeting with her agent.

Jess had lived in California her entire life but rarely made it to the ocean. It seemed like too much preparation—the sand, the crowds, finding parking—but once she was there, she'd invariably wonder why she didn't do it more often.

Kind of like sex.

Jess thought of the kiss again, the way River had angled his head to capture her mouth more deeply, how he'd held his breath, then let out a shaking exhale when they pulled apart. She wondered whether it would have been hard to stop if they'd been alone. She wondered whether he fucked like he kissed.

Her phone rang in her hand, startling her. She expected to see Fizzy's face filling the screen, but instead there were three words: SCRIPPS MERCY HOSPITAL.

"Hello?" Jess said in a rush, eyes raking over the horizon as her heart began to thump *Juno, Juno, Juno* against her breastbone.

"May I speak to Jessica Davis?" a woman asked. In the background, Jess heard voices, an elevator ding, phones ringing, and the distant murmur of an intercom.

"This is Jessica." Her pulse pounded her daughter's name.

"This is Scripps Mercy Hospital. We have a Joanne Davis here. Your grandfather, Ronald, is asking for you. Please come as soon as possible."

JESS DIDN'T REMEMBER the wait at the valet or the drive to the hospital, the walk from the parking lot or talking to anyone at the front desk, but she would never forget the sight of Nana in the hospital bed. Jess stood rooted in the doorway, motionless as machines hummed and beeped around Nana, and Pops hovered at his wife's side, holding her hand. Both of Nana's legs were immobilized and strapped to a splint. There was an IV in her left arm. The smell of antiseptic burned Jess's nose. A nurse scooted past her into the hallway, and she managed to step into the room.

"Nana?"

Pops turned to face her; every ounce of Nana's pain was mirrored in his expression. He opened his mouth, but nothing came out.

"I'm here," Jess said, crossing the room to wrap an arm around him. "What happened?"

"She fell."

"I'm fine," Nana said through a shaky breath. "Just lost my footing."

Pops squeezed her hand, eyes trained on her face. Jess's grandfather had always been the strongest, steadiest person she knew. But right now, he looked like a slight wind might knock him down.

"They think it's a fractured femur," he said, "but we're waiting for the doctor. We were bowling at that new place in Kearny Mesa and she slipped." He put a hand over his mouth. "They took the X-rays twenty minutes ago, but nobody will goddamn tell me—"

Nana winced and, if possible, Pops's face went even paler.

"Okay, okay," Jess said, guiding him away from the bed and to a chair. "Let's have you sit down, and I'll see what's happening. Have they given her anything for pain?"

His fingers trembled as he pushed them through his thin, fluffy hair. "I think in the IV."

"I'll be right back," Jess said, and leaned in so Nana could see her. "Nana Jo, I'll be right back."

Jess stopped the first nurse she saw in the hallway. "Excuse me, I was just in room 213. Can you tell me what's happening with Joanne Davis?"

"You're family?"

"I'm her granddaughter, yes."

"We've given her some pain meds and are expecting her X-ray results any second." The nurse pointed to a woman in blue scrubs striding down the hall toward them. "Dr. Reynolds is coming. She'll talk you through it."

Dr. Reynolds returned with Jess to the room, where Pops had moved his chair over to the bed and resumed holding Nana's hand. Sweat beaded her brow, and it was clear that she was in pain but working valiantly to hide it.

Dr. Reynolds greeted Nana and Pops, and a new nurse took Nana's vitals. Clipping the X-ray film to a lighted board, the physician explained that Nana had a subtrochanteric fracture, between the two bony protrusions of the femur.

"We'll have to operate," she explained. "We'll put in a rod that goes down here." Dr. Reynolds drew along the image with her fingertip. "And a screw that goes up into your hip. Yours won't be that long because your fracture is pretty high. It'll probably go to about here." She traced a finger over the X-ray where the metal rod would end. "And then you'll have another rod that will go up through the fracture into your hip. This is stronger than your actual bone, so you'll be able to walk and get up and move around pretty quickly. But no more bowling for at least eight weeks."

"How long will she be here?" Pops asked.

"Let's say five days if everything goes as planned and you're able to work on mobility quickly. Possibly sooner." Dr. Reynolds shrugged. "Or longer if there are complications or we have other concerns."

Jess's stomach dropped. She imagined Pops sleeping in the stiff hospital chair every night until Nana was discharged and knew he would be miserable. But she tried to imagine him at home while Nana was *here*, and that seemed even less likely. If he and Jess could take turns being with Nana, she might be able to convince him to eat, to rest, to take care of himself. Jess glanced at her watch, mentally rearranging deadlines and schedules and pickups.

Panic bubbled up: Juno was out of school in less than an hour.

The doctor left, and Nana's eyes were heavy from sedation.

"Pops," Jess whispered. "I need to make some calls, okay? I'll be right back."

He nodded, numb, and she excused herself to the hall. Her

safety net had a hole in it: Fizzy was in LA. Nana and Pops were obviously indisposed. She scrolled through her contacts, feeling very, very alone. Pausing on her mom's name, Jess sifted through every possible outcome. Jamie would be on time, but smoking. She'd be late, and Juno would be alone and worried. Jamie would be on time, not smoking, but would fill Juno's head with weird criticisms and jabs. She'd be on time, not smoking, wouldn't fill Juno's head with garbage, but would find the open bottle of wine in Jess's fridge and figure *why not.*

Jess didn't like any of the options. She dropped heavily into a chair.

Her phone rang in her hand, and she looked down to see River's name.

Jess didn't even think; she picked up after one ring, her voice breaking on his name. "River?"

"Hey. I . . ." A pause. "Is everything okay?"

She swiped at her eyes, chin trembling. "No."

His tone went soft with concern. "What's happening?"

"I'm at the hospital." Her words came out strangled.

It sounded like he'd just stood up. "Oh, no."

"Nana broke her hip, and I need someone to get Juno from school." Jess swiped at her eyes again. "I know this wasn't part of the bargain, but Fizzy is gone and my mom—"

"No, hey. Of course I'll get her. Will they let me pick her up?"

"I can call and . . ." Tears spilled over, and Jess bent, pressing her face into her hand. "Oh my God, I had a call at four. And tomorrow—"

"Let's make a list," he cut in gently. *Yes, a plan.* Order. Her brain held on to the lifeline. "First things first: Call the school. I'll text you a photo of my license with all my information so you can just read it off to them, okay?"

Call the school, let them know. "Okay."

"Does she have anything after school on Tuesdays?"

Jess felt clearer, but slow. She imagined the calendar in the kitchen, the tiny little boxes with Juno's hearts and bubbly handwriting. "She has ballet, but she can skip it. Can you bring her here? We're at Scripps."

"Jess, I can take her to ballet."

Jess immediately shook her head; she'd already crossed too many boundaries. "No, it's okay, I—"

"I promise, it's not a problem, and I'm sure having her at the hospital won't be easier on you."

She went silent, unable to disagree.

"I've attended plenty of ballet recitals. Remember the meddling sisters?" he said. "I know what a plié is and everything."

Letting out a soft sound, not a laugh, not a sob, Jess was too drained to argue. "They've never been apart," she said. She needed someone else to know how much her grandparents loved each other. "Fifty-six years. I don't know what Pops would do if something happened to her."

"It's going to be okay," River said soothingly. Jess nodded. She needed to believe it, too.

SHE CALLED THE school and made arrangements for River to pick up Juno. He texted as soon as he had her, sending a photo of the two of them making silly faces, and then another of Juno safely buckled into the back seat of his shiny black Audi. Frankly, Juno looked *delighted* to be there. Jess could only imagine the harassment she would get to buy a new car, "like River Nicolas's."

Nana was wheeled into surgery a couple of hours later, and a nurse handed Pops a small pager that looked like the kind restaurants used.

"That'll vibrate when we have news," the nurse told them. "Bring it up to the desk and we'll update you. If it doesn't go off, there's nothing new to tell you."

Pops alternated between holding Jess's hand in the waiting room and taking long walks around the building. His eyes were red-rimmed when he returned, his body heavy as he sank into the chair facing hers.

"Anything?" he asked.

"Not yet." Jess leaned forward, taking his hands and pulling them into her lap. "Do you remember that time Nana bought us all gardening gloves and didn't realize the 'floral print' was actually marijuana?"

"The way she kept insisting it was a Japanese maple." His shoulders shook with quiet laughter. "And Junebug still pointing out 'Nana's favorite plant' whenever she sees one on a T-shirt or a sign."

The sound of familiar laughter carried down the hall, and Jess looked up in time to see River and Juno turning the corner into the waiting room. Juno was still dressed for ballet in her pale pink leotard and tights, but her favorite pink cowboy boots clomped across the linoleum floor. Her hair was pulled up in a lopsided bun, and she held on to River with one hand, clutching a bouquet of sunflowers in the other. The sight of their clasped hands yanked a breath from Jess's throat.

"There's my girl," Pops said, eyes lighting up.

"We brought sandwiches!" Juno whisper-yelled, and Jess glanced up to River. He must have explained to her that this was a hospital, and sick people were trying to rest. Jess couldn't imagine another scenario where Juno Merriam Davis didn't burst into this room at full volume looking for her nana.

She handed Jess the flowers, pressed a kiss to her mom's lips, and then climbed onto Pops's lap.

Jess stood, taking the white paper bag River offered. "You didn't have to do that."

"We figured the last thing on your mind would be dinner," he said.

She smelled meatball subs, and her mouth watered. "Thank God, because I am famished."

"How is she?"

"Yeah, how is Nana Jo?" Juno asked.

"She's still in surgery," Jess said. "They're expecting her to be fine, we're just waiting." She handed Pops a sandwich and pointed with hers up at the hunk of male magic in front of them. "Pops, this is River Peña. River, this is my grandfather Ronald Davis."

River reached to shake Pops's hand. "It's a pleasure to meet you. I've heard great things."

"Likewise." Pops returned the handshake, and Jess had to bite her lip to keep from smiling. "And thank you for taking care of our little Junebug here. It's been quite an afternoon."

"It was no problem," River said. "Sometimes it's fun to take a Muppet to ballet."

Juno wiggled wildly on Pops's lap, sticking her fingers in her ears, screwing up her face.

"There she is," River said fondly.

Juno came to an abrupt stop, seeming to remember something. "Will Nana have her scooter again?"

"I'm not sure," Pops told her. "We better get my steel-toed boots out of storage just in case."

The pager went off in Jess's lap: the disk illuminated with red lights, vibrating across her thigh. Pops stood abruptly, depositing Juno in his seat before he picked up the pager and hustled to the nurses' station.

"She must be out of surgery," Jess said, watching him.

"I'm going to let you get to it, then." River glanced at Juno. "Thank you for spending the afternoon with me, Juno Merriam. It's been a long time since I went to a ballet class."

"You're welcome," she said. "You can come again if you want."

"Well, maybe I will." He smiled, turning to Jess. "Call me if you need anything else?"

"I will." Words she wanted to say tangled up in her chest in an emotional clog. Gratitude and lust and fear and longing. She didn't want him to leave. She wanted to stand, slide her arms around his waist under his jacket, and whisper her thanks into the warmth of his neck. But instead, she simply said, "Thank you, River."

NANA CAME THROUGH surgery with flying colors. She was wheeled into recovery, and while Pops was able to have some time with her, Jess and Juno had a little picnic with sandwiches, fruit, and cookies in the family waiting room.

"How was your afternoon with Dr. Peña?"

"I call him River Nicolas, and he calls me Juno Merriam," she corrected around a mouthful of mandarin orange. "We went to ballet class and he met Ms. Mia, and he was going to wait in the parents' room, but I asked Ms. Mia if he could watch us practice our recital. He sat on the floor by the mirror and watched us, Mom. He saw how good we were."

"I bet he was impressed." Jess's chest pinched tightly at the image of six-foot-four-inch River sitting cross-legged on the floor of the dance studio.

"*Then* we got a pretzel and some flowers, but he thought you guys might be hungry, so we got sandwiches, too." She munched on her orange and then looked up at Jess with wide blue eyes. "Did you know, I told him that you don't like raw onions and he said he doesn't like raw onions, either?"

"I didn't know that, but it was very nice of you guys to bring us dinner." She ran her hand through Juno's coppery hair.

"Now is he your boyfriend?" Juno met her eyes and then looked away in a rare display of shyness. "Because today he picked me up at school sort of like a daddy would."

"Oh." A sharp ache pressed up from Jess's stomach to her

breastbone. "Well, we're friends. So, when I needed help picking you up, he offered to help me like friends do."

Juno looked disappointed. "Oh."

"But I'm really glad you like him." Jess leaned forward, kissing her daughter's forehead. "It's been a long day, hasn't it?"

"I'm not tired," Juno claimed through a yawn. "But I bet Pigeon is wondering where we are."

Jess smiled as they cleaned up their food, watching Juno grow droopier with every passing second. She thought she was a big kid, but as soon as eight o'clock came around, exhaustion rolled over her like an offshore drift. With Nana asleep, they said goodbye to Pops. Jess made him promise to get some sleep, too, and promised him that she'd be back in the morning. She lifted Juno, and wiped-out little arms made their way around Jess's neck, her legs around Jess's waist.

The elevator doors opened to the ground floor, and Jess stepped out, stopping in her tracks when she saw River perched in a chair near the exit. Approaching him, Jess balanced Juno in her arms. "River, oh my God, you're still here?"

He looked up from his phone and abruptly stood. "Hey."

"Hi." Jess laughed uncomfortably. Guilt oozed through her. "I hope you didn't feel like you had to stay."

He looked sheepish and sleepy. Jess wasn't sure why, but it made her want to cry. "I wanted to see how she was," he said. "Your grandmother."

"She's a champ. Everything went fine." Jess smiled. "She's sleeping now, but I'm sure she'll start hassling them to let her go tomorrow."

"Good." He tucked his phone in his pocket and glanced at Juno, asleep like a sack of potatoes over her shoulder. "I also wanted to thank you for trusting me today." He leaned to the side, confirming that Juno was out. "She mentioned something in the car to me about Krista and Naomi?"

"Those are her two best friends at school."

He clicked his tongue, wincing a little. "I think maybe she had a rough day. We talked it out a bit, but sounds like they weren't being super nice to her at lunch. Just wanted to let you know."

Jess's heart twisted. Her sunshine girl rarely spoke about school; it must have been rough if she mentioned it. "I'll ask her about it. Thank you. You're amazing."

"*She's* amazing, Jess. You're doing a great job."

She had to swallow twice before she could get the words out. "Thank you for saying that." Pride warmed her from the inside out. Juno *was* an amazing kid, proof that Jess was a good mom—most of the time. It hadn't been easy, but they were doing it. His compliment loosened something in her, though, and Jess was suddenly exhausted, too.

"Can I walk you to your car?"

She nodded and they turned, passing through the automatic doors and out into the humid, cool night. At her car, Jess fumbled in her purse for the keys.

"Can I help you with something?" he asked, laughing like he felt useless.

"Nah. You should have seen me when she was younger. A car seat, diaper bag, stroller, and groceries. I'd make an excellent octopus." Remote in hand, she unlocked the car.

"I'm beginning to see that."

River opened the back door and she bent to carefully deposit a floppy Juno into the seat, buckling her in. When she straightened, closing the door, he was still there. The sky was dark; the parking lot had mostly emptied out. Crickets chirped from a nearby bush. Jess wondered if he was going to kiss her. The ache for him seemed to expand inside her like a star.

"Thank you again," she said.

The moment stretched and then he was leaning in, diverting slightly to the left at the very last second so that his lips pressed to the corner of her mouth. It would have been so easy for her to turn her head slightly one way or the other, and they both knew it. She could have made it more intimate, or she could have refused him. Instead, she kept them there in this weird limbo, feeling his lips so close to hers, his breath fanning warm across her skin. She was equal parts caution and lust. She needed to protect her little family; she wanted his mouth open, the heat of him. She needed proof that this wasn't all fake; she wanted his hands shoving her clothes away.

She was being a coward.

He straightened and gave her one last, lingering smile. "Night, Jess."

Before he could turn away, she caught his fingers with hers. "River. Hey."

He frowned down at her, waiting, but the longer she stood there looking up at him, the more his expression transitioned from concern to understanding. Finally, he turned his hand over in hers, threading their fingers together. "You okay?"

She nodded, swallowing down the tangle of angst in her throat.

Pressing her hand to his chest, she stretched, and he stood carefully still as she brushed her mouth over his. When she stepped away, he stared down at her with the same unreadable restraint. If she'd been any less exhausted, Jess would have felt like a complete idiot. "Yeah—sorry. Just. Wanted to do that."

River reached up, gently guiding her hair behind her shoulder. "Even without an audience?" he asked quietly.

"I'm amazed we did it *with* an audience."

A smile broke slowly across his face, starting with his eyes and moving down to lips that curved up in shy relief. Bending, River set those lips on hers, and the same sensation of floating hit her like a narcotic. He gave her a series of sweet, brief kisses, and finally tilted his head to pull at her lower lip, nudging her mouth, coaxing it open so he could taste her.

The first contact with his tongue was like a shot of adrenaline into her heart, sent with shocking clarity and speed down every extremity. A quiet sound of relief escaped her throat and it turned something over in him; his hands flew around her back, pulling her flush against him.

Jess had the acute urge to crawl inside him somehow, kissing him with the kind of concentrated, building intensity she'd never felt before. Not even at the cocktail party. Alone together in the darkness of the parking lot, with a black sky all around and fingers of the cold, damp February air dipping beneath their collars, River left no room, holding her close and sending his warm, broad hand up under the hem of her sweater, pressing his hand flat to the small of her back.

Tight, hungry sounds escaped whenever they pulled away and

came back for more. He bent possessively, one hand holding firm at her back, the other sliding up her neck, cupping her jaw, digging into her hair. Jess could, in an instant, see how easily he would devour her. A current vibrated when they came together; he became less man than pure energy, arms shaking with restraint. She imagined scooting back on a bed, watching him prowl forward, anticipating how it would feel to let him do whatever he wanted to her. Begging him to.

River broke the kiss, breathing hard and resting his forehead on hers. "Jess."

She waited for more, but that seemed to be all of it, the quiet exhalation of her name.

Slowly, with the clarity of the sharp, cool air in her lungs and space from the intoxicating weight of his body against hers, she returned to herself. The night sky tickled the back of her neck; a sodium light buzzed overhead.

"Wow," she said quietly.

"Yeah."

He pulled back and looked down at her, a tether connecting something inside her to him. They were quiet, but the air didn't feel empty.

River pulled his hand out from beneath her shirt, leaving the skin on her back suddenly chilly without the heat of his palm. And then the sensation doubled—as she leaned back into the cold side of her car, a violent shiver ran through her.

All at once, their proximity sank in.

Her car.

Juno.

Jess whipped around, horrified to remember only for the first time in several minutes that her child could possibly watch this through the window. Jess deflated in relief to find that Juno was still out cold.

What was I thinking?

River stepped away, cupping his neck. "Shit. I'm sorry."

"Oh my God." Jess lifted her hands to her face, breathless for an entirely new reason. "No, I started it. I'm—sorry."

She walked around to the driver's side, meeting his eyes over the top of the car. She was losing her head. This was all moving way too fast, and she had the sense that neither of them was behind the wheel. "Thank you," she said, aware of the knowing, calculating way he watched her. Inwardly, Jess shook herself; she barely knew him. She was letting this soulmate stuff get to her.

"Good night," he said quietly.

"Night," Jess replied, her voice hoarse. She worried her panic and lust and confusion showed plainly on her face. She must have looked like a lunatic—wide-eyed and breathless—but fondness warmed his gaze from the inside out, as if he was seeing exactly the person he wanted to see.

SEVENTEEN

———⌐———

POPS WASN'T ANSWERING his phone. He probably forgot to charge it.

Despite the draw of good coffee and the emotional ballast of her best friend—Fizzy'd gotten back from LA late last night—Jess decided to take her chances with hospital coffee and headed straight there, finding Pops standing at Nana's bedside, just . . . staring worriedly down at her. Nana remained hooked up to all manner of hospital monitors, with one leg carefully propped and wrapped from calf to hip, but she was peacefully asleep. Despite this, a glance at Pops's face told Jess he hadn't closed his eyes for longer than a blink since she and Juno had left him last night.

She crossed the room, wrapping her arms around him from behind and kissing his shoulder. "Hey, you."

He patted her hand, turning his face toward her. "Hey, honey."

"You been standing here like this all night?"

His laugh came out as a cough. "No. Up and down, though.

There's so much beeping, so much checking in, lights on, lights off. Glad she slept through most of it."

"She has the benefit of painkillers and a bed," Jess said. "You must feel like hell."

He nodded, reaching up to scratch his stubbly cheek with the ends of his blunt, thick fingers. "Just worried about her."

Jess opened her mouth, but immediately closed it again. Halt this vigilance for a half hour? Jessica Davis knew better. She wouldn't even consider suggesting he go home to shower and get a few hours of sleep in his own bed.

Might as well give him some fortification in the form of caffeine. "I was going to grab some coffee downstairs. Want some?"

"Yes," he rasped, grateful. "And something to eat, please."

Jess kissed his shoulder again. "Of course. Back in a few."

Out in the hallway, it was impossible to ignore the stressful energy of the hospital. Nurses wheeled monitors into rooms; doctors flipped through charts, frowning. A constant white noise of unsynchronized beeping emanated from all directions.

Statistics wheeled through her thoughts—life expectancy after a hip fracture: one-year mortality rate ranged from 14 to 58 percent, with a mean of 21.2 percent. Odds of survival worsened with increasing age, of course; thankfully males were more vulnerable and mobility scores significantly influenced outcome. Nana was active and female . . .

Meaning at best she only had a one-in-five chance of dying this year.

Numbly, Jess ordered coffee in the cafeteria, grabbing a fruit salad and bagel for Pops. She bent, inhaling the cups, trying to trick her brain and divert it from a panic spiral. A whiff of the weak brew barely registered.

She sat in a hard cafeteria chair and took a second to check her emails—Kenneth Marshall had sent over some sample data sets, and she had a new request through her website from a wholesale jewelry dealer in Chula Vista. She would need to reschedule the meeting she'd had to postpone yesterday, and bump up a deep dive on analytic epidemiology for some data that was coming in from UCSD. There was no way she was going to get through all of it today, get Pops to rest, talk to Nana's surgeon, and be there for school pickup. At least Juno had run enthusiastically toward Krista and Naomi at drop-off, so Jess didn't have to worry about her.

Swallowing a bitter sip of coffee, she texted Fizzy:

> My inbox is terrifying, and I think I'll need to stay here today so Pops can get some rest.

Fizzy replied immediately, anticipating what Jess was going to ask even as she was typing out the question:

> Does that mean I get Juno today? Yesssssss!

Jess closed her eyes, tilting her face to the ceiling. Gratitude and guilt prickled hot and cold through her.

> Thanks. I won't be late.

I have nothing else going on. Rob is on a work trip, and I missed your kid.

Thank you. I'm sorry—I swear I'll get home as early as I can.

Shut up. I mean it.

Unexpected tears erupted across the surface of her eyes, and the sting pulled her into awareness. Pops was probably starving; Nana might wake up soon. *Pull it together, Jess.*

Back up on the orthopedic floor, voices filtered down the hall from Nana's room. Jess heard the low rumble of Pops, Nana's sluggish, soft words . . . and then the deep, quiet voice that had left her tossing and turning all night.

She turned the corner to see River standing with his back to the door, right next to Pops at the side of Nana's bed. Nana Jo was awake, blurry-eyed but smiling. From behind, Pops's posture looked perkier than it had in twenty-four hours, and he held a to-go cup in his left hand.

"It's good to see you awake," River was saying. "I met Mr. Davis but didn't get to meet you yesterday."

Nana still hadn't seen Jess in the doorway—she was mostly hidden by River's body—but Jess caught a glimpse of her beaming up at him. Jess couldn't blame her grandmother; Dr. Peña was undoubtedly better-looking than she had let on. "Well, you're sweet to come by, hon. Jess has told us all about you."

This made him laugh. "Has she? Uh-oh."

"Well," Nana hedged, laughing lightly, "not as much as I'd like, I admit. That girl is a steel trap."

"That sounds about right." This time, they laughed knowingly together, and Jess scowled from behind them. "I'm glad you seem to be feeling better today."

Nana Jo pushed to sit up, wincing. "They'll probably get me out of bed and walking here soon."

Pops nodded. "That's right. You up for it, Jellybean?"

"I'm gonna give it my best," Nana said quietly. Uneasily.

Frozen in the doorway, Jess didn't know what to do or say. River wasn't throwing Nana and Pops into We Have Company mode in the slightest.

"Sounds like you've got a pretty fancy operation over there in La Jolla," Pops said.

River nodded, tucking a hand into his pocket. "We're hoping. If you two ever want to get tested, you'd be a nice addition to our Diamond Match data."

Nana laughed, waving him off. "Oh, you're sweet."

"But he's right," Pops said, bending to kiss her forehead. "What do you think? Should we see if we're meant for each other?"

Nana smacked his chest, laughing, and Jess felt another mysterious urge to cry.

But when she took a step backward to ease out of view, her shoe squeaked on the linoleum, and all heads turned in her direction. River pivoted fully, breaking into a smile.

"Hey, Nana," Jess said, walking to her bedside and bending to kiss her soft cheek. "How're you feeling, superstar?"

"Much better with two handsome men and my favorite granddaughter in my room."

River laughed and extended a coffee from Twiggs to Jess. "I don't think you got your flat white this morning," he said. "Fizzy said you hadn't been in."

Their eyes met briefly, and Jess was the first to look away. She flushed at the memory of his mouth on hers.

"Came straight here after school drop-off." She set the crappy hospital coffee on the windowsill (in case of emergency) and Pops's food on the little table by Nana's bedside. "Thanks," Jess said, taking the cup from River. Their fingers brushed and it felt like clothes-ripping foreplay.

River curled his hand into a fist, shoving it into the front pocket of his pants. "Just wanted to stop in on the way to work."

"That's really nice of you."

Nana Jo gave Jess a *Is that all you have to say to him?* frown, and when River glanced to the side at the sound of a monitor beeping, Jess returned a helpless *What else do you want me to say?* shrug.

Nana Jo rolled her eyes and Jess looked back to River, who unfortunately had caught the tail end of this nonverbal conversation. He cleared his throat and pulled his sleeve back to look at his watch. "I should probably head out."

"Thank you for stopping by," Jess managed.

"Yeah," River said haltingly. "Of course."

Jess tried again. "Can I walk you out?"

He nodded, and she followed him into the hallway.

"I'm sorry if I'm intruding," he said immediately.

"No." She lifted her coffee to him. "This will save me today."

Frowning, he murmured, "Well, I'm glad."

What would really be helpful would be to step into his arms and let him worry about everything for a few hours. River seemed willing to be that person.

Last night had felt like falling into a deep well filled with stars. Jess could have stayed in his arms for hours without coming up for air. But right now was not the time to be distracted by constant thoughts of getting into River's pants.

He straightened. "I brought something for Juno." Digging into his messenger bag, he pulled out a few sheets of paper. "Some roller coaster stuff I printed off last night."

Jess took the papers without looking at them, unable to shift her gaze from his face. Her heart was ramping up to a crescendo, but her mind had gone unexpectedly mute.

These small, easy ways of caring: sandwiches, coffee, school pickups, roller coaster research.

Juno's heart was built to expand. *He picked me up at school sort of like a daddy would*. She was going to get attached, but if his relationship with Jess didn't pan out after their experiment, he would be gone. Juno would know abandonment—after every tiny and enormous effort Jess had made to build a lasting, secure world for her.

And Jess couldn't deny: she would feel the loss, too. She didn't want him to become indispensable and precious to her. She'd never needed anyone except her tiny circle. She didn't know if she was even capable of trust-falling backward into anyone else's arms.

It was unfair after everything he'd done for her in the past twenty-four hours, but fear crawled up inside her like a creeping, strangling vine anyway. "Thank you for doing that," she managed robotically, lifting the papers.

River frowned, at a loss against her blank tone. "Okay—well, that's all I've got." He adjusted the strap on his shoulder, brow furrowed in confusion. This morning's Jess was not the same woman he'd kissed outside of the car last night. "I'll catch you later."

He turned, stiffly, and began walking toward the elevator.

Stride, stride, stride.

Something thawed in her. "River." She heard the way her voice rang down the hall, its odd, desperate pitch. "Wait."

He turned slowly, expression guarded.

"I'm sorry I'm so—" She approached him, stopping a few feet away as she struggled for the right words. "I'm sorry I'm oddly nonverbal today. I'm really grateful for your help with Juno last night, and I love that you brought me a coffee."

He stared at her, waiting for the rest.

"It's just—none of this is part of our contract. I hope you know I know that. I would never want to take advantage."

If she thought his expression was flat before, she was wrong. Because at this, his mouth straightened, brow went completely smooth. "You're right," he said. He stared at his shoes for a clarifying beat, and then smiled stiffly at her. "I'm sorry if I made you feel uncomfortable last night, or today. Let me know if you need anything else."

He started to turn again, and a clawing desperation rose in her at the sight of him walking away. She wanted him here, she wanted him *right fucking here*, but that exact feeling was making her want to reach forward and shove him away.

"It's just that I don't know what to do with what I'm feeling," Jess admitted in a burst.

Slowly, River turned back to her and let out a gently bewildered laugh. "Neither of us does."

"You stand to make so much money," she said. "How can that not be constantly on my mind? What would I have done if you hadn't helped with Juno yesterday? But it's always right here," she said, urgently tapping her temple with an index finger, "to question whether it's genuine. It's one thing if you're fooling me, it's another when it's my kid."

His brow relaxed. "I'm not here for the stock price, Jess. I've said it before. It isn't about the money."

"That's something only people who aren't worried about money say."

River sighed, blinking away and then back to her. "Did last night feel like an act to you?" When she didn't answer, he took a step closer, tone softening. "Do you understand what I'm trying to tell you? The DNADuo can bring us together, but it can't make us fall for each other. It can't know your past or mine, or predict what would scare us off, or entice us to be together. All of that is up to us, not the algorithm."

Jess closed her eyes and reached up, rubbing her hand over her face. Everything he said sounded so logical. But still. She was scared.

She resented her infatuation's persistent stab into every waking moment. She was attracted to River beyond anything she'd felt before, but it was emotional, too. It was the kind of attraction that sent down roots below the surface.

This new, tender kind of torture made her want him in all aspects of her life. On the pillow next to hers. Across the table at dinner. Holding her hand at the hospital. River was kind, and thoughtful, and vulnerable. He was brilliant and quietly funny. He was everything she ever wanted in a partner, even if she didn't realize it until he was standing right here, telling her that it was all up to them to try, or not.

Jess released a tiny stream of anxiety: "I'm scared, okay? I don't want to get hurt, and I *really* don't want Juno to get hurt. She's never—" She stopped short, rephrasing. "Juno's never had someone she loved disappear on her."

River's unwavering gaze softened, and he took another step closer to her. "I don't want that, either. But I'm not a soldier or a robot. I'm not here on GeneticAlly business. I'm following what I'm *feeling*." He looked back and forth between her eyes for a bit before something in his expression cleared, relaxing. "You'd have no way of knowing this, but I'm terrible at faking emotions." Jess laughed through a quiet sob. "And I get that it's more complicated because of Juno, but what else am I supposed to do but ask? I *want* to spend time with you."

"We *are* spending time together," Jess said lamely.

"Official events and conversations in hospital hallways?" he asked, frowning. "Is this enough for you?"

Could he see the *no* in her eyes? "I don't know what else is possible right now."

"What does that mean?" River closed the last bit of distance between them, reaching for her free hand. It felt cold against the heat of his fingers. He looked around the hallway surrounding them. "This is part of life, Jess. Emergencies and responsibility and managing small fires all the time—but it's only part of it. There are quiet moments, too. Good moments. Moments when we can ask for more."

"It's not the part I'm very good at."

"I hadn't noticed." He unleashed a wry smile.

This made her laugh. "What are you saying?"

"I thought it was obvious." His grin turned shy. "Really?"

"Really."

"I *want* to be here to bring you coffee. I want to take you out to dinner and order the same food and hear you recite the odds that we would have met. I want to hate-attend fancy social events together." Jess laughed, a surprised burst of sound, and his tone softened. "I want you to call me for help—without an apology already on the tip of your tongue. I want to feel like I can kiss you again by your car at the end of the night." He swallowed. "I want you in my bed."

Jess was a little afraid that her feet would melt into the floor. That flames would travel up her legs and burn a hole straight through her. She wanted that. But if she let herself fall for River, there would be no easy way out.

"I can tell you're not sure what to say," he said, bending to kiss her cheek. "That's okay. You know where to find me when you're ready."

EIGHTEEN

P OPS, WOULD YOU get out of here for just a little while?"

He ignored her. "What's a thirteen-letter word for 'old'?"

"I'd say Ronald Davis," Jess said, "but that's only eleven."

Nana chuckled from the bed, where she was drowsily half watching TV on mute.

"Well?" he prompted, tired and irritable.

Jess shook her head. "Nope."

"What do you mean, 'nope'?" he gruffed.

"I'm not helping you," she told him. "You stink and you're falling asleep in your chair."

"She's right," Nana murmured.

He stared at Nana Jo, then at Jess, and then blinked down, forlorn, at the puzzle. "Octogenarian?" He counted on his fingers, and grunted in annoyance. "Septuagenarian?" Victorious, he moved to write it in.

"That's fourteen letters," Jess said. "You're forgetting the U in there, aren't you?"

Irked, Pops dropped the crossword onto the table in defeat.

"Go home for a bit," Nana said sleepily. "I don't need you watching me all day."

"Well, it's not my fault I can't take my eyes off you. You're just too pretty."

Nana Jo rolled her eyes, but his words made her glow like a Christmas tree.

"Fine, I'll go home and shower and sleep." He stood, stretching. Something cracked in his back and he let out a tight moan before kissing Nana on the forehead. He looked over his shoulder at Jess. "You won't leave her?" Jess forgave him the accusatory tone; he was exhausted.

It was on the tip of her tongue to joke that she promised to only leave if she got bored or hungry, or if a hot male nurse wanted to sneak into a supply closet, but now was not the time. "I won't leave her." Quietly, she added, "Superannuated."

Letting out a quiet "Dammit, I should have known that one," he walked back over and scribbled the word into the puzzle.

POPS RETURNED AROUND three, looking significantly cleaner and marginally better rested. He arrived only a handful of minutes before the physical therapist came to get Nana up and out of bed for the first time, and Jess was glad because it took all three of them to talk the normally fearless woman through the panic of putting weight on her leg.

Jess didn't have time to reel in the emotional hit of seeing Nana so frail and scared; it took an hour to get her up and taking the ten assisted steps to the door, where a wheelchair took her to the PT room, and another hour there, working on strength and balance.

By the time Nana Jo was back in bed for the night it was just after five, and although Jess had been sitting for most of the day, she was so mentally drained that she just wanted to curl up in her bed—hell, she'd happily find a spot on the linoleum floor. But more than that, she wanted some time with Juno while her daughter was awake. And food. She hadn't eaten since she'd picked at a dry bran muffin around ten that morning, and her stomach gnarled in annoyance.

Texting Fizzy that she'd have some dinner delivered, Jess climbed into her car, called an order in to Rama, and turned on the mellow rumble of the National. Music filled the car, and it was an intoxicating hit of calm.

You said love fills you up . . .
I got it worse than anyone else

Her shoulders tensed, and she turned the music off.

In the silence, her thoughts immediately flooded with River. The paradoxical brew of hospital tedium and chaos had held everything back, but in the dark solitude of her own car, emotion poured over her.

I thought it was obvious.
I want to hear you recite the odds that we would have met.
"'I want you in my bed,'" she repeated aloud.

Jess pulled into her parking spot in the alley, listened to the engine tick in the silence. She could smell duck curry all the way down the path and sent a silent thanks to Rama.

Inside, Juno and Fizzy were at the table, feasting and playing cards. They were wearing handmade paper hats and Fizzy had put . . . a lot of makeup on Juno.

"We're filming makeup tutorials for my mom," Fizzy said, standing to walk over and give Jess a hug.

Jess stifled a laugh at her daughter's exaggerated lips. "I see."

With an irrepressible urge to deflate in fatigue, Jess considered simply lowering her body to the floor. But she wanted her arms around her kid so bad they ached. At the table, Jess lifted Juno up and set her on her lap while her daughter finished eating, pressing her face to the small stretch between the delicate shoulder blades. "I missed you, Bug."

"I haven't been gone, silly!" Juno bent in her grip, maneuvering a bite into her mouth.

Once they'd stuffed themselves to the point of discomfort, Juno settled on the couch to watch *The Lion King*, and Fizzy and Jess lingered in the kitchen with glasses of wine.

"I don't like when you're out of town," Jess said through a yawn. "I blame you for yesterday."

"Seems reasonable." Fizzy swallowed a sip and bit her lip, studying Jess with narrowed eyes. "Juno says *River Nicolas* picked her up and took her to ballet?"

Jess waved a hand, unprepared to talk about it yet. "How are things with you and Banker Rob?"

"Hot and fantastic."

She raised an eyebrow. "Will he be coming to your place later?"

Fizzy shook her head, waving her glass with a delicately bent wrist. "He's out of town, remember? Which means you won't get to avoid the River conversation." Her best friend sat at the table and patted the seat next to her.

"Oh. Right." Jess sat, but immediately crumpled, resting her head on her arms. "I'm too tired, Fizz."

"Tell me what's going on. You look . . ." She leaned in, lifting Jess's hair to peek at her face. "This looks like more than just worry about Jo."

Straightening, Jess quietly unloaded it all, parcel by parcel. She admitted she was starting to feel for River—feelings too big to ponder when it seemed like everything else in her life was pounding at the door to be dealt with. She admitted she didn't know whether River's intentions were completely trustworthy, even though he swore they were. She told Fizzy about the cocktail party, about honest-to-God one of the most intense make-outs the parking lot of Scripps Mercy had ever seen. She told Fizzy about how she couldn't stop thinking about him. She told Fizzy every detail she could think to tell, like she was purging her sins.

"He said that?" Fizzy whispered, wary of the small but excellent ears in the other room. "He actually said the words 'I want you in my bed'? Just like that?"

Jess nodded.

"With eye contact?"

"Steady, ardent, I'm-going-to-fuck-you-until-you-find-religion eye contact," Jess confirmed.

Fizzy groaned, reaching for her purse, pulling her notebook out, and writing it down.

Jess bent over her arms again, exhaling an enormous sigh. "I just need some time to figure this all out. It's happening so fast."

Fizzy dropped her pen, scoffing at this. "Come on. No, you don't."

Surprised, Jess looked up at her. "What do you mean I don't?"

"You've known him for weeks now. You're telling me he told you he wanted to take you to dinner and hear you be nerdy. He wants to be there for you without you feeling guilty. He admitted he wants you *in his bed*—this poor boy is *sprung*, Jess, and you're going to—what? Shove it aside?"

Jess stared at her, uncomprehending.

"You're looking for a way out of feeling anything," Fizzy said, "but you're clearly bonkers for this guy."

"I'm not sure 'bonkers'—"

"You're scared, and it's cliché."

She exhaled a shocked laugh. "Wow, give it to me straight, Felicity."

"You think having feelings for River is selfish."

"I mean, this situation does actually take me away from both work and Juno," she said. "I've barely seen her the past two days."

"So?" Fizzy challenged.

"What . . . ? I—" Jess grew flustered. "She's my kid. I want to see her."

"Of course you do," Fizzy said, "but she's Jo's and Pops's and mine, too. She and I had a blast tonight, and I wish I could see her more. But you act like asking for help is selfish, you see wanting something just for yourself as selfish, you see taking any time away from your kid as selfish, and if you're selfish, then you must be turning into your mother."

Hearing it aloud was like being punched.

"But you're not your mom, Jess." Fizzy took her hand, lifting it to her mouth to kiss it. "There isn't even a drop of Jamie Davis in you."

Jess's voice broke. "I know."

"And if you could do anything tonight when Juno goes to bed, what would it be?"

She expected the word *Sleep* to drop out of her mouth. But instead: "I'd go to his place."

Fizzy's dark eyes flashed with smug victory. "Then go. I'll stay here with the kid as long as you need me to."

"Fizz, you don't have to do that."

"I know I don't." She kissed Jess's hand again. "That's the whole point. You do things for me because you love me. I do things for you because I love you. Duh."

Jess scrounged around for the last remaining excuse. Luckily, it was a good one: "I don't know where he lives."

"Well, you could text him. Or . . ." Fizzy reached across the table for a piece of paper and handed it to her. On it, in small, cramped handwriting, was the name *River Nicolas Peña* and an address in North Park.

"Wait," Jess said, laughing incredulously, "how did this end up on my table?"

"I asked the same thing when I found it in Juno's backpack," Fizzy said with mock bewilderment. "And Juno explained that she wanted to mail him some drawings of Pigeon. How kind of him to give this to her."

———————

RIVER OPENED THE door and his mouth went slack.

"Jess." He reached for her shoulder, concerned. "What are you—? Are you okay?"

All at once, she had no idea what to say. He was standing in front of her in lounge pants that hung low on his hips and a thread-bare Stanford T-shirt. He was barefoot and freshly showered. His hair was wet and finger-brushed back off his face; his lips were smooth and perfect. Unraveled and bare, Jess knew in her bones that he was her ninety-eight.

"I wanted to see you."

Realization altered his expression, and his eyes darted behind her and then quickly back. He licked his lips. "Is Ju—"

"Fizzy."

He stared, breaths coming out in shorter and shorter gusts. Maybe three seconds later, Jess didn't know who was moving first, whether he pulled her inside or she stepped in out of the cool, humid night, but she was in his entryway only a moment before the door slammed and she was pushed back against it. River braced his hands beside her head, staring with wild disbelief. And then he bent, pressing a groaning kiss to her mouth.

The feel of it, the perfect pressure and angle, transformed her longing into a staggering hunger. Jess's hands shook as they made fists in the soft fabric of his shirt, and when he tasted her—lips parted, tongue teasing—she was hit with a desire so intense it felt like taking a breath too big to hold. She had to pull away, gasping for air.

"I can't believe you're here," he growled, scraping his teeth down her jaw, sucking, biting at her neck. "Did you come here for this?"

Jess nodded, and greedy hands bunched her sweater as they moved up her torso, seeking skin. The loss of contact while he pulled away to yank it up and over her head was torture, and Jess jerked him back, wedging her hands between them to get his T-shirt off as quickly as her frantic fingers would let her. Beneath her touch he was hard and smooth, candy for her feverish hands.

Jess laughed an apology into his mouth as she managed to get his elbow briefly tangled in one of his sleeves. "It's okay," he breathed, tossing the shirt away. His eyes met hers for an electric beat before his hair fell forward and he bent to kiss her.

While his mouth moved down her jaw and neck, over her shoulder and along the sensitive inside of her wrist, she watched her fingers memorize each perfect inch of his torso. River's shoulders were broad but not massive, defined but not bulky. His chest, too, and lower, where his stomach clenched under her touch. Jess wanted to dig in, bite, consume. And when her nails scratched up his back, over the curves of his shoulders, tracing his perfect collarbones, his breath caught in his throat.

With his gaze on her face, River reached back, releasing the clasp of her bra. His hands were rough and warm, and Jess wanted to catch every tiny shift in his expression, every reaction to the feel of her. The way he looked at her—the sweet devastation pinching his brow—made Jess feel like she'd been plugged directly into the sun. Urging him back, she fell to her knees, drugged and nearly delirious with need.

He let out a whispered "Oh, God" as she worked his pants and boxers down; River turned her into Medusa with his fingers in her hair, and with a voice that had grown hoarse, he quietly begged for more than the heat of her breath. She looked up, and when their eyes met, hunger speared painfully through her. Jess hadn't ever felt this desired or this powerful. Having never craved anything in excess like this before, she wanted to pull him into every bit of her body at once, wanted to break off pieces too big to consume.

River's voice went from whispered pleas into broken, growling warnings, and with a cry, he pulled his hips away, wrapping a hand around her arm and guiding her to her feet. Jerking her close, he tucked her head beneath his chin while he caught his breath. With the pause in the frenzy, Jess grew aware of how fast her own breaths were coming, how it felt like their hearts were hammering on opposite sides of the same door.

I want to never get used to this, she thought, holding him. *If tonight is about being selfish, then here's my selfish wish: I hope we never get used to this.*

He pulled away, sending his hands over her body—hungrily touching chest, and ribs, and the curved small of her back—and Jess closed her eyes, tilting her head as his mouth slid up her throat. Teasing, his fingers toyed with the button on her jeans.

"Can I take these off?"

At her nod, River worked the button loose, smiling and kicking his own clothing free as he peeled hers down her legs. Leaning away, he grabbed and threw something to the floor, and when he carefully lowered her down, Jess realized he'd pulled a plush blanket from the couch.

Her back met the blanket, and his hips slid between her thighs. She got one gentle kiss before the heat of his mouth moved down her neck, sucking and kissing at her breasts, fingers digging into hips and navel and then gently feeling, stroking, before his kiss was there, too. The relief of it was like being uncapped and poured across his floor, and her fingers made fists in his hair as Jess closed her eyes against the overload of sensation.

She felt blindly for the purse she must have dropped as soon as her back hit the door, and fumbled through the fog of lust, pulling the square of foil free.

River heard the tear, lifting his head and dragging his mouth up her body. He tasted like her, but sounded like a man on the verge of breaking when she gripped him, rolling on the condom.

But he went still over her, and she paused, too, moving her hands to rest them on his hips. "Too fast?"

He shook his head and smiled down at her. "Just making sure."

Jess reached up to push the hair out of his eyes and nodded, unable to get the words out.

"Say it," he said, bending to kiss her. "I'm sure. Are you?"

She couldn't spread her hands out wide enough; even with his body aligned all along hers, she needed to get closer. "I want to," she said. "Please."

River dropped his forehead to her temple, letting her be the one to take him in. They both went still for a breathless pause, and in that time Jess existed only on the razor-sharp edge of bliss and discomfort. Carefully, holding still, he kissed her—so sweet and searching—and she could finally exhale.

"You okay?" River kissed her mouth again, and Jess felt him pull back and take in her expression. "We can stop."

Was he serious? They absolutely could not. Her drama-queen body was certain they'd die if they tried.

"No. Don't go."

"Okay." His lips dragged across her jaw and she could feel his smile. "I won't."

He kissed her again, pulling away with a gentle bite. When he whispered through a laugh, "I'm sorry. I don't know why I'm shaking," and she felt the truth of it under her hands, she could exhale some more because it made her think maybe she wasn't alone in this feeling—so desperate for him that she might cry.

River moved over her—slow, then building in tempo, pressing into her again and again, releasing a quiet grunt with every forward pitch and—

—and suddenly she felt the weight rolling down her spine like a steel boulder in a trap ready to spring.

Jess got only one word out—"I'm"—before it hit her like an explosion, the inside-out splitting of heat and relief spreading through her entire body. She was still too tangled up to appreciate River's abandon, but it imprinted in the back of her mind how he groaned her name against her neck, going tightly still over her.

After a pause filled only with the sounds of their short, stuttering breaths, River pushed up on his arms and stared down at her. His hair was a mess of dark curls falling into his eyes, but Jess had the weird sense of looking into a mirror anyway; his gaze was brimming with the same shock and amazement she felt vibrating in her blood. It hit her in a sharp, startling truth: her whole life she had been put together wrong in one tiny, invisible, and critical way. And having that piece altered just enough for it to slide into place suddenly changed everything.

"Can you stay?" he asked, catching his breath. "Stay here tonight?"

Her heart pinched painfully and Jess ran a hand down his sweaty chest, over his stomach. "I don't think so."

Nodding, he pulled back with a wince, and she immediately ached for him. River sat back on his heels and ran a warm palm along her leg, from hip to knee.

She marveled at this man who, a month ago, she'd known only as "Americano," as surly and quiet and selfish. This shy, brilliant man kneeling in front of her who showed up without having to be asked, who put the ball in her court, who asked her if she was sure and told her they could stop. She felt her control slipping out of her grip, and the two syllables of his name tattooed a permanent echo inside her.

River's shoulders rose and fell with his still-labored breathing, and he closed his eyes, sliding his hands up over her hips again, across her navel. "I don't have to say it, do I?"

"Maybe not," Jess said, gazing up at him. "I still want you to."

Somehow she'd known exactly what he would look like without a stitch of clothing on, but she took a leisurely visual perusal anyway.

"That was unreal, wasn't it?" he finally said. "I don't feel like the same person I was an hour ago."

"I was just thinking the exact same thing."

He laughed quietly. "I can't believe we did it on the floor. In all the times I imagined it, I did not imagine the floor."

"I probably wouldn't have let you get much farther than the entryway."

"I like a woman on a mission."

With hungry, curious eyes, Jess watched him stand and stride unselfconsciously naked across the foyer to his sleek, austere kitchen. She hadn't even taken a moment to look around his place, but it was exactly what she expected: open floor plan, clean lines, simple furniture, understated wall decor. There were, for example, no crayon drawings of hippos taped to his refrigerator or unpaired socks strewn on the floor.

He returned a moment later, coming over her like a shadowed, predatory animal. "I'm going to think about this constantly now."

Jess laughed, admitting, "I already do."

"Like when?" he whispered.

She rolled her eyes away, thinking. "Um. Shelter Island—"

"Same."

Her eyes met his again. "And the kiss at the party—"

"Of course."

"The parking lot at the hospital."

"I almost asked to follow you home."

She reached up, sliding her thumb over his bottom lip. "I'm glad you didn't. I would have said yes, but I wasn't ready yesterday."

He opened his mouth, gently biting the tip of her finger. "I know. I hope you were tonight."

She nodded, mesmerized by the sight of his teeth around her finger. "I was. It lived up to the mental hype. It exceeded the mental hype."

"I wanted you before Shelter Island," he said quietly.

Jess pulled back a little, surprised. "When?"

"The night we found out about the match, when we were outside. I wondered what it would feel like to kiss you." He bent, giving her a tiny peck. "And at dinner, with Dave and Brandon." He kissed her again. "In the lab when I took your blood. Our first date. Pretty much every time I thought about you."

"Do you think it's because the number told you to want me?"

He shook his head. "I believe in the algorithm, but not that much. I fought it. Just like you did."

Jess stared up at him, running her palm up his chest. A faint echo of discomfort registered in her back, and he must have felt her wince because he pushed up, reaching for and helping her stand.

River bent, pulling on his boxers before draping the throw blanket around her shoulders. Taking her hand, he led them to the couch, gesturing for her to sit first, but Jess stepped forward, gently pushing him until he sat, and then placed a knee on either side of his hips, straddling him. Bringing the blanket around her shoulders, she sealed them in together below their necks.

Beneath the blanket, River ran his hands up her bare thighs and let out a long, slow breath. "You're going to kill me."

Suddenly it all felt very surreal. "I honestly can't believe that I'm here and we just had sex on your floor."

River went in for a kiss and laughed against her mouth. "Does Juno know you're here?"

"No."

He lifted a brow. "Does she know we're . . . ?"

"She's asked me a couple times if you were my boyfriend,

but . . ." Jess shook her head. "I'm not really talking about it with her yet."

He gave a little *That's fair* frown and pushed the blanket off her shoulders, drawing lazy spirals over her collarbones. "But I assume Fizzy knows."

"She practically shoved me out the door with your address in my hand."

He looked up at her face, realization dawning. "Shit. I forgot to tell you about the cat drawings and giving her my address. I didn't mean to overstep, but that kid is persuasive."

With a laugh, Jess waved this off. "Trust me, I know how she operates. It's why we joke that she's half Fizzy's."

"Still. I'm sorry I didn't mention it."

"Are you kidding?" She kissed him again. "*I'm* sorry because no doubt she made you feel incredibly guilty, questioning everything about yourself, before you finally relented."

He laughed, tilting his head back and giving her a delightful view of his throat. "I guess I shouldn't be surprised you know exactly how it went down."

"She definitely does not get the evil-genius persuasiveness from me."

River's smile stuttered; Alec was there with them now. River reached up to twist a long strand of her hair around his finger.

Jess cleared her throat. "Or her father, for that matter. Like I said: she's half Fizzy's."

"Her father's not in the picture at all?" River asked quietly.

"Alec, and no."

"So he won't ever—"

"Try to share custody?" Jess anticipated the end to the question, shaking her head. "No. He signed away his rights before Juno was born."

River blew out a surprised breath. "What a dick."

She loved that this was his reaction, but she didn't need it. "I'm glad he did."

He smiled up at her, unsure, and she got a tiny glimpse of River from before, the cautious, shy man who hadn't yet pulled her proverbial pin and made her come undone.

"What?" she asked, reaching up and drawing a line over the crease in his forehead.

"Has Juno ever met one of your boyfriends?"

Jess laughed and he shifted her forward, closer. She deflected. "Is that what this is? Boyfriend?"

"As soon as I said that word, it seemed both a presumption and an underrepresentation."

"Because ninety-eight," she said, grinning.

He leaned in, kissing her neck. "Because ninety-eight."

"The more accurate question," she said as he kissed his way around the curve of her jaw, "is whether I've had a boyfriend since Juno."

River stilled, and then pulled back, looking at her. "Isn't she seven?"

"She is. I've seen a few people here and there, but no one I would consider a boyfriend."

He drew another gently looping shape across her collarbone, humming. "Wow."

"Is that weird?" Jess asked.

"I don't know. I'm not sure how I would handle it, either, if I had a kid."

"Do you date a lot?"

He brought both hands below the blanket again and laid them on her hips. It made it hard to focus on his words even when he said, "Not a lot. Some. A couple times a month, maybe? I work a hundred hours a week."

"Not this week."

River grinned. "No, not this week. This week I've been unable to stop checking in on my Diamond Match."

She kissed him again, deeper. "I'm glad you're persistent."

"One of us has to be."

NINETEEN

"OKAY, ONE ON each hand." She waited until Juno tugged the lobster claw oven mitts all the way on. "It'll be hot, so be careful."

Juno opened the oven door and they both winced from the hot wash of air as it passed over their faces. Jess helped her carefully pull the cookie sheet from the top rack and set it on the stove to cool. The entire apartment smelled like cinnamon and warm oatmeal, Nana's favorite.

Juno growled like a hungry little creature and inhaled deeply over the pan. "Nana is gonna be so happy. What day does she come home?"

Using a spatula, they moved each cookie to the cooling rack. "Three days," Jess said. "Normally people only stay a few days, but she's older so they want to make sure she's up and moving okay before they let her go."

Juno pursed her lips in concentration. "So, Sunday?"

"That's right."

"Maybe Try Something New Sunday can be bringing Nana home from the hospital. We've never done that before."

"Excellent plan."

"We could just have cuddles and movie day here. Nana will probably be tired."

"I bet you're right. I think she'd love that."

"So, we can take her cookies tonight; Friday is my sleepover at Naomi's house." She gasped as if just remembering something. "Did I tell you she got a dog? He's part poodle so he's very sweet and doesn't shed." She batted her eyelashes up at her mom. "A dog wouldn't eat our cat."

"Child, we are bursting at the seams. Maybe when we have a yard where a dog can run." Gently redirecting, she continued, "So Friday is the sleepover . . ."

Juno huffed out a little sound, but relented. "Yeah, then Saturday maybe I can stay at Naomi's for a little while? And Nana will be back Sunday." A twinge of unease worked up Jess's spine at the mention of Naomi's name. When she'd asked, Juno said that they'd had a fight, but it seemed to have been forgotten. She knew kids needed to learn how to resolve conflict on their own, but the mama bear in her never hibernated too deep below the surface.

"You sure you want to do a sleepover?" Jess asked. "We could go to the movies together. Maybe the zoo?"

"No, it's Naomi's birthday, and I already got her a present. They're doing a hula night."

"You got her a present?"

"I used my good citizen tickets and got her two slap bracelets and some glitter stickers."

Offering a high five, Jess told her, "I have some gift bags in the closet; maybe we can use one of them and put a gift certificate in there, too?"

With the plan in place, they slid the rest of the cookie dough toward them to load up another sheet just as the doorbell rang. "Let's get these finished so we can go before visiting hours end," Jess said. "Use the spoon to scoop the rest on the pan, and I'll be right back. Don't touch the oven."

Out in the living room, her heart tripped over itself when she peeked out the window and saw River standing on the other side.

Jess glanced down, groaning. Would it kill her to wear something other than sweats?

He looked up at the sound of the door swinging open and her breath went thin. His smile was somehow both shy and naughty; the muscular curves of his shoulders and chest were visible beneath the fabric of his shirt, and Jess wanted to rip it open like a bag of chips.

"Hey." She tried to keep it together.

His voice was a low, secretive burr: "I hope it's okay that I stopped by."

"It's fine." Jess swallowed. "Do you—um, do you want to come in?"

He stepped inside, hesitating for only a second before bending and carefully putting his mouth on hers. Heat erupted in her veins, and even though it was only a touch and he pulled away before they were busted, Jess knew she looked like she was about to catch fire anyway.

"Hi," he said quietly.

"Hi."

"You good?"

She nodded. "Definitely good now."

Beaming, he looked past her, and she found herself following every point of his attention, trying to see the apartment through his eyes. It wasn't tiny, but it wasn't big, either. She'd splurged on the yellow couch and bright blue chairs, but repainting the kitchen cabinets wasn't the same as getting new ones, and instead of art covering the walls, she had framed photos and elementary school art projects.

"Your place is great," he said, turning in a circle. "It's so cozy."

Jess closed the door with a laugh. "*Cozy* means *small*. I think this whole place could fit in your living room."

"Yeah, but my house feels like a showroom you walk through to pick out cabinet fixtures." He smiled up at a photo of Jess and Juno at the beach. "It's not a home."

"Who's here?" Juno shouted from the kitchen, followed by the sound of the step stool scraping over the tiles and her feet padding across the floor. "River Nicolas, are you here to make cookies with us?"

"Are you kidding, Juno Merriam?" They executed some complicated knuckle-bump, hand-slap, dance greeting. "I am always here to make cookies."

"Wow, what was that?" Jess asked.

They both ignored her—obviously it was a secret handshake—and Juno beamed up at him. "We're making them to take to Nana Jo. Do you want to see my room?"

River grinned. "I would love to see your room. But do you think I could talk to your mom for a second first?"

"Okay! I'm gonna go get it ready. Also, Mom said we can get a dog!" She raced out of the living room and down the hall. "I'll be waiting!"

"I said when we have a yard," Jess shouted after her. She turned back to River, who was biting back a smile. "A warning, her room is a disaster," Jess told him confidentially, "so that buys us a few minutes at least."

When she looked back at him, he was already staring at her, eyes fixed on her mouth. Tension tightened his shoulders, and he ran a hand through his hair. "Maybe we can talk outside?"

"Sure." Unease sent a cool film over her mood. "Juno," she called, "we'll be in the courtyard. Give us ten minutes."

Just outside the apartment, hidden from view, River reached for Jess's arm and pulled her toward him. His mouth came over hers, and he pressed her against the door, kissing her with a hunger that matched her own. But again he pulled away, clearly conscious of the risk. His bright eyes, when he looked down at her, simmered with that familiar, heated intensity.

And then they fell closed and he bent, releasing a long, frustrated growl against her neck.

Jess laughed out a sympathetic "Yeah, me, too."

She pushed her fingers into the back of his hair, relishing the quiet moment. His arms came around her waist, banding all around her until he was pressed so close it was like having another heartbeat. They couldn't stay this way for long, but Jess closed her eyes and breathed him in. The weird hollow ache in her chest settled.

She was relieved he was so clearly as wrapped up in it as she was. She was anxious to get her hands back on his skin, to feel that connection reverberating along her bones. She felt guilty that she couldn't just invite him to stay over, but also worried how they would keep the relationship from Juno, or whether that was even the right thing to do. And she was sure these feelings showed plainly on her face when she pulled back and looked at him.

But then she remembered.

River straightened at her gasp, alarmed. "What?"

"Guess whose kid has a sleepover at Naomi's tomorrow?"

"If the answer isn't you," he said, frowning, "then I'm going to admit that I don't like this game very much."

Jess laughed. "You're right! It's me!"

"Does that mean that Juno's mom also gets a sleepover?"

"She sure does."

He leaned in again, kissing her jaw, her cheek, her—

River's phone vibrated against her hip.

"Save the vibrations for tomorrow," Jess joke-whispered as he pulled it out.

He swallowed a laugh, answering with an easy "Hey, Brandon." River paused, listening and shaking his head at her in mock exasperation as she gave him a dorky, Brandon-toothy smile. But then his expression smoothed in shock. "What? Hang on, wait, wait, we're both here." River put it on speaker and held it between them.

"Oh, good!" Brandon said. "How are you, Jess?"

She leaned forward. "I'm good. How are you?"

"I'm fantastic. And as I was just telling River, you two are about to be fantastic, too, because the *Today* show wants you."

Her gaze bolted to River's, and she mouthed, *What?*

He shrugged, eyes wide.

"They already filmed footage for a segment on GeneticAlly," Brandon continued, "but after hearing about our Diamond Match they changed things up and want you in New York City tomorrow for an interview. Can we make it happen?"

"Tomorrow?" Her mind raced. They'd have to take a red-eye and go straight to the studio. She should say yes, because this was literally what they were paying her for, but Nana would come home from the hospital on Sunday, then start at the rehabilitation clinic on Monday. Someone needed to take care of Pops. And Juno would never forgive her mother if she had to miss a sleepover because of schedule complications. "Um—"

River smoothly cut in. "That's not going to work," he said. "If they want it in the next couple days, let's see if they can shoot our portion of the interview locally."

She opened her mouth to tell him it wasn't necessary, they could figure something out, it was the *Today* show, for crying out loud—but he firmly shook his head.

"It's better for us to do it there," Brandon insisted.

"No, I get that," River said with finality, playfully cupping a hand over Jess's mouth to keep her from committing to something she shouldn't out of guilt, "but Jess's grandmother just had surgery, and she needs to be here. You're in marketing, Brandon. Sell them on this." She stared at him from behind his hand, wanting to kiss him until they both had to come up for air. How did he know exactly what she needed?

There was a pause before Brandon spoke again. "You got it. We'll figure it out and get back to you."

"Thanks," River said. "Let us know." He ended the call.

The silence stretched between them. "Well, hello, Mr. Decisive Executive."

He tilted his head, giving her a flirty eyebrow. "You liked that?"

"It was so vintage Americano." Jess stretched, kissing him.

"Well," he said, kissing her one more time before straightening, "I admit that I'd like to stick around town for a selfish reason, too."

"Sleepovers and vibrations, am I right?"

"Yeah." He frowned. "But . . . also because of my sisters."

"Oh?"

"They're in town from San Francisco." He winced. "I may have mentioned that you and I would love to join them for dinner tomorrow night. You can always say no."

Elated, Jess looked up at him. "Embarrassing stories?"

"They have them all."

"Dirt on your pre-hot days?"

He laughed. "You have no idea. I'm sure they'll bring photos of the time they gave me a haircut before a school dance. It did not look awesome. It was also during the phase where my orthodontist's word was law, and I wore my headgear around the clock. I'm absolutely certain I'm going to regret this."

TODAY SHOW TRANSCRIPT

Natalie Morales [voiceover]: What if someone told you that dating was a thing of the past? That finding your soulmate was just a simple mouth swab away? It might sound too good to be true, but in San Diego, California, a burgeoning biotech company claims it can do just that.

Through a series of personality tests, brain scans, and yes, DNA analysis, GeneticAlly can identify your biological soulmate.

Using a patented algorithm called DNADuo, your DNA will be compared to hundreds of thousands of other individuals in GeneticAlly's database. Their proprietary software then places your compatibility scores, from zero to one hundred, in a range of categories: Base Match. Silver. Gold. Platinum. Titanium. Three out of four Titanium Matches end up in committed relationships. So, what about the couples who score over that coveted ninety? Only four Diamond Matches have been found to date, and in a startling twist, one of them is a member of the GeneticAlly team. Specifically, the DNADuo inventor and lead scientist, Dr. River Peña. Peña, a thirty-five-year-old geneticist, started his research in the labs of the Salk Institute.

River Peña: I wanted to see if I could find a common genetic factor in couples who described themselves as being in loving, long-term relationships for over two decades.

Natalie: How many couples did you study in that first test?

River: Three hundred.

Natalie: And what did you find?

River: In all of the couples who reported long-term relationship satisfaction, I found a compatibility pattern across two hundred genes.

Natalie voiceover: But Dr. Peña and his team didn't stop there. A study of one thousand test subjects grew to over one hundred thousand, and the initial pattern of two hundred genes is now a patented assay of over thirty-five hundred.

Natalie: So, humans have twenty thousand genes.

River: Between twenty and twenty-five thousand, yes.

Natalie: And your company has now found correlations between thirty-five hundred of those that lead to compatibility? That seems like a lot.

River: It is. But think about it: Everything we become is encoded by our genes. The way we react to stimulus, the way we learn and grow. Thirty-five hundred is likely just the start.

Natalie voiceover: GeneticAlly has plans to go public in May and hopes to have their DNADuo kits in retail and online stores by summer. With online dating revenue this year topping nine hundred million dollars in the U.S. alone, investors are lining up.

River: Compatibility isn't limited to just romantic relationships. Imagine finding the caretaker who's most compatible with your children, or a doctor for your parents, the right management team to lead your business.

Natalie voiceover: The sky's the limit. But back to that Diamond DNADuo score. In January, Jessica Davis, a thirty-year-old statistician, took the DNADuo test kit on a whim.

Jessica: I'd completely forgotten about it until I got the message from GeneticAlly asking me to come in.

Natalie voiceover: Jessica was Client 144326. Her match? Client 000001, Dr. River Peña.

Natalie: What was the highest match you'd found up to that point?

River: Ninety-three.

Natalie: And what was your and Jessica's score?

River: Ninety-eight.

Natalie voiceover: A ninety-eight. That means that of the thirty-five hundred gene pairs that score compatibility, ninety-eight percent of them were found to be ideally compatible.

Natalie: River, as the lead scientist, what was your initial reaction?

River: Disbelief. We did a blood test to confirm.

Natalie: And?

River: Ninety-eight.

Natalie: So, biologically, the two of you are compatible in almost every way? What's that like?

Jessica: It's . . . hard to describe.

Natalie: Is there attraction?

River: [laughs] There's definitely attraction.

Natalie voiceover: Attraction may be putting it mildly. Off-camera, crew members commented that it felt like there was something palpable between the pair.

Natalie: So, what comes next for you two? Are you dating?

Jessica: Let's just say . . . we're enjoying getting to know each other.

River: [laughs] What she said.

/Cut to hosts/

Savannah Guthrie: Is it hot in here or is it just me?

Natalie: I was just going to say! I'm sweating.

Savannah: GeneticAlly is set to launch widely in May. I have to admit, I think this could change the entire face of the e-dating industry.

Natalie: Without a doubt.

TWENTY

T HE DAY HAD been so chaotic that it didn't occur to Jess to be
anxious about dinner with River's sisters until the two of them
were literally walking into the restaurant. But just outside the arched
glass doors, her feet became glued to the pavement and she took a
few steps away, pressing herself to the side of the building.

"Oh, shit." Leaning back, Jess stared up at the sky, incandes-
cent blue in twilight. Today had been fine—better than fine, it went
perfectly—so why was she freaking out?

River kept walking, looking back only when he noticed she was
no longer next to him. He returned to her. "Everything okay?"

"I'm meeting your family."

He smiled patiently and tucked a hand into the pocket of his
perfectly tailored pants. Perfect pants, perfect shirt, perfect face.
Perfectly at ease waiting for her panic to subside.

People passed on the sidewalk, and cars inched along Fifth,
turning down G Street. "I've never done this before," Jess con-
fessed. A hot flush crawled up her neck. "Like, met someone's

family. Alec and I were together while we were both at school, and his family was from Florida. I never met them."

River's eyes searched her face, lashes brushing his cheeks with every amused blink. Finally, he crowded into her space, hands on her waist. "I promise this will be much more painful for me than for you."

"It's easy to say that now, when your awkward years are behind you." She pointed to her forehead. "Don't you see my stress pimple?"

"Nope, sorry, I only see pretty." He leaned in, settled his mouth on hers for a sweet kiss. "You three are going to have fun at my expense, and then we'll go back to my place and maybe actually make it to my bed this time."

"Sir, are you bribing me with mind-bending sex?"

He laughed, his gaze glimmering in the dim light. The longer she stared, the more reassured she was. He communicated so much with those eyes. Reassurance, sure, but also attraction, mirth, and something else—something that looked a lot like adoration.

"I like you a lot, Jessica Marie," he said quietly.

A fist wrapped around her heart. "I like you, too."

"And if it makes you feel better," he said, "I've never introduced a girlfriend to my family, either." River reached down, threaded their fingers together, and led her inside.

The restaurant was wide open and glaringly loud, pop music pumping out of speakers and the sounds of laughter and conversation throbbing from the walls. With high ceilings and a bar in the center of the room, the decor was eclectic and trendy. Couches and armchairs formed a funky mix of seating configurations, and lights fashioned from glass globes, vases, and mason jars swung from the ceiling by thick, bristly rope. A waifish hostess led them across planked wooden floors to a table situated beneath a giant metal print emblazoned *EAT*.

Two women sitting side by side glanced up from their cocktails as Jess and River approached. The resemblance was undeniable. One had long dark hair, the ends cut blunt, bangs razor-straight and smooth as gloss under the bright lights. The other was a few years younger, with curly hair that'd been highlighted with a coppery red. Both women shared River's golden-brown eyes, perfect olive skin, and heart-shaped mouth. The Peña family genes were a wonder.

Shouting over each other, they stood, wrapping River in a tight group hug before pulling back to fuss at him simultaneously.

"Your hair is so long!"

"I'm telling Mom, you're so skinny. Your pants look like trash bags!"

Jess followed their attention to his expensive charcoal trousers, ironed to smooth perfection. They . . . did not look like trash bags, but Jess appreciated the sisterly ribbing anyway. Clearly the entire family could step into and out of the pages of a fashion magazine comfortably.

River managed to extract himself, reaching up to smooth his ruffled hair. He had lipstick on each cheek—which both women tried to smudge away.

"Jess, these are my obnoxious sisters, Natalia and Pilar. Please don't believe anything they tell you."

The older one—Natalia—wrapped Jess in a tight hug. "Holy

crap, you are so pretty." She turned to her sister. "Isn't she so pretty?"

"Way too pretty for him," Pilar said, pulling Jess in for a hug of her own.

"It's nice to meet you. River's told me so much about you."

Natalia glanced warily at her brother. "I'm sure he has."

They sat down, ordered cocktails for Jess and River and a few appetizers to share. Jess learned that their mom was a pharmacist, and their dad sold insurance. Natalia was married and a research analyst in Palo Alto; Pilar had recently gone back to school to be a nurse and lived with her girlfriend in Oakland. It was clear they adored their brother. But as River had promised, they loved giving him shit.

"So." Natalia rested her chin in her hand. "I hear you two didn't exactly get along before all this."

Jess glanced at River, passing this one off to him. But then questions of her own bubbled to the surface. Did they know about the money? How honest was she supposed to be here?

River eyed Natalia across the table. "My not-so-subtle sister is trying to ask if I was the asshole."

They both grinned, and Jess perked up. "Oh, he definitely was."

"*Hey*," he said. "I wasn't that bad."

Jess turned in her seat to face him. "You called me 'entirely average.'"

Pilar let out a low whistle. "Child, are you blind?"

"Not to her face!" he corrected, and turned back to Jess. "And in my defense, the first time you spoke to me, you—"

"Don't do it," Pilar whispered, laughing. "Trust me."

"—were wearing an old baggy sweatshirt."

They all stared blankly at him. River finally exhaled. "I was the asshole."

Pilar lifted her chin. "Jess, can I tell you an important family secret?"

"If I left here without any, I would be devastated."

She laughed. "I get that my brother looks like this now, but that wasn't always true. Nitpicking other people's clothing choices would have been the least of his worries."

"He said it," Jess said, "but I find it hard to believe."

Pilar bent, scrolling through her phone, quickly locating what she wanted . . . almost as if she'd put it there for easy access. Jess stared when Pilar turned the screen to face her. "Stop it." She looked at River and then back at the photo. "That isn't you."

A scrawny kid with a bowl haircut and headgear looked out from Pilar's phone. Searching for any resemblance to her boyfriend, she stared at it long enough for River to laughingly shove the phone away.

"Until he was twenty-one, he had no game to speak of," Pilar said.

River laughed. "It's true. But I managed."

"Yeah, you did," Natalia said. "I remember in high school there was this football player who was constantly bothering him. Anthony something. River tutored half the class to bring up the curve. Anthony failed and was kicked off the team."

"That's called problem solving," River mumbled into his glass.

"He did the same thing when I ran against Nikki Ruthers for student council," Pilar said. "He offered group tutoring sessions to everyone who voted for me. I won by a landslide."

River thoughtfully selected a piece of prosciutto-wrapped grilled endive from a plate. "Longest summer of my life."

"Okay, that's actually really sweet," Jess said, taking his hand under the table and giving it a little squeeze.

"I know it's hard to imagine with his grumbly exterior, but he was the softest little boy." Natalia put her hand on Pilar's arm. "Do you remember the way he followed Abuela around?"

Pilar's face crumpled into a dramatic tender sob. "And watched her stories with her!"

"Oh man, I did not anticipate this one coming up," River said.

"I'm two years older than River," Natalia told Jess, "and Pilar is a year older than me, so he was like our baby, too. Our parents both worked full-time, and back then there's no way they could have afforded summer camp for all three kids, so our summers were spent with Abuela. River was her little helper, and every afternoon they would sit together and watch soap operas."

River examined the appetizers like they were data sets.

"Closet soap opera fan?" Jess said. "We all have a secret identity, but this? It would be easier to believe you were an assassin."

"They're just being dramatic," he said, and then laughed at her, murmuring, "Assassin? Really?"

"Don't listen to him, Jess," Natalia said. "He watched so many of them and got in deep. I thought he'd grow up to be a telenovela star or something, but the whole DNA-love thing makes sense when you think about it."

Jess turned to look at him and found him watching her with such tender amusement it was almost like he'd just wrapped his arms around her right at the table.

"The DNA-love thing does make sense when you think about it," she agreed quietly.

THEIR HANDS ENTWINED on the drive to his place, both resting on his thigh, and the Audi's seat warmers made Jess feel like she was melting into a pile of happy goo.

"That was fun," she mumbled, full of fantastic food and just past tipsy from all the wine.

"Natalia texted me already that they both adored you and if I mess this up, they'll neuter me."

Jess grimaced. "Please don't mess it up. You have such a big, beautiful—"

River turned and smirked at her.

"Personality," she finished, grinning back. "And being neutered would be kind of a downer."

"I'm glad you have such a fondness for my personality," he said, turning his attention forward again.

"A soft spot, one might even say," she joked.

He looked at her again, playfully scandalized. "How much wine did you have, woman?"

"The perfect amount."

They'd stayed at the restaurant too late, eating and drinking, and laughing harder than Jess had in years. She'd been comfortable with his sisters almost the way she was with Fizzy; the way they spoke over each other and didn't take themselves too seriously had felt like sitting down to dinner with old friends, rather than people she was meeting for the first time. And right now, contentment flowed, warm and honeyed, through her. Nana Jo was going to be okay; Juno was thriving. Fizzy was falling for someone, and for the first time in her life Jess had money and a sense of security, and a person of her own. She turned and stared at the side of River's face.

"I like you."

"I like you, too." He squeezed her hand. "Very, very much."

Was this what joy felt like? Safety?

She nodded toward his house as they neared. "Are we gonna get freaky?"

"Without a doubt." He laughed, pulling into his driveway and leaning over to kiss her after he put the car in park.

Inside, River turned on a lamp in the spacious living room, turned another light on in the kitchen, and excused himself to get them each a glass of water. Jess texted Naomi's mom to check in on her kid, pleasantly surprised to hear that Juno was having the time of her life.

Setting her phone down, she turned around on the couch to watch River as he futzed in the kitchen. "I don't know what to do with myself," she said. "Nobody needs me right now."

River came back with two glasses, set them on the side table, and then crawled over her on the couch. His mouth moved from her neck up to her lips. "I do."

And then he pulled back and smiled, like maybe he was just

teasing, but Jess saw the sincerity in his expression. Her own fondness rose to the surface, the quiet thrumming of infatuation.

She was starting to need him, too.

Her phone was trapped beneath her back, and she reached for it, tossing it to the floor. Tracking it with his eyes, River asked, "How's Juno doing?"

"Good. Naomi's mom says they're watching a movie out by the pool."

"Things are good with her friends, then?"

Jess lifted a shoulder. "Some days one of them is mean or mad or tired and it creates a little drama tornado that takes a week to get over. I'm learning it's best if the moms stay out of it. Kids argue. Sometimes it hits our own buttons, and we make it into more than it needs to be."

He hummed at this, braced over her on his elbows and playing with the ends of her hair. It was still curled from the interview that morning, and he absently looped a strand around his finger. "I bet it's hard to not get overprotective sometimes. I felt that way when she talked about it on the drive to ballet, and I'm only just getting to know her."

Jess stretched up, kissing him for that. And then she remembered something. "I can't get over the idea of you being obsessed with soap operas. No wonder you and Fizzy get along."

He buried his face in her neck. "I hadn't thought about that in a long time. Sisters never forget."

"When did you go from telenovelas to intense geneticist?"

"My grandmother died when I was fourteen," he said, pushing

up to sit and pulling her legs over his lap. "She moved in with us for the last seven or so years of her life, and she was absolutely the happiest aspect of my childhood. My parents didn't get along great, and without her there as a buffer, that resentment bled into everything."

Jess frowned, reaching forward to pull one of his hands into hers.

"Also, they're not very . . . warm people by nature, so it got really quiet when Abuela died. Dad was never a fan of me sitting with her, watching the shows. He didn't get it—and when I tried to watch them after she died, sort of as a way to stay connected to her, he was not having it. He wanted me to get my head out of the clouds and think about a future that could support a family."

"My mother, Jamie, is the same, sort of." Jess smiled sardonically. "But her version was to always remind me what men want and look for. Suggesting my time was better spent finding a way to be taken care of, rather than learning how to do shit on my own."

It was his turn to frown sympathetically. "I'd always been good in school," he said, "so I just . . . got better. Science came naturally to me."

"Had it occurred to you before Natalia said it tonight that what you're doing now is—in a roundabout way—sort of connected to all that? I bet your abuela would *love* it."

"It didn't, but I think it's true. Think about how many love stories we'll build."

Jess tilted her head and stared at him. She couldn't believe she got to be naked with this man.

He did a self-conscious double take. "What?"

"You're really hot, you know that?" Jess said. "And sort of wonderful. I think I'm even more into you now than I was earlier today."

The corner of his mouth turned up. "How is that possible? I thought I had you on lock already."

Jess stretched out on the couch, grinning up at him and slowly peeling her shirt off. "Didn't someone say something about getting freaky in here?"

TWENTY-ONE

———————/———————

J ESS AND JUNO were about a block away from school one morning when Juno stopped and asked, "*Now* is River Nicolas your boyfriend?"

"What made you think of that on the way to school?" Jess deflected.

"Just wondering if you're going to see him this morning."

She carefully considered this statement; her kid was fishing. "I'll probably see him at Twiggs later."

"Oh." Juno slanted her eyes up to her. "I thought I saw his stuff at home."

Jess's neck heated, her mind starting to race. The last week, River had come over every morning for an hour or so after school drop-off and before they both started work for the day—it was their only time totally alone—but Jess'd had no idea that he'd been leaving evidence behind. She guessed in the haze of sex on the floor, on the bed, in the shower, bent over the dresser, and once on the kitchen island, even a hyperorganized scientist was prone to forget something.

"Huh," she said, stalling.

"Yesterday," Juno said casually, her eyes straight ahead, "he left some shorts."

"Oh." Jess scrambled to come up with a suitable explanation, but the image of River suffering his way through a workday without underwear made her cough out a tiny laugh. "He probably used our place to change after, um, going for a run?"

Juno nodded at this and kicked a stick into the street. "Yeah, probably."

They stopped at the border of school property, and Jess turned to face her daughter, needing to see her eyes when she asked, "How would you feel about it if we were dating each other?"

"I would like it," Juno said absently, and her eyes veered to the side as she started scanning the playground for her friends.

Jess guided her chin so Juno was looking at her again. "Are you sure? Because it means sometimes he'll be with us, doing things."

Her daughter's eyes glazed over. "I know."

"But you are still the most important thing in the world to me."

Juno's attention started to drift to the side again. "I know."

God, it was not the time or the place to be having this conversation.

"Juno," Jess said with gentle authority. "Look at me."

Her eyes cleared. "What?"

"It's important to me that you hear this," Jess said. "You asked about River, so I want to say this now. You are my family. It's you and me, and nobody can change that, do you understand?"

Juno nodded. "I know, Mama. I like River. And I know you love me."

From a few yards away, Naomi and Krista called out Juno's name. She tensed in excitement, bouncing on her feet, but obediently kept her gaze on her mother, waiting for the release of the goodbye kiss.

Jess pressed it to her forehead. "I do love you, Juno Merriam."

"I love you, too, Jessica *Nicolas!*" With a delighted giggle, she tore off toward her friends.

RIVER'S HAIR WAS a tangled mess from Jess's fingers as he kissed his way back up her body, and his expression quickly turned cocky at the view of her rag doll prostration on the bed.

"That was inspired," she mumbled.

He kissed her once, breathless and smiling, and then fell to the side in his own exhausted puddle. "Good."

Jess rolled over, half sprawling across his chest, and grinned up at him. "How was going commando at work yesterday?"

Letting out a laugh-groan, he reached with his free arm and wiped a hand down his face. "You'd think I would notice the lack of boxers sometime before leaving for work."

"Sex drunk."

Humming, he smiled into a kiss, and then went completely still as realization dawned. "Shit. We had sex in the kitchen yesterday." He squinted apologetically down at her. "Juno found them, didn't she?"

Jess waved this off. "She thought they were shorts."

He winced, face grim. "I'm sorry, Jess."

"No, it's good." She rested her chin on her fist, gazing up at him. "I did tell her we're together, though. I hope that's okay."

River bit back a smile. "Of course it is."

"Honestly, I'm amazed her friends at school didn't ask about the *U-T* article. Or the *Today* show, for that matter."

"Was she okay with us?"

She stretched to kiss him, because that was the perfect first question. "I think she's thrilled, River Nicolas." Returning to her perch on his chest, she added, "I don't want her to worry that things are going to change too fast."

He dragged long, lazy fingers through her hair and gazed unfocused at her face.

"I'd ask you what you're thinking," she said, "but I bet the answer is, like, RNA editing or restriction enzymes."

"Actually, wiseass, I was thinking how beautiful you are."

An important circuit shorted out in her brain; she had no idea how to respond articulately while elation simmered in her veins. "Oh. So . . . *not* RNA editing."

River smiled, curling to kiss her. "No." He settled back on the pillow. "I was thinking how happy I am."

Her blood cells stood up, gave a roaring standing ovation. "Just like your fancy machine predicted."

"I haven't felt this way before," he said, ignoring her joking. "Is it too soon to say that?"

Jess grew short of breath. "Of course not."

"I haven't been home in years, but I feel that way with you."

She bent and pressed her face to his chest, squeezing her eyes closed and trying not to hyperventilate.

"You okay?"

"Just trying not to freak out," she said, and quickly added, "Good freak out. Deeply infatuated freak out."

"That's a good freak ou— Oh." When she looked up in response to his tone, an uneasy smile spread across his mouth and he pushed back into the pillow to be able to see her better. "I meant to tell you this as soon as I got here, but—"

"But I was waiting for you naked?" she interrupted with a grin.

"Yes, exactly." He laughed. "We have people coming into the offices on Monday."

". . . Okay?"

He gazed at her, and then laughed at her misunderstanding. "We have *People* magazine coming into the offices on Monday. They're meeting with us in the morning, I guess," he said, gesturing to include her, "and then David, Brandon, Lisa, and I will have an interview in the afternoon. So, unless you and Fizzy are going to re-move every copy in the grocery store, it's probably good Juno found out today."

AFTER A TRY Something New Sunday—River joined all four Davises at the zoo, and holding his hand in public was the novelty—Monday came along, and she didn't even wake up in a panic. She was getting used to all these high-pressure situations—interviews, parties, photo sessions—though no doubt it helped that her relationship with River felt like a cornet-blaring, red-carpet-unfurling, fireworks-over-the-ocean, first of its kind in all of history.

It helped, too, that he slept in her bed Sunday night. In life, River was restrained and cautious. As a lover, he was expressive and generous. And in sleep, he was a cuddler: pressed up against her all night, her long, big spoon.

At six, his alarm went off and he jerked awake like he'd been hoisted by strings, sleepily tugging on clothes—double-checking that he had on *all* of his clothes—kissing her, and silently sneaking out before Juno was awake.

Half an hour later, he was at their door "surprising" Jess and Juno with coffee and hot chocolate.

Juno shuffled out of her bedroom, and the three of them sat down at the dining table for breakfast. River pulled out some papers to review; his foot came over Jess's, reminding her that not even an hour ago he was beside her, in her bed. She tried not to let the thought unspool, imagining the three of them sitting there in easy silence every morning for the rest of their lives.

Juno poked sleepily at her cereal. "Why did you leave so early to get coffee? Mama has a coffee machine in the kitchen."

River and Jess went completely still. Finally, he managed a deeply unconvincing "Huh, does she?"

They followed the path of Juno's pointed finger to the counter, and River let out a murmured "Oh, I didn't know that. Thank you."

He looked at Jess over the top of Juno's head and winced for help. Jess had to bite her lips to keep from losing it.

They walked Juno to school together, bracketing her, each

holding one of her hands. She crab-walked; they swung her. "You need to be taller, Mom," Juno said. "River Nicolas can swing me way higher."

He looked over at her, gloating.

And all of it felt like the tip-top of the roller coaster, the feeling of anticipation before the thrill of the drop.

So obviously, Jess was terrified.

WHICH WAS OKAY, because there was plenty to distract her from those enormous, scary feelings. When they arrived at the Genetic-Ally offices—the parking lot more crowded than Jess had ever seen it—everything exploded into motion and excitement. Lisa greeted them at the curb, firing information off about the schedule as soon as they climbed out of the car. Jess and River were up first for two hours, then the reporter, Aneesha, would take River to meet with David, Lisa, and Brandon over near the Salk. Before she'd even had a chance to put her purse down, Jess was being ushered into Lisa's office, where a makeup artist and hairstylist got right to work.

"You look like you've been carried here upside down," Aneesha said, laughing. She was a gorgeous Black woman with glowing skin and the most perfect crab-apple cheekbones Jess had seen in her entire life. "Totally shell-shocked."

Jess laughed as the makeup artist worked around her. "I am not—to put it mildly—*accustomed* to this treatment."

Over the next twenty minutes, Jess learned that Aneesha Sampson had interviewed Brad Pitt last weekend, had an irrepressible laugh, called River "Keanu Banderas," and embraced both plunging necklines *and* shoulder-grazing dangly earrings in her personal style. Jess didn't know if she wanted to propose or propose a life swap.

"We're going to start in the lab, if that works for you," Aneesha said as they all stepped out into the hall. "Just River at first."

Lisa looked a little harried. "Jess, are you okay just hanging out?"

Jess held up her laptop. "I have a ton of work to do. You can put me anywhere."

As Aneesha headed toward the elevator and Lisa bent to reply to a text on her phone, River leaned in, kissing Jess. "Okay. I'll see you in a bit. I love you."

White noise roared in her ears and her eyes went wide. "What?"

River stared down at her, his expression slack with shock. But he didn't take it back. He just . . . started laughing. He nodded sideways to Lisa, saying quietly, "Not the place I'd planned to say it, but hallways and audiences do seem to be our thing."

Lisa turned to take a call, and Jess broke into a grin, throwing her arms around his neck. She planted a dozen tiny kisses all over his face. "I love you, too."

The truth of it was so obvious; Jess didn't know how they hadn't been saying *I love you* from that very first day.

With his smile straightening and a bright heat flashing like lightning in his eyes, he moved his lips to her cheek, and over to her ear. "I'll see you in a few."

"River, they're ready for you." Lisa waved him down the hall.

With one final peck, he disappeared into the elevator and Lisa returned. "Jess, I'd put you in River's office, but they're setting up for some stills." Hooking her thumb to the office directly behind her, Lisa said, "Let's just put you in David's for now. He won't mind."

Jess lifted her laptop. "I'm cool anywhere."

Lisa tried the door, then pulled out her keys and unlocked it, immediately wincing as she turned back to Jess. "This okay? I forgot how messy he is. I never go in here."

And . . . *wow*. David's office was the upside-down version of River's. Where River's desk was bare but for his computer, David's had the look of a desk found in the rubble post-hurricane. It was covered with printed-out data sheets, empty paper cups, wadded-up napkins, Post-its, and stacks of journal articles. His shelves were lined with a dusty and disorganized array of convention freebies: a Merck-branded stress ball, a Sanofi travel mug, a plastic DNA molecule from Genentech, a pile of branded pens.

But listen. River Nicolas Peña had just told her he loved her. Lisa could drop Jess off on Bourbon Street early on a Saturday morning and she'd be fine. "This is great."

"We'll come grab you when Aneesha is ready." Lisa grinned before ducking out, closing the door behind her.

Staring at David's desk, Jess wondered whether she should use her laptop on her actual lap, before figuring she could just carefully set it on top and not disturb the mayhem. While her computer booted up, Jess glanced around the sciencey detritus. Among the papers were sheets and sheets filled with hundreds of rows of data. An electrical current passed over her. Maybe that was a thread of why she and River were a Diamond Match—they were both deeply enthralled by numbers.

About halfway down a messy pile of papers, a corner of one stuck out. Jess's eye caught on something written in the top left corner, and she carefully pulled free the thick binder-clipped cluster.

Client 144326.

Her blood turned carbonated as she registered what she was seeing. That was her. Jess's data. And beneath her number was another: *Client 000001.*

River.

Below, in bold, was the information they'd heard a thousand times in the past month: *Compatibility quotient: 98.*

She'd never seen their raw scores before, but there was something oddly holy about holding the data in her hands.

Okay. I'll see you in a bit. I love you. His words echoed in her mind.

Smiling, Jess scanned the rows and rows of numbers reverently. The client numbers and compatibility score were in the top left corner, and in the top right was the assay information: date, time, which DNADuo machine had run the assay, et cetera. Below that were about sixty rows of numbers, broken into three groups of columns, each three columns wide. Behind this sheet, there were pages and pages of solid numbers.

Jess got chills realizing she was currently holding the information on the roughly 3,500 genes for which she and River aligned. Was it really possible that their connection—their love—was encoded in their cells? Was she programmed from the day she was born to feel this happy—even when Jamie was leaving her over and over, when girls teased her on the soccer field for her drunk mother on the sidelines, when Alec stared mutely at the pregnancy test for a handful of minutes and finally said, "I've never wanted kids"? Of all the men Jess could connect with, was River her perfect fit all along?

The idea made her both queasy and high. She looked back down, leaning in to focus on each tiny row of information. The first two columns on each set showed what she assumed was the gene information—gene names and GenBank session number. The third columns held raw compatibility scores, with numbers that seemed to range from zero to four. Nearly all of their scores were higher than 2.5. So, somehow these scores came together in the neural network's algorithm, and *ninety-eight* popped out at the end. Clearly, Jess could see now, the data was scientific, but it also felt deeply magical. She was a convert. Show her to the GeneticAltar.

She dragged a finger across the page, wanting to feel the information for herself.

Their most recent assay had been completed on January 30—River'd drawn her blood the night before with such careful formality. They'd been so awkward around each other, so wary. Jess bit back a laugh remembering. Holy shit, she'd had no idea: he'd wanted her even then.

Looking up to confirm David's office door was closed, she quickly took a picture. She knew she shouldn't; it might have even been illegal—besides, she could just ask River for a copy of it anyway. But Jess knew she'd want to look at it again and again. Flipping through, she began snapping photos of every page, rows upon rows upon rows of data. Each one had a few values circled, annotated, called out—she guessed—for being totally fucking awesome.

Maybe she'd frame this for him as a gift at some point.

Maybe they'd each pick their favorite gene and get that value tattooed.

Maybe she was starting to sound like one of Fizzy's heroines right now and should probably shut the hell up.

Grinning like an idiot, Jess flipped to the next page, ready to snap a picture, but stopped. This next set of data was from their first DNADuo assay, the one from her spit kit. In this stack, some cells were circled in pencil and some notes were scribbled in the margins, barely legible. Jess marveled that their data had been pored over like this. Her soaring-soundtrack brain sang that their data might even unlock larger truths about love and emotional connection.

And there was still more. Jess flipped more pages, expecting notes and correspondence, but she found another first page. *A duplicate?* No. It was a different first page—someone else's—from an assay run in 2014.

Client 05954

Client 05955

Compatibility quotient: 93

This must be David's Diamond Match pile, Jess assumed. But her brain tripped over a coincidence in the upper right corner. She flipped between this one and her and River's top sheet, comparing.

The assay dates were different in all three cases, but the assay end time was exactly the same.

Every time.

Jess blinked, tilting gently toward uneasy, flipping back to their first pages to confirm. Yes: for all three assays, the run time ended at 15:45:23.

Her stomach tightened. Statistically, that was . . . deeply un-likely. Out of 86,400 seconds in each twenty-four hours, there was only a 0.0012 percent chance of *two* events landing on the same second. Even if Jess assumed the assays were usually started and finished at roughly the same time—say within the same four-hour window—that was still only a likelihood of 0.007 percent, or a 7 out of 100,000 chance, that Jess and River's assay and another assay completed on a different day would have finished at the *exact same time*. But all three? It was nearly impossible. The chances—Jess closed her eyes to do the math—of three assays randomly end-ing at the same exact second on different days were roughly 1 in 2.5 million.

Jess tried to think logically. She pushed back the roaring in her ears. Maybe the machines were programmed to begin and end at the same time to reduce certain variables? It wouldn't be unheard of.

Except on January 29, River had started the assay almost im-mediately after taking her blood. In fact, he'd double-gloved and rolled up to the fume hood before she'd even left the room. The following morning, he'd texted her, asking for a date, and said the test had been confirmed. But although the date on the printout was right, how was it possible River had the data in the morning if the assay wasn't complete until 3:45 that afternoon? Did he lie to her that he'd gotten the confirmation? That didn't sound like River.

"What the fuck?" Jess exhaled the words, confused. *I have . . . I have to be missing something.*

Her lungs hurt. Her stomach rolled. Her eyes burned from the strain of her intense focus. She couldn't blink. And then—her heart seemed to fill with needles—Jess noticed that all three assays were run on the DNADuo 2. She remembered seeing the two machines the night he ran the blood samples and asking about them.

"Are those the DNADuos?"

"Creatively named DNADuo One and DNADuo Two. DNADuo Two is down right now. Getting serviced next week. It'll be up and running by May, I hope."

A thought crashed into her head. She was frantic now. Flipping through the respective pages on the two data sets, she scanned down the columns on the two pieces of paper. She tried to find differences in the data sets between her and River's ninety-eight, and this other couple's ninety-three.

She couldn't; they were identical. Every value—as far as she could tell—was exactly the same. It all went blurry the harder she stared. It was too many rows. Too many tiny numbers. It would be like looking for a needle in a haystack while her hair and the haystack were both on fire. And, she thought desperately, for scores this high, maybe most of the raw scores *would* be identical? What was she missing?

With dread sinking in her chest, Jess registered that the circled numbers on their first data sheet were circled for a reason. Her gaze slid to a penciled oval on the original spreadsheet from January 19.

Jess brought a shaking hand to her mouth. On her and River's sheet, she saw:

OT-R GeneID 5021 3.5

But on the other couple's:

OT-R GeneID 5021 1.2

Inside another circle on their original sheet—for the gene

PDE4D—Jess and River had a 2.8. Her heart vaulted into her throat. The other couple had a 1.1.

Jess only had the stomach to confirm two more circled values— an AVP of 3.1 on hers and River's, a 2.1 on the other couple's; for DRD4, a 2.9 on theirs, a 1.3 on the other couple's.

As far as Jess could see, the *only* values that were different— maybe only thirty in the entire data set of nearly 3,500—were the ones that had been circled in their first DNADuo. To draw attention to them. If it weren't for the identical time stamp and the DNADuo 2 mystery, Jess could have told herself a lie, that those values were circled because they differentiated her and River from the other assay. But she knew they weren't circled because they were special. They were circled to keep track of which ones had been altered. Someone had, on purpose, changed a compatibility score of ninety-three into a ninety-eight.

Johan and Dotty were our very first Diamond Match, River had said at the cocktail party. *Their granddaughter brought them to us back in 2014, and she was right: they came through with a score of ninety-three.*

She might throw up. With shaking hands, Jess took a picture of every page of the assay she was almost certain belonged to Johan and Dotty Fuchs. She nearly knocked over the pile twice. She was numb as she bent and stowed her laptop. She put her phone away. And then she sat quietly. Waiting for Aneesha to come for her, Jess had no idea how she was going to get through the interview, knowing what she knew now.

River and Jess had never been a Diamond Match.

TWENTY-TWO

———————⌇———————

IN THE PAST twenty minutes, River had asked her four times whether she was okay.

Of course he had; any creature with a pulse could sense that there was something Not Right about her at the moment. But she couldn't talk about it yet, and couldn't talk about it *here* at the office, and even if she could—she wasn't sure she was prepared to hear his answer to the simplest question: *Did you know this whole time?*

So she put on a flimsy blissful mask and answered Aneesha's questions. But River's quiet concern repeatedly reminded Jess that her stress was as clear on her face as a fever. The shock felt like the flu.

They took some photos together outside; they took some in the lab, laughing and gazing adoringly into each other's eyes. But behind her smile, the question rammed into Jess's thoughts like the piercing siren of a police car. Until she knew the answer, she couldn't even let the next question slot into place, though it pressed against the glass anyway: *Is what I feel even real?*

Statistically speaking, she and River were many thousand times more likely to find their soulmate in a Base Match than they were to ever get an authentic Diamond Match, so even if their true score was a twenty-five, it wasn't like they couldn't be right together. But it was so much easier to trust those early, deep reactions when the numbers supported her.

But she was getting ahead of herself, and without information—without data—it was the last thing she could let herself do. Jess mentally crumpled the thoughts into a wadded-up ball of paper and set it on fire. One moment at a time, and now was not the moment for a meltdown.

Aneesha finished up on-site and gave Jess and River time to say goodbye before he had to leave with the *People* team to meet up with David and Brandon. Even thinking of David right then made Jess's stomach sour. And if River knew . . . she didn't know what she would do; her emotions would be too hot and giant and impossible to manage.

The moment they were alone, River pulled Jess into an alcove, bending to look her directly in the eye.

"I feel like I'm missing something," he said quietly. "Are you mad at me?"

This one she could actually field. *Are you okay?* had been too big to answer under her breath with Aneesha and her photographer ten feet away.

"I'm not mad at you. But can we get together later?"

He laughed, confused. "Of course. I assumed we'd—"

"Just us."

The smile evaporated, and a frown lined his forehead. River took a step closer, sliding a hand down her arm and linking his warm fingers with her cold ones. "Have I done something wrong?"

Jess hated to say "I don't know," but it was true.

"Something happened," she admitted, "and I need to ask you about it, but now isn't the time." She swallowed. "I know it sucks, and I'm sure you're going to be worrying about this until we can talk about it."

"Uh, yeah."

"I will, too. You just have to trust me that we can't do it here, and we need more than the ten minutes we have before you and Aneesha have to go."

River gazed down at her and seemed to decide this was the best he was going to get right then. "Okay. I trust you." He pulled her into his chest. There was honestly nothing Jess wanted more than to be able to confidently put her arms around his waist and lose herself in the clean citrus smell of him. But her joints were locked, posture stiff. "We'll talk later?" he asked, pulling back to look at her, cupping her elbows.

"Yeah." Her phone buzzed in her back pocket and she retrieved it, expecting notification of some work email, or a text from Pops about dinner plans.

But it was from Fizzy, and worry immediately pushed all of the tightness in Jess's chest up into her throat.

I need you ASAP.
Best friend bat signal.

"Sorry," Jess whispered. "It's Fizzy. She . . ."

Jess quickly replied:

> Are you ok?

> I am safe and not injured.
> But no. I'm not ok.

Heart pounding, Jess looked up at River. She didn't like leaving things like this, but she was going to have to. "I really need to go."

His voice was a low blend of exasperated and worried, and he reached for her arm. "*Jess*—"

"She needs me. Fizzy never needs me. Call me when you're all done?"

He nodded and took a step back, letting her go.

Turning away, Jess typed as she walked:

> Where are you?

> My place. Are you coming?

> Yes. Be there in 20.

FIZZY'S FRONT DOOR was open; the interior of the house was shaded behind the screen door. Jess didn't hear sobbing or screaming—which was reassuring—but Bon Iver played quietly from the living room speakers. For someone like Fizzy, whose general mood leaned more upbeat bop than quiet ballad, Bon Iver gave Jess a legitimate reason to worry.

And like that, River was put aside for later. Jess had a great deal of experience compartmentalizing. Jamie had shown up at Jess's high school graduation toward the end of a four-day-long meth bender and stalked the aisles looking for her among the sea of classmates. About thirty seconds after she loudly climbed over Jerome Damiano and Alexa Davidson to get to her daughter, Jamie was escorted out by the campus security guard. Even so, Jess stood and made her way to the front of the auditorium when her name was called.

And, Jess remembered, she and Alec broke up about an hour before she presented her thesis to the entire mathematics department, when she was six months pregnant with Juno. She'd shoved all of her anger and disappointment aside, gone into the presentation with an enormous smile and beautifully designed slides, and gotten an A.

One look at Fizzy curled up in a ball on her couch, eyes red-rimmed, hair in an uncharacteristically messy bun, and a familiar wall slid into place.

She sat down, pulling one of Fizzy's bare feet into her lap. "Tell me."

Reaching up to wipe her nose, Fizzy said simply, "He's married."

"Who's married?"

Fizzy turned her watery dark eyes up to Jess's face. "*Rob*."

"*Banker* Rob?"

"Yeah."

"Married? To a person?"

"Yeah."

Jess stared at her, disbelieving. "Wasn't he Daniel's brother's friend? How did no one say anything to you?"

"Apparently he's, like, a friend of a friend of a friend, and Rob got married sometime in the past two years, when they hadn't been hanging out as much."

"What a—a *garbage human*." Jess's jaw hung open. "How did you find out?"

"He found me at Twiggs and told me."

"He told you in public?"

Fizzy nodded, grim. "He sat in your chair."

She gasped. "How dare he!"

"I know."

"So what did you do?"

Fizzy took a deep, fortifying breath. "I got up, asked Daniel for a pitcher of ice water, and dumped it in Rob's lap."

"*Applause*," Jess whispered, impressed.

"I think he started to freak out that he was going to get caught. One night in Little Italy we ran into someone he knew, and he introduced me to the guy as his 'friend Felicity,' which at the time, I was like—'That's fair, we're pretty new still,' but now I know why." Fizzy's face crumpled. "I really liked him, Jess, and you know me," she said, hiccupping, "I never like anyone. I cooked for him, and talked about books with him, and we had inside jokes—and he's fucking married. And I swear he wanted credit for coming clean with me. Like, he was genuinely shocked that I was so pissed." She wiped her nose again.

"Come here." Jess shifted Fizz's foot away and pulled the whole Fizzy into her arms, squeezing tight while her friend cried.

"You know the crazy thing?" Fizzy asked, her voice muffled by Jess's shirt.

"What?"

"We just sent in his spit samples."

"To GeneticAlly?" Jess asked, and Fizzy nodded. "I thought you weren't going to do that."

Fizzy wailed. "We weren't!"

"God," Jess said, "what a dumbass. What was he expecting to happen?"

"Right?" Her best friend laughed through a sob. "And now, what if I find out that we're, like, perfect for each other, and it doesn't matter because he's married? I don't want to know if we're supposed to be together!"

The feelings from the other room peeked around Jess's neat little compartmentalized corner, asking if it was time to come out yet. Jess shook her head. It was not.

"Well, logistically, you can request that his account never be linked to yours so you never have to know, but I'm fairly sure that he doesn't belong anywhere near your perfect, kind, sassy ass, anyway. Anyone who would do something like that is rotten from the inside. I bet his DNA looks like black bathroom mold."

"Like long strings of mucus," Fizzy agreed.

"I could keep this metaphor going, but it's only going to get grosser." Jess squeezed her again. "I'm sorry, cutie. I want to know where he lives so I can go shove his head up his ass so far he can lick his own ear."

"His wife would be there," Fizzy said quietly. "I guess that's why we never went to his place."

"Garbage human," Jess whispered angrily.

Fizzy wiped her nose on Jess's shirt before pulling back and inspecting it. Suspicion straightened her frown as her attention moved up Jess's neck to her face and hair. She sniffled. "Why are you all dressed up?"

"We did *People* today at the offices."

The watery, puffy version of her best friend groaned, falling dramatically back on the throw pillows. "I sent the bat signal when you were with *People* magazine, oh my God." After a thoughtful beat, she sat up and threw her arms around Jess again. "And you came!"

"It would be in my best interest to take these golden friend points and not tell you that we'd already finished when I got your text," Jess said. "But the lying would negate the golden friend points. And I swear I would have come anyway."

"But you could be off having celebratory sex with your soulmate, and I could have just used wine and cheese for emotional support."

Soulmate.

Jess shot a warning look at the feelings now plotting their escape. "I would always rather you lean on me than on wine and cheese." She paused before adding, "And River isn't done with the interview."

"I'm honored to be your second choice."

"Third," Jess reminded her.

Fizzy leaned back and laughed. "You suck."

"Maybe, but I love you."

"I love you, too." She glanced at the clock on the wall. "Speaking of, do you need to pick up your first choice from school?"

"It's Monday," Jess said. "Pops'll get her, and they'll do the library thing. I have three hours to do whatever I can to make you feel better."

FIZZY AND JESS lounged on the couch with *Sense and Sensibility* playing quietly alongside their cheese-and-cracker feast. Eventually, Jess gave her one last squeeze, headed home, and got Juno fed, bathed, snuggled, and tucked in—and then got a full glass of wine in herself—before she opened the proverbial floodgates.

But then they were open, and thoughts of River drowned out everything else. The upside to pushing it all behind a wall was that she'd been able to function pretty normally all day; the downside was that she wasn't at all mentally prepared for the conversation awaiting her.

There was no use putting it off. Jess pulled out her phone, texting him.

> Can you come over?

He answered immediately, almost like he'd been waiting with his phone in his hand:

> Yes. Now?

> Now is good.

She hit Send and then immediately replied again.

> Wait.

She typed as fast as she could because she knew the *Wait* had probably sent him panic-spiraling.

> This may sound strange, but did you ever see our raw data?

> Of course.

Jess chewed her thumbnail as she considered how to phrase what she wanted to say next without giving him time to prepare an excuse if he had been in on the data fabrication all along. She wanted to be able to read the truth on his face. On the other hand, if he had a copy of the data at home, she wanted him to bring it.

Luckily, River saved her the trouble of phrasing the question.

> I have the plot here.
> Want me to bring it over?

Jess exhaled a slow, hot stream of tension.

> That would be great.

> I should have offered that ages ago. I'm sorry. Is that what this is about?

She chose not to answer this.

> Are you leaving now?

Yes.

HE LIVED ONLY ten minutes away, but River was at her door in eight. Before, if he'd shown up at her apartment after Juno was asleep, Jess would have been in his arms immediately. But tonight, they both seemed to know that affection was on hold.

Wordlessly, he stepped inside, breathless from what Jess could only guess was a jog from his car. "Hey."

She swallowed back a sob that seemed to rise out of nowhere. "Hey. How was the rest of the interview?"

He nodded, wiping a hand over his forehead, still catching his breath. "Good. Yeah, I think it was good. Is Fizzy okay?"

Shaking her head, Jess walked over to the dining table and sat down, shoulders slumped. "Rob is married."

River slowly removed his messenger bag from his shoulder, setting it down on the table. "You're kidding."

"No. And I guess they just sent in his DNADuo kit."

River winced. "Shit."

And then they fell quiet. The proverbial elephant was standing directly on top of them. With a mumbled "Well . . ." River pulled out a sheet of paper from his bag and handed it to her. It was well-loved, wrinkled and worn, like it'd been picked up and put down again and again, studied a thousand times.

"Our data." He reached up, wiping his forehead again. "Are you going to tell me what's going on?"

The colorful scatter plot was printed in a landscape view and took up the entire page. A masterful display of computational skill, and a statistician's best friend: principal component analysis. After only a handful of seconds, Jess could tell it captured every data point she saw on the tables in David's office.

The plot had two axes: The vertical Y-axis was labeled zero to four—the composite scores Jess was already familiar with. The horizontal X-axis had twelve different labels. She assumed they represented the categories of the gene families included in the DNADuo: Neuroendocrine, Immunoglobulin, Metabolic, Signal Transduction, MHC Class I/II, Olfactory, Regulatory Proteins, Transporters, Heat-Shock, SNARE, Ion Channel, and FGF/FGFR. And on the graph itself, there were thousands of tiny dots, seemingly one for each of their scores on each individual gene, color-coded and clustered by category.

It was a much easier way to look at the raw scores—Jess could immediately see trends here that she couldn't in the table—but because there was so much data, it was clear to her that if this was all River had seen, it would have been almost impossible to decipher that it was nearly identical to a plot he'd seen years ago.

And, most importantly, the information that tipped her off—the run end time, the date, the DNADuo machine—wasn't included in this plot. This graph only had client numbers, the compatibility score, and, in the lower right corner in tiny print, the date this plot was generated.

Maybe River didn't know. Hope was a weak light shining on the darkness of her mood. As casually as possible, Jess asked, "Is this the way you always look at the data?"

He laughed quietly. "I'm sure for a mathematician, it's maddening to not look at actual numbers, but we've come to rely on these scatter plots. It's easier to see outliers this way and to know if we need to rerun the assay for any reason." He leaned in, pointing to a large cluster of dots in their plot. "See, you can tell that we are particularly well aligned in metabolic genes and immunoglobulin. And our lowest scores seem to be for regulatory proteins, but that's not a very meaningful conclusion because even those scores are all pretty high. Once you get a score above eighty, most of the plots look similar."

She swallowed back a relieved gasp. It confirmed that it might not immediately jump out to him that the data had been manipulated. "How do you generate these?"

"This actually *is* the raw data. Everything in a table is shown here. Tiffany just worked with the Caltech guys to have the neural network create this plot for us as a team because it's way easier to look at. But we can generate one of these for any couple who matches."

"So Fizzy would have a million of these," she said.

He laughed again. "I mean, in theory. We don't upload these to the apps or even routinely generate them anymore unless requested because the files are huge, but sure, you could theoretically create scatter plots like this comparing you to every other individual in the world. That just wouldn't be very useful." He met her eyes, almost shyly. "But of course we did one for our assay. I wanted to look at it really closely. At first because I was skeptical, and then because it was sort of amazing."

Tears filled her eyes, and she bent to rest her head on the table. Relief washed over her like an analgesic, a paralytic. Jess's head felt so heavy, and before she could stop it, a sob ripped from her throat.

"Holy— Jess." River leaned over, pulling her into his arms. "Sweetheart, what's wrong?"

He'd never called her "sweetheart" before, and it only made her cry harder. She was relieved that he hadn't been lying to her this whole time. But now she had to tell him that they weren't a ninety-eight. She was in love with him—and Jess hated how much this was going to hurt him. His trust in David was going to be irreparably damaged. Until she'd come along, GeneticAlly had been River's entire life.

"I hate what I'm about to tell you."

He went still around her. "What is it? Just say it."

She moved away from him, standing and going to the kitchen to retrieve the photos she'd printed earlier. Her hands shook as she handed them over.

River seemed familiar enough with the tables to immediately know what he was holding. "Where did you get these?"

"David's office," Jess admitted. "Be mad at me after you look at them. They were on his desk when Lisa put me in there to wait for my part of the interview. It wasn't my intention to snoop, but when I saw our client numbers, I got really excited. Like you said, it's sort of amazing to look at it and know it's how we started." She bit her lip. "And then there were some things about it that were strange to me."

He frowned, looking down, not seeing it yet. "Like what?"

Jess reached up, wiping her eyes. "Just look at them for a few minutes."

She left him to study, walking into the kitchen to get a glass of water. Ice-cold, it burned a frigid path from her lips to her stomach.

About thirty seconds later, a quiet *"What the fuck?"* came from the dining room.

Jess closed her eyes. Papers rustled with renewed urgency, and the sound of them spreading out on the table was rushed.

"Jess." She could tell from the strain in his voice that his jaw was clenched. "Can you come back here, please?"

Taking a deep breath, she set her glass in the sink and joined him in the dining room. He was standing, arms braced on the table as he bent and stared down.

"Who circled these values?"

"I don't know." She put her arms around his waist from behind and rested her forehead between his shoulder blades. Relieved that he knew, Jess thought they could start to figure this out together. "You okay?"

A dry laugh, and then, "No. What am I seeing? Is this for real?"

"Did you know?" she asked quietly.

His voice came out tight, as if through clenched teeth. "Of course not."

Closing her eyes, Jess squeezed him tighter. But he didn't turn around; in fact, Jess realized he remained completely stiff in her embrace. And for the first time it occurred to her—*how was it only occurring to her now*—that although Jess trusted the magic in statistical anomaly, River might look at their doctored score and see that they were never meant to be.

TWENTY-THREE

———⌐———

AFTER A STUNNED beat, Jess stepped away and let her arms fall to her sides. River didn't seem to notice; his attention was still shifting over the rows of numbers as he went from page to page and back again. Her heart had lodged somewhere in her windpipe.

River let out a low groan and hung his head. "I should have seen it."

"How?" Jess asked, incredulous. "There are thirty-five *hundred* numbers there. At this point, you send this information into the black box and it's simplified so extensively you'd never know if something was off."

"You don't understand," he said, turning around and ducking past her, out into the living room. "The amount of time I spent poring over the Fuchses' data. I should have seen."

"Not even a brain like yours can memorize *thirty-five hundred* numbers from almost a decade ago." Jess moved to put a hand on his arm, but he shrugged away, turning to face the window.

His hands ripped into his hair and he let out a quiet growl. "This is a catastrophe."

Jess stared at his back. He was right. It was a terrible thing to uncover, and David was going to have hell to pay, but wasn't there a touch of serendipity in it, too? It had still brought them together. "I know you have a lot on your mind," she started quietly, "but I want you to know that I love you. This doesn't change that."

He went still, like he was thinking about how to react to this, but then abruptly looked down at his watch. "Shit. David's probably still at the office. I need to head over there right now."

Jess pivoted as quickly as her heart and brain would let her. "Okay. Yes. Good." *A plan.* She reached for her phone, swiping to Favorites and pressing Pops's photo. It was already ringing when she brought it to her ear. "Let me just get Pops to sit with Juno—"

"Jess." He reached for the phone, gently pulling it from her grip. With his eyes on the screen, he ended the call before Pops answered.

"What are you doing? I can't leave without—"

Oh.

River was still staring at her screen, at the photo of four-year-old Juno dressed as an octopus for Halloween. His eyes were glued to the image. Had he looked at Jess once since he saw the data? "I need to talk to him alone."

Jess exhaled a shocked laugh. "You're not serious."

"This is my company, Jess."

"But this situation involves me, too. I have a right to know why he did this."

His shoulders stiffened. "*If* he did this. We don't know that this wasn't an oversight or mistake or, or—some kind of computer glitch. I've known the man forever. I have to give him a chance to explain it, and I need to do it myself."

Jess felt her jaw clench. "You seriously expect me to just cool my heels here, alone?"

He nodded tightly.

"Will you come over later?"

"I'm not sure." River took a deep breath and finally met her eyes. "I'm sorry, I've really got to go, now." He reached for his bag on the table and shoved everything inside before heading for the door. Jess trailed after him, but he couldn't leave fast enough. Mentally, River was already gone.

She stood at the door, watching the burning, familiar sight of someone she loved walk away. "*River.*"

He muttered, "I'll call you," and then disappeared through the dark courtyard.

BUT RIVER DIDN'T call. Jess stayed up until almost three, alternating between watching TV and checking her phone. Finally she fell asleep propped awkwardly against her pillows, waking to find the TV still on and her phone still empty of messages.

She was in a terrible mood by the time the morning routine began.

"Juno, I'm trying to make your lunch. Can you leave the cat alone and get dressed? Now, please."

Juno pouted from where she was crouched on the carpet waving one of Pigeon's toy feathers back and forth. "I don't know what to wear."

"You had clothes out last night. And bring me your dishes, Bug."

"But we have PE today, and I want to wear leggings."

Jess swore her kid had some sort of radar that zeroed in on exactly how short her Mom Fuse was on any given day, and then turned lighting it into an Olympic sport. "So wear leggings."

"I don't know where they are."

"You have at least ten pairs of them."

"I want the black ones with the stars."

"Did you put them in the laundry?" Jess reached for the grapes in the fridge and tucked a bunch into Juno's lunch box. Her phone was facedown on the counter, but she left it untouched. Looking would only make her feel worse.

Juno rolled around on the floor, squealing as the cat began chewing on the ends of her hair. "I think so."

"Then look in the dryer." Jess threw in a cup of applesauce, a bag of carrot sticks, and the last tube of yogurt, making a mental note to go to the store.

"Can you get them for me?" More laughing, more squealing. No getting dressed.

"*Juno!*" Jess yelled. Her voice was so loud it startled even her.

Quietly, Juno pushed herself up and skulked out of the room.

Frantically, Jess wiped down the counter and closed the refrigerator door so hard it bounced back open. Another glance at her watch. Shit. The dryer door slammed and a startled cat bolted down the hall, jumping on the coffee table and knocking over Juno's half-eaten bowl of cereal. Milk and soggy Rice Krispies dripped slowly to the floor.

"How many times do I need to tell you no food in the living room!"

"It was Pigeon's fault!"

"Get dressed!" Her voice seemed to echo through the suddenly silent apartment.

Juno's bottom lip jutted out and she stomped into her room again. Jess dropped onto the couch, exhausted. It was barely eight.

They walked to school in tense silence; Juno was mad, but not nearly as mad as Jess was at herself. She cycled through memories of Jamie having an argument with whatever man she was with at the time and taking it out on Jess or Nana or Pops.

Jess was in a shame spiral by the time they reached the monkey bars.

Needing to fix this, Jess crouched on the grass in front of Juno. "You have your outline for the art fair?"

She nodded but didn't meet Jess's eyes, instead focusing on the playground over her mom's shoulder. Her little forehead was so grumpy.

"And your lunch is in your backpack?"

Another curt nod.

"I'm sorry I yelled this morning. I didn't get enough sleep and woke up in a bad mood. I should have counted to ten."

"Can Pops pick me up after school?"

Betrayal was a sharp knife twisting in her chest. "He'll be with Nana Jo at rehabilitation. I don't have any meetings, so I get to pick you up today."

"Can River Nicolas instead?"

The knife pushed in deeper. It wasn't that Juno wanted someone specific, it was that she specifically didn't want Jess. Jess knew that it was irrational to feel hurt—Juno was mad, and this was what mad kids did—but being a shitty mom this morning was the last thing Jess's heart needed. How could she say that she had no idea where River would be after school? Or next week? Or next year?

If she were Jamie, she would either show up later today with a present two years too young for Jess's interests or call Jess a brat and not show up at all. *I am not my mom.* Jess wrapped her little girl in a hug. "I'll ask him, but either way, I'll be here at pickup," she said. "I love you the mostest."

Juno softened in her arms. "I love you the mostest, too."

FIZZY AND SHE had been sitting at their table at Twiggs for twenty minutes, but Jess had yet to log into her computer.

"Earth to Jess."

She tore her eyes away from the window. "Sorry, what?"

"I was asking about Nana."

"Right." Jess looked down at the frothy top of her untouched flat white. "She's doing okay. Better than okay, actually. She has outpatient PT every day for a couple weeks. They're working on strengthening exercises and putting some weight on that leg. Her bone density is good, so they aren't too worried about the pins shifting. She's a lightning bolt on that scooter."

"And Pops?"

"He's happier now that she's home with him," Jess said flatly. "He's charmed most of the staff at the rehab facility, so of course gets whatever he wants."

"Let me find my surprised face," Fizzy said, and then went quiet and still across from Jess as she turned her phone over and glanced at the screen. Nothing. "Do you want to tell me what's with you today?"

"Me?"

Fizzy smiled. "Jess. My bestie intuition is god tier, level five thousand, the top one percent. You think I can't tell when something's off? Are you worried about Nana or those children of the corn in Juno's class?"

Jess laughed for the first time all day. The problem was that she couldn't talk about this. Not only wasn't it her problem to share, she wasn't even sure how big the problem *was*.

"I'm fine, just slept like crap and snapped a little at Juno this morning." Lifting her cup to her lips, she asked, "Any update on Rob?"

"I'm sure he's tried to call," Fizzy said, "but I blocked him. From my phone, Insta, Facebook, Snapchat, WhatsApp, TikTok, Twitter, and . . ." She lifted her phone, tapped the screen a few times, and added, "LinkedIn."

"You have all those?"

Fizzy shrugged, tearing off a piece of muffin.

Jess reached across the table to take Fizzy's free hand. "Do you think you'll see any more of your matches?"

"Who knows. My social boner is pretty limp right now."

"That sentence makes so much sense."

The bell rang over the door, and Jess's attention flew toward the sound. *River*. She glanced at her phone. It was well past nine. He was late.

Bypassing the front counter, he walked straight toward their table. His hair was a bit more mussed than usual, and his eyes looked heavy and red, but his clothes were pressed, his posture perfect. Jess hated how quickly her traitorous body wanted to forget about his abrupt departure yesterday, his lack of communication, and just stand up and step into his arms.

"Hey," he said to her, and then turned to Fizzy. "I heard about the asshole."

"Today I'm affectionately referring to him as the douchebaguette."

"Well, I didn't want you to get an alert, so I deactivated your matching for now, and banned the douchebaguette from the platform. The system may have accidentally sent a duplicate receipt to his billing address, but I obviously wouldn't know anything about that. With any luck his wife is the one getting the mail."

Fizzy smiled warmly at him and reached for his hand. "I knew you were my favorite of Jess's many lovers."

Jess just sat there, watching the two of them interact like everything was normal. But it wasn't. He hadn't looked at her again. A rough fissure was forming in the center of her heart.

River gave an awkward laugh. "Well, this is yours if you want it." He handed Fizzy an envelope with the colorful DNADuo logo embossed on one side.

Wary, she took it from him, turning it over in her hands. "Is this what I think it is?"

"It's your compatibility score with Rob."

She dropped it like it was on fire. "Ugh. I don't think I can open it."

True to type, River didn't say anything. He only stared at her with gentle empathy. "Your call."

"What if it says we're a match?" Fizzy said, heartbreakingly vulnerable. "I'm never going to be with someone who cheated on his wife, no matter how perfect biology says we are for each other." She slid it back across the table. "Just shred it."

"You're sure?" he asked. He didn't reach to pick it up.

"If you thought you and Jess might not be soulmates, would you want to know?"

Leave it to Felicity Chen to hit the proverbial nail on the head without even knowing it.

River's gaze flew to Jess's and then away, visibly pained. He reached for the envelope, tucking it into his blazer. "Maybe. I don't know." When he dragged in a stuttering breath, it felt to Jess like she was witnessing him fraying at the edges. Did River need a particular score to be sure about her?

"Can I talk to you for a minute?" Jess asked.

He met her eyes and nodded once.

With a little wince to Fizzy—who was no doubt picking up on every weird vibe they were throwing off—Jess followed him out the door, turning on him as soon as they were outside. "Dude."

"I know I didn't call last night and I'm sorry," he said immediately, sending an agitated hand into his hair. "It was a lot to process."

"Would you like to share any of your process with me?"

"He admitted everything . . . all of it. He and Brandon both."

Jess felt unsteady where she stood. "*Both* of them?" She needed to sit down.

"They knew I would take it seriously. That I'd . . ." He paused, blowing out a breath. "That for a score like that, I would do my best to try."

"Holy shit."

"They changed the values from the Fuchses' assay. They weren't wrong that it would be a huge boost for the company. I don't even know what we're facing, honestly."

"What were our actual scores?"

He shrugged. "David never let any of our assays finish. He didn't want a data trail."

Jess stared at him, stunned. They didn't even have a score? *Ever?* "Was this the first time or were there others? Is the whole thing fake?"

River shook his head vehemently. "I've had my hands in all of the data until about six months ago, when things got much busier," he said, words all smashed together. Jess had never seen him like this: eyes wild and bloodshot, energy tumultuous. Whatever power had kept him composed in Twiggs was crumbling out here on the sidewalk. "I mean, until I was out meeting with investors constantly. Dave and Brandon claim our profiles are the only ones they forged." He sent both hands into his hair now and stared down at the pavement. "I'll have to confirm that."

"I don't understand. If they were only going to pick one set of scores to fabricate, why include me? You're gorgeous and can sell this better than anyone. I'm a thirty-year-old, broke single mother. Why not keep things simple and pick a model-slash-PR-superstar?"

"Dave saw you when you and Fizzy came into the office," River said, voice tight. "He thought you were beautiful and would look great on camera."

Jess thought back to that day. "I was in jeans and a sweatshirt. I looked like a fifth grader."

"Dave's known me for almost thirteen years. As he put it, he 'knew what I'd be into.'"

Her brows rose slowly.

River quickly clarified. "He meant *you*. To be fair, he wasn't wrong." River attempted a smile, but at best it was a grimace. "The idea cemented when they learned more about you. A statistician, a local, helping take care of your grandparents. They didn't know about Juno until later and—"

"And I said I didn't want her involved."

"Exactly." He looked back toward the café, eyes narrowed against the morning light. "You didn't tell Fizzy?"

"What would I tell her? Five minutes ago, I wasn't even sure what was going on. Besides," she said, and stepped forward, coaxing one of his hands from his tightly crossed arms, "this is a mess for your company, but it isn't a mess for us." She tried to pull him closer, but he was as tight as a lock; nowhere in his present demeanor was her deliberate, focused boyfriend. "Hey. Look at me. No matter what our score actually is, I'm in for the long haul. Statistics can't tell us what will happen, they can only tell us what *might* happen."

He didn't respond, didn't look at her. Instead, he lowered his head and carefully pulled his hand free from hers. River's silence pressed down all around her, heavy and choking.

"Right?" she pressed.

He looked up. "Of course, yes. I'm just a mess this morning."

She didn't feel at all comforted. "What will happen to them?"

"The board will meet, and we'll have some really difficult conversations. What they did was unethical at best and illegal at worst.

They'll likely be replaced, and all the data from the past six months—about fourteen thousand samples—will have to be rerun." He paled, staring down the enormity of it.

A question bloomed, pushing itself out of her mouth. "Did you run our samples?"

"No," he said immediately. Flatly. "I took my profile offline."

Jess couldn't decide whether that was a relief or a gut punch. They didn't have a score of their own, and now they never would. It was hard for her to imagine that River wouldn't need to know his compatibility score with his girlfriend.

Unless . . .

"Oh." She stared down at their shoes—his polished, hers scuffed. They were only a couple of feet apart, but it felt like he was standing a mile away. "I guess that's that."

His restless energy bled into her heartache and made her feel restless, too.

"Go," she said, finally. "It's a lot to digest."

River exhaled slowly, turning his gaze up to her face. "It is."

He searched her eyes for a long beat before bending to deliver a quick peck on her cheek. After jogging back inside to pick up his Americano, he didn't stop at their table again on the way out the door.

TWENTY-FOUR

———/———

S TANDING IN VONS the next evening, Jess looked up from her grocery list and realized Juno was still staring at the half mile of cereal options. "Junebug, can you pick one? We still have to drive home, unload this, and get you bathed and into bed." Jess glanced at her watch, dreading the amount of work she still had to do when she got home. With her nights suddenly River-free, she should have been all caught up, with plenty of time to spare. And yet. Her focus had been terrible, and when she wasn't busy being sad and staring off into space, she was helping Juno with homework or, like earlier tonight, going to the physical rehabilitation center with Nana and Pops.

Juno gazed up at the colorful boxes, eyes narrowed as she considered. When a seven-year-old is told for the first time in their life that they can pick whatever cereal they want, it's a big decision. "Hmm." She tapped her chin. "Cinnamon Toast Crunch looks good but Trix is fruity." She reached for the box. "I'll get Trix."

"You know it's not real fruit, right?"

Her daughter: ever confident. "Yes, it is. Look, it says 'natural fruit flavors.'"

Jess saved the lesson on tricky advertising for a better mood and tossed the box into the cart.

A shocking amount of money later, they were loading groceries into the trunk when her phone rang with an unknown number. "Go ahead and get in. I'll finish," Jess told Juno, and motioned that she had a call. "Hello?"

"Jessie!"

Tinny music filled the line and Jess glanced at the number again. "This is Jessica. Who is this?"

"Jessie? It's Mama."

"Mom? I can barely hear you."

In the background, the sound of shuffling and muffled laugher, and then Jamie was back, the line quieter from whatever room she'd moved to. She let out an annoyed scoff and sounded like she was speaking to someone else when she said, "Assholes wouldn't turn it down."

Jess loaded the last bag and leaned against the back of her car, listening closely. "Whose phone are you using? I didn't recognize the number."

"I got a new one. Was getting so many unwanted calls. Just all the time."

Jess's heart sank. Bill collectors. This was Jamie's third new number in as many years. And now that Jess could hear better, she registered a definite slurring.

"Mom, are you drinking?"

Her *Jusalilbit* came out as one fluid syllable, meaning what she said next lacked any credibility: "Only beer. Not drunk, though. I promise."

Closing her eyes, Jess took a deep, steadying breath, and then slammed the trunk shut. So much for *clean for eighteen months*.

"Listen, Jamie, I'm out with Juno, and we have a car full of groceries. I have your new number now, so I'll call you later."

"No, wait. Baby, I need you to come get me."

Jess worked to keep the annoyed edge from her voice. "Sorry, I can't tonight. I need to get Juno home and I have a lot of work to do. Sleep it off, and I'll talk to you tomorrow." She turned to take the cart back.

"Jessie, I think I'm in trouble."

Jess stopped. "What kind of trouble?"

"With the cops," she said, sounding like she'd put a cupped hand around the phone. "I'd drive myself over to your place, but I had a little to drink and probably shouldn't."

Jess returned to the car. "Mom, you can't come to my place if the police are looking for you, are you serious right now?"

"That's all you have to say?" her mother asked. "Aren't you even a little bit proud of me?"

Jess's mouth dropped open and for a few seconds she honestly had no idea what to say. "Am I—? For getting drunk? For having a problem with the police?"

"For not driving," Jamie snapped. "You know what, never mind. I'll just wait twenty minutes and then drive myself."

"Mom, wait." Jess closed her eyes, counted to five. The sun was already starting to set. Nana and Pops were out with some of his navy friends; Fizzy was on a deadline, and Jess couldn't keep running to her anyway. River—River was apparently out of the picture. She was on her own.

"Don't drive," she said. "Just . . . send me the address. I'll come now."

THE ADDRESS JAMIE sent was to her friend Ann's house in Vista, over half an hour's drive away. Jess had met Ann a few times and knew she wasn't the worst of Jamie's people—she was, after all, responsible enough to have a steady home. A few cars littered the long, wide driveway—Jess didn't see Jamie's, but that didn't mean anything— and the sound of classic rock filtered through the open windows.

"Whose house is this?" Juno asked, peering through the windshield at the two-story orange stucco house. She scrunched her nose. "It smells like that comic book shop we went to."

Weed. It smelled like weed. But that was the least of Jess's worries.

"It's Grandma Jamie's friend's house." Jess helped her daughter from the back seat and took her hand. "I want you to hold on to my hand the whole time, and don't talk to anyone." They made their way up the driveway, but Jess stopped. Who knew what they would find inside? "Just—don't look at anything if you can help it."

Juno nodded, gripping her mom's hand in her clammy little one. Jess tried to keep most of the bad stuff from her kid, but Juno knew enough about Jamie to not ask too many questions.

The front door was partially ajar and Def Leppard blasted sharply out onto the front porch. Juno gave her mom a wary frown before Jess pushed the door open and took a step inside. "Hello?"

Jamie walked around the corner with a tumbler of amber liquid in her hand, but when she saw her daughter, she immediately put it down on a cluttered table. She was barefoot and wearing a knee-length sundress; Jess tightened her grip on Juno as she glanced uneasily around the room. There was a man passed out on a couch, a woman in the kitchen anxiously pacing as she murmured into a phone. God only knew what was happening upstairs. "Get your things, Mom. Time to go."

Jamie spotted Juno, and her face brightened, arms went wide. "There's my baby girl." Her voice was too big, smile too wide. "Give Grandma a hug." Juno took a step back, wrapping her arms around Jess's waist and hiding behind her legs. Dejected, Jamie straightened and turned her attention to her daughter. "Didn't think you'd be here so soon."

Jamie didn't seem falling-down drunk, but her complexion was pallid and vaguely sweaty. She swayed where she stood. As if reading Jess's thoughts, Jamie swiped self-consciously at the mascara smeared under her eyes and ran two shaking hands through her hair.

"It's late," Jess said flatly. "It's a school night. Everyone in this house is probably drunk or high, including you."

"Why do you always assume the worst of me?"

Jess wasn't in the mood to argue. Picking up Juno, she turned toward the door. "I'll be in the car. If you're not out there in three minutes, I'm leaving without you."

Almost exactly three minutes later, Jamie walked out, still barefoot, and climbed into the front seat. As she passed in front of the headlights, Jess could instantly see that she'd lost weight. Jamie had always been slim, but she got rail thin when she was using.

"Where are your shoes?" Jess asked, putting the car into reverse and backing out of the driveway. Not that it mattered; Jess wouldn't turn back for them. She'd give up her own shoes first.

Jamie looked down at her dirty feet and frowned. "Oh . . . I'm not sure."

It took intense effort for Jess to focus on driving safely. She was so furious, so disappointed, she was afraid to even open her mouth. A glance in the rearview mirror reassured her that Juno was watching *Lady and the Tramp* on Jess's iPhone, eyes heavy with exhaustion and headphones firmly in place. With any luck she'd be asleep before they were even on the freeway.

The miles passed in tense silence as they headed toward Jamie's apartment farther inland—a new address since only a handful of months ago.

"You didn't have to come," Jamie finally said, clearly trying to smooth things over by sitting up pin-straight and enunciating. Jess was very rarely *mad* at her. Her mother had forgotten holidays, mostly missed her high school graduation, and outright lied to Jess about her sobriety more times than she could count, but Jess always let it go. Jamie was her mom. She didn't have any other choice.

But right now, Jess was so tired. "You asked me to come get you."

"I could have called an Uber or something in the morning."

"You said you were in trouble."

"I did?"

Jess exhaled a slow, calming stream of air. It wasn't worth getting into it. "You said you've been sober for eighteen months, so what are you doing drinking at Ann's?"

"I had *one* beer." Jamie let out a curt laugh and turned toward the passenger window. "Of course, to you that ruins everything. You're always so quick to judge."

"I'm not judging. I'm upset that I have a hundred and fifty dollars' worth of groceries in my trunk, including frozen stuff that's probably ruined. I'm upset that I dropped everything, and instead of having my daughter asleep in her own bed, I had to drag her to some drug party, and you can't even be straight with me. What's going on? How on earth did you get in trouble with the police?"

"It's a stupid misunderstanding."

"With who?"

"Skin Glow," Jamie said. "I ordered some product to sell. But now the owner says she's going to press charges if I don't pay her. It's ridiculous. How am I supposed to pay her for product I haven't even sold yet?"

"Product?"

"Some creams and serums, vitamins. That kind of stuff."

"So, you bought stock on credit, and pay it back from the profit, I'm guessing?"

"Yeah."

"Mom, I'm sure all of that is in the terms of whatever agreement you signed to buy it."

Jamie shook her head. "When I went in for the consult, they said I'm really good at sales, and should come in at the Blue level. It's a really big deal to be told that, trust me, and Trish understood that I was taking on a lot of inventory." She lifted her chin. "But I had a lot of people who wanted to buy the stuff, and a lot more who are interested in buying, they're just waiting to get paid."

Jess felt like she couldn't breathe, like she knew what was coming but didn't want to hear it.

"Some bills got a little ahead of me, so I used the money from my first sales to cover them. I was planning to pay it back. I just haven't had the chance yet, and she's being such a bitch about it. She says she'll report all of the inventory as stolen." Her mother squinted over at her, indignant. "Can you even believe that?"

"You ordered product, sold some, and used the money for your bills instead of paying for the product you ordered?"

Jamie nodded, turning her face to the window again. "It's not like I'm not good for it. If Trish trusted me to come in at Blue level, then why can't she trust me to get these orders sold?"

Jess tightened her grip on the steering wheel. "How much?" Jamie didn't answer, and ice-cold dread slipped over her skin. "Mom, how much do you owe?"

"I don't know. Like ten thousand."

Jess gaped at her, eyes wide with horror, and had to swerve to stay in her lane. "Ten thousand *dollars*?"

Rolling her eyes, Jamie mumbled, "Here we go."

"You ordered ten thousand dollars in *face cream*? *Wholesale*?" Jess . . . couldn't even wrap her mind around that. And then it hit her.

Trish was most likely not the only person her mom owed money to.

"You have two felonies," Jess said, and her hands were shaking on the wheel now. "California is a three-strike state. Do you understand what that means? If this woman presses charges, you could go to prison for twenty-five years."

Jamie waved this away. "It's not going to come to that. I just have to pay Trish back."

"Mom—*how*? How are you going to do that?"

Her nostrils flared, and she clenched her jaw. "I'll pay her back out of my cut of the product I have left to sell."

"You really think you can sell ten thousand dollars of skin care product to your friends?" Jess glanced at her and then back to the road. Jamie's friends didn't have money, either.

"Yeah, that's not going to be a problem, seriously everyone loves this stuff. But I might need you to loan it to me so I can get her off my ass—"

Tearing her eyes away from the road again, Jess cried, "What in the world makes you think I have that kind of money lying around?"

Jamie studied her shrewdly. After a long pause, she said, "I figured you could ask your new boyfriend."

Jess felt like she'd been punched in the chest. "What?"

"I saw the *Today* show." Jamie had the nerve to appear wounded when she looked back over at her daughter. "The guy who started that company that's going to be such a big deal?"

Jess had to push the words up her throat. "I don't know if he and I are—"

"You weren't even going to tell me. Probably because you assumed I'd just come to you looking for money."

She gaped at the black asphalt ahead, at the mile marker she passed, the speed limit sign. "Isn't that what you're doing?"

"Not for a handout! Jesus Christ, Jessica, I'm talking about paying it back within a month! I only need it now because fucking

Trish has me backed into a corner! Hasn't she ever been late on a bill? Haven't you?"

Glancing into the back seat, Jess was relieved to find that Juno had fallen asleep. She turned and stared straight ahead, blinking back tears. Jess had the money. She'd been holding it for braces and insurance and a rainy day, but she still had it.

Why can't you just be my mom?

"It's fine," Jamie said. "I'll figure something out or I'll go to prison, but either way it's not your problem."

Jess blinked up to the mirror again. Juno's mouth was softly open, her head bobbing gently with the tiny bumps in the road. Jess couldn't keep doing this anymore.

"I'll give you the money."

Jamie's face whipped to Jess. "You will? I'll pay you back with my first check. I'm telling you, Jessie, before all this happened Trish said she'd never seen anyone sell like me."

She pulled into the apartment complex that made her own look like a palace and parked in the first empty spot she found. "Don't pay me back," Jess said flatly. "I'm giving this to you. But after I do, I don't want you to call me anymore, and I don't want you to come by."

"What? Why—"

"I'll transfer the money, but that's the end. I don't want to ever see you again."

The car idled, and the silence stretched between them. Jess had no idea what else to say. Would Jamie even pay her debts, or would she take the money and run?

It honestly didn't matter. Jess was done.

Jamie looked at her granddaughter in the back seat, and her gaze seemed to sober as it moved over Juno's sleeping face.

Resolved, she turned back around. "You still have my account number?"

Sadness and relief braided hot and painful through Jess's limbs. "Yes."

Her mother nodded and slowly faced forward again. "Okay." Her fingers wrapped around the door handle. "Okay." She pushed it open and stepped out into the darkness.

TWENTY-FIVE

———⌐———

SURPRISINGLY, THE WORLD didn't stop turning when Jess cut off her mother.

Juno and Jess got up the next morning, and got ready in a sweet, easy rhythm. Juno seemed to know to be tender with her mom, and didn't need to be reminded to get dressed or bring her dishes to the kitchen or brush her teeth.

She held Jess's hand all the way to school.

"I was thinking we could go out to dinner tonight," Jess said, "just me and you. Somewhere special."

With an enthusiastic nod, Juno stretched, kissing Jess's cheek, and then ran off to meet up with her friends.

Jess watched her until the bell rang and Juno disappeared into her classroom. After transferring the money, Jess had to remind herself that she was still better off than she'd been before all this craziness began. She had new clients, new visibility. She could re-build.

She was much better off than she could have been, she knew. Plus, she had a pretty fucking awesome kid.

SIX DAYS LATER, Fizzy whined plaintively into her fancy headset: "This setup doesn't feel the same."

Jess looked at Fizzy's glowering image over Zoom on her iPad. "Well, it's the best you get. You said you didn't want to go back."

"I know, but . . . don't you miss Daniel?"

"And good coffee and reliable Wi-Fi?" Jess replied. "Yes, of course I do."

Other things Jess missed:

Her boyfriend.

Her good mood.

The ten thousand dollars that had been in her checking account a few days ago.

The possibility that her mother would change.

Fizzy growled again and disappeared from view as, Jess presumed, she left to make herself another cup of mediocre coffee.

Three things Fizzy reminded her of constantly now that they'd stopped going to Twiggs:

1. She hated drip coffee but was too lazy to get even a basic Nespresso.

2. Her Wi-Fi sucked.

3. The lack of people-watching killed her meet-cute mojo.

But even though Jess's coffee was also less satisfying than a Twiggs flat white, and she had a hard time focusing on work at her dining table, she couldn't find it in herself to go back to Twiggs and pretend like there weren't a million memories imprinted on every scuffed surface. Twiggs was where she met River, where she first got the notification from DNADuo, where she saw him last, and—most importantly—where she absolutely did not want to risk running into him at 8:24 on a weekday morning.

Though to be totally frank, it might be harder if Jess found out that he wasn't going to Twiggs at all anymore, either. That he'd erased every bit of their shared history completely.

And it wasn't like Fizzy was genuinely pushing to go back. Rob had spread his gross cheater vibes all over their table before Fizzy doused him with ice water. God, Twiggs had been tainted by the ghosts of their carefree former selves. The ones who, two months before, happily ogled Americano, gossiped with impunity, hadn't had their hearts broken. Jess missed those women.

But working from home wasn't all bad. Jess was saving money and might even lose a few pounds without her daily intake of blueberry muffins. She could work at home with her screen door open, wearing a T-shirt and no pants because it was warm outside and no pants beat pants every time. She could be at Nana Jo's side in twenty seconds (after putting on pants) if needed.

Jess and Fizzy pretended they were sitting at the table together; they'd tried to actually work together in person, but they'd ended up on the couch watching Netflix after about a half hour. Zoom was better for deadlines.

Her phone dinged on the table, and she glanced down at the Wells Fargo notification just as Fizzy returned.

Fizzy settled in her seat and adjusted her screen. "What's that expression?"

"Probably my mom's bank accepting the—" Jess paused, and bent to look closer. A chill ran through her. "Um, no. This is me reacting to ten thousand dollars being *deposited* into my account."

"Tax refund?" Fizzy screwed her face up, not understanding.

Had Jamie refused the money? Jess tapped open the app and felt her heart drop. "Oh. It's a GeneticAlly payment."

Fizzy went quiet on the other side of the screen, eyes wide. "*Yikes.*" And then her brow cleared. "But . . . convenient timing?"

Looking up at her, Jess winced. "I can't keep this."

"The hell you can't," Fizzy responded. "You kept up your end of the deal."

Jess knew Fizzy was right, but she wasn't sure it mattered. At least to her. "I wonder if River knows that the company is still paying me?"

"Maybe that detail got lost in the scandal," Fizzy mumbled, blowing on her hot coffee.

"How awkward would that conversation be?" she asked. "'I realize you're ghosting me but I just wanted to send one more note to thank you for continuing to pay me to be your girlfriend. It's nice to be just heartbroken, instead of heartbroken *and* broke.'"

What could her best friend say to that? So, the heartbroken to the heartbroken said only, "I'm sorry, honey."

Jess nearly startled out of her chair when a sharp knock rapped on the screen door, jarringly loud, followed by a deep, smoke-scraped voice. "Hey-ho, Jess."

"Oh my God," she hissed. "UPS is here for a pickup, and I don't have any pants on."

Fizzy reached for her notebook, quietly whispering as she jotted down: "UPS guy . . . no . . . pants." Jess yanked her shirt as far down her thighs as it would go, grabbed the shipping envelope from the table, and shuffled to the door.

Pat—midfifties now, kind eyes, and deep wrinkles from years of sun exposure—was the same delivery guy they'd had for nearly a decade. He averted his gaze as soon as he registered the way Jess was hiding her lower half behind the door, and Jess handed him the envelope with signed contracts for Kenneth Marshall. "Sorry," she mumbled. "Let's pretend this never happened."

"Deal." He turned and made his way down the path to the gate.

"Maybe being away from Twiggs isn't so bad for my writing mojo," Fizzy said when Jess returned to the table. "That might be the best start to a story I've had in a couple weeks. Maybe I'll finally be able to write something other than sex scenes that transition into aggressive and intentional penile injury."

"Please don't write a romance starring me and UPS Pat."

"Do you know that penises can be fractured and strangled?" Fizzy paused. "But don't Google it."

"Fizzy, I swear to Go—"

If possible, Jess startled even harder when the second knock came. *Did I forget to tape the label on?* Defeated, she called out, "Pat, hold on, I need to go put on pants."

A low, quiet voice resonated down her spine. "Who's Pat?"

Jess's eyes went wide, and she turned to gape at Fizzy on the screen.

"What?" Fizz whispered, angling as if she could see through her screen to the door, moving so close that her nose and mouth loomed. "Who is it?"

"River!" Jess whisper-yelled.

Fizzy leaned back and made a shooing motion with her hand, whispering, "Go!"

"What do I say?" Jess hissed.

"Make him do the talking!" She shadowboxed in her chair and forgot to whisper the rest: "Fuck him! Tell him I said so!"

River cleared his throat and offered a dry "Hi, Fizzy" through the screen door.

"Oh, *great*." Growling at her, Jess stood, stomped over to the door, and jerked it open.

River stared at her face and then dropped his eyes before immediately looking back up. A hot blush crawled up his neck. Right. Pants. And as they stood facing each other, River made a valiant effort to not let his eyes drop below her shoulders again.

Or . . . maybe it wasn't valiant. Maybe it wasn't hard at all. Maybe for him, turning off feelings was like flicking the switch off at the end of an experiment.

Score over ninety: interest on.

Score unknown: interest off.

"Hi," Jess said. Well, even if he could shut off his feelings, the same was certainly not true for her. If anything, her love for River had somehow solidified into a brick in her chest: If she wasn't truly in love with him, then why did she cry herself to sleep every night?

Why was he the first person she'd wanted to hold when she finally got home from dropping Jamie off the other night?

But at the sight of him—how Jess could immediately tell he'd gotten a haircut recently, how he was still the most gorgeous man she'd ever seen, even with the dark circles under his eyes, and how being this close to him still made a cord of longing pull tight from her throat to her stomach—the sadness melted away and she was angry. More than angry, Jess was livid. It had been eight days. Eight days of complete silence from someone who'd told her he hadn't felt like he'd been home in forever until he met her. Who'd kissed her like he needed her to breathe. Who said "I love you" out of the blue and didn't try to take it back. And then he left.

"What are you doing here?"

His jaw clenched and he closed his eyes, swallowing with effort. "Do you . . . want to go put on pants?"

Jess stared at him, mute with shock. This was the first thing he said to her? Go get dressed? Honestly, being confronted with the uppity, asshole version of River made it so much easier to dial down the love and crank up the hate.

"No." Jess waited for him to look at her face again and then put a hand on her hip, deliberately ignoring when her shirt rose up. "What are you doing here?"

River exhaled shakily, blinking to the side and then looking back to her. "Do you mind if I come in?"

Her first instinct was to tell him that she did mind. She minded very much, in fact, because having him in her space would remind her that he'd started treating it like *his* space, too. She'd thrown out the deodorant he'd left in her bathroom, the socks she'd fished out of the laundry basket, the oat milk he'd kept in her fridge. But she knew they needed to have this conversation. They had to break up, officially.

Stepping to the side, Jess let him in and then turned and stalked down the hall, calling out, "Stay there."

When she returned, she had pants on, but her mood, if anything, had darkened. Walking past Juno's room was like pouring lemon juice on a cut. River hadn't just vanished from Jess's life; he'd vanished from her kid's, too. Her little girl who'd never been left before had lost two people in a week. Would it be hitting below the belt to tell him that Juno had asked to see River no fewer than four times? Jess berated herself for telling Juno about their relationship at all.

Jess found him perched on the edge of the couch cushion, hands pinned between his knees. He looked up at her and seemed to relax the smallest bit, shoulders slumping.

"Why are you here, River?"

"I was hoping we could talk." He said it like it was obvious, but was he kidding?

Her jaw dropped. "What do you think I was trying to do when I called you last week? When I texted? You never replied."

He took a deep breath and let it out slowly. "I wasn't ready."

"Oh?" she said in quiet shock. "I was here totally losing my mind thinking we were over. I was heartsick, River. Am I supposed to feel better hearing that you didn't call because you weren't ready to have a relatively simple conversation?"

"Jess, come on. You said it was a lot to digest, too. I was neck-deep in data. And when you didn't call again, I—I wasn't sure whether you needed space."

"Do not make me the bad guy here." She immediately pointed her finger at him. "I get that this threw you—"

His eyes flashed as he cut in. "Do you?"

"Of course I do. It threw me, too!"

"It isn't the same," he said, voice sharp.

"Maybe not, but you had no right to dump me the way you did."

"What?" His eyes went wide. "I didn't dump you."

"Reality check: When someone goes completely silent for eight days, it isn't because they're off planning an elaborate grand gesture." Crossing her arms, Jess leaned against the wall. "And you know that, River. I realize that I'm easy to leave, but I was hoping you were better than that."

He looked like he'd been punched. "You aren't *'easy to leave.'* None of this has been about my feelings for *you*. I was a total fucking wreck about work, worrying we would have to disclose the tampering, worrying my entire company would go under."

Jess looked away, clenching her jaw while she struggled not to cry. Was she being unfair? His entire world had come apart, but she could only focus on all the shrapnel he left in her. "I understand that, but it doesn't make my feelings any less valid," she said, careful to keep her voice from trembling, "I had a really shitty week. I needed you. Even if you were going through it, too, I needed you. And you don't get to do that, you know? Just vanish? Remember this for the next time, with the next woman. If you say feelings like 'love,' you owe her more than what you gave me this week."

He stared at her in confusion for a few long moments before bending and putting his head in his hands. "I know it doesn't change anything," he said quietly, "but I felt shattered." He didn't move for several long moments. "I was totally humiliated, Jess. Yes, it's just data, but it was the cruelest thing they could have done. People I've known and trusted for nearly fifteen years took advantage of my genuine belief in this technology. They manipulated me personally and the project I've spent my entire adult life on—because they knew that if I got that score, I would do everything in my power to explore the personal implication of it." River looked up at her, and Jess saw that his eyes were red-rimmed. "I got crushed as a scientist and duped as a man. I felt like the entire world was"—he coughed—"laughing at me."

"I wasn't laughing at you," Jess reminded him. "We were already so much more than a number on a piece of paper. And if you'd come to me, you would have had someone in your corner, ready to fight anyone who hurt you. Ready to fight for you."

"I didn't even know how to understand it in my own mind. I—I—" He struggled to find the words, sitting up and looking at her in earnest. "I didn't leave my office for days. I pored through every line of data from every Gold or higher pairing we've had. Sanjeev and I reran samples twenty-four hours a day to make sure the company wasn't going to have to fold."

"You still could have called."

He opened his mouth to defend himself and then exhaled, tilting his face to the ceiling before meeting her eyes. "I could have. I should have. I'm sorry, Jess. Time just flies for me when I'm like this. But I've only been home to shower and change."

She couldn't help but let her gaze rise, studying his new haircut.

He shook his head, understanding immediately. "I got a haircut just before coming to see you."

"So you could look handsome for our breakup?"

Abruptly, River stood. "Is that what you think this is?"

Jess let out a sharp breath. "I'm sorry, what?"

"We're breaking up?" he asked, voice tight.

"What are the other options?" She pretended to check her watch. "I mean, it's a little late for our standing sex date, and it's been a weird week, but why not, for old times'—"

"Jess," he rasped, "stop it."

She crossed the room and got right up in his face. "*You* stop it. Why are you even here? I get that you needed space. But I fell in love with you. Juno fell in love with you." He reacted like he'd taken a shove to the stomach, and Jess pushed on. "Do you know what that means?" She pressed her fingertips to her chest, mortified when her throat started to burn. "I opened my life to you. I gave you the power to gut me if you disappeared, and you knew that, and you did it anyway. I understand that you were struggling, too. But just a word—a *text*—and I would have waited."

He scrubbed his hands over his face. "I wish I'd handled it differently. I fucked up."

"You did."

"I'm sorry." He bowed his head. "I didn't know how you'd feel once you weren't obligated to be with me."

That pulled her up short. "River, I never felt *obligated* to be with you. Not the way that we were together by the end."

He took a step closer, growling, "Stop calling it the end."

"I don't understand what you think is happening here! You don't get to drop off the face of the earth for a week and then act confused."

"Do you remember what you said to me the last time we saw each other?" he asked, closing the distance between them. "You said, 'Statistics can't tell us what will happen, they can only tell us what *might* happen.' And you were right. A Diamond Match is so rare that two random people are ten thousand times more likely to find their soulmate with a Base Match than they are to ever score above a ninety with someone else."

"I could have told you that," Jess said quietly, adding with a reluctant smile, "And I bet you didn't even use the right analysis to calculate it."

He laughed dryly. "I guess I needed to see it for myself."

Jess couldn't help but give him an exasperated look.

Tentatively, he smiled. But it ebbed away in the face of her stony silence. "Do you really want to break up?"

Jess had no idea what to say to that. She hadn't expected to be given the option. She'd thought it was a done deal. "I *didn't*, but, I mean—"

"It's a yes or no," he said, but gently, reaching forward to take her hand. "And for me the answer is a no. I love you. I love Juno. I needed to get my head on straight, but once I did, the first person I wanted to talk to was you."

"About a week ago," Jess said, "my mom called. She was drunk at a friend's house in Vista. I had to drive up to get her on a school night, walk into a house full of fucked-up people with my seven-year-old, and give my mother ten thousand dollars so she could avoid being arrested for stealing a huge amount of merchandise."

River paled. "What?"

"I told her that if I gave her the money, she was never to contact me or Juno again. When *I* came home to get my head on straight, the first person I wanted to talk to was you. But I didn't have that option."

To his credit, River didn't wince or frown or tense his jaw defensively. He just swallowed, nodded once, and absorbed it. "I should have been here. I hate that I wasn't."

"How do I know you'll be here the next time?" she asked. "I get that this was terrible for you. I can absolutely imagine how you don't even look up when you're in a work panic. But I really, truly wanted to be the person you turned to during all of this. And you said it yourself to me once: Bad things happen all the time. That's life. So, if something huge happens at work, and you don't know how to process it, do I have to worry that you're going to retreat into yourself and not speak to me for eight days?"

"No. I'm going to work on that. I promise."

Jess stared up at him. Dark eyes, thick lashes, full mouth. That smooth neck she fantasized about licking and biting her way down to the world's most perfectly muscled collarbones. Inside that cranium was a genius-level brain, and—when he let himself out of the lab for a breath—River Peña had the emotional depth of a man who'd already lived an entire lifetime. He talked stats with her, and the little heart that watched stories with his abuela still beat in his chest. *He loves me, and he loves my kid.*

"I don't want to break up, either," Jess admitted.

He bowed his head, exhaling slowly. "Oh my God. I really wasn't sure which way that was going to go." Reaching forward, he cupped the back of her neck and gently guided her forward, into his arms. "Holy shit, about your mom. I . . . this is a bigger conversation, I know."

"Later," Jess said, pulling back and resting her hand on his chest. "Is the company going under?"

He shook his head. "In the end, they only fabricated our score. Everything else reproduced within the standard margin of error."

The next question Jess had rose shakily to the surface. "Did you ever run our samples together?"

"I did." Reaching into his blazer pocket, he pulled out a small sealed envelope. "For you."

A potent mixture of dread and excitement streaked through her. "Do you know what the answer is?"

He shrugged, smiling.

"Is that a yes or a no?"

Nodding once, River admitted, "I do. I didn't trust anyone else to run it, but I worried someone would, eventually, out of curiosity."

Chewing on her lip, she fought the internal battle. Should she look? Should she not? Voice tight, Jess told him, "I don't care what our score is. I never have."

He laughed. "So don't look."

"Do *you* care what our score is?"

River slowly shook his head. "No."

"It's easy for you to say that because you've seen it." She paused. "Does that mean it's bad?"

Again he shook his head. "No."

"Is it something wild? Like the ninety-eight was actually right?" He paused, chewed his lip, and then slowly shook his head a third time. Jess blew out a frustrated breath. "Do you feel better about it now?"

"Jess," he said gently, "all you have to do is open the envelope to know."

She squeezed her eyes closed. "I don't *want* to. I understand that you needed to see the data, but I hate that you needed to see it to choose me."

He quickly reacted, shooting an arm around her waist. "I don't. I'm telling you; this score doesn't matter to me. I love you because I love you, whether or not I'm supposed to."

Jess squinted up at him, picking these words apart. "Okay, I'm going to assume that we're a Base Match."

He nodded, satisfied, and put the envelope away. "Sounds good."

"Are we?"

River grinned, saying, "No," and she growled.

His expression softened, and he glanced at her mouth and then back up to her eyes. "Do you want me to tell you or not?"

"*Not.* You know what we statisticians say: all models are wrong, but some are useful." He laughed. "I don't want to know the score, River."

"I won't ever offer again." He stepped forward and wrapped his other arm around her waist. "Can I do this?"

Jess nodded, looking up at him through her lashes. It felt so good to have him this close. When she closed her eyes, she was able to focus on the desire thrumming through her blood like a drug. They had hours before Juno came home.

She reached forward and ran her hand up his chest, along his neck, and traced his lower lip with her thumb. "I can't believe you're here."

"I missed you."

"I've been here the whole time." She gently pinched his chin.

"I'm feeling incredibly clingy." River bent and rested his lips over hers. "I love you."

Emotion welled up in her throat, and Jess wrapped her arms around his neck. "I love you, too."

"FYI," a disembodied voice said from the iPad, "if you think I haven't written down every word of this, you're both high."

WITH A SMIRK, River turned and walked over to the iPad, ending the Zoom meeting with a quick tap of a finger. When he looked back at Jess, his smile immediately took on a ravenous edge. "Guess I wasn't the only one who forgot she was there."

Jess's "Sorry" dissolved between them as River stalked over to her, gaze darkening; adrenaline poured warm and insistent into her bloodstream. Sliding his arms around her waist, he leaned in to kiss her neck. "What is it with us and audiences?"

"I don't know, but I sure am glad we don't have one now." She closed her eyes, focused on the sweet, tiny kisses he dropped on her skin, from her collarbone up to her jaw.

Bending and reaching around to the back of her thighs, River lifted her, wrapping her legs around his waist to carry her down the hall. "This okay?"

"If by 'this' you mean makeup sex with no child in the house, then yes. It is very okay."

As he walked, their kisses took on the kind of aching, bruised-lip intensity that told Jess, even more than his words had, how much he missed her. But when he set her down on the bed, and braced over her in that hungry way of his, he lifted a gentle hand to coax a few strands of her hair out of her face and said, "We never really talked about it—it was so unimportant at the time—but I haven't really been in a relationship since we founded GeneticAlly."

Jess pushed back into the pillow, staring up at him. "Seriously?"

River nodded. "Work was everything," he said carefully. "I just wasn't emotionally engaged anywhere else. Until you. So, I know it isn't an excuse, but now I know to be aware of it if we have another work crisis." He paused, reconsidering. "*When* we have another work crisis. I slipped back into that mode so fast, everything else fell away. Until this morning, I thought it had only been two or three days since we spoke."

Jess had to take a beat to absorb this. "Why didn't you tell me that the second you walked in the door?"

"I wanted your forgiveness before I defended myself."

She reached up, bringing a hand around his neck and drawing him down to her. His kiss started slow, his lips absorbing her relieved exhale, but then he opened to taste her.

The flirtatious tease reminded Jess so much of what it had felt like to make love to him, how he could be commanding and sweet in an almost impossible balance. Her hands turned greedy, moving up under his clothes, pushing them off. She wanted his skin right up against hers, smooth and warm with friction. They got there quickly, bare together in a stretch of afternoon sunlight streaking across her bed. River reached with a long arm for her bedside table, and then kneeled in front of her, tearing the condom wrapper with his teeth.

Jess trailed her fingers up over her own stomach, biting her lip as she looked. "I really enjoy watching you do that."

He grinned down at his hands. "Yeah?" And then he shifted, bracing a palm near her head, and bent, kissing her. "I think I prefer watching you do it."

His smile lingered—playful and seductive—and that familiar, charged pulse echoed in her like a second heartbeat. With enduring focus, River moved, teasing at first, staring transfixed at the look of bliss on her face. He watched her fall and then, exhaling a breath of disbelief, turned his face to the ceiling and followed her into pleasure.

He stayed over her for a long time, arms caging her protectively, his face pressed to her neck. Once they'd both caught their breath, he dealt with the condom and then returned exactly where he'd been. Jess had never had this before: someone who was, without question, hers. She held him with her arms banded around his waist and legs draped lazily around his thighs, wordlessly falling back in love.

WHICH MEANT THAT they woke up like this a good while later, stiff and hot and groaning. River rolled away, falling onto his back and reaching up to cup the back of his stiff neck. Beside him, Jess attempted to straighten her legs, whimpering.

"I don't want to sound paranoid," she said, "but I swear someone must've hit us with a Benadryl dart from my doorway. We literally just passed out."

He laughed. "I haven't napped like that since I was in kindergarten." Rolling to face her, he pulled her close again, with sweet, sleepy eyes. "I think our bodies needed our brains to shut down for a few minutes."

"I think you're right." Jess kissed him, unable to close her eyes. She thought she'd felt secure in this before, but the love they'd just made cemented something different between them. With the tip of her finger, she traced the shape of his jaw, his mouth, and then a thought occurred to her. "Can I ask you something about the company, or do you want to stay in the bubble a little longer?"

"I plan to live in this bubble with you, so ask anything you want. It won't harsh my Jess buzz."

She grinned, but then it faded. "What's happening with your executive team?"

"David and Brandon are gone. The board fired them the same day I saw you at Twiggs. Tiffany, too."

Jess gasped. "She knew?"

"I think she sort of had to," River said, and reached up to rub his eyes. "The only ones left from the original team are me, Lisa, and Sanjeev." When he pulled his hand away, he gazed at her, unguarded, and Jess caught a glimpse of just how exhausted he was. "We brought on a geneticist from UCSD and the head of chemistry from Genentech to sit on the interim board. I've been promoted to

CEO. Sanjeev will step up as CSO. We're bringing on a new head of marketing, who'll hopefully start in the next week."

"Are you going to have to make some sort of official announcement?"

"Yeah, tomorrow. We're just waiting on Amalia to confirm the CMO package we've offered, and then the new executive slate will go up on our site."

She shook her head. "No, I meant an announcement about the results."

"The results?" His brows pulled together in confusion.

"Just—" Jess faltered, hoping this wasn't insensitive or intrusive. "I mean, what about the *U-T*, and the *Today* show, and the *People* issue comes out Friday, right?"

River looked back and forth between her eyes for a second, and then said quietly, "We had to include it in the IPO audit, but otherwise, no. We're not making a statement on that."

"Is that . . ." Again, she hated the possibility that this would insult him. "Is that legal? I mean—"

"Jess."

"—the original score affected your valuation and—"

He leaned in, kissed her slowly, and then pulled back. "Genetic-Ally isn't going to release a statement."

Unease ballooned in her chest, making her feel like a boat on rocky water. Was he speaking in legalese? "Okay," she said, frowning.

He studied her reaction and chewed his lip, smiling. "Stop it."

"Stop what?" she said, blinking up to his eyes.

"I know what you're thinking. That I'm being unethical or evasive. I'm not. You just have to trust me."

"I do, it's just—"

He quieted her with another kiss, a longer one, deep and searching with his hand cupping her jaw and his torso rising back over hers. "Listen, I don't know how to answer this question any other way, so I'm just going to kiss you until you stop asking."

"I'm saying, because I love you and I don't want your company to—"

"*Jess*." He kissed her again. A loud, definitive smooch. "You've told me you don't want to know our results." He stared at her intently. "So, you have to let this one go."

In shock, she watched him push up and climb out of bed, smirking over his shoulder at her before walking to the bathroom. She heard the water running, and the entire time Jess stared unfocused at the doorway he'd just stepped through. They weren't going to release a statement. River didn't seem to think they would need to. Did that mean . . . ?

Her heart had somehow transformed into a bird inside her.

River returned and reached near the foot of the bed for his boxers, pulling them on. Jess had a million questions but couldn't ask any of them.

Well, maybe one more. She frowned as he stepped into his pants. "Are you . . . going in to work?"

He buckled his belt and, before reaching for his shirt, bent over to kiss her again. "No. I'm not going in to work." Straightening, he went silent for a second, and then said, "But do you think it would be okay if I got Juno from school?"

Jess bolted upright, diving for her phone. *Shit*. They had two minutes to make the seven-minute walk.

"I mean," he clarified, "I want to go get her."

"I know. Just let me—" She stood, reaching for her clothes.

"Jess." Putting his hands on her shoulders, he eased her back onto the bed. "I'm saying *I* want to get her. Let me help you." And then he ran his hands through his hair and took a deep, steadying breath. "If that's okay. I've got to fix things with both of my girls today."

TWENTY-SIX

———————

Two Months Later

IN THE COMMOTION of parents passing by and kids jabbering excitedly about their creations, Fizzy slid a small plastic item into Jess's hand, then curled her fingers around it. "Surprise!"

Jess stared down at the USB drive, coming to a stop in the crowded hallway. "Is this what I think it is?"

"If what you think it is is the newest Felicity Chen novel, *Base Paired*, about a hot scientist and a sexy single mom making a love connection through a DNA-based dating app," Fizzy said, "then *yes*."

River hovered behind, leaning a curious chin over Jess's shoulder. "Is it as dirty as your other books?"

Fizzy nodded proudly. "Probably dirtier."

His eyebrows went up. "It's hard to know whether I should be weirded out by that," he mused, "or proud." Reaching around Jess's waist, River took the USB. "I'll start it tonight." At Jess's look, he added, "Consider it research."

Jess laughed, and his big hand came around hers, guiding her through the maze of tables and exhibits, knowing exactly where to go because he'd been here at one o'clock that afternoon helping Juno set up. For almost a month, River and Juno had worked tirelessly on the roller coaster. To suggest that he had grown more invested in it than Juno had would be unfair—she was, after all, often found awake when she was supposed to be in bed, triple-checking the glue on any one of the two thousand points of contact between all of the Popsicle sticks—but he had also been predictably intense about it. They had abandoned the art tape for something sturdier (read: bigger and faster), and had built four different cars to test on the coaster before finally settling on wheels that had to be ordered from Germany. In the hall closet, Jess now had three remaining boxes of HO-gauge model train track she had no idea what she would do with.

In the end, the coaster was more than four feet long and two feet tall. It had been painstaking work, and after a few nights of watching them with ovary-bursting bliss, Jess had finally registered that her presence wasn't at all needed and spent the time happily reading or watching her shows alone in bed. When the project had finally been completed three nights ago, River took them both for ice cream to celebrate.

So she knew better than to think even GeneticAlly's official IPO the next day would keep him away. Still, they had a company dinner tonight, and she expected River to be at the office until well past midnight—and probably gone again before Jess was awake. The starting price for the stock was higher than even the underwriter had dreamed it could be, and everyone was on tenterhooks hoping it wouldn't drop in the aftermarket. If it held steady, or climbed, the original GeneticAlly team—minus David, Brandon, and Tiffany, who'd breached an important contractual clause— would each be worth tens of millions overnight.

"What time do you need to leave?" she asked.

He shrugged distractedly, and she wasn't able to pester an answer out of him because then they were at Juno's table, and both River and Juno were beaming with such pride that for a second Jess wanted to ask whose second-grade art-science assignment it had been. But how could she tease those faces? As parents, teachers, and fellow students came around the room to hear Juno's presentation— River was obediently quiet but stood proudly nearby—Jess felt the weight of the past few months press down on her chest like a sand- bag. Destiny could also be a choice, she'd realized. To believe or not, to be vulnerable or not, to go all in or not. Tears pricked the surface of her eyes and she turned to Fizzy, pretending an eyelash had gotten in one. Fizzy, to her credit, pulled a tissue and a mirror out of her purse, allowing Jess her dignity.

"He's pretty amazing," Fizzy agreed in a whisper. She watched River without a trace of tightness or envy in her expression; after moving on from the Rob debacle, Fizzy had realized she was ready for the real deal, updated her DNADuo criteria, and was confident her own Titanium-or-higher wasn't too far away.

When the judges were finished viewing the projects and tabu- lating the scores, students were encouraged to find their families and wait in the auditorium for results.

It was a familiar scene: rows of folding chairs and excited chat- ter. Younger kids darted between the aisles while parents took time to catch up with each other. It wasn't too far in the rearview mirror when a night like this would have stoked the embers of loneliness and been followed by days of smoldering in her own insistence that Single Was Better. But tonight, she felt like the contented heart of a very sturdy family. Her perfect village took up an entire row: Nana Jo and Pops at the end of the aisle with Nana's scooter; Fizzy on her left, and River, then Juno on her right. No buffer zone of empty chairs anymore.

"I'm not saying the other projects weren't great," River said, leaning in to whisper. "I mean, some were terrible, and some were great, but completely objectively Juno should win this thing."

"Completely objectively, huh?" Jess bit back a laugh. River's competitive streak ran deep; second-grade art-science competitions were apparently not immune. "Win or lose, I'm impressed with you both." She pulled back his sleeve, glancing at his watch. It was already six thirty. "Don't you have to leave soon?"

He followed her attention to his wrist. A couple of months ago, Jess imagined, River would have bolted up at the sight of the time. But he just exhaled, calculating, and said, "They're about to do the awards. I'll leave after that."

"How're you feeling about tomorrow?"

The moment of truth. "Nervous," he admitted, "but mostly relieved that it's finally here."

He took her hand in his, and she lifted them, kissing his knuckles. It was as if David's betrayal had eased some tension in him: Things had gone horribly wrong, but it'd turned out okay in the end. Better, even. The new executive team was invigorated and had a tight, instant connection. River had personally retested hundreds of samples. There was so much media buzz about GeneticAlly lately, Jess was aware that many parents knew who she and River were and not because their children were in school together.

And as much as he insisted it didn't matter, Jess knew that their new Diamond score had confirmed that once upon a time he had discovered something authentic, and he'd actually managed to do something with it to make the world better.

Beside him, Juno was busy talking to a friend in the row ahead, enthusiastically debating the merits of corn snakes versus California kings. Jess made a mental note to remind River not to give an inch on the snake front.

"Juno is such a curious, creative kid," River said, following Jess's attention. "We need to make sure we get a house with enough space for her projects—"

His words came to an abrupt stop, their eyes meeting as they each seemed to register the magnitude of what he'd just said. *We need to make sure we get a house.* They were together—of course—but they hadn't really talked about what came next.

River turned his face to the front, giving Jess a sweet view of his cheeks darkening. "I was going to talk to you later, but"—he cleared his throat—"one of the teachers earlier mistook me for Juno's dad. Juno explained, but she paused for a second first. It made me think that maybe I haven't been clear enough about what I want."

Jess's heart pounded and her palm grew clammy against his. She briefly turned her eyes to the left, to confirm that Fizzy and Pops were still cracking up together over some goat videos on Instagram. "You have an IPO tomorrow," she reminded him. "This conversation can wait."

"Why?" he asked, angling his gaze to her and grinning. "Is it going to be hard or stressful in some way?"

She smiled around her bottom lip. "Okay. Point taken. What *do* you want?"

"You." He let the syllable hang for a meaningful beat. River wanted her, and he *wanted* her. His whiskey-brown eyes held the same heat they had in the middle of the night, when he'd woken her with a kiss and turned on the muted bedside lamp before guiding her over him.

But then his intensity broke, and he continued with quiet sincerity, "And Juno. Maybe a dog." He peeked over her shoulder. "I want Fizzy's insanity and Jo's cooking. Fishing on weekends with Ron. I know it's too early to really decide anything, but when you're ready to take the next step—whatever it is—I'm in."

"You're saying you want to move in together?"

He laughed a little at this. "Of course I do. My place has more room, but it doesn't feel like a home, and I know how much you guys love the apartment. But we could find something big enough for all of us. With a giant kitchen and bedrooms on the ground floor for your grandparents, or even their own place out back."

Jess didn't know what to say. She had so much already, it felt almost greedy to want more. Waking up together every morning or the quiet intimacy of mundane tasks like grocery shopping and budgeting and just . . . sharing the daily load. She imagined moving around each other at the end of the night—putting the last glass in the dishwasher, sharing a quiet groan that Juno left her socks on the couch again. She imagined not having to say goodbye to him on the doorstep, ever.

Ask for all of it. What do you have to lose?

"This summer," Jess said, lifting her chin as if daring him to balk. "June or July. If you mean it, let's find a place."

His mouth turned up at the corner. "Yeah?"

She couldn't resist; he was too sweet. Jess leaned in for a kiss. "Yeah."

But it was cut short by the appearance of Mrs. Klein at the front of the room. River jerked himself away, tapping Juno's shoulder. Jess watched as they looked at each other, and then ahead, and smothered a laugh with her fingertips. She'd always joked that Juno was half Fizzy's, but now she had to admit there was an even more dominant influence afoot. Because, in unison, Juno's and River's eyes went big and round, their spines went ramrod straight.

So, Jess wished for one more thing.

And as the room broke out into applause, and River lifted Juno up into a celebratory hug, Jess quickly threw a few more wishes out there for good measure. But even if nothing went the way they'd planned tomorrow, GeneticAlly had already done at least one spectacular, extraordinary thing.

Juno closed her eyes as she wrapped her arms around his neck. "We did it, River Nicolas!"

Yeah, Jess thought, watching them. *We did.*

ACKNOWLEDGMENTS

———————‿———————

I T CERTAINLY WASN'T intentional, in an era where the word of scientists seems to be continually disregarded, to write a book about the power of data, but here we are. Although we conceived of the idea before the pandemic fully hit, we wrote it during our respective states' shelter-in-place orders, and this book will forever hold a sacred place in our hearts for the distraction and joy it brought us during such a dark time for the world. There was nothing about the process of writing this book that wasn't escapist and rewarding, and for this reason (and about a million others) we are so incredibly privileged to do this.

We are also grateful for the group of spectacular people we not only get to work with but who've been our ride-or-die team this past year. We've taken turns propping each other up, which is the best possible scenario in a crappy year such as this. Before 2020, our love ran bone-deep, but the devotion now runs DNA-deep: Holly Root and Kristin Dwyer, we are your forever ride-or-die. Beyond what you've done for this book, what you give us daily as friends and colleagues is invaluable and we cherish both of you. Kate Dresser, your capability and warmth has kept our careers and spirits alive even when the world was (sometimes actually) on fire. Thank you for always being present—both emotionally and professionally—responsive, enthusiastic, and reassuring. We are the luckiest authors. Jen Bergstrom, thank you for always believing in us and, specifically, for believing in this novel. Your decision to put us in hardcover still makes us glow inside. We've been through every step of our career with you, and that means the world to us. Rachel Brenner, you are always a bright spot even on the crappiest days. Thank you for hustling, but also—and we mean this with our deepest sincerity and gravitas—thank you for always, *always* being willing to crack a dad joke.

To our entire Gallery team—Molly Gregory, Aimée Bell, Jen Long, Abby Zidle, Anne Jaconette, Anabel Jimenez, Sally Marvin, Lisa Litwak, John Vairo, the Gallery Sales team and foreign rights group: WE ADORE ALL OF YOU A WHOLE LOT.

The primary setting of the book, namely the apartment complex, is based on a real place! A place that is truly beloved to me (Lauren), in fact, and is owned by my much-adored aunt and uncle, Sharon and Clayton Haven, who retired, sold their house with a million stairs, and made the dream a reality, living at the apartment complex with my grown cousins and their families. We took some fictional license with the setting so that it worked for Jess and Juno, but in most ways our descriptions of the apartment complex are based on reality, and you can find more about this place in an *LA Times* story from February 15, 2019, entitled, "3 Generations in One Apartment Building? That Was the Grandparents' Idea." My aunt and uncle are two of the most precious people on this planet, and I am indebted to them not only for too many wild nights to count but for their enthusiasm, for their support, and for modeling a sense of adventure that has driven them for their entire lives. They find joy in everything; it's so inspiring (example: Unc was seventy-five when he had the pleasure of seeing a reader ask us to sign her boobs, and I can still hear his laugh). You would have a hard time finding two more curious, thoughtful, and open souls in this world. S&C, I love you madly.

Thank you to Keith Luhrs, Iqra Ashad, Erica Lewis, and Rebecca Clark for your scientific expertise and for reading the manuscript. For something entirely theoretical and probably scientifically impossible, you helped us get as close as we could. It goes without saying that any remaining errors are ours and ours alone.

To our bookish friends who have been in it with us this year, we heart you so much. If we are ever thriving, it is because our community is strong and powerful and loving: Kate Clayborn, Kresley Cole, Jen Frederick, Cassie Sanders, Sarah MacLean, Rebekah Weatherspoon, Sally Thorne, Sarah J. Maas, Jen Prokop, Leslie Philips, Alexa Martin, Sonali Dev, Gretchen Schreiber, Alisha Rai, Christopher Rice, Jillian Stein, Liz Berry, Candice Montgomery, and Catherine Lu.

We've been cooped up with our families for eight months by this point so there's nothing we can say here that we haven't said (or shouted) . . . except maybe this: there have been challenges, and there have been victories, but none of the low points were ever because our love faltered. For that we are very lucky indeed. We love you, R, C, K, O, V.

This section of the book would be remiss if we didn't mention

Kim Namjoon, Kim Seokjin, Min Yoongi, Jung Hoseok, Park Jimin, Kim Taehyung, and Jeon Jungkook. BTS has been a brilliant ray of sunshine in this gloomy, tragic year, and we adore the members as if they were our own family. Enough said. ARMY knows how it is, and we purple you.

To all of the librarians, booksellers, readers, and our beloved members of CLo and Friends: we hope when this note reaches you that you are safe, secure, well-fed, deeply loved, and know that when you read these words we are speaking to you. Thank you for picking up our books, but more importantly, thank you for being the bedrock of a community that, without you, would crumble. In all sincerity, we write to make you happy. We hope we succeed.

And, finally, to each other we say: You are my best, and here you are my only. And look . . . we just wrote a book about soulmates. Funny thing, that.